Once a Jolly Swagman

Sara Powter

Bible Quotes from the King James Version

ISBN: 9780645110753
Paperback edition

ABN 99 768 734 831
Pacific Wanderland Publications
Kincumber, NSW, 2251, Australia

saragpowter@gmail.com
www.sarapowter.com.au

1st edition 2022 printed by Kindle
an Amazon Company; available on Kindle Unlimited & KDP
2nd edition, paperback 2022 Pacific Wanderland Publications
3rd edition, hardback 2022, Pacific Wanderland Publications
4th edition large print paperback 2023. Pacific Wanderland Publications
All Revised and updated 2025

*Inasmuch as ye have done it unto
one of the least of these my brethren,
ye have done it unto me.*

Matthew 25 v 40

Australian Historical Novels
(All stand-alone books)

A First Fleet Stories (1788+)
Gentle Annie Soames
The Emancipated Potter
Paternity Unknown

The Hunter to Macquarie Collection (1795-1822)
When Upon Life's Billows
The Saddler's Song
Tuppence to Pass
His Majesty's Pageboy (2026)
A Fist Full of Holey Dollars (2026)
Far From the Whispering Sheoaks (2026)
Bound Down in Iron Chains (2026)

Unlikely Convict Ladies Trilogy (1792-1840s)
Dancing to Her Own Tune
(co-authored by Sheila Hunter & Sara Powter)
Amelia's Tears
A Lady in Irons

The Lockleys of Parramatta (1800-1901)
Unshackled Lives - *Prequel novella - **free** with newsletter signup*
Hands Upon the Anvil
Out Where the Brolgas Dance
Diamonds in the Dirt
The Earl's Shadow
Once a Jolly Swagman
Jonty's Journey

The Convict Birthstain Collection (1820-1840s)
No More, My Love
The Vine Weaver
Scotch at The Rocks
Waiting at the Sliprails
Convict Shadows of the Past
In Defence of Her Honour
I Can't Stop Tomorrow
Madeline's Boy
Jam or Marmalade for Tea

Shelia Hunter's
Australian Colonial Trilogy (1840-1850s)
Mattie
Ricky
The Heather to the Hawkesbury

Dedication

This story was inspired by listening to

The Seekers

As we travelled through the wonderful country, Australia.
As I write these words, the news has been released that

Judith Durham

has gone to be with our Lord.

Judith and the three amazing men she sang with
brought joy to many through their music and song.

(Song list at the back)
As described by The Seekers, a Swagman,
is a 'vagabond' or a 'tramp,'
a character who lives along the roads and byways,
living from what he can catch and working where he can.
He is a character often mentioned in Australian folklore.

Thanks to
my husband,
Steve, for all his support in my writing.

To Roby Aiken
for your patience in correcting my punctuation
and
Jan Threlfo, Alana Baines, Noreen Robertson
doing the final read-through edit.
And Anna Marie Leffew for helping with promotions.

Family Tree and Character list at the end of the book

Table of Contents

*The grammar and language in this book are
Australian English spelling.*

KEY

~ - Time passing in the same locality

- Different locality/country

Chapter 1   Darned Weddings
1872 Parramatta

*R*ick was standing in front of the wall mirror in his room, trying to get the cravat to sit neatly. He had already messed up six and was getting very frustrated. He let out a groan of desperation, and as he did so, he heard a familiar knock.

His mother had come to his rescue.

"I hate darned weddings, Mother. Why do I have to get dolled up like some toff when all I want to do is go back to work?"

"Well, son, I think if you missed your sister's wedding, she would not be too impressed," his mother said gently as she dextrously tied the crisp cravat with little effort. It looked superb, and this frustrated him even more.

"If she weren't marrying Alfred, I wouldn't bother to go," he said petulantly.

Cathy said, "Just remember that Mary Louise is one of the bridesmaids, and you, my dearest young son, are to escort her to the party at Uncle Charlie's after the wedding."

His mother smiled in a resigned manner and gently stroked his cheek. She watched the blush of embarrassment creep down his neck.

Rick shrugged. "Aw, Mother, leave off. I'm only just seventeen, and she's even younger than me. There's no way I'll be getting leg-shackled any time soon." He looked away, unable to meet her eyes, although his heart was beating faster at even the mention of her name. It was because she was going to be there that he'd decided to 'don the togs' as he called it, and 'frock-up' for Goldie's wedding.

His sister was marrying Alfred Evans; they were in a way distantly related because Uncle Eddie's son Neddie had married his cousin. But they were as close to family as any of the rest of his blood cousins. The families had known each other for 'simply forever'. He rolled his eyes and then thought of Mary Louise.

Cathy Lockley watched as her youngest son blushed. She knew he had a 'thing' for Mary Louise, but they were far too young for anything more to happen as yet, at only sixteen and seventeen. She smiled and stood holding his coat.

His physique was such as to make a grown man weep in envy. He had spent many an hour at the family forge with his cousins and Uncle Eddie. He knew and loved the work.

At seventeen, his muscles were more developed than most men's. His arms bulged, and his shirts already had to be made to order, especially for him. His wavy hair fell with one lock drooping over his forehead, and no matter what he did, it would not stay in place. He was six feet two inches tall, with a heart-shaped face and two deep dimples that appeared when he returned his mother's smile.

Cathy smiled, "Richard Edward Lockley, you are cutting things fine. Will you please put this on and join the rest of us? She will be here shortly, and Goldie is already waiting. Uncle Jim is collecting us in his new carriage, and… well, just put this on, will you?"

Cathy rarely got edgy, and she did not know why she was so now. Yes, she did; he was her baby, and she realised he was now grown up.

"Rick, other than the fact that your hair is a light brown rather than blonde, you are the image of your father at the same age. He ran away with his six English friends and 'went to find his fortune'. As you know, on his return trip, he also found me. We had actually known each other for four years, but he hadn't mentioned his interest until he returned. Oh, you know the story. I can't believe that we were married only a year older than you are now."

She wiped a single tear from her eye. "I remember the day that you and Bette were born. How can you both be seventeen now? Where have those years gone?"

She gave him a hug, and he returned it, bending down to kiss his mother on the top of her head.

"I love you too, Mother, but I'm nearly fully grown up now. Yes, I think I'm a bit like Father, but I don't want people to presume they know what I want. Lukie and Pip love working for Father, as I do, but I don't want to spend my entire life in a shop." He took a breath before saying with an excited tone in his voice, "I want to see the world, go places and make something of myself. I feel stifled here sometimes. I suppose it's the 'youngest son syndrome' and all, but sometimes... ahhhh," he almost yelled. "I just want to break free from the confines around me."

Rick had just finished his schooling at The King's School in Parramatta. He should have done another year, and then he could have gone on to university, but he had no wish to study further. He could already walk into any one of a dozen family jobs, but he wanted more than that in his life.

"Rick, wait until today is over, and then we'll talk to Father." Again, she stroked his cheek. "In the meantime, come on."

They left his bedroom arm in arm.

Cathy and Wills owned *Roseneath* in Parramatta and Emu Hall at Emu Plains, which was their primary residence.

Wills had the central Hardware Emporium Warehouse in town, so they spent at least one night a week in Parramatta, sometimes more.

As Cathy arrived in the front sitting room with her son, her daughter Goldie stood looking out the window. Next to her were her sisters, Bette and Tilda.

Both were dressed in lovely light lavender gowns and looked glorious. The colour had been chosen as the third bridesmaid, Mary Louise, who was yet to arrive. She had dark curls and blue-grey eyes, and the dress made them look almost violet. The shade of lavender Goldie had chosen was perfect for all three girls.

"She's here, Mother," Goldie exclaimed as a carriage pulled up at the front gate.

Phillip Evans alighted, handed his daughter down, and walked her to the front door.

Cathy's husband, William Lockley, known as Wills, was waiting for them and stood back so she could enter.

Wills gave a warm greeting, and Phil raised his hand in both greeting and farewell. "See you all at the church," he said as he walked back down the garden path.

"We're just waiting for Brodie to bring around the new carriage Jim delivered last week. Tell Alfred we may be a few minutes late, but not embarrassingly so." Wills laughed.

Wills hated it when the bride was late for a wedding. Now, his own daughter was to be five minutes late to the church, but it was out of his control. He smiled and then walked indoors.

~

Wills walked up to his middle daughter. "Aurelia Lucy, I never seem to connect you with that name. You've been Goldie since Pip named you on the day you were born. You had a shock of white hair and the most adorable smile. It was the month that the gold finds got out, and the world went crazy for a while." Wills stood looking at the stunning blonde girl in front of him. Her blue eyes sparkled with happiness, and her smile brightened his day just by seeing it. His pet name for her was Stardust, and she seemed to sprinkle happiness wherever she went. When she fell in love with Alfred Evans, it was almost a dream come true.

Alfred had mooned over her for years, but she had never shown she was interested. Alfred announced that he might move to Melbourne as a lawyer and follow in his father's footsteps, but expand the business down there. Only then did Goldie realise the depth of her feelings.

Cathy had found her in the stables, sobbing her heart out behind a pile of chaff bags when Cathy asked her why she had never let on about her feelings.

Goldie admitted she had not realised the depth of her feelings for Alfred until she knew he was leaving. It hit her hard.

Unbeknownst to them both, Alfred had arrived with a delivery for Wills and had overheard their conversation.

Alfred was six years older than Goldie and had adored her all his grown life. He was disappointed that she had never encouraged him or shown interest in singling him out. So he decided to move away. He stood rooted to the spot in the barn doorway.

Goldie looked up and saw the silhouette of her heart's desire and promptly collapsed.

Alfred was beside her instantly, and soon she was in his arms, being carried back into the house.

Cathy escorted them into the sitting room and left to get assistance.

"Did you mean what I overheard, Goldie? Did you really mean it?" Alfred asked in earnest.

She was unable to reply, so she just nodded.

A tear slid unnoticed down her cheek. She had no idea the effect this had on a young man's heart.

He thumbed the tear away, and when another followed it, he leaned forward and kissed the next one gone.

Goldie leaned into his shoulder and was gathered close to his heart.

Now, six months later, they were getting married.

With the change in marital situation, Alfred's father, Phil, has asked if he would like to open a new law branch in Emu Plains instead of moving to Melbourne.

The town had grown enough to have its own lawyer in residence, and it would be a good start for the young couple.

Now Rick stood at his sister's wedding, looking at the stunning vision his sister's bridesmaid made in the room's doorway. He swallowed and went to greet Mary Louise Evans.

Mary Lou raised her eyes and gasped when she realised who it was. "Oh, Ricky, oh wow! You look fabulous." She then blushed scarlet, having realised what she'd said. She wished she could sink into the floorboard cracks.

Rick saw her delightful flush and replied quietly, "So do you, Mary Lou. You look smashing, too. Mayhap frocking up isn't such a bad thing after all, eh?" He smiled down at her adorable face. "Occasionally, anyway."

His mother, Cathy, watched on as he greeted his young friend. His face lit up as she arrived.

Wills walked in and announced that both Jim and Brodie were now waiting outside for everyone.

The family group gathered around Goldie and had a quick prayer before leaving for St John's church.

Rick escorted Mary Louise into the second bridal carriage before he hopped into the front one with his mother and other family members not in the bridal party.

"Maybe today would turn out all right after all," he thought, smiling to himself.

The carriages arrived at the beautiful grounds of St John's church, and the occupants of the first one hurried inside and joined the rest of the waiting family.

Cathy walked down the aisle and sat next to her elderly parents and Sal, her mother-in-law.

All this generation was now seventy-two, and this was the first family wedding since the funeral of Charles, the Earl of Coxheath.

Everyone was somewhat sad but knew that life continued on.

On the morning of her wedding, Jim had delivered a letter to Goldie from her grandfather. It was a joyous, loving and uplifting letter that brought joy to her heart.

"Be not afraid, but be of good cheer," it read along with a swathe of blessings and a list of things she had done of which he was proud. Her grandfather had also written about how proud he was of her. He encouraged her to keep her faith alive and to instruct their children in the teachings of Jesus.

Wills had been unsure if she should have been given it, but when he saw the glorious glow on her face after reading it. However, after reading it for himself, he knew his father had been right to leave instructions for its delivery on this day.

The family were now all seated and awaited the beginning of the wedding music.

When the music started, Cathy stood in her seat and turned to watch for her daughter.

Tilda, followed by Bette and then Mary Louise, all preceded the bride down the long aisle.

The music was regal, and the atmosphere serene.

Then Goldie began the long walk down the aisle of St John's Church of England in Parramatta, on her father's arm, towards her future.

Her face was glowing with happiness.

Alfred awaited her.

Chapter 2 Powerful Words

*R*ick escorted Mary Louise from the church to the party venue at his Uncle Charlie's inn.

It had been two years since his grandfather had died, and it was strange to think that the innkeeper in Parramatta, his Uncle Charlie, was, in reality, the 4th Earl of Coxheath. Uncle Charlie and Aunt Gracie were the typical Australian innkeepers for most of the time. They also happened now to be Earl and Countess of Coxheath, and Uncle Charlie was the Viceroy for Western Sydney, so they had to 'frock-up' and attend the Governor's many official functions, and they hated it.

As did most of the family, Rick included. Oh, it had its perks, of course, like unrestricted use of a town carriage when in Sydney and permanent access to the best suites at the King's Arms Inn in Sydney, but it also carried responsibility, and it was these that irked the family.

Rick had grown up with the knowledge and still hated it. His Uncle Charlie had it thrust upon him when he was nearly the same age as Rick is now. As he walked from the church with Mary Louise on his arm, this was all flowing through his mind. He should have been chatting to her, but he wasn't in the mood. A single overheard comment had ruined his day.

Mary Louise was silent. She, too, had heard the remark and fell to wondering if they had a future together. Her mother should learn to keep her voice down and mouth shut. She knew Rick was hurt; she was too.

Alice Evans found that her tongue often ran away on her. The comment was intended for Sal's ears only, but she'd spoken far too loudly. There had been a cacophony of noise when she started talking, but everyone had fallen silent at once.

"Wouldn't it be lovely if Rick and Mary Louise made a match of it?" She realised both had heard the comment. She had the courtesy to blush as quite a few eyes turned to hers.

"Rick, I'm sorry," Mary Louise said as they fell behind some of the other young folk.

He turned and looked at the stunning girl on his arm. "Mary Lou, if I were older and had done some travelling, I'd be on one knee right now, but we're not even adults yet. I haven't even officially left school. How can parents throw this sort of thing at us and expect us to dance to their wishes? It's not you that I have a problem with. I hope you know that... It's them, all of them," he said with a harrumph.

She gently squeezed her fingers on his arm. "I know, Rick, I'm just sixteen, and my mother is on at me to find a man and settle down. Ricky, look at me…"

He turned and looked at her adorable face. "If, when we're older, you're interested, I would listen to that question, but no way do I want to consider it for years. I want to keep our friendship as it has been forever. Do you understand what I'm saying? Don't let them push you. Do what you have to do, Ricky; I'm not going anywhere." She blushed as she spoke.

"I'm sorry, Mary Lou, I hate being pushed to do things too. You know I want to, well, be more than friends, but heck, I'm only seventeen. I don't want to think about even growing up." He squeezed the fingers resting on his arm. "Let's forget about it and enjoy the party. As I have said before, you look stunning. The colour of your dress makes your eyes the most amazing lavender hue."

Her rosebud lips broke into a beaming smile. "Deal, Ricky, and thank you. You scrub up nicely, too." She chuckled. "I like dressing up for a 'do' like this, but hate the formality of the Law Balls Papa makes us attend. 'Do this,' or 'Don't do that', 'Dance with this man', and 'Behave yourself'. As if I don't anyway." This time, it was her turn to harrumph.

Rick grimaced, but with a smile. "Okay, let's throw off our moods and enjoy ourselves?"

She nodded. "Okay, Rick. Will you still dance with me? You don't ever tread on my toes like some of the others. You're so light on your feet."

He grinned and nodded. "Willingly, Mary Lou, willingly."

The party was about to start by the time they arrived. They had dawdled so much that they were two of the last to walk into the yard.

Mary Louise caught her mother's eyes and frowned at her.

Food had been prepared earlier and was now placed on the back of a flatbed wagon. It was brought down from Rick's Uncle Eddie's house, located up the street a bit; the wagon was unhitched and left at the edge of the courtyard, becoming the servery. They had performed this task for many functions over the years, and everyone was familiar with the system.

Rick saw his grandmother standing, just looking at the family. He knew what she was thinking and how deeply she was still affected. He pointed her out to Mary Louise, and together, they went to her side.

"I'm sorry, Grandmother, we all miss him. Do you know he wrote a letter for Goldie, and she was given it this morning? Jim had it in his possession. I wonder how many more he's got."

Sal turned to her grandson.

He was so like his father, Wills, that it made her gasp slightly. Wills was the dreamer of the family. He had run away at eighteen and returned overwhelmingly wealthy, and he used that wealth to build his empire. Wills had constructed his Emporium empire and now had over twenty stores across the state, as well as a colossal warehouse in Parramatta. Not that he showed it. He wore his simple, elegant, and understated clothing with dignity. Rick had inherited his father's style when he chose to 'tog up', as he called it. Like her beloved Charles, he, too, hated it.

"Thanks, Ricky boy. We all miss him. I aim to get through just one day at a time. As to the letters, there is one for each of you, and Jim has them all. I have no idea what is in them or when you are each to receive them. Each one is dated for a specific time, date or reason." She smiled at Rick and Mary Louise, and they assisted her to a seat so she could watch the party.

At seventy-two, Sal was still active and not at all wandering in mind. She was now the linchpin of the family. She still officially lived in 'Christina's Cottage' but spent little time there. She would spend a week or two at each of her six children's houses, but she was now mainly based at Eddie's house. They all loved having her whenever she stayed. She could not bear to surrender the cottage that she and Charles had lived in for so long, and no one asked her to leave it. She would when she was ready. If Sal chose to stay in the cottage for a while, one of the grandchildren or great-grandchildren would come for a 'visit'. These were always great fun. Everyone adored her. Luke's twins were her youngest grandchildren, and they were now twelve. One or other of them was often the occupant of the 'spare room'. It only had a single bed, so a roster was made as to who would 'sleepover' when she lived there.

The party was a success and went on for many hours. With early services the following day, it finished at dusk. Ricky and Mary Louise danced often. If it had not been a family party, that could not have occurred. The two dance rules still stood at official functions unless they were engaged.

As the two families were now twice related, that rule was considered obsolete. Rick's cousin, Neddie, had married Mary Louise's cousin Miriam; now, his sister, Goldie, married her brother. He was still trying to get his head around that Goldie was married. At twenty-one, she was older than most colony brides. She had waited for her beloved Albert, but hid her affection for him a shade too long.

Sunday morning, the family had gathered once again. Rick stood looking around at the vast number of family members that surrounded him. Many were nearing adulthood like he was, and he guessed that there would be an enormous quantity of marriages soon. He groaned, knowing that this meant he must 'tog up' for each one. But he didn't want to be one of them, no matter what his feelings for Mary Louise were, not yet anyway. Last night, his heart rate quickened when his eyes fell on her across the dance floor. She was in his older brother's arms, but he wasn't worried, as he knew that Lukie was interested in another girl present that evening. Rick expected a proposal to be announced soon and was surprised that it had not been announced already. At twenty-five, he thought Lukie was old enough to settle down.

At seventeen, Rick wanted to see what was over the hills and around the next bend and then the next. Well, further than the hills, as he had already travelled with his father. He wanted to see things before settling and not just be expected to take over the warehouse as his father wished. Not that he hated it, he didn't; he loved it. Every day was different, and you never knew who you would meet, but he wanted to do something first.

Yesterday, he and Mary Lou had discussed it often. Now, as he sat listening, he could hear his Uncle Eddie's voice wafting across the table of other voices. "Wills, you were only seventeen when you ran away to see the world. You came back stinking rich, and now look what you have done. Yes, okay, we all put a lot of hard work into it, but I only had one small Emporium; how many do you have now? Twenty?"

Rick saw the look on both their faces, and then he heard his father's reply, "Currently, yes, but five more are being built. It's why I want Rick to finish school and take over the warehouse full time. I need to treble its size and ..." his voice was overwhelmed by others.

Rick's heart sank. "No! Absolutely no way," he thought. How to get out of it, though. It was his father's dream, not his. All the arrangements had been made. He was to head in there as soon as school finished, which was the end of next week. Classes were already done for the year, but two essay submissions had yet to be presented. Then that was it. He'd do those and then leave. But how?

Mr Barlow at King's School was prepared to help Rick with some of the background information, and so after church the next day, the geography teacher spent a few minutes discussing the issues with Rick. Rick could not remember how the conversation had come up, but they had discussed the massive gold nugget found some years earlier in Ballarat, Victoria. "They called it the 'Welcome Stranger', you know. I'd darned well 'welcome' it too. Apparently, smaller ones are often found, but nowhere near their size. Still worth the miners' time looking for them." Mr Barlow looked at the student, knowing that Rick's father had found gold. No one had ever heard exactly how much he'd found, but all knew it was a lot. It had turned the entire colony around when the Bathurst boom had taken off, but Rick's father, Wills, had never let his wealth go to his head. Mr Barlow was proud of Rick and his work ethic. He was prepared to help him on the weekend, even though it was a Sunday. As the minister walked by, he changed the subject, and Rick realised and followed suit, switching back to their original topic when he was out of earshot.

"Thanks, sir; I really appreciate this information. Now, I can get cracking and finish the final essay. Then I'm done with learning." Rick stated adamantly.

"What? No university, young Richard?" Mr Barlow was shocked.

"Oh, no way, sir, my father wants me to run the warehouse. Lukie and Pip are being 'prepped' to take over the Emporiums while I 'do' the local one." He gave a soft groan. "I've got some growing to do first — so it's the warehouse he has in line for me." He sounded somewhat sulky.

"Not to your liking, lad?" Mr Barlow asked with a smile as he nodded to Wills across the yard.

"No, not exactly, sir, I want to see things and go places, not be stuck behind a shop counter all my life," Rick admitted.

"Tried talking to him? Fathers always want the best for their children; being the youngest son is sometimes hard, I know, as I am one too. My father wanted me to study law; I could think of nothing worse. I enrolled in university and changed courses without his knowledge. I graduated and started teaching. He was livid, but I have never regretted that decision. A teacher has a significant responsibility in shaping the minds of their students. No, lad, I do not regret my decision one bit."

As he spoke, Luke walked by and nodded to him. "Rick, your Uncle Luke is one of the very best teachers I've worked with. He can instil a love of learning in his students. If you can learn that from him, then you're made."

Mr Barlow did not know he'd just sown a seed in Rick's mind.

Rick had tried talking to his father, but he was always just too busy. Rick knew that his father had run away when he was eighteen and came back rich. It was a story he'd heard often as a child. He'd been sworn to secrecy, but he knew all the details by heart. He knew his father had proposed to his mother on the return trip before she knew of any gold finds. She thought he was just a penniless schoolboy. They had married when his mother, Cathy, turned eighteen. Only then did Wills tell her how much he had found. She didn't care, and it didn't change either of them. He stood looking at them both, then swung on his heel and walked off. He said to himself, "I'm going too! Father did it, so I'm leaving as soon as I can get sorted."

Mary Louise saw a look on his face and knew he'd made a decision. She came and stood beside him. "Ricky, what are you up to? I saw your face. What's happened?" She gently placed a hand on his arm as was appropriate.

He looked down into her violet eyes. "Father wants me to start work in the warehouse next Monday. I won't even get a break. I'm not going to do it, Mary Lou. I'm going to get out of here. I'll come back, I promise, but I need to go; I need to do this. I'm not going to tell you anymore, as I don't want to get you into trouble, but Mary Lou, please know that I care. More than that, I won't say now. I'll write, I promise. It may not be regular, but I'll send your letters to Hamish."

"Ricky, are you sure? You have everything here you could want." She was stunned. There was no way she wanted him to leave. She was nearly old enough to start courting, and she had always hoped he'd be the one to ask her.

"I have everything but freedom, Mary Lou; I'm not given a choice; everyone just expects me to do what they want and toe the line, their line, not mine. Father has not asked me once if I *want* to do the warehouse; I'm just expected to front up." He was exasperated and frustrated. "I'll get out of here somehow; just you watch."

As they were standing in the middle of the churchyard, many of the family observed their intimate and intense conversation. The deep concentration on both young faces led many to jump to the wrong conclusion.

"Such a lovely couple, aren't they?" Alice said a little too loudly again.

"A bit young for an engagement, but Rick's father was about that age when he married Cathy," said another.

"Mary Louise is a sweet girl; she'd be a good match for young Lockley," a third chipped in.

He looked up and saw his mother eyeing them, and she gave him a smile and a half twist of her face. That look told Rick that she, too, had heard the comments.

Rick growled quietly to Mary Louise, "See what I mean? They are all darned busybodies, and I won't stand around and see you hurt. If that means I leave… I'll come back, Mary Lou, but I have to go and do some growing away from here. Can you understand that?" Rick looked pleadingly at her.

"Yes, Ricky, but I'm going to hate it. You are special to me, you know that. I'll say our goodbyes now because we won't be able to later. I don't know if it would ever be more, but we're friends. Okay, very good friends, Ricky. Yes, I would like letters and Hamish and Effy are great. I would like to know where you are and what you're doing, if possible."

"Thanks, Mary Lou." He saw a tear well up in her eye and trickle down her face. He reached out and thumbed it away.

The action made him catch his breath; unfamiliar feelings made his heart skip a beat. "I'll come back, and... and... well, I'll come back to you."

"Be careful, Rick, but I'll be here, waiting. To make things easier, I'm going to throw a scene when we are near the inn. I know lunch is on there, and near the end... well, follow my lead."

"Are you sure?" he asked.

"Yes, if this is what you are intending to do, then we have to make a reason for you to go. As I know the real reason, and I know you will return, I don't want that door closed to you on your return. This will work, Ricky. Trust me." Mary Louise's heart was almost breaking, but she knew they could have no future unless he were settled.

"I do, Mary Lou; I do trust you totally. I even think I'm half in love with you, but we're just not old enough to do anything about it. I can't stay and put you through more innuendo than we are getting already." He offered her his arm, and they followed the bulk of the family as they all walked back to Uncle Eddie's backyard for a picnic Sunday lunch.

~

Three hours later, the luncheon was drawing to a close. The Evans family was due to leave on the ferry in less than half an hour. Rick was so nervous. He had no idea what Mary Louise had in mind, but yes, he trusted her, absolutely and totally.

"Put your arm around me, Rick," she said softly.

"What? I can't do that. I'd almost compromise you; then we'd..." his horrified look spoke volumes.

"Oh, for goodness' sake, Ricky, we're both too young. Just do it," she said with a beatific smile on her rose-red lips.

Nervously, he slid his arm along her shoulder, and suddenly, she was in his arms, her hands against his chest. A place where she had always wished to be, but now was not that time.

"Ricky, just know that I do care for you very much; now, here goes. I even wish I could kiss you properly, but bend and kiss me anyway." She had her face lifted to his as she spoke.

He did as she suggested, dropping his lips to hers and kissing her briefly on the lips.

She raised her voice. "Richard Lockley, what do you think I am? I'm not that sort of girl, and... well, you get your hand off me. How dare you treat me like that? Just don't presume you can kiss me because we're with family." She turned and stomped off, tears streaming down her face. They were genuine, as she knew she'd not see him now for some time, but she would wait, and he knew that. She would wait forever.

The stunned look on Rick's face was mirrored in many of the other faces watching.

A shaky voice was heard over the rippling river water nearby.

All had fallen silent, and all eyes turned from her to Rick.

"Father, I want to leave. Now! Right now." She turned her tear-stained face and looked at the faces of so many of her loved ones, but especially at the look of shock on Rick's face. Her heart broke. "Go find another girl to lavish your kisses on, Rick!" She turned her back to him. His face was sheet white.

Rick stood rooted to the spot.

He had no idea that was what she was intending to do. She said for him to go, so go he would. It was just as well he knew the situation for what it was because he felt his heart was not just breaking but shattered.

He turned and left the courtyard. He walked out of the gate and down to the riverbank in the opposite direction from the way they had gone. He made it to the bridge pylon and almost collapsed against the base of the bridge. He could not even catch his breath. If he was in two minds before about going, it was now a certainty. The ramifications of what was to follow would be unbearable for some time to come. He would not return with the family to Emu Plains, but he would pack his things and ostensibly head to the warehouse tomorrow to do the day's work as arranged. The two essays would be handed in on Monday, and then he would leave.

The decision was made; he stood and walked back to *Roseneath* to finish the essays. He'd sort the gear he needed and go on Monday. He had already set up some 'swaggie' kits for sale for the Emporiums, but he'd prepare a special one for himself. All he then had to do was collect it and leave. He had some savings from working at the various stores over the holidays, so his £10 would be stored, and he'd have to stretch it. He thought about catching the mail coach, but that was traceable. No, he'd become a swagman, humping a bluey or a matilda along the streets and byways. He had no real direction. He'd just leave. No fixed address and no destination.

The family returned to the house not long after he arrived on foot. His dress shoes pinched; he took them off and angrily threw them in the corner. They would not be going with him. He would take his riding boots and a change of work clothing. His oiled leather coat and a sheepskin waterproof. He could sleep on or under that, too. He packed the basics he usually took when travelling with his father and stowed them in a tied bundle under his bed.

When his mother looked in an hour later, he was feigning sleep, and he had no intention of facing them. He hurt too much. How could he explain what had occurred? It needed to look natural, and it did, far too real. He had no idea his heart would hurt so much, but now the dice were thrown, and he would be leaving.

He got up once his mother had closed the door and wrote a letter to his parents, which he would leave on his made bed and be gone before they woke. It would only be to leave the two essays at school, but they wouldn't know that. He would finish them after everyone else had gone to bed. He wouldn't return to *Roseneath* until they had left to go home. They had to leave soon after dawn themselves, as his father had a meeting at lunchtime at Emu Plains.

He loved his parents dearly and hated hurting them. This wasn't what he had planned. Well, he had not actually planned anything beyond leaving.

~

On the ferry back to Sydney, Mary Louise was inconsolable, weeping on her mother's shoulder. Her heart, too, was breaking. She had no idea how long it would be before she saw him again, but she'd wait as she told him.

Alice knew they had heard what she said, and guilt ate at her. She sent Phillipa out of the cabin to her father and brother.

Mary Louise hiccupped; she was so angry at all the silly busybodies who had caused Rick to wish to leave, including her mother. She pulled out of her arms and sat staring out the window, her arms folded. She was angry and sad simultaneously. Angry at her Mother for her thoughtless comments and sad that it had come to this. Rick had gone, or would be soon.

~

The morning was quite well advanced when Rick's parents gave up waiting for his return.

Cathy was in tears, and Wills was still angry at Rick. At dawn, when they had awoken, Wills let fly at his absent son. "The young whippersnapper, what the heck was he thinking, making a pass at her in front of all the family?" Wills was livid, and Cathy had never seen him so angry in the nearly twenty-eight years they had been married. "How did we bring up our son with so few manners?"

"Wills, for goodness' sake, calm down. I feel there's way more to this than meets the eye. It's not like Rick to do something like this, is it? Something else is going on. I can feel there's much more." She grabbed at his flaying hands and stilled them. "William Wentworth Lockley, look at me." Cathy held his eyes, and he calmed down a bit. "Wills, you trust me, I know that. Trust me now. Something has occurred. Go and see if he's up. I somehow doubt he'll even be there." She stroked his cheek, and he'd calmed down somewhat.

Wills walked down the corridor and knocked on Rick's door. When there was no answer and silence inside, he opened the door and saw the letter propped on the pillow. His heart sank. He also recognised the remorse in himself, as now he knew how his brothers felt when he'd done the same thing to them nearly thirty years before. He tore open the screed.

> *Dear Father,*
>
> *I know it will be you who finds this, and I'm sorry it must be this way, but I'm leaving. I shall write, but I must go. I have gone to submit my two final essays, and then I'll leave.*
>
> *Do not wait for me, for I won't return until you have left. Yes, I'll be watching. I love you both dearly and am sorry that I have caused you grief. Please know that I will take care and write when I can. I have no direction and will stay hidden. I may not even be using my real name, so do not seek me.*
>
> *I love you more than I can say. Be assured of that. Also, know that Mary Lou is dear to me. I would never willingly hurt her. Be assured of that, too.*
>
> *Pray for me. Tell Mother I love her, too. Comfort her as best you can.*
> *Rick*

Cathy found Wills sitting on the end of Rick's bed, a letter in hand. "He's gone, hasn't he?"

Wills nodded. "Yes, at least he will be. Cathy, it's me all over again. I have to let him go; I know that. I need to reply, and then we'll leave. He's coming back for his things but will wait until we've gone." He blew his nose on the crisp white handkerchief he always carried and rarely used, and then he released a long breath. "Oh, Cathy love, now I know how gutted Ed felt when I did this to him. Cath, what have I done?"

He looked more like a pleading twelve-year-old child rather than a forty-six-year-old man.

Cathy sat next to him. "Love, for some reason, I feel that what happened yesterday was for show. It's just not in Rick's nature to do that, and not to Mary Louise. He cares far too much for her to hurt her in any way. I'm sure… no, I'll leave that unfinished." She looked at her grieving husband. Her heart was hurting too.

~

Wills penned a long reply to Rick and left it on his pillow. Inside the letter, he left £50 in small notes and coins. It was all the cash he had on him. He told him to write often. Wills had written to Ed when he had left and left a letter on his desk without any farewells. He suggested that Cathy also pen a note at the end of the letter, and then they packed and departed.

It nearly broke Rick's heart when he saw his father assisting his weeping mother into the carriage. She turned and searched up and down the street. They did not see him sitting in the tree across the street. He waited until they were out of sight before climbing down and going inside through the kitchen door.

Brodie was still in the stables; he would soon lock the front door. He grabbed his bundle and the letter he was sure his father had left.

Rick quickly read it, surprised at the money it contained and the blessing his father had given him, too. Then, silently, he left again by the kitchen door. Rick would head to the warehouse and gather a kit of swaggie gear as his father suggested.

He had smiled when he had read his letter. They knew him far too well. Mother had even guessed that Mary Louise had put on a bit of a performance for everyone. It made the leaving easier for all, although this was not easy at all.

Rick hoped the return welcome in the years to come would be as easy.

Brodie saw him leaving. He, too, had been a witness to the incident and wasn't quite sure what to say. "You okay, Mr Rick?" he simply said.

Rick was just managing to hold himself together. He nodded. "I will be Brodie; look after them for me. I'll see you when I return," Rick muttered.

"You be going somewhere, Mr Rick?" Brodie met his eyes in an honest, loving look.

Brodie was only four years younger than Wills, and he had married Shauna Connor, who had lived with Eddie and Jenna since her parents' death.

Cara and Paddy Connor were lifers and had been assigned to Ed a few years after their marriage. Their two youngest daughters, Moira and Shauna, had moved in with them. They married two of the Murphy brothers and had all become like an extended family. Brodie cared for Rick like a second father. "Rick, don't go and do something you'll regret. Your father told me there was a letter for you. Did you get it? He also said you must write when you can. Will you promise to do that?" Brodie was concerned for the young man whom he loved like a son.

"Brodie, I promise. I will write, I just need to go. Will you drop me off at the warehouse? Father said I could help myself from the warehouse. Sorry, Brodie, but it means I won't be doing shifts there now as Father intended." Rick had a large lump in his throat. He hated goodbyes at the best of times, and this situation had escalated way beyond his intentions.

"Of course, Rick. Your papa said that you may need a lift. I've harnessed up the gig. Is that all right?"

"Sure, Brodie, and thanks. I've only got a bit here, but nothing to carry it in until I grab something from the warehouse. I will only take what I can carry, so it won't be much. Let me throw this in the gig." Rick took the small, tied bundle from his back and threw it on the floor of the gig. He hopped up and grabbed the reins.

Brodie opened the gate and hopped up beside him.

Rick drove the gig out the gate and, when he was halfway down the street, handed the reins back to Brodie. "Sorry, Brodie, I just wanted a last drive. It will be a while before I'm in the position to do so again."

Rick sat looking around the town and saw Ed come out of the Emporium. He must have been waiting for Brodie when he appeared at the door. When Ed lifted his hand in a farewell wave, Rick knew his father had spoken to him and told him of his plans.

Rick saw Ed put his hand on his heart and then, together in prayer, pointed to him.

Rick nodded and waved; he teared up.

Who knew leaving could be so darned hard?

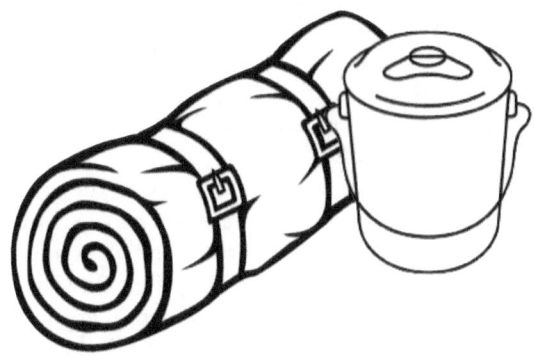

Chapter 3   Packing a Swag

$\mathcal{B}$rodie deposited Rick at the back entrance of the warehouse and tied the gig to the hitching rail. Rick had been inside hundreds of times before, but today was different. This time, he had to sort out what he would need to live on the road for goodness knows how long. He'd made up swag packs before, and so had Brodie, so they knew the basics of what was required. Hundreds had been sold to the miners heading to Bathurst.

Brodie insisted that he take a water bag, a billy, a frying pan, and some bags of dried goods, such as tea, flour, and salt. He was insistent on the salt and explained that sugar was a treat and salt was a necessity. He added packets of dried meat and other goods to the clothing, so the pile was cumbersome and quite heavy.

They repacked it, and Brodie grabbed two thick leather straps, making a sort of harness for the swag. It had two shoulder straps and one short one that held them together at the front; he added some smaller ones off the roll at the back and tied on the bulky fry pan and billy. Then he told Rick to grab a leather money belt.

"I've worn those before, Brodie, and they are darned uncomfortable. The leather digs in. I'll take a neck pouch sort." Rick knew that one of the things his mother made for the warehouse was small pouches on a coarse rawhide leather thong. It was far more comfortable to carry than a stiff leather belt under the shirt. He grabbed one and split his money, putting most of it in the pouch. Then, a note or two was placed under the sole of each shoe, and some notes were in his pocket with the coins.

All he then had to carry was his hat, as the rest sat on his back. It was bulky but quite comfortable, and with the thick straps, the weight was much easier to bear.

When Brodie asked Rick where he was heading, Rick returned a blank look. "I have no idea, Brodie; I'm just going. South, I suppose. It's as good a direction as any. I may work my way down to Ballarat and see what the goldfields down there are like. I've seen Bathurst. It's not the gold that draws me but the lure of adventure, I suppose. I'll write as often as I can." Rick swallowed again. "Okay, south, at least I know where I'm heading," he thought. "Cor, what have I done?"

Nearly two hours later, Brodie took Rick to the gig and left him at the railway station at Parramatta Junction. They had decided that it would be better for him to travel as far as the train line went and then see what happened from there. Rick had made that trip often with his father and was familiar with the area around Campbelltown. From there, it was all new. He hoped to pick up jobs at farms along the way. He could do blacksmithing, leatherwork, knife sharpening and all sorts of other jobs. Even fencing, but he wasn't too good at that. Labouring was something that he expected, too, even droving. He'd take what came and pray he'd have enough to eat. Pray, yes, he'd be doing lots of that too. Rick decided to leave it for a week before he wrote for the first time. He wanted to assure his folks that he was okay, especially his mother. He also wanted to thank his father for both the money and the goods. He sat in the rattling train as it carried him far from home. Click-y-clack, rocking and rolling, as it took him mile after mile further away from the comforts and luxury trappings of Emu Hall.

He had already written to Mary Lou. He would either deliver the letter to her or send it via Hamish upon his arrival in Sydney. So, first, he'd go to Sydney, then to Campbelltown and south. He wasn't actually sure how far the line went, but if it could take him as far away as possible, then he would walk cross-country. He didn't want to pay for a travelling carriage to take him to Ballarat. He knew Cobb and Co. were still running them. That wasn't his purpose. He intended that the trip would be mostly on foot. Seeing everything he could and experiencing life.

Once in Sydney, after posting Mary Lou's letter, he caught the train south and lay back relaxing. Listening to the rhythmic clacking of the rails as the miles passed. The rocking and rolling of the train was soothing to his hurting heart. At least Mary Lou knew the reasons he was going, and she knew he cared. The soot of the engine smoke blew in through the open window, and he decided to move to the other side of the carriage so he could keep the window open. It was the first time he'd travelled 'cattle class', as his father called it: no compartments but just rows of seats in the carriage with an aisle in the middle.

He watched out the window as long as he could, then closed his eyes. He'd had little sleep the night before and soon was deeply asleep. He was lying on his arm and knew it would be numb if he didn't move, but he was just too tired to care. The train carried him far away, and he was blissfully unaware that the distance between him and his family grew farther each minute he slept. He had curled up and was using his swag as a pillow. Otherwise, the stranger who was watching him may have ransacked it. Rick was totally unaware of the scrutiny of the man in the next seat. He had noticed his dirty teeth and food stuck in his beard. He also noticed the absence of a smell, which surprised him. Even the old man's clothing wasn't too dirty. He woke when he felt a hand creep into his jacket, which was empty anyway, as his valuables were now hanging around his neck in the pouch. He grabbed the hand and twisted it backwards, catching the man unawares.

Without a word, Rick looked up and raised one eyebrow.

"Cor, Gov, you be mighty young to be swagging. I figured you for a green new chum, but you'se is a cluey one you is." The man looked filthy, but his hands were clean, his nails clipped, and there was no noticeable odour. "Not to mention you'se got the grip of a bloody vice."

"Good, because as a blacksmith, I should. Now, can I help you?" Rick was shaking like a leaf. He'd barely been gone from home for half a day, and he was a potential victim of a robbery.

"Help? Well, I'se not sure about that, but ya got any tucker? I haven't eaten for a day," the old man said.

"Why did you waste money on the train then?" Rick asked, intrigued.

"Ha, that's some joke! I just jumped on the last stop where they refill water. The conductor won't be around until Goulburn or just before. I'll jump orf before then. It's the end of the line anyway." The dirty man grinned, and his filthy teeth looked black and smelled horrible. "I'll use shanks' pony from there to the border. How far is youse goin'?" he said, patting his legs.

"As far as the line goes. Now shove off. Here's some dried beef, but that's all I can give you." Rick handed over a large chunk of freshly dried beef. The old man looked hungry, and Rick had a stash of it. "Here's an apple, too; it looks like you need it more than I do."

"Ta, lad, tasty tucker you got. Thanks, mate."

The old swagman didn't leave; he stayed and ate his food, keeping his mouth closed and eating politely. He had manners that surprised Rick.

They had talked for some time; Rick wasn't sure how long, but he did notice the old man dropped his guard and spoke beautifully.

The swagman saw the conductor coming down the carriages and said a hasty goodbye. "I gotta fly, matey. May catch you by some billabong somewhere. Safe travels, lad, and thanks for the tucker." He shoved the apple down his jacket and had the dried meat hanging out of his mouth. He stood and heaved his own swag onto his back and headed for the rear of the train. His blackened billy was clanging on his frypan as he walked.

The train was due to refill the water tanks just before the last stop, and Rick wondered if that was when the swagman would get off. He sat watching until the conductor drew next to him. He produced his ticket and was informed that this coming station was the last stop. The train would terminate here, so all had to get off. They would arrive in less than thirty minutes.

He didn't notice the old man get off the train, but he watched the conductor open the back door and check that no one was free-riding on the back deck. It was empty. Rick hoped the old man was uninjured, then fell back to his own concerns.

Rick wondered where he would go on arrival at the train's destination. He wasn't even sure where that was. He picked up his clean-looking swag. It was obviously brand new, and he looked pristinely clean and far too young. Life for him now was going to be vastly different to how he'd grown up. He had roughed it camping with his family in Hartley, but this was going to be real roughing it. He hoped he'd cope. He knew he'd have to find work first. He figured that the police might direct him to a suitable job, perhaps with a needy farmer looking for assistance. It wasn't that he needed money; he needed a purpose, direction, experience and, above all, a distraction. The train pulled into the station with a screeching of the brakes, and a belch of black sooty smoke engulfed the platform. It stopped with a jolt that nearly sent Rick flying down the aisle. He gave a grunt, regained balance, and then walked to the door. He looked down at the platform to his left, only to see that it was some distance away. The rear carriage had not quite reached it, and there was a yard jump to reach the ground. With a soft groan, he heaved off the pack again and placed it half in the doorway, climbed down the metal stairs and then grabbed his pack again and hoisted it on his back once more. He thanked Brodie in a silent prayer for the design of the straps.

"The driver stopped short again, sorry, lad. Here, give us your hand, and I'll heave you up." All this had occurred under the watchful eye of a stationmaster.

Rick handed up his swag and was then given a helping hand onto the platform. "Thanks, sir." Rick settled his bundle on his back. "Any idea where I could get any work? Anything from smithing to fencing, sir, I can turn my hand to most things."

The firm grasp of the handshake that the stationmaster received from the lad gave a hint of the strength hidden under the lad's shirt. He was clean and well-spoken, too. The stationmaster looked at the immaculately clean lad and the brand-new swag. "The new smithy in town is currently trying to work with an injured ankle. I'd try there first if you're really genuine about your smithing skills. Dylan could do with some assistance. No one else here knows the work. Are you sure, though?" The stationmaster stood looking at the young man. He was hardly old enough to shave, but he was built solidly. His hands belied his boast.

Rick nodded. "Yes, sir, my family run a forge, and I grew up working on it. I know the trade well, but I've just finished school. Hence the soft hands. Can you give me directions, please?"

"His name is Dylan Davies. Head down the street that way and turn left at the end. Tell him Daniel sent you." The stationmaster smiled at the young man after he had given him directions.

"Thank you, Daniel. I will." Again, Rick shook his hand in an almost bone-crushing shake and then walked off.

Daniel stood rubbing his fingers, watching the lad go.

Within an hour, Rick's swag was ensconced in the tiny back storeroom at the forge, and he was already making his first horseshoe. The smithy, Dylan, was happy with his work and employed him for a month. After that, he'd probably not need him, but he'd see. As Rick had no intention of staying that long, he accepted, saying that he'd only stay until the man's ankle was mended. So, with the first month on the road sorted, Rick slept that night in the safety of the blacksmith's storeroom.

Rick was tired, but he was happy.

~

He woke the next morning at dawn, the sun beaming in through the open door. He had heard rustling in the rafters above his head during the night but was too tired to investigate.

He was met with the flickering tongue of a python only inches from his face upon opening his eyes. "Ahh, so that's what the noises were." He eased out from on top of his swag and crept away from the gentle beast. He thought, "At least there would be no rats or mice in here." Once up, he realised the snake was ten feet long and then some. Not something he would want around his throat. He heard noises from the cottage next door and had enough time to pull on his trousers before the smith's wife appeared. She called him in to have breakfast. She saw his visitor and gave a squeal, banging the door on her hasty departure.

He grinned and said through the door, "Thanks, ma'am."

There was a bucket of cleanish water, and he dunked his head in it and rubbed his face on an old but clean towel she'd brought out for him. He had already decided at home not to bring a razor. Not that any beard he could grow would be bushy, but it would make him look a bit older. His fuzz would probably be fair or red. His Uncle Charlie had apparently had red sideburns, and he eventually shaved them off.

Once washed and clothed, he headed into the kitchen. He was warmly welcomed, and a massive plate of bacon, eggs and toast was placed before him. "Gee, thanks, Missus Davies, this will hit the spot. I expected some porridge." He gave her a cheeky grin, and the dimples in his cheeks popped momentarily.

She smiled warmly at him. "You be a good boy and eat up. If you can help my Dylan while he is injured, you're worth your food. You may not want to be paid, but when you leave, I'll stock up your stores with whatever you can carry."

"Thanks again, Missus Davies; I'd appreciate that," Rick said while happily hoeing into the plateful of hot food. He doubted that life as a swagman would generally start with a full hot breakfast and a job.

The meal over, the two men headed into the forge. Dylan was leaning on a rough-looking walking stick. The coals were still warm from the day before, and Rick gathered them together, soon having the fire going. He hunted around and soon found everything; then, he worked out what orders were for the day. Dylan's foot was severely swollen, and he was having trouble even standing. Rick suggested that Dylan work the bellows while sitting, and Rick would get on with the items required. He tied a rope on the top handle so Dylan could work them while seated.

Dylan was amazed at how quickly the lad worked. He streamlined the method, and Dylan watched him in awe. Rick created the rough shapes first and then honed each one to meet the individual requirements as per the orders. He sorted the work so that he had four horseshoes heating in the coals while working on a fifth. As each step needed particular heating, this reduced the time necessary to complete a single shoe. Dylan had never seen it done this way before. He usually made only one horseshoe at a time, and it was a laborious and meticulous process that often resulted in much wasted time. With a stock of rough shapes now done, a single shoe could be completed quickly. Rick had made these in two basic sizes: draught horse size and riding horse. These can be easily adapted to other sizes.

Rick explained that their forge mass-produced them, which meant they could produce more in a day. He gave no hint about his family connections.

The following item was six scythe blades for an order. This, too, was done with a minimum of fuss. Rick demonstrated his prowess with the tools, and Dylan watched in awe once again. The final sharpening Dylan could do with a file while sitting at the vice. The pile of stock items grew as whatever Rick made added some extra 'blanks', as he called them. Soon, they had finished the few orders that were on the board, each now crossed out. Dylan was obviously not the most efficient blacksmith, and the ankle was also not the only reason the workshop was messy.

When Rick was busy sharpening the sixth scythe blade he had made, Dylan hobbled into the house after finishing the first five. He was exhausted. The pain of his injury was wearing, and he'd had enough.

As the heat of the day was now upon them, Rick scattered the coals and cooled the fire. As Dylan had not given him more work to do, he decided to organise the workroom. He found a box of long nails and, knowing he could make more, used some. He soon had the tools sorted, and he was quickly mounting them in an orderly fashion on an empty wall using the nails he had found. He had earlier spent some ten minutes hunting for a set of callipers that were supposedly on the bench. He had found them on the anvil.

When Dylan returned nearly an hour later, most of the tools were now in their new homes. Each position was outlined with chalk to indicate where each tool was located, and each was grouped into various categories.

Dylan walked in and stood with his mouth open. "Cor lad, that's fabulous. I'm always losing me stuff, and by the time I find what I'm looking for, the iron is cold." He stood grinning. "I thinks we is gonna get along jus' fine." His hands were on his hips, looking around the now organised room.

"So, you don't mind, sir?" Rick asked, somewhat concerned at what he'd done.

"Mind? Why should I mind, lad? It's blooming brilliant. Go to it, do what you think is best." Dylan slapped Rick on the back and roared with laughter. "You're the cheapest labour I've ever heard of, bed and board. I can deal with whatever you do. Oh, and that reminds me, Bronwyn said tucker is on. Something about special pasties and cheese on toast."

Rick was already ravenous. He had worked off breakfast and was ready for a good feed. If the pasties were like Aunty Betsy's, he'd be thrilled, but he doubted they would be; few were. Some were like glue. He washed again in the bucket of water at the storeroom door and vigorously rubbed his face and hands to rid himself of the dust, grime and sweat. He felt a little cleaner and refreshed. He walked to the kitchen door and was greeted by the most delicious scents wafting out the door.

"Come in, lad, take a seat. The Welsh rarebit is nearly done, and I have made you some pasties, too. Dig in; there are plenty." She greeted Rick with a smile.

"Thanks, Missus Davies. They smell delicious." He waited until they were both seated, and this time, he bowed his head and gave thanks. He noticed that they did not pause and say, "Thanks," so he said his own.

"It's Bron or Bronwyn, lad; Missus Davies is my mother-in-law, and she's in Wales," she giggled at Dylan's rolling eyes. "Sorry, lad, we forget the niceties of life sometimes; Dylan, would you please give thanks?" She'd seen Rick's action and felt embarrassed that they had forgotten to do this.

The three joined hands, and in a deep and respectful voice, Dylan gave thanks to the Lord for the meal and assistance Rick had brought to them. He prayed in a manner that only a believer would.

Rick's eyes flew open. "You believe, too? Seriously?"

"Yes, lad, we both do. And you are an answer to our prayers." Dylan grinned at him. "Sometimes we forget to thank the good Lord for his blessings. This food and your arrival are two of them. Now let's eat."

Bronwyn placed a platter piled high with pasties on the table but said, "Eat the Welsh rarebit first; it's delicious hot."

"Thanks, Bronwyn, they smell divine. I've not had this before." He helped himself to a half slice. Once he'd taken a bite, he groaned with desire. "Oh, this is delicious." He munched on a second bite.

Bronwyn smiled. "Mother's secret ingredient is called garlic. She bought some bulbs from an Italian sailor, and I brought some growing bulbs out with me. I grow it myself, as I can't buy the stuff. I grate the cheese and mix in some garlic, then melt it into the buttered toast. Certainly not traditional, but it's delicious. Sometimes I add some finely diced garlic or onion tops too."

"It certainly is, Bronwyn. I'll have to work this off this afternoon. If your pasties are as good, I'll be huge by the end of the month," he chuckled. He bit into one of those, and it was equally as good as Betsy's crisp, flaky pastry. The filling was stuffed full of vegetables and minced meat, and the best thing was that there were no turnips. "Gee, Dylan, you're on a good wicket here." He grinned while still chewing.

Dylan nodded, smiling at his wife.

~

Three months in Goulburn passed quickly. Rick had no intention of staying past the one month, but Dylan's ankle took time to heal. It was ten weeks before he could stand on it easily, and another two weeks before it was totally healed.

Rick had been moved from the storeroom into a sleepout on the side of the house. The snake had decided to 'snuggle' him in the middle of the night. Rick had been found asleep in his swag on the lawn on the second night of his stay. When he explained that his sleeping quarters were not a 'single' as expected, they said he could bunk down on the meshed verandah. This was a delight as Rick didn't like snakes.

Rick discovered soon after he started that they had only been married for six months and were still adjusting to life in town. They had arrived from Wales with little more than their clothing and found that the forge in town was vacant. The previous smithy had drowned in the flood nine years before, and no one else knew the skill. Dylan took over, and while moving the anvil in his first week, he injured his ankle. Rick had arrived and did the sorting Dylan needed. Hence, the disorganisation in the smithy's shop, no wonder it looked filthy. It had nine years of neglect.

With the two working closely together, they knocked the forge, shop and storeroom into shape. Dylan had no idea what some of the tools were for, and Rick was able to explain them to him. Dylan had only ever done basic smithing in Wales and never expected to use it again. Rick taught him some skills and showed Dylan some easy ways to stock up on what would be most likely needed. He also gave Dylan the address for Eddie and told him to write there for supplies. He suggested he order a few coach springs and moulded tool heads, as they lasted longer than the welded ones. Plough heads they could make, and Rick and he drafted a list of what he should keep in stock. The storeroom contained a vast amount of raw pig iron and basic supplies; he just needed to work it into saleable items.

Dylan took note of all the information, and before Rick left, the load had arrived from Eddie, along with three letters for Rick.

His Uncle Luke's logistics company delivered it, and Rick introduced the drivers. Rick knew most of them as he had often done trips assisting with large loads, but he had not been this far south before.

The storeroom was now just that. It, too, had now been reorganised and was sorted with spare items. The partially made horseshoes were sorted into various sizes, and they had made shelves and stacked everything so that it was findable. The snake had watched the proceedings from a distance for some time, and Dylan was not sure he wanted it to stay there, so Rick suggested they place orange peels and cedar offcuts around the room. This should eliminate the rodents, and then the snake would move on. Sure enough, it was gone within a week.

Daniel Jones, the station master, had come to see how Rick had settled in. He was surprised that the smithy shop now looked neat and tidy after just a week. "Gee's lad, you're a blooming miracle worker. I know Dylan needed help, but you've done wonders."

Daniel became a regular visitor. He, too, was from Wales, but since he was unmarried, he had been adopted by the Davies couple. Daniel was a boon for the business as soon as word spread that the new smithy was now open for orders.

Dylan and Rick also sorted the bookkeeping side of things, and with Rick's two uncles, Eddie and Luke, now assisting with deliveries, business was soon brisk. Rick knew that some of the items had come from his father's warehouse, but he couldn't bring himself to write directly to him to ask for things, not yet anyway.

Dylan now had a handle on the basics.

~

By March, Rick knew Dylan had everything under control. It was time to move on. The clinching decision came one morning when Bronwyn served them soft fried eggs. Dylan squished him onto the toast as he loved to do, and Bronwyn raced outside. Both men watched her flee, and Dylan grinned. "She's gonna have a bub."

"Ahh, that's great, Dylan; congratulations to you both! I was going to say that it's time I pushed off. I had only intended to stay for a month, at most. I've been here three. But you're all sorted now, and business has already picked up. If you have any questions, ask Uncle Eddie. He'll help with whatever you need."

"Thanks, laddie, I will. You've been a boon, and I really don't know what I would have done without you."

They both turned as Bronwyn walked back into the kitchen.

"Congratulations, Bron, I was just saying to Dylan that it's fabulous news." Rick ate a hearty breakfast and headed out to the forge. However, he knew it was time to go. He left Dylan to tell Bronwyn.

A week later, they were waving farewell to their blacksmith angel.

Daniel, too, had come to say farewell the night before and thanked Rick for assisting his friend.

The town now had a fully equipped blacksmith and one who knew where to turn for assistance. Daniel had arranged that Dylan could send letters to Ed by train with the guardsman, and small orders could be delivered by the next train if urgent. Large ones would come by Lockley's Logistics.

With a trustworthy backstop, Dylan was now far more confident. He waved a farewell to an overloaded Rick and watched until he was out of sight; with a deep sigh, he returned to the now silent forge, almost wishing that his ankle had not healed as well.

Chapter 4 Moving On

*R*ick was awoken by a splodge of dribble sliding down the stubble on his cheek. The first thing he saw when he opened his eyes was a huge brown eye gazing at him. He both groaned and laughed. The cow licked his cheek, and more drool oozed from its mouth. "Oh yuck! Move off, Daisy or whatever your name is." He groaned and pushed the cow's face away from him. It let out a loud bellow and slowly moved away. He'd arrived on dusk and found he was sleeping on a lovely grassy bank of a large billabong. He knew he was on the Wollondilly River on the outskirts of Goulburn. It was obviously near the watering hole of a dairy herd. He sat up and saw some thirty other cows in the area. One behind him lifted its tail and splattered him with excrement. "Oh, that's disgusting!" Thankfully, only a few spots of the obnoxious greenish ooze had landed on him. He heard loud laughing from down at the water's edge. His eyes focused in the early morning light, and he could see the old swagman from the train washing in the river. His torso was bare, and he was washing his shirt.

"One got me, too. We chose a bad spot, lad; at least there's water to wash in. I might even do a spot more washing." The old man chuckled as he yelled. "Got any more tucker? I could do with a bite to eat."

Rick noticed his now-perfect English; he had a small campfire a little further along the riverbank. "I do, actually, more than I can eat, and much of it is fresh and won't keep." The old man hadn't hurt him before; he had even looked concerned, so Rick decided to share his bounteous gifts of food with him.

"Roll your swag and dump it next to mine; they don't like fires so that they will stay away," the old swaggie said.

"Will do, thanks, mate," Rick replied.

"The name is Jack, lad. Just Jack, nothing more, nothing less." The old codger grinned at Rick. His teeth were no longer black but pearly white and even. "Hey, at least you kept your clothes on; some don't. Makes for a fun sight the next morning."

Rick grinned. He knew that sleeping in the buff may have been more comfortable, but he had been brought up in a house with girls, and his mother would often come and wake him, so he always made sure he was adequately covered. Rick rolled up his worldly possessions and dumped them next to Jack's fire.

"Bring your shirt down and wash it. The sun will dry it pretty quick today," Jack shouted up to him.

"Will do; I might have a swim too. Is the river okay for that?"

"I dunno, I don't swim; I can't, actually. It's blooming cold, though; I'll tell you that much. Me fingers is freezing jus' washing me clothing." Jack got busy washing his fouled shirt again.

"Hey, Jack, lay off the accent. You forget, I've heard you speak perfectly," Rick said softly as he eventually joined him at the water's edge. He didn't wait for a reply. Rick would have loved to dive in, but his father had taught him never to dive into a river, as you never knew what was underwater unless you could see it clearly. He couldn't, and he was glad he listened as about six feet out, a dead tree had wedged itself in the bank. It was totally invisible from above. He had stripped off and gingerly waded into the frigid water, giving himself a complete wash. Once wet, the initial chill of the water became bearable. He swam across the river and back, the cold invading his limbs. "Brrr," he said as he emerged.

Jack met his eyes with a wicked grin when Rick came back. "Sprung me, lad. You are correct; I throw on the slang as a defence. I've been burned a few times by speaking, well, normally. I blacken my teeth with charcoal when I travel. Puts off people approaching me." No more explanation was forthcoming, but none was really needed. "Now you said something about tucker?"

They laid out their washed clothing in the sun and headed back to the fire and their swags. Each wondering who would say something…

Rick spoke first. "I have spent the last three months working with Dylan at the blacksmith's forge. His wife loaded me up with so much food that I found it hard to carry it all. There's jerky, dried fruit, damper, beans, flour, sugar, tea, and so much more. That will all be kept, but there are fresh pasties, six hard-boiled eggs, four fresh ones, cheese, and even some stew. If you're happy, we'll have a feast for a few days, at least until we eat the perishable stuff. I was hoping I'd meet someone to share with; I'm glad it's you."

"Are you kidding? I haven't seen food like this for… well, for ages." Jack gave him a broad, toothy grin. "Did you say bacon too?"

"I didn't, but there is some and the eggs. Have you ever had French toast? My father makes a mean Australian version with emu eggs and damper; we'll go halfway and make damper toast with bacon on top. How does that sound?"

"You really have some bacon? I've died and gone to heaven. And French toast used to be my favourite breakfast with crispy fried bacon on top." For him to even know what it was surprised Rick. He didn't ask.

The two got busy with both frypans and billy cans. Soon, the fire was covered in two frying pans: one with some dripping and French toast damper, and the other with long slices of home-cured bacon. Rick's Billy was off to the side, sitting, waiting for the water to boil, were two tin mugs. Jack's billy, which was black and badly dented, was larger and had a lid, and Rick asked if he'd mind if they could have a hot wash with his water.

Jack nodded. "Cor, you even have tea and sugar. Oh joy, oh bliss. I'm sick of lemon myrtle tea with honey." Jack released a sigh of contentment and a chuckle. "I have a sweet tooth, I'm afraid." His accent and laugh reminded Rick of his now-deceased grandfather. Now, he spoke without hiding it; his English accent was similar to his Uncle Ned's and the cousins from Kent. Both of these dear men were now gone, and Rick missed them, especially his grandfather. Jack's voice reminded him of them if he closed his eyes. However, his unkempt hair and long flowing beard were filthy, but there was no smell. He was clean, as were his hands. Even his nails were trimmed and clean.

They heard the cows bellowing from the other side of the paddock and saw a farmer come and open the gate so they could get into the dairy shed. Jack watched them. "I've been working over there and have got sick of milk, cream, and cheese; however, they gave me a large chunk to take with me. We can add that to our feast, lad." Jack waved to the farmer, who replied with the lift of his arm.

"Hold off on the cheese, Jack; we can have 'Welsh rarebit' for lunch, at least a campfire version." Rick smiled at his new friend. Dylan had shown him how to melt the cheese over the coals by using a camp oven. Rick only had one frying pan and needed two to follow Dylan's instructions, but with Jack's, he could try it. Dylan explained that the trick was to toast the bread first and then melt the cheese on top. Jack's frying pan could work as a lid.

"So much for roughing it, laddie; we're supposed to be swagmen living rough." Jack served the French toast and bacon, bowed his head and gave silent thanks.

"No need to hide the 'grace' from me, Jack. I also believe. We have much to praise God for. Good food and companionship are two blessings given to us by our Lord." Rick saw a smile spread over Jack's face.

"They are that laddie." The old man's eyes twinkled with delight.

Together, they bowed their heads and gave thanks for the bounteous gifts. Rick caught the twinkle in Jack's eye. "What?" he asked while munching.

The old swaggie's eyes sparkled with joy, "Nothing, lad. You're the first person in years who believes in God and has been prepared to admit it. Many are ashamed of their faith in the Almighty. I am not, but I have had many occasions in past years where my faith was tested. Never be ashamed, lad. Take it from someone who has seen many sides of life."

Rick smiled and replied. "Jack, my Christian faith to me is a bit like one swagman telling another swagman where food is, or in our case, sharing what one has. In other words, sharing the food is sharing the faith. It's so necessary to who I am that I can't exist without it."

"Oh, I so agree; I have often used the five points of Evangelism I heard many years ago at home to tell others of my beliefs. I tell whoever will listen; sadly, not many will," Jack muttered. "Rick, I speak to the sky every night, you know. Then I lay back and look up at the myriad of stars; I see God in everything. I speak to him like a friend."

"I've heard of those before, and I wonder if they are the same? My Uncle Ned told me about them; he had heard about them from a minister in West Sussex, and he had told my cousin Kit. He called them evangelism points and told me that if I wanted to share my faith with others, I should remember these five points and use them as my personal 'prompt'. They are:- 'God, Man, and God. What if you do? What if you don't'?'"

Jack looked at him intently. "Mine are the same, and word-for-word too. Ned, you say, eh?" His eyebrows flicked up, and then he shrugged. He wondered if it was the same person, but said nothing. "I heard them in a church in Kent many years ago. I suppose that as they are not far from each other, it's possible that one Minister heard it from another."

After a laugh about the coincidence, or God-incidence as Rick called it, the two fell to eating their delicious meal. Once the pans were empty, both used another half-slice of damper to mop up the drippings.

"I have a treat for dessert, too, Jack. Do you like 'cockies joy'?"

"No idea what that is, son." Jack's eyes grew round. His bushy eyebrows hid the stunningly blue orbs, and he looked intently at Rick. "But I'm not eating another cockatoo ever again. You know what they say about them, don't you?"

Rick shook his head.

"Throw a cocky and a rock into a pot; when the rock is soft, eat it and throw out the cocky." A smile slid across his face.

Rick grinned. "No way is it like a dead cocky, Jack. This is sweet, like honey. I'm sure you've heard of golden syrup. Well, here it's called 'cockies joy' because 'cockie farmers' used to buy it by huge tins and used it instead of butter."

The old man chuckled again, "Oh, that stuff, yep, delicious tipple. I mix a spoonful of water and drink it. How do you eat it, lad?"

"On damper or in doughboys, Jack, with thick butter, and Bronwyn gave me some butter too. As it won't keep, we get to eat it tonight."

The two pairs of blue eyes twinkled at the thought of a delicious, sweet treat.

"But what's a doughboy?" Jack was intrigued.

Rick didn't answer but made them for Jack, and they devoured the delicious, gooey meal. They set to making another damper, then lay back on their swags and chatted.

Jack started singing the hymn, 'Amazing Grace,' and Rick joined him, followed by other hymns. They stayed by the billabong near Goulburn for a few days, eating the perishable food that Rick had been given. No mention of future plans had been discussed by either man. On the third night, Jack came straight out and asked. "Rick, what the heck are you doing here, you know… doing this. I'm sure you have a good home and a loving family, and you're living as a swagman like me?"

Rick gave a half-laugh, "It's a bit of a long story, Jack, but at seventeen, I'm too young to marry and don't want my life planned for me. Yes, I have a loving family and a great life, and I will return to them; they know that, too, but I need to find myself. I need to do this."

"Do what, lad?" Jack's stare was like he was looking into Rick's soul.

"I need to see the world that I live in, my way. If that means humping a swag or a bluey from one end of the country to another, then so be it. Jack, my father, did the same at seventeen. He ran away. I at least wrote and have gone with their blessing. Okay, I didn't actually say goodbye with loving hugs and all that, but they know where I am and what I'm up to. I've even written and put Dylan in touch with the family business and have received loving, supportive letters back. I'll go home when I'm good and ready, and they know that, too."

Rick was not telling him everything; Jack knew that, but as he'd not said a thing about his past, he wasn't one to criticise. His own story would take more than a few nights around a campfire to tell. So, he just nodded and left it there. Jack took a deep breath. "Fine, so where do we go next? Feel like sticking with me for a bit? At least until the novelty wears off?" Jack was afraid to meet the young lad's eyes. He had never made that suggestion before, but he wanted to stick with this boy.

"You mean it? Really? I'd love that. But what about your plans?" Rick asked.

"Got none. Been everywhere I've heard about. Where do you want to go? I've been around on the roads for years. Seen most places, meant to return to a few; one, in particular, I wouldn't mind heading back to, but I didn't want to travel by myself. My own company is wearing thin." Jack was tickled pink that he now had a travelling companion. "So, as I said, where to next?"

Rick blew out his cheeks and thought hard. "Ooh, I don't know, Ballarat, I suppose. Father found gold in Bathurst, and we've been back often for work. Jack, it's not the gold I want to pursue, but to see the diggings there and observe how different they are. Bathurst is alluvial, but Father found reef gold. I'm not sure what Ballarat is, but I've heard that nuggets are even found in the bush."

"There are, you're so right there, but the nuggets are few and far between. Don't just expect to bend down and pick them up. For every thousand miners, one may strike it lucky to some degree; of those lucky ones, only one of them will hit the jackpot. The people who make money are the storekeepers and shops. Many miners find a fortune and have lost it in a week. Drinking, gambling, and, excuse the term, whoring. The girls on the goldfields must be the richest in the place. The undertaker also gets a cut, as does the blacksmith. Most miners go broke or just die. Having said that, let's give it a crack, eh, sonny? At least it gives us a destination. So Gunning and Yass are the next stops, followed by Gundagai. We'll see how the money holds out from there. I usually work as I go. Fruit picking is hard. Strawberries are the worst, as they are backbreaking. Hence, I've been milking and churning butter. How does that suit?" Jack grinned. He'd been itching to go back south but didn't want to make the long, arduous journey alone.

"Suits me just fine, Jack, but are you sure? I must admit to being somewhat fearful being by myself, and that, admittedly, is partially your fault." He looked sheepishly at the old man.

"Why so, lad?" Jack looked shocked.

Rick didn't want to admit how scared he had been when he grabbed the man's hand as it crept into his shirt. So, he just said, "The train incident, Jack, I didn't think to protect my valuables much until then. Not that I have much, but it made me do a double-take as to how easily things could go awry."

"Well, you had me, too. Only I thought you were dead. I was feeling for your heartbeat, hence the hand in the shirt. Your pouch, by the way, was sticking out of your shirt buttons. I sat watching over you while you slept. You reminded me of a school friend I knew a long time ago, and I couldn't help but notice the similarity between you and him. Same fair hair and blue eyes, you're a dead ringer for Paul if the truth be known. It took me back to happier times, lad. As you had not moved in some time, I felt for your pulse and couldn't get one. Your hand was cold as ice. I admit I panicked a bit, too." Jack looked deeply into the flames as they danced around the billy base. The fear that had made his heart skip a beat surprised him.

Rick remembered that Jack had looked concerned when he had awoken and that, too, had surprised him. He was more concerned with his numb arm and the fact that he could have lost everything. It turned out that Jack was more like a guardian angel rather than a thief.

"Well, if you have known any of my extended family, we all have a family likeness." Rick thought back to the first time he saw the two paintings in London and Kent. At least when he saw the artworks, he was old enough to realise they were not of his father and uncle. They were over one hundred and fifty years old by then, but both looked as though they had been recently painted. Rick fell silent. There's no way this old swaggie would have known his extended family, though. Dukes and earls would not have been in this man's circle of school friends, would they? Rick remained silent. Neither had shared their surnames. And neither had asked for more information about the other's background, and that's how it stayed.

Jack and Rick headed south, walking the long miles in companionable friendship. Old and young, wise, and keen to learn. The two were odd friends. Each taught the other many new skills and hunting tactics, from tickling trout in icy streams to making fish traps and collecting the fish from the rock-lined pools. They walked through Yass, Gundagai, Holbrook, Albury, Glenrowan, and Violet Town, working where they could. From there, they decided to enjoy the sights of Melbourne before heading to Ballarat. By the time they had arrived in Glenrowan, winter was not far away. Jack said that Ballarat was not a place to be in winter as it was so cold. So, they decided to head to Melbourne and board at a place Jack knew. They had earned a fair bit working *en route*. They could both work making bootlaces over winter and head out to the goldfields when it started warming up. Spring was a good time to be there; not too hot and not too cold. Their arrival in Melbourne was on the back of a train. They had hopped on again when the engine had stopped to refill and jumped off when it slowed before reaching Melbourne. Rick was scared stiff he'd fall and even more concerned that Jack would hurt himself. Neither thing occurred, and they hot-footed it off the rail lines before being caught. They slept rough a few nights in town, and Rick was in awe at the things he saw. When Jack showed him the post office, Rick stood awestruck at the amazing building. It had a clock tower on one corner of the double-story arched building.

Rick's home was Emu Plains, a small village just across the Nepean River west of Parramatta. He had been to Sydney, London and even to Kent, and Melbourne reminded him of some of the buildings he had seen in London. There was nothing like it at Emu Plains. He stayed silent. Not many seventeen-year-olds had travelled, let alone so often. Some of the buildings were larger than those in Sydney, but overall, he was impressed with what he saw. Jack showed him the river in town and waited for Rick's reaction. "Oh yuck. It's filthy. Do they drink that? It's like it's flowing upside down." Rick exclaimed in horror at the muddy brown river water.

Jack sniggered and smiled, just the reaction he expected.

Rick wandered around with his eyes wide open, absorbing all he saw.

Jack suggested that he write to his folks and tell them of their plans. He could post his letter at the new post office.

Rick did.

~

Every few weeks, Jack would insist that Rick write again. He had no idea that Rick had already posted a few letters in secret. Mary Louise had already received a couple from Melbourne, and so had Uncle Ed, mostly to thank him for his help with Dylan. His parents were the most difficult to write to. His guilt over how he left still hurt. He knew his mother would worry. It's what mothers did, wasn't it? So, he settled down to write a long screed. He'd purchased a special letter sheet from the post office. It was light blue and gigantic. He wondered if he'd have enough news to fill the four pages of paper. He didn't fill in the address until he was just about to post it, in case Jack saw it. One day, he may tell him his full name, but not just yet.

~

They spent the three months of winter in Melbourne making leather bootlaces and leather hide strips for mattress bases for Mr Tyzzer. They made overnight, weekend, or even week-long trips to various other areas, including Portland and Geelong.

In October, they decided to look around the western part of the state. Jack had not been out near Clunes, and he wanted to see it. Gold was still being found in reasonable quantities there, and Rick, too, was interested in the mines out that way. They had done little exercise over the cold months and were now out of condition. Jack had caught a cold soon after arrival, and it had gone to his chest. Rick had worried about him. He was now fully recovered but weakened. So walking was out of the question.

Mr Tyzzer, the bootmaker, had the pair of them cutting up leather hides, and as jobs go, there were worse. However, the stench of the leather tanning solution was unbearable. It permeated their clothing and their swags, as well as stained their hands. Both were pleased they would not be there in the summer.

They left Melbourne on the first weekend in October and headed to Clunes and the other goldfield towns in their sights. The weather was quite pleasant during the days. Nights were still cold, and they huddled close to the campfire.

Jack would regale Rick about the many adventures he'd had along his journey through various countries on the overland route to Australia. He'd stowed away twice and cut his trip short. The last leg from India was the worst, as the cargo storeroom was filled with rats and smelled of decay.

Rick soaked them all in. He found that Jack sometimes called his swag a "Matilda". Rick smirked as his older sister's middle name was Matilda, although she was known as Tilda. He'd tease her about that when he saw her next.

~

They celebrated the anniversary of a year since Rick had left home. He'd not told Jack that it had been his eighteenth birthday the week before. They sat again around a campfire and ate doughboys and cockies joy again. The treat Rick had introduced Jack to the night they met. It had been easier just to make them rather than explain them. Rick's mother had made these for all his siblings whenever they camped at Hartley. It was a simple damper mix, pulled out into long dough strips and wrapped around a gum tree branch. The end must be sealed. This glob of dough was then held over the coals until it was puffed up and cooked. The baked dough would be hollow when pulled off the stick and filled with golden syrup and a dob of either butter or thick cream. Eaten hot, it was one of the treats of camping.

Jack had fallen for this young man as he now was.

Rick's beard was still sparse, but he was maturing quickly. He was surprised his beard was not red but a light brown.

They had some incidents on their travels, having narrowly avoided the occasional snake.

Once, they nearly set up camp under a large gum tree, Rick remembered Uncle Ed's story from his honeymoon when a branch had fallen just after his Aunt Jenna had used the tree. They moved some distance away into the open. Through the night, a huge branch just dropped. It woke them both, of course, and they stood looking at it the next morning, both speechless. The size of the branch was thicker than Rick's leg. They raised their eyes and thanked God for their protection once more.

Another incident involved a bull, and Jack discovered he could still run fast after all. However, the most dangerous incident was when they accidentally came across a bushranger hideout while stomping noisily along a bush track to scare off snakes.

Rick 'quick-talked' them out of danger by offering them supplies and cooking them a meal. He had heard many bushranger stories from his father's friend, Jim Leslie. Jim had been a Cobb and Co. coach driver and had been held up some four times by Ben Hall and company, which Rick knew about. This had occurred before Jim had retired to train draught horses on Uncle Harry Harlow's farm, just down the road a bit from their house in Emu Plains. Rick adored hearing Jim's tales. Rick also knew about one bushranger named Gilbert, who had shot Jimmy Saunders, his cousin, Mattie's husband, but Rick knew John Gilbert to be dead some years ago. He wondered who this person was—just their confounded luck to run into some criminals. So, Rick knew enough to keep his mouth shut and butter them up with the promise of food.

By now, both men were dirty, and no matter how much they washed, they could not get the stench of leather tanning solution from the bootlace making out of their clothing. This actually worked in their favour. They smelled so bad that they were told to keep away from the bushranger camp.

Jack was alarmed when they discovered that the bushranger was Andrew Scott, better known as Captain Moonlight, who was in charge of this band of ruffians. He'd read about his escape from Ballarat Gaol the year before. It never occurred to him that he'd stay in the area. Jack whispered to Rick who it was and that they were in grave danger.

Rick remembered Jim also saying that the bushrangers had always wanted food from the Ellisons' when they were raided. Rick hoped and prayed that this mob were the same and enjoyed a free feed. They had passed a pond not far from their campsite, and Rick noticed duck poo around the edges. Surprising Jack, Rick offered them all roast duck for dinner. The leader had his arm slung affectionately around the shoulders of a younger, clean-shaven man whom he later discovered was called Nisbett. The group laughed disbelievingly, but each answered Rick in the affirmative when questioned.

Rick figured he would need at least eight birds to feed everyone; however, more wouldn't hurt. He would let only Jack come with him, so that Jack could mind their gear without it being ransacked. Just before dusk, Rick stripped off and silently entered the cold, murky water of the duck pond. He had cut a thick reed and top and tail it, leaving a long, straw-like tube. He waited in the water, half-submerged.

The ducks flew in and settled for the evening.

In the gloom, Jack watched as the first one bird, then another, was pulled below the surface. Jack smiled quietly to himself when he saw that the hole in the centre of the ducks was getting bigger and bigger. Not a sound was made. Jack saw bubbles amongst the ducks, then he heard a gentle splash and saw Rick struggling to hold his catch. The birds quacked and took off.

"Jack, grab some of these damned things, will you please?" Rick had five pairs of legs in each hand. All the birds had drowned and now hung limply from his hands. "I would have got more, but I couldn't hold them."

Jack took four that Rick was having trouble holding and laid them on the pond bank. He reached down and took the rest, a few at a time, then helped Rick out of the pond.

"Good job, lad, but how did you hold your breath for that long?" Jack was impressed with his prowess.

"I didn't, Jack. That's what I use the straw for; you breathe in through that and out through your nose. It takes practice, but I've done it heaps of times before. If you only need one or two, you don't bother with the straw. Father taught me long ago. He learned it from the aboriginal children when he was little," Rick explained, then said, "Head back to camp, Jack, and be careful. I'll be along in about ten minutes. Oh, and leave your big billy, please."

Rick helped Jack up, and he went to sling both swags over his shoulder.

"No, just take your own, Jack, and a couple of the ducks if you can manage them. Can you find your way?" Rick said. He grabbed a handful of duck legs and passed them over.

"Tell them to build up the fire. I need lots of hot coals." Rick found the outcrop of clay he'd seen while passing earlier and filled the big billy with clay and added a slosh of water to the top.

Jack frowned but did as he was asked. He left the moonlight, allowing him to see the way. He followed the narrow path, humping his swag and some of the ducks that Rick had just handed him.

On arrival at the bushranger's encampment, some ten minutes after Jack, Rick got busy mixing the clay to the correct consistency, then encasing the ten ducks in grey clay and setting them near the fire to harden. Soon, ten mud-encrusted balls sat ready for the fire. Coals were scraped back, and the duck balls were placed around the edge of the fire and covered in coals. "Now to wait," he said.

"How blooming long though? I'm famished," Scott asked.

"For them, about an hour or a bit more, but we're having Australian French toast first. Because look..." Rick pulled two enormous green emu eggs from his billy. "I found a nest on the way here today. They have only started laying this week, so these are fresh. I saw you with some dampers. Can I use them?"

Scott nodded, intrigued by the lad. He thought damper was just damper, a bit chewy and bland. He shrugged and pointed to where they had them stored.

"I need about six frypans. You got any butter or dripping?" Rick set about making the French toast with their dripping. Soon, everyone was exclaiming how delicious it was. By the time everyone had eaten their fill of Australian French Toast, the ducks were cooked. They had each been turned once. Rick had cracked one open and saw it was ready. All the feathers were now stuck to the hardened clay. The juices from the birds were soaked up with more damper, and the cooked flesh was delicious.

Jack watched on, impressed. This lad was a never-ending source of amazing things. Rick had taught Jack more about making tasty things than he'd ever known before. Meals were no longer plain dried beans and jerky. Jack did his fair share of teaching, too, but Rick was still only really a boy, and Jack had been 'on the road' for thirty years; hence, it was unexpected. Jack again chuckled to himself; nothing disconcerted the lad either.

The next morning, Scott and his cronies released the two men, issuing a strong warning. "Speak about us, and we'll know." Rick didn't expect to be thanked, and he wasn't, but escaping alive was reward enough. They were pleased to leave the camp at dawn. Scott had kicked them awake and told them to 'scarper'. They did.

They went directly to Clunes and reported the incident and location. The police didn't seem too interested and virtually ignored the report.

Both shrugged. Jack and Rick had done their bit and reported it; if the police had chosen not to listen, that was their call. There would, however, be no repercussions from the bushrangers. From there, they hot-footed it out of town, staying only one night in Clunes.

~

When they finally arrived in Ballarat some three days later, it was now the week before Christmas. Word had travelled faster than they had. A riot had occurred in Clunes over the miners' work schedules. No wonder the police didn't care. It must have happened soon after they left. They knew they could have easily covered the thirty miles between towns in one day, but they were not in a hurry. They took a long detour around the bushrangers and the duck pond, avoiding the felon's encampment. Thankfully, they avoided any more encounters with the wild men of the bush and hoped there would be no further incidents like that.

Jack finally admitted that the one place he had wished to return to was to his friend Mac in Ballarat. His heart had soared when Rick had said it was his destination. Mac's wife, Mary, was Mr Tyzzer's daughter, and they had met many years before. It was also how he knew they could get work in Melbourne. Jack admitted that Mac was also a blacksmith, and he was sure they could find work either with him or nearby.

Rick was content to follow Jack wherever he went. To walk into another job suited Rick perfectly. He still had most of the money his father had left him. Food was usually all they asked for when working, as money wasn't often needed. They had to buy tea and flour, but the rest was earned.

Chapter 5 Ballarat

$\mathcal{T}$he diggings were much like Bathurst, with most miners living in tents and lean-tos. Squabbles occurred over nearly everything. Theft was rife, and nothing was sacred. Rick had been with his father to Spring Gully and Ophir when they made the last trip to Bathurst, but neither was as extensive as this. There were tents and lean-tos everywhere. "Cor Jack, where do we go?" Rick asked, stunned at what he saw. "What happens if we walk through someone's claim? Will they shoot us?"

"Nah, but be careful. If you intend to mine, you'll need a mining licence, and as they cost some shillings a month, well, it's why the miners get cranky. If you don't and you want to work in a shop or at the smithy, then that's how you'll make some good money if that's what you're looking to do. It's your call. I've done it all before. I'm too old for the digging, but I'm getting a permit in case I trip over a giant nugget. They don't cost much in the scheme of things, and it means we can fossick in our downtime. That's the best bet if you ask me. The smithy – Mac Wallace is his name; he is often looking for some help. He's getting on a bit, not a young fellow like Dylan." Jack led them along the hot, dusty, and twisted streets; he turned a few corners until they reached the ramshackle smithy's forge.

"Hey, Mac, long time no see, eh?" Jack shouted out to the smithy, who had his back turned to them.

The blacksmith swung around, obviously recognising the voice. "Jack. Look who the cat dragged in, eh? What are you doing back on the diggings, man? I thought you said you were going north." Mac asked with the ten-pound hammer still raised easily above his head. He let the hammer fall, and it bounced as it hit the wooden log he used as a block.

"I did, got bored, so came back. I've brought this young lad to see the diggings. This sensible boy decided to look for a job rather than slave over the mud and dust." The two older men looked Rick up and down.

"Can he work?" Mac asked.

"And how! Just wait until you see his skills. Says his family are smiths, so he knows his stuff. Give him a go, and you won't regret it. Trust me. Know of any jobs for an old codger?" Jack wasn't hopeful.

"Actually, you're in luck, Jack. Feel like manning the till in the shop? Mary must go up and see Elsie in Bendigo. She's due any day. I was going to close it up, but that would be great if you could take over the store for a month or so. Same deal? Bed and board with some stores and a few shillings thrown in?"

Jack was thrilled. "Deal, Mac. Only instead of the shillings, grab us each a mining licence each, along with bed and tucker, and we'll call it square, eh? I'll cook while Mary is away; I know what your tucker is like. We'll leave when young Rick gets sick of the place. We just got out of Clunes before the riot. So, it will be nice to have some safe lodgings over the summer." Jack looked at his friend. "Many fires around this year?"

"Nah, Jack, all quiet this year. Hope it stays like that," Mac replied.

Rick sat listening to the two men. They obviously had a history and were friends. Mac asked if they had this month's mining licences yet, as they were going to close the office soon. "Go down now, just in case. Have you got the money for them?"

Both newcomers nodded. They dumped their swags where Mac pointed and headed down to the licensing office, if that's what it could be called. It was a slab hut on the edge of town. Jack pointed out various sites in town and points of interest as they walked.

Rick was pleased he had once again walked into a job. Who knew his blacksmithing skills would prove so useful?

An hour later, they were back at the blacksmith's forge. Their swags were nowhere in sight, and neither was Mac. The fire was out, the tools stowed, and the doors shut.

"Come, Rick, he'll have gone home or to the shop. It's in the middle of the block, but we'll go around the front gate so you can see where the shop is." Jack led the way down the short side street to a white-painted picket fence and a neat yard. As he opened it, a bell rang. It backed onto the blacksmiths' forge.

A red-haired lady appeared at the door and greeted him warmly. "Jack. Welcome. How long is it? Five years?"

"Eight, Mary, love." The old bushman greeted her with a hug. "Thank you for your warm welcome. This is Rick. He's going to start with Mac for a while. We've just bought our licences, just in case." Jack said hopefully.

She kissed his wrinkled cheek and told him that Mac had brought both swags home. "If you have anything you need to be washed, let me know. I'm just putting on a half-load as I'm heading to Elsie's. She's due soon, and I want to be around for the birth. Mac said you could man the store while I'm gone?" Mary was the epitome of a Scottish lass, only older. She reminded Rick of a female version of Hamish and Fergus Macdonald. She still had a Scottish lilt and looked out of place in a colonial town. She was, however, in her element in the rough place. She'd made a home from a slab hut and turned it into a business. Mac had turned that slab hut into the store and built her a proper house with a verandah. From the store, she sold preserves and a variety of homemade items. The store had a supply of local honey and giant bags of dry goods lined up on the floor. She measured out produce by weight and sold it in a paper bag by the pound. Each large sack had some pre-measured bags sitting on the top, weighed into half-pound and one pound bags and two-pound cloth sacks.

Jack was in awe of this tiny lady. He knew she had lost three children of the eight she had birthed. One to a snake bite, one to drowning, and one to illness. The scars of hurt she buried deep. He had been there when the snake had bitten the little boy, and he was dead before they even realised he had been bitten. The five who survived all still lived in town except Elsie. She had married and moved up to Bendigo.

They found Mac in the back room, where he had just placed their swags on two single horsehair mattresses.

"Cor, Mac, thanks," Rick said. He smiled when he thought of his colossal feather four-post bed at home. His father had bought it for his mother, who hated it on sight. She preferred her horsehair one and a slab bed. Rick had loved it, and since no one else claimed it, he was given it on the condition that it would become a visitors' room should it be required. As there were six other spare bedrooms, that had never occurred. Now, he was excited to have a bed. And a roof over his head would even be nice. He thought, "Mind you, it was so hot that a spot on the verandah would be as welcome."

Again, they settled in for a stay. Rick didn't know how long for, but as they were welcome and both pulling their weight, they stayed. Mac was a great boss, and Rick worked hard for him. There was always a wait time getting things made on the goldfields, as everyone wanted things yesterday. The system Mac used was similar to the one used by Tindale and Lockley, and soon Rick was powering through the work. Mac was astonished at the speed at which the lad worked. Mac did not have a smelter of any sort, so tools, like pick heads and mattocks, had to be made from scratch and heat-welded together. They were not as strong and took more time to complete. He decided to have a fiddle and investigated making a simple one-pot smelter. This way, he could pour one pick head at a time.

Rick wrote secretly to Uncle Ed and asked if he had a spare mould for either a pick or a mattock, preferably both. Ed sent both a crucible for melting the iron as well as a plan for a small brick-built smelter furnace. It was like the first one he had built soon after he had married.

Mac said to him, "Rick, me, boy, have a go and see if it works. If it does, we can sell them as quickly as we can produce them. If it doesn't, then, well, turn it into a bread oven for my Mary." Mac chuckled and showed Rick where to find a stash of bricks he had been given instead of payment for a job he had done a short time ago.

The following weekend, Rick made a start on creating a furnace, following Uncle Eddie's plans. It looked all right; the draw and heat worked. Accessing the coal was initially problematic, but Mac bought a big bag of it for Rick.

Mac watched his efforts intently. The first firing didn't get quite hot enough, so Rick closed the opening a little so it was just large enough for the crucible. The second test run worked perfectly. They could now smelt and pour pick heads.

Mac danced a jig when the first one was quenched. "It worked, lad. It worked, and what a thing of beauty."

Mac shouted so loudly that Jack raced out from the back door of the store, thinking someone had been injured.

"Who's hurt?" Jack shouted when he appeared at the door, puffing.

"No one, Jack, we just poured the first pick head, and it worked," Rick said with glee. "We'll get cracking on making as many as we can now, as these will sell faster than hotcakes."

"Too right, they will, lad. I'm forever trying to fix the welded pick heads; they are just not strong enough." Mac had the new tool in his hand and compared its weight to that of the welded ones. "I wish I could buy a stack until I can get them made."

Seeing no one was injured, Jack nodded, chuckled and headed back into the store.

Rick said, "Hold that thought, Mac. How many could you use? I have a source. I could send the order and payment by wire, and they could be shipped down to Melbourne by sea and then come up by rail. Say two weeks from ordering? Anything else that is desperately needed?" Rick knew his father had a vast stock of gold mining supplies still in stock, and the rush was beginning to slow considerably in Bathurst—some he even classed as dead stock. If Mac wired £10, Rick would ask his father to send what he could. If this worked, he would teach Mac how to place an order at the post office and get more later.

"Oh gee, Rick, gold pans, pick and mattock heads, shovels, buckets and even sieves, all the usual gold-finding items. They dig a bucket full and take it to the creek to pan out. Those things are sold out in Melbourne, and I have to try to make them from scratch." Mac looked puzzled. "How do you know all these things? And who are these people?"

Rick ignored some of the questions and just answered, "I used to work at the forge in Parramatta and know the family well. I know they have a lot of stock, and Bathurst gold mining is slowing down quite a bit. It's where I learned my skills." All the truth and no lies, he thought.

Jack had long ago worked out just who Rick was. He had seen his name on some of the mail he collected for him, but he stayed silent. He'd also put more than one and one together. Things started falling into place.

Rick would see Jack sitting and staring at him. He would return his glances with a friendly smile.

~

Three weeks later, a large wooden crate with rope handles arrived addressed to 'Mac Wallace, Blacksmith, Ballarat'. The three men pried off the top slats and started to unpack a treasure trove of goods. Rick discovered a fat envelope addressed to him sticking out of one of the cast-iron camp ovens. It was just addressed as 'Rick'. Relief flooded through him. Rick stuffed it quickly into his pocket and said he'd read it later.

The giant crate contained gold pans, pick and mattock heads, a sluice, and an instruction sheet on how to make them from scratch, as well as additional washboards and gold mats with ridges or riffles to place in the homemade sluices. Other items included sheets of mesh in various sizes, which could be used to make their own sieves. Mac was elated. "Are you kidding? All this for a measly £10?" The grin on his face was a delight to Rick, who stayed mute. He knew his father would be pleased to shift the gold panning stock. The boom of twenty years ago brought considerable wealth to his family and gave his father the means to build two Emporiums and a warehouse initially. They, in turn, have been so successful that he now has a massive chain of stores across the state. If Mac knew... well, Rick didn't want him to find out.

With the extra items now in stock, Mac suggested that Rick and Jack should take a break. He had a suggestion that they visit Tasmania over the summer, as it was easier to travel at that time.

~

Some years earlier, Jack had come across a man named Marcus Clarke while in Melbourne. He wanted to reconnect with him after he'd seen some of his articles in the newspaper and wanted to congratulate him. They were all particularly enjoying the serial story, 'For the Term of his Natural Life'.

Rick thought that it reminded him of what his own grandfather had gone through.

The two men caught a Cobb and Co coach to Melbourne rather than walk. They planned to spend a week in Melbourne, then head to Hobart and see the sights there before returning to Portland.

Rick was keen as it was a new area for him. Jack had been there before and told Rick what it was like. Jack particularly wanted Rick to see a place called Port Arthur. Jack still shuddered when he thought about the inhumane, silent prison. He felt that Rick would appreciate seeing it. But there was much more to see in this fantastic place. They had two weeks to see as much as they could. They decided to spend Christmas in Hobart.

~

The following winter came and went, with the two men still ensconced at Mac's place in Ballarat. They had panned for gold and fossicked on weekends without much success. If work were slow, Jack and Rick would take a week off and go bush. Returning, refreshed, and ready to work again. The smithy and shop had developed into a thriving mine supply store, and business was booming.

Rick had long ago shown Mac how to place an order for the goods and how to wire the money. The problem was that Mac didn't know what else was available. Each order grew, and word spread that the quality of tools was better than you could obtain elsewhere on the goldfields.

Mary had left again to be with Elsie for another birth—this time for her second child.

Rick realised they had been in Ballarat for over eighteen months.

~

1874 came and went. Rick was content but felt that he still hadn't done much himself. He often thought about Mary Lou and missed her dreadfully. A particular letter from her made him realise that she was missing him too. She said something about standing on the slip rails at Jim's in Emu Plains and watching him break in a horse. They had done this often together. She said that she missed him. Reading this made him somewhat sad; he missed her so much, too.

~

By Easter in 1875, Rick was getting restless. They had fossicked occasionally and found a few small nuggets. He was nearing twenty-one; he really should have started thinking about heading homeward. Letters to and fro occurred spasmodically. He received more from Mary Louise and his mother than anyone else. He wrote regular, lengthy letters to Mary Lou and received some equally lengthy ones back; they were kept close to his heart. Yet, the letters that were hardest to read were from his mother. He missed her in a way that was different to Mary Lou, but at least she knew the reason he had gone, and they had shared much in the long screeds they wrote to each other. He had never been able to admit everything to his mother. Doing so could hurt Mary Lou's reputation. He felt guilty.

Jack noticed the wistful look appear on his face more and more often. He knew that feeling well—the longing for home. Only Rick had a home to go back to; he could not go back to his. He felt somewhat guilty that he had not done more to send the lad on his way. Maybe it was time.

One evening in May, Mac surprised both men after they had finished work. "I have tickets to the new theatre in town, lads, and you two are coming with us, as a thank-you for all your hard work. I still can't believe neither of you will work for money. Only bed and board. So, this is our treat."

"What? Mac, you don't need to do that. Does he, Jack?" Rick was flummoxed as to what to say. And he was also anxious about what he was supposed to wear. Both sets of clothing he owned were nearly worn out.

"Nice gesture, Mac, what's on?" Jack asked, thrilled to be included.

"Well, it's opening night at the new Her Majesty's Theatre next month, and it's 'The Filly do Ma'am Angout' or some such. I've got no idea what that is, but it is supposed to be some silly Frenchy operee or some such."

"It's '*La Fille de Madame Angot*', and yes, it's a funny French opera. Not really something any of you would enjoy, I'm thinking," Jack said. "What else is on Mac?"

Rick looked at Jack, surprised that his French was perfect. His was, too, but he would not let on about that. "Well, I was thinking of the 'Variety performance' that's on the week later. That sounded more our 'cup of tea', don't you think?"

Everyone nodded. Mary noted Rick's expression. She had joined them for a mug of tea after dinner. "Jack, you can wear some of Mac's clothes as you're much the same size. Rick, I made you a new shirt. I don't know when your birthday is, but as you won't let us pay you, this is the least we can do. Mac has some new trousers that I haven't yet taken up, and they should fit you. You can also borrow some braces. I've just finished a new dress for myself, and I haven't worn it yet. So, we'll all tog up to the nines as you say, Rick, and let our hair down. What do you say?" She smiled so sweetly at the two men that they didn't have the heart to refuse.

Both nodded, looking forward to the treat outing.

The special day in June came around quickly, and the evening performance was hilarious. One man played a saw blade with a bow, another played a tune on a gum leaf, and a third played on a comb with some paper on it. There were acrobats, jugglers and singers who sang some beautiful songs and ballads. One poet brought the house down with his ability to string together many of the well-known characters in town into hilarious verse. Another recited a beautiful ballad, and one nervous young man stood and recited the poem 'Australia's Daughters' by Robert Wisdom.

Australia's gentle daughters
The beautiful, the bright
With hearts like crystal waters,
And eyes like heaven's own light;
Wreath every brow with gladness,
Crown every cup with wine
And be the toast our own dear girls of Australy divine."

Rick was lost in thought about Mary Louise. She had eyes like heaven's own light. They were grey, but they took on whatever colour she wore, sometimes blue, sometimes violet, but lovely. He released a deep sigh.

Come, each to his loved maiden,
Fill high the sparkling bowl;
What heart can be grief-laden
That owns her sweet control?
Oh, not so rich a treasure
The honey-bee e'er sips,
As he, who, heart exchanged for heart, Saluteth her ripe lips.

Rick could not get Mary Louise's violet-grey eyes out of his mind. His heart hurt, and he was homesick. Her last letter had affected his mood more than he realised. He realised he had had enough. He sat lost in his thoughts for the rest of the performance.

The laughter gurgled all around him, but his mind was in Sydney with a rosebud mouth and a pair of violet eyes.

Jack watched Rick's face. He saw the micro-frowns and looks of sadness. Jack saw Rick smile and then was sad again. He knew it was time for the lad to go home. "Homesick, boy?" He asked quietly. He saw Rick's eyes go glassy with unshed tears.

Rick nodded. "I miss her, Jack, and I miss Mother too. I feel guilty that my mother thinks I did something wrong. I had no idea what Mary Louise was going to do. I would have stopped her as it could have harmed her irretrievably. I would never let that happen, Jack, never." He had finally told Jack a little about the incident and the real reason he left home. It had taken nearly three years, but Jack knew he'd tell him when he was good and ready. "So much for being grown-up, eh Jack?" Rick sniffed.

"Sonny, let me tell you something: many say, 'Big boys don't cry;' well, that's plain stupid, so I add, 'real men do' to the end of the previous comment. Trust me, I've shed my fair share and then some. God gave us the tears for a good reason. And remember, even Jesus wept over Jerusalem." He smiled. "Shortest verse in the Bible that you know? 'Jesus Wept.' It says so much in those two words. Jesus also showed love, anger, compassion, and almost every other emotion in His life, but not laughter, funny that."

As the four walked home after the fabulously hilarious show, Jack slowed his walk so he could speak privately to Rick.

"It's time, Rick, you know that. I'll stay here with Mac and Mary. They'll keep their eyes on me; I won't go back on the road. At least not the way I was." Jack sounded determined that Rick would listen to his counsel. He felt selfish that he'd kept the lad so long. He knew it was now time for him to return to his hearth and heart. He took a deep breath. He had finally said what he'd needed to.

"Do you promise me that, Jack? I know you've never told me your story, and I'll never ask, but you're much more to me than just a friend, Jack. I owe you my life many times over; you know that. Black snakes, brown ones too; bushrangers, wild bulls, feral pigs, and so much more. Not to mention train hopping and every other adventure we've had. Oh, Jack, we've had so much fun, though."

"It works both ways, lad." Jack stood and looked hard at the young man before him. Then he turned, and they kept walking. "Rick, I will confess I was contemplating my mortal demise the morning that cow licked you. The river looked very inviting, and since I couldn't swim, I knew it would be quick. Then I saw that cow wake you, and for some reason, I knew that my life still had a purpose. At the very least, I could keep you safe. But I laughed so hard, and well... the last few years have been an absolute joy. You are like the son I never had but wanted, oh so dearly." Jack was speaking softly so Mac, with Mary on his arm just in front of them, could not hear.

"Seriously, you could come with me, Jack. My family would welcome you. I've told them about you, and Father said you would always have a room if you wanted one." Rick still hated goodbyes, and he knew he'd be unlikely to see Jack after he left.

They walked for some time in silence. Rick said after some time, "Jack, I have no idea how old you are. Under all that fur, you could be fifty or ninety. I have absolutely no idea."

Jack grinned. "I turned seventy-five today, son. June twenty-four is my birthday, lad. Mac has no idea either, but I won't stop you from telling them. So, tonight was a real treat for me. Three-quarters of a century, lad. It's St John's Day, you know; it's how, or should I say, why I got my name. No one should live this long, especially alone. Hence, I've enjoyed your company. Rick, go home to Mary Louise. You know she's waited for you this long, but for how long? Marry the girl and name a child Jack after your old friend. That would make me happy. To know my name would live on in one form or another." He looked so sad.

"Jack, I'll do that if she'll have me." Rick's heart skipped a beat. Excited at the thought.

"Rick, if you're sure of her, keep her. I married in haste."

A look of surprise crossed Rick's face.

Jack continued, not giving him time to comment. "Yes, I still have a wife, and she's still alive. We married in 1843. I was forty-three myself, and I thought she was much younger than I. I was fooled in more ways than one. Thinking she was younger, I had hoped to have children. I discovered the error of my thoughts too late, for by then, we were married. She was not thirty, as she claimed; she was over forty as well, so no children were likely. Anyway, a mere three weeks after our wedding, I arrived home early from a meeting. I was in haste to see my bride and walked straight into our bedroom. Let us say she was not alone in our bed. Nor did they hear me enter until I cleared my throat." He released a long sigh. "I left that week. I've been on the road here for over twenty years, and before that, I walked through Europe, across India, and arrived here on a Chinese junk with a load of miners. I had stowed away; that's a story in itself. I've had a great life, Rick. I write to my lawyers every so often so that they know I'm still alive and so she can't have me declared dead. I collect mail from them, so I know she's still alive. So, my wife's punishment is, in essence, banishment from society. She has little money, and according to the terms of her allowance, she can't leave the house; otherwise, it will stop. As I'm still her husband, she has no say about that and no means to leave." He sniffed and drew another long and deep breath. He turned to face Rick. "So, Richard Lockley, if you are sure of your love, marry her and stay close. She is something worth far more than mere gold. Yes, we've had fun panning for the few specks we found, but our adventure was worth so much more. You're a grown man now and will be a worthy husband for any woman. Go home, lad, and be the man she needs you to be." Jack was grinning as he saw Rick's face.

"You know who I am? How?" Rick was stunned.

"Yes, it was your mail, lad. It has your name on it." Jack confessed to his knowledge.

"But… oh heck, how long have you known, Jack?" Rick was flabbergasted. "You could have said."

Jack grinned. "Oh, a couple of years ago, one fell from your bag while you slept. It was while we were in Melbourne and not long before we left. I picked it up and tucked it back in. You were none the wiser. I knew the name; I've come across it before, lad. It certainly explained why you were so good at blacksmithing, though. Rick, my boy, you have a wonderful family heritage there. Go home, son, and make the family complete again, lad." Jack laid a caring hand on Rick's shoulder. "… And Rick, I'd go sooner rather than later. She won't wait forever, you know."

Rick lifted his eyes to the knowing blue eyes he'd come to love so dearly. "Will you come too? Please, Jack."

"No, not yet; maybe I'll come in a year or so, son. Mac has said I can stay here for a bit, so I will. Mac and I go back a long way, and Mary is a delight. She'll look after me; she has done so before. I can help in the shop and pay my way by doing that. I can even do the bellows for Mac. I can be useful here, Rick, so I'll stay. But please write to me. I'd love to know what she says."

Rick nodded. He had no idea that you could be both so sad and happy at the same time.

Chapter 6   Going Home

$\mathcal{I}$f Rick was nervous about leaving Jack and travelling home, he didn't let on. He knew Jack was right, and he decided to write to Mary Louise, letting her know that he was thinking of returning. If she replied, he would go and go soon. The wait was hard.

~

Jack collected the mail, which included a wired telegram reply from the post office in town when he placed an order for Mac. On return to the forge, he stood waiting anxiously for Rick to finish the job he was doing. He knew that interrupting him would ruin the project, and he couldn't talk over the noise anyway.

The reply Rick received back was short and to the point. It contained three words other than the signature: "Come. I'm waiting." Rick devoured those three words with a slow smile spreading across his face. His smiling eyes raised and met Jack's.

He, too, was grinning. "She said, 'Come home,' didn't she?" he asked quietly.

Rick nodded and handed him the brief message.

Jack's furry eyebrows raised, and his blue, blue eyes glinted back at him. "Whoa, I knew it! Go, lad, and go by train if you can. Don't waste a minute of this lassie's life. She seems to be one in a million. Savour her, lad, for good girls are hard to find. That's more than just a reply; that's a full-blown invitation," Jack slid his arm along Rick's shoulder. "Let's go and tell Mac and Mary you are leaving, eh?" They walked into the kitchen where the Wallaces were sitting, drinking tea.

Mary saw he had a telegram, but noticed a smile on his face. "Everything all right, Rick?"

"Better than that, she's waited for him, Mary. I'm sending him home, hot-footed, and we'll hear they are getting married very soon after he arrives, I bet." Jack turned to Rick. "She's waited long enough for you, lad, don't make her wait anymore. Most lassies at twenty are mothers already."

Rick blushed. He was blissfully ignorant of how this occurred and knew that the night before the family wedding, his father would have 'the talk' with him. Since he left home, he had virtually not spoken to any unwed girl.

A brief version had already occurred when he turned twelve, and his father had taken him into their cellar one evening, and they sat in the dark. He gave Rick the basic facts of life and told him that he had responsibilities as an Earl's grandson and that not all girls were the 'nice' sort. Some would try to entice him into compromising with them so that he would have to marry them. Wills explained that everyone around Emu Plains was aware of their incredible wealth, and that alone would make Rick and his brothers a target for the local girls, and his sisters a target for gold diggers. So, Rick had steered clear of them all except Mary Louise. She was special, and had always been, and was almost like family anyway, as her brother had married his sister. Since leaving home at seventeen, he had been with Dylan or Jack for the entire time, and the situation had not occurred where he'd met anyone else. "I will if she will have me, Jack. If not… I may even come back. But, by this," he said, waving the telegram, "I'm pretty sure she'll have me." Rick grinned so much that his dimples were visible under his sparse beard. He turned to Mac and Mary and said, "Did I ever tell you all how she gave me an *out* for leaving?" He sat and told the Wallaces his story.

After all the years together, Rick finally told Jack of the complete unadulterated version of the incident and its aftermath. "I was so anxious about leaving and hurting Father that she was prepared to take things on her own shoulders. I had no idea what she would do, and I would have stopped her if I had known. She and I had walked down to my Uncle Eddie's house after church. She had her arm on mine as was proper, but we overheard certain inappropriate things being said about us. Remember, she was only sixteen at the time, and I was a little older; we didn't have time to think through the plan or its repercussions. We got through the luncheon, and it was nearly time for her family to leave. She sidled up to me and asked if I was determined to leave, and when I assured her that I was but didn't wish to hurt the family, she just asked if I trusted her. I still do, so I replied, 'of course'. She told me to slide my arm along her shoulder and bend to kiss her. I did as she said, and she yelled so everyone could hear, 'Richard, I'm not that kind of girl.' She did a marvellous performance of being insulted. She was in tears and demanded to be taken home immediately. Well, the die was well and truly cast. I left the next day. I had time to complete my two school essays. I have not got the results from those yet; anyway, I wrote a few letters too. Mary Lou was the only one who knew my real reason. The comments made about us at the wedding horrified us both. We were both so young that we got angry. Some were made by her mother, by the way, so it was coming from both sides. We hatched our plan; it just worked far better than we realised it would." Rick watched his three friends dissolve into laughter. "So, I had to say farewell to Mary Lou and goodbye to my heart. I left it with her." Rick had spilled the entire story and was now somewhat embarrassed.

Jack was finding it hard to stop himself laughing. Mac caught his eye, and the pair of them let fly. Mary Macdonald had her head on her arms, and her shoulders, too, were shaking with laughter.

Finally, Jack looked at Rick. "I knew you were hiding something, but boy, that's some story. You only had told me a bit about being forced into working for the family, and she gave you an out. You didn't elaborate. Running away from the girl you love with only her assistance. The funny side is that you're now going home to marry her anyway. Can't you see the funny side?"

Rick smiled; he certainly could. "Oh, trust me, I can, but Jack, remember, I was only seventeen back then. I turn twenty-one this coming October. I've now seen some of our country and made new friends, but, Jack, I've still relied on you a lot; oh, but I've had a wonderful time." He fell silent.

"There's more, isn't there, lad?" Mac asked.

Rick grinned and nodded. "I've been keeping her informed of where I am and what I've been doing. Even more than I have told my folks." He smiled sheepishly. "Some letters to her were a little longer than I had planned. We set up a way for me to write so none of the family knew. I sent them to a mutual friend who's Scottish too, by the way, and a hopeless romantic." Rick was holding his lips hard, trying not to smile, but his eyes gave him away. They all dissolved into laughter once more.

Jack was still chuckling. "Eh, Mac, looks like I'm on the bellows for you from next week." He turned to Rick. "Soon enough, lad?"

Again, Rick nodded. "Are you sure you won't come, Jack?"

"No, lad, not yet, but you let me know when you've had your first kiddie, and I will come and meet the little chap or lassie."

"I will, Jack. Then you'll come?" Rick asked in earnest.

"Yes, lad, if I'm still here, I'll come," Jack said.

Four days later, Rick packed his swag and headed north. He planned to walk until he reached Goulburn and then catch the train back to Sydney. He could have arrived faster by ship, but in those months, he would turn twenty-one. He had replied to Mary Louise, in essence the letter said, "I am coming, expect by Christmas." However, he gave her some details of the route he planned to take and how long he had hoped to be.

Mac, Jack, and Rick sat and planned his trip. He was to first head to Bendigo and deliver a parcel to Elsie from her parents. Jack gave Rick directions. "From Bendigo, go to Shepparton, head cross-country to Wangaratta, and follow the road to Albury. It's the same way we came down, lad. That way, you miss most of the cold country and may pick up some work picking fruit on the way home if you need a job. Do you have enough funds?"

Rick replied that he had ample. His father had included a few pounds here and there; he had spent little.

Jack nodded and continued his itinerary. "From there, head northeast to Holbrook, then up through Gundagai and Jugiong. Goulburn is still the end of the rail line, or at least it was when we came south, but they may have built a bit more since then. See if they have reached Gunning. I know Yass was the next planned station, but they didn't expect that bit to be done until next year. Having said that, as Gunning is halfway, it might be done."

Rick and Mac both looked surprised that Jack knew so much about the trains.

"Hey, I'm getting on, Mac, and it's easier to hop on a train when I can. It saved the legs. So, I have kept my ears open to how far it has reached. The Yass line is due to be opened next year." He shrugged and smiled at Mary. "Rick, don't be tempted to take the shortcut across the mountains; there's snow, and you don't have the gear. Stick to that route, and you'll be fine. You even look like a 'bushy' now and not a 'green new chum', so you'll be okay." He leaned back in his chair and folded his arms. "You'll do, lad, and it will be good for you to fend for yourself for a bit. You'll cope now. I'm not so sure how you would have gone back then. God led me to stay on the bank that night. I've thanked him often since then."

Rick was a bit nervous but also excited. With his swag packed again, he set off. Mary stocked him up with food and the parcel he had to deliver to Elsie. He'd met her daughter a few times over the years they had been with Mac and Mary. She was expecting again and already had five children. Mary would travel up when her time drew closer, but that was yet some months away. The parcel was clothing Mary had made for the other children, so it was not too burdensome to carry.

~

He stayed overnight with Elsie and her husband, Keith, and headed for Shepparton. He thought he'd have a good feed and decided to buy a meal in the inn. While devouring a steak, a man asked if he could share his table. They fell into chatting, and Rick ended up accepting a week's work on the new house the man was building.

"I've dreamed of this house for some years, and now I'm finding it hard to get labourers. Interested in a few days' work? My name is Thomas

Swallow. The house is going to be called '*The Pines*'.'

Rick said yes, he would, and the money he'd make would cover the train fare. He intended to buy a ticket and go home honestly, not train-hopping as Jack did. He grinned and lifted his eyes skyward, thanking God again for his bounteous blessings.

Mr Swallow saw the action and smiled. "Keep that going, lad. He won't ever let you down. It may not work out as you plan, but it will always be for the best. Trust me on this."

~

Rick stayed for three weeks and ended up begging to leave; he could have stayed for the entire build, but was itching to get home. He'd be cutting it fine now as it was.

Mr Swallow was so thrilled with Rick's work that he offered him a lift to Albury. "I have a load to collect, and it's coming up the river. If you're heading that way, I can save you some time."

As this saved some two weeks of walking, Rick accepted the offer gleefully. His schedule was again back on track. Albury had just opened its new post office a few weeks before, and Rick posted another long screed to Mary Louise and a shorter one to his parents. He didn't say he was returning to them, only that he was passing through Albury and he'd been working in Shepparton labouring. To Mary Louise, he filled her in on his latest adventure and outlined the route of his return trip, as well as his expected dates. He said he would wire her from Goulburn and let her know what train he'd be on. He hoped to try and catch a train from Gunning; he'd heard the line was about to open. If she could arrange with Hamish to open his father's townhouse, he'd appreciate it. He didn't say that he now looked like a filthy swagman and needed the services of a barber and tailor.

~

The miles fell away as he walked. He was following the river at Gundagai when he saw a horse rearing in its traces. A man and a boy were on board. He saw the son jump from the cart, but the man stayed on the galloping vehicle. The boy rolled after he jumped and then stood watching his father with a look of absolute horror on his face. Rick saw from the corner of his eye that he was safe. Rick dumped his gear and ran to try to hold the beast, but it was too quick for him. The man was thrown clear just before the horse reared again and headed for the river and down a steep embankment. The horse and attached spring cart disappeared underwater as Rick ran. He was able to assist the man up the last few feet of the riverbank. The three stood watching the horse struggle in the water. The cart finally pulled the horse under. There had been nothing they could have done.

"Damn thing. It was going so well. I had a buyer lined up for that next week. £15 down the gurgler, literally." The man was muddy but uninjured. "The name is Turner; thank you for your assistance, sir." The boy cuddled close to his father for comfort. Both were thankfully mostly unscathed—a few bruises, but nothing more than scratches.

Finally, the dead horse surfaced near a dead tree, and while the lad went and fetched Rick's swag, Rick swam out and dragged the dead horse to the river's edge. He tried to get the cart to shore using the flow of the river to assist. It was useless. The weight of the dead horse was too much.

"Will I unharness it? It's no use to anyone now, and we'll be able to rescue the cart," Rick yelled from the water.

"Can you? I can't swim, so that would be wonderful. There's a rope looped around the front of the footrest. It's tied on, so it should still be there. Throw it to me, and I'll pull the cart close."

Rick dived underwater and grabbed the now trailing rope. He threw the end to Mr Turner and proceeded to attempt to unharness the dead beast while Mr Turner held the cart steady on the riverbank. "It's going to take a bit of time; it's a bit twisted," Rick shouted as he surfaced.

"Laddie, don't take any risks; it's not worth your life," Mr Turner yelled. "The beast is dead anyway."

Rick dived down again and, each time, managed to undo another bit of the harness. "I'll have to let the bit go; I can't get it undone. He has clenched his teeth on it." He dived down again before the man could answer. Three more times, Rick dived and was eventually able to release the dead horse. The poor animal floated downstream with the current. The only straps Rick had been unable to do were the animal's bit and halter. "Sorry, sir, but they were mangled and twisted anyway. At least we have the cart and most of the traces and reins."

The two men and the boy were able to secure the cart to a tree, but they would need help from others to remove it from the river. The current was too strong for the two of them to get it out by themselves, and the boy was too young to assist.

The man thanked Rick for his assistance and offered him a bed for the night and a warm meal. Rick thanked him but refused the offer. He did, however, dig into his swag and swap his wet clothing for some dry ones. Mr Turner helped wring out the saturated items, and he tied them to the top of his swag. "Hey, at least I've had a good wash." Rick laughed, then shivered. "I might camp early and light a big fire, though. I passed a good firewood tree back a bit. Are you right? Do you want to join me?"

"Nah, we're right, thanks, mate; we've got about a mile to walk home, so not far, that-a-way." Pointing in the direction they had been heading. "Are you sure you won't join us?" Mr Turner asked, concerned for Rick's welfare.

"No thanks, I'm good," Rick said. He'd seen a well-dead, fallen tree back a bit and knew he could get some good firewood from it. Rick waved his hand in farewell and walked in the opposite direction from them. His walk took him back over the area he'd just come; he didn't have far to go. Rick soon had a fire roaring and started drying his clothing. He had filled his billy before leaving the cart accident site, so he shoved that in the fire. Something warm in his belly would be good. He'd just made some tea and was going to settle down to some damper and honey when he heard a shout.

Mr Turner had returned in another cart and had some food for Rick. His wife had ladled some thick beef stew with vegetables into an old billy with a lid for him and had added some cake and other sweet treats into a leather bag. These he accepted willingly and waved a farewell again. Rick set the stew pot on the coals and waited for it to heat up. There was enough for two nights, and as this billy had a lid, he could keep the flies out of it. He again raised his eyes heavenward and gave thanks.

With a full belly and warm clothes, he slept well. He remembered Jack's lesson, which he called 'speaking to the sky'. They had prayed together nearly every day.

He knew that it was a bit over a hundred miles from Gundagai to Goulburn and wondered how much he could cut off if he went cross-country. If he could hitch a ride occasionally, he might even be able to catch a train next week from Goulburn.

~

The miles passed slowly, as did the towns; Coolac, Jugiong, and Berremangra were all non-events to Rick. He barely looked around as he passed through them. He purchased food and just kept walking; his eyes were now firmly fixed on home. Now, he was just interested in getting back to Mary Louise.

Upon arrival in Browning, he heard that the line had reached Gunning. He had heard from Jack that sometimes swagmen could hitch a ride on the pump-wagon cart the railway men used. He'd seen them being moved, and they looked fun.

When he reached Yass, he headed down to the rail line site office and asked if they needed any muscles. At twenty-one, having spent much time blacksmithing, his muscles were bursting out of his shirts. The overseer took one look at the muscular lad and hired him for a trip pumping a Kalamazoo. The rails had been laid just two miles from Yass; the ballast in the tracks was yet to be done along the route, but it was suitable for the push wagons, just not a train. The man told Rick that there were about thirty-five miles of track laid and ready to use to Gunning. That's where he needed Rick to go.

Rick figured that it was fair payment for not having to walk over fifty miles to get to Goulburn. It was a long hike, but still easier than walking. For payment, he asked about the possibility of a free fare to

Sydney. He had enough money for it, but if they would give it to him for free, that was even better.

The pumping was much easier than swinging a ten-pound hammer for eight hours a day, and it wasn't as hot. It was easier than pumping the bellows. He discovered that the line was finished to Gunning from Goulburn, and as Jack said, the Yass line should be open the following year. The Gunning line was opening soon. He was told that he could have his free ticket if Rick could get the Line Inspector, Iain Campbell, to Gunning by the next day, he would get not only his free passage but a night in a hotel as well, plus a bath and a hot meal at night and again the following day.

Rick agreed; he would pump all night if he had to, not knowing what was ahead of him. He knew he would be sore for a day or so, but it couldn't be much worse than smithing for Mac. His equipment had been so primitive that it made the work hard when he'd first arrived. He'd helped modernise the forge and the smithing techniques before he left.

Rick pumped the two-man cart by himself. It was easy on the flat sections, but he'd even had to get Mr Campbell to assist up one particularly steep bend on a hill. His arms were sore by the time he had reached his destination just on nightfall. Rick earned his free meals, bed and free ticket as he made the thirty-five-mile trip in good time.

The inspector was thrilled. He thought it would be nearer to midnight when they arrived. They had talked about his years on the road for the trip. Rick asked why the contraptions were called Kalamazoos.

Iain laughed. "It's where the carts are made in America, lad, simple as that."

Rick smiled and nodded in understanding. His tough, callused hands had some small blisters on them from the movement of the handle. One had ruptured; he doused it in brandy, cringing as the alcohol hit the raw skin.

Iain had called in at the hotel a little later and handed Rick a small glass bottle. "Soak your hands in warm water with a small amount of this, lad. It's eucalyptus oil, which will help stop the infection. Keep the bottle – I have another one." Iain smiled as Rick looked embarrassed at the man's kindness. "You got me here on time; it's the least I can do."

Rick did as Iain suggested. If nothing else, the eucalyptus smell was heavenly and also covered the odour from his clothing.

He relished his large stew for dinner and an apple cider or two, followed by hot steamed spotted dick pudding and custard for dessert.

After pumping a Kalamazoo for nearly forty miles, Rick slept well. He was surprised when he was called at seven, having slept well past dawn, his usual time of waking. The chambermaid told him Mr Campbell was again waiting for him downstairs.

Rick hastily donned his clothing and packed his swag, sad that his night of luxury was cut short. He was greeted warmly by Mr Campbell downstairs. "Morning, lad, I'm guessing you've not yet eaten, so join me for breakfast." He turned to the waitress. "A stockman's special for the lad, please, with three slices of toast and a large mug of tea. Charge it to the rail account. Tea and toast for me, please."

She nodded and went to get the order.

Rick wished he'd ordered for himself as he was hungry and wanted a large steak. He'd not had one for ages, and he was so hungry he could eat half the beast.

"I suppose I should have told you why I needed to be here today; you never asked. We open the new station today. Rick, I want you there, if possible. As you're going to Sydney, I'll send you back with some films for the head office. They will want them for the papers. I've wired through, and someone will meet you at Central Station. Did you know the new station building is now open? Happened last year. Will you take them for me?"

Rick willingly agreed. "Absolutely, sir, who would meet me? I have an appointment nearby and will need to go directly from the station. I need to clean myself up somewhat."

"Clive Johnson will meet you in Sydney. Ask the stationmaster, and he'll take you to him. You're a lifesaver, Rick. Thanks." Iain sat talking to Rick until the waitress arrived with a massive platter of food. Another one followed her with a rack of toast and a steaming pot of tea. A third one brought another plate of toast, jams, marmalades, and butter curls for Iain.

As she placed the enormous platter of food down in front of Rick, she breezily said, "The tea and toast are bottomless, so eat up. I hope the eggs are how you like them, just set 'cause they don't dribble that way."

Rick looked at the huge T-bone steak, two fat sausages, three eggs, bacon, fried black pudding, fried onion, bubble and squeak and a large pile of beans in sauce. His mouth was already salivating. "Oh wow! This will fill my void. My tummy has been rumbling for the past half hour, sir." He bowed his head and gave thanks. Then started eating. Not hurriedly and with perfect manners.

Iain looked on as the lad munched through the enormous platter of breakfast.

"Oh, sir, this is delicious. Mother cooks food like this. I'm looking forward to seeing her again next week," he said between mouthfuls. He ate until he was full. Only a few of the beans and a bit of the onion remained, knowing what they did to his anatomy, but he had cleaned up the lot. He had always been taught to leave some of everything to show he'd had enough. He had been so hungry that only a tiny bit remained. The toast was also eaten, and the pot of tea was emptied. He leaned back in his chair, sated and content, a big grin on his face.

Iain responded to Rick with an enormous grin on his face. "You're the first person I've seen who's made it through a stockman's breakfast, lad. My railway men have good appetites, but no one has ever done justice to the entire stockman's plate. Congratulations!" He chuckled, leaning back in his chair, watching the young man's face.

They sat chatting about the opening for some time. Eventually, Iain said, "Now, one more thing, I'm going to 'tog you out' as I want you to be at the official party. You'll be working, so the clothing is instead of payment."

He saw Rick's face and noted the concern it showed.

"No, no, lad, you'll get your ticket too. Don't worry about that; this is an extra. It's a uniform of sorts, but you can keep them: blue dungarees, a white shirt, and a straw hat. I must have a 'labourer', and you're well-spoken and mannered enough to assist me in what I have to do. Savvy? Not a free handout, but a form of payment. Will you do it?" Iain asked anxiously. "… And there's someone I want you to meet." He looked embarrassed.

This puzzled Rick; why would he look embarrassed? However, Rick grinned again. "Of course, sir. I'd be honoured." He laughed to himself, knowing his Uncle Charlie often did this sort of official opening of things either with or without the current governor. He fully expected to see one or both there this afternoon. Either way, he'd be back in Sydney some six hours after he caught the train. He had only met Governor Robinson once before he left, so that it wouldn't be him, but he knew he had asked his uncle to stay on as Viceroy, as this had occurred only weeks before the wedding.

"Can you come now?" Iain asked.

Rick stood feeling like he had eaten a month's worth of food in one sitting. "Yes, sir, but I just have to grab my swag. It will take me a bit to pack properly."

Iain nodded. "Oh, come now, and I'll show you where to bring your stuff when it's packed. I'll come and get you when I need you." Iain took Rick along to the railway headquarters and togged him out in work clothing. He told him he could safely leave his swag in his own office and collect it again after everything was over.

On return to his room, Rick had taken the opportunity of a long, hot bath the night before, and he had washed everything he could. His hair was long but clean, and he had brushed it while wet, and he now had it tied back neatly in a queue. His light brown beard was a decent length, and it, too, had had a good scrub. When he was in his new uniform, he folded his clothes and wrapped them into his swag, then retied it, ready to grab; the two billies swung off the end, and the frypan stuck out the top. The thick leather straps were worn but still strong.

Chapter 7   A Day of Surprises

*J*ain collected him at ten o'clock. They had to arrive at the official launch early, as it began at noon. Iain loaded Rick up with various items he needed to be carried into his office. "Ready?"

Rick nodded, wondering which of his family would be there.

Iain did not know his full name, but he accepted him for who he was. An honest, hardworking man. It was who Rick wanted to be, just himself, and as Jack said, nothing more, nothing less.

As they arrived at the station in Gunning, he saw, as he expected, his eldest uncle, Charlie, standing waiting for him, with his arms folded but smiling.

Rick looked not at him but at Iain.

Iain smiled and shrugged. "You look too much like him not to be related. We got talking last night, and one thing led to another. I thought you might like to travel home with him in luxury. We did promise a fully paid ticket." Iain grinned.

Rick carefully put down his armload of goods and embraced his uncle. "Hi, Uncle Charlie, it's so good to see you again. Did Mr Campbell tell you I'm on my way home?"

Charlie hugged his nephew, then held Rick at arm's length. "Yes, lad, you've matured well, son. Your father will be glad to see you come back. I should ask, are you well? You look it." Charlie's eyes were devouring his nephew's physique and glowing health.

With a laugh, Rick replied, "I'm fine, Uncle Charlie; I've been working in Ballarat, as I'm sure Uncle Ed told you. How is everyone at home?"

Their conversation kept up for some time.

Charlie called over the governor and reintroduced them. "Sir Hercules, this is my nephew, the wandering Richard. He has been on the road as a swagman for… how many years, Rick? Three?" Charlie asked.

"No, nearly four, Uncle Charlie, but it feels longer. I worked my way around blacksmithing and labouring," he added.

The balding, rotund governor roared with laughter. "You can take the boy from the anvil, but you can't take the anvil from the boy, eh? So you've had enough and are heading home?"

"Sort of, sir! I'm now old enough to get married and… well, that's the next plan." Rick's reply made his uncle's fair bushy eyebrows raise quickly.

Stunned, his uncle inquired, "What's this lad? Does the family know?"

"Err, no, Uncle Charlie, neither does her family. Although I am intending to remedy this very soon." Rick's confidence in Mary Lou's reply was strong. Her words, conveyed by wire, were almost confirmation of his unspoken proposal. He was sure that Phil Evans, her father, would allow them to at least court, even though they both had a lot of explaining to do.

The governor chortled. "Well, if it comes off, congratulations, lad. Now, come and meet the rest of the official party. I think another of your uncles, Tim Miller, is one of them, with some others from his firm." Sir Hercules walked off, expecting them to follow.

Strolling beside Rick, Charlie noticed him freeze. He followed where his eyes were looking, and they fell on a beautiful, smiling vision.

A dark-haired lady with the most adorable grey, almost lavender-coloured eyes, also stood frozen on the spot. Before he realised, Charlie stood alone on the platform.

Rick was walking quickly to her. He arrived in front of her and took both her hands in his. "You are here? Why? No, don't answer that; I don't care why; I'm just thrilled you're here."

She whispered, "I couldn't wait any longer, Ricky, so I came halfway with Father." A tear of happiness slid down her cheek unchecked.

Rick thumbed it away. "I missed you so much, Mary Lou. I left my heart with you that day, do you know that?" he said softly.

Her misty eyes drank in his face, "No, I don't because Rick, you took mine with you. It seems both have been lonely. It's always only ever been you in my heart, Ricky." She could not look away from his lips; she wished that he would kiss her. She had dreamed of their first kiss for so long. She noticed a slow smile sneak across his lips, "Rick?"

With a full grin that made his dimples pop, he said, "I'm going to kiss you properly, you know. I just thought I had better tell you first in case you yelled again," he said laughingly.

She giggled naughtily. "I won't. I've dreamed of this for ever so long," Mary Lou admitted. She took her hand from his and laid it possessively on Rick's chest.

"So have I," he murmured as he cupped his hand on her cheek. He bent his head slowly and kissed her, gently drawing her into his arms. They stood locked together, almost devouring each other with the depth of their very first kiss.

He pulled back, cupping her beautiful face in his hands, then bent and kissed her eyes, her cheek, and her nose. "I love you, Mary Lou. So very much! I want you to know that."

She hid her face in his chest with her arms wrapped tightly around him.

He was about to kiss her again when he heard a cough behind him. He lifted his cheek from the top of her head.

Her father stood with his arms folded, watching them with a smile on his face. Phil said, "I'm guessing that after what I have just witnessed, the scene after the wedding was a set-up after all? And I bet you have been in on this the whole time, haven't you, miss?"

Mary Louise's eyes were laughing; she nodded, "Yes, sorry, Father. There were reasons."

"Well, I presume by that public display of affection, you wish to ask me something, young Richard?" Phil enquired.

Rick still had not released Mary Louise; she was snuggled under his arm. "Yes, please, sir, I was going to see you tomorrow and ask if I could court her; if not, ask for her hand in marriage. Do you mind if I do so now instead?"

"I suppose you've made your fortune and are going to become more famous than your father?" Phil said.

"No, sir, I'm skint. I have about £5 to my name, no job, and no home. Having said that, I'm sure Father will have some work for me somewhere. I have not even told him I'm coming home," Rick admitted honestly.

"Father dear, if you say no, then I'll leave with him anyway. Although I would rather you make it official, and that we have your blessing, for I'll marry no other man, you realise. I'm going to marry Ricky, whatever you say," Mary Louise said adamantly.

Phil just laughed. "I'm not going to say no, Rick, but she's a handful. And you're correct, I'm sure your father won't shun you. He was boasting to me last week about what you've been doing in Ballarat, not to mention Melbourne, Goulburn and was it Gundagai? Oh, trust me – I've heard all about your travels."

"No, Shepparton, but you mean it, sir? I can marry her?" Rick was grinning so much that his eyes danced, and his dimples once again made an appearance.

"Yes, lad, if you're game. What's more, you've compromised her now in public; you'll have to now," he chuckled. He threw his hands up in jest. "And Rick, no returns."

"Father!" Mary Louise said indignantly, but she laughed and snuggled closer to Rick.

"Thank you, sir, and I might do it again soon, but I'll not do that in public." Rick smiled down at his fiancée. "Well, my love, will you marry me? I have absolutely nothing, so if you do, we'll have to start from scratch."

"Let me answer you this way: I don't care if we have to live in a tent and hump a swag, or I think you called it a matilda, around the country roads; I'm not letting you out of my sight again, at least, not for long. So that's a yes, an absolute Yes! Now kiss me again, Ricky, my love." She looked so adorable that he couldn't resist. Her violet eyes were dancing with laughter.

Rick looked at her father, who nodded and said, "Go on, congratulations, son." Phil turned his back and tried to hide them from the public eye.

Rick again cradled her face in his hands, looking lovingly into her eyes. "I love you so very much, Mary Lou. I have done so since we were children. I have never looked at anyone else. This is because I *want* to be with you, not because I *have* to be with you." He gently bent down and brushed his lips over hers.

She stepped closer and, this time, she wrapped her arms around his neck.

He groaned and crushed her to him.

His passionate kiss parted her lips, and her response sent his emotions spiralling almost out of control. Having never kissed a girl before, he was vastly unprepared for the surge of desire that raced through him. He raised his head and just held her close. "It's not going to be a long engagement, Mary Lou. Just so you know."

"Good," was all she said.

Phil cleared his throat, trying to hide the cuddling couple behind him. The official party arrived, and she had stepped out of Rick's arms as they walked closer.

Iain came over and asked for an introduction. He had seen the passionate welcome from the other side of the station, and he watched on in delighted shock and surprise.

With Mary Louise now on his arm, Rick introduced her to Iain as his fiancée. It was only then that Rick realised Iain already knew Phil as one of the railway's lawyers.

Iain was stunned. "Rick, when you said you had a girl, I had no idea it was Phil's daughter. I would have told you she would be here if I had."

Mary Louise's musical chuckle was followed by, "But that would have spoiled the surprise, sir," Mary Louise said sweetly. She was clinging tightly to Rick's arm and had no intention of letting him out of her sight.

Rick looked at Iain and realised he was supposed to be working. "Is there something you would like me to do, sir? I am at your disposal."

"No, lad! Once I met your uncle last night, it was just a ruse to get you here. You are free to spend time with your young lady love; I don't need you. Except to maybe deliver the film in Sydney as previously requested. That I do need." Iain looked at the young lovers. "Oh, to be young again," he thought to himself. He so missed his beloved wife. In the ten years since she had died, he had done everything he could to not be at home. Hence, he had taken this job.

The official opening duly took place, and the extended family group joined the official party for the luncheon.

Rick was included at Iain's invitation. He was placed next to Mary Louise, and they sat holding hands under the table. They did all the correct things and spoke to the people on either side, but wished the long luncheon would finish. Rick wanted to kiss her again; oh, the feelings she had awakened in him were unbelievable.

Mary Lou was finding it hard to concentrate on the conversation with the man on the other side of her. She had missed his name and just kept calling him 'sir'. She started tracing hearts on Rick's hand while she kept up a banter with the man next to her. He was talking something about horse racing. She was not interested and let him talk... and talk... and talk. She nodded occasionally.

Rick was stuck with the wife of one of the dignitaries. He thought she was the Mayor's wife, but he, too, had missed her name. He was also unable to concentrate.

Mary Lou was tracing hearts on his hand, and it was having an amazing effect on his lower stomach area.

Rick leaned over just before the meal finished and whispered that she had to stop it, as he had to stand up soon.

She had brothers, so she knew what he meant. As an unmarried young lady, she was not supposed to be aware of such things. She stifled a giggle and gave his hand a quick squeeze before releasing it.

It gave him time to get his emotions and body under control. There was no way they would have had a long engagement, even if they did have to live in a tent.

Their eyes met frequently, and hers were dancing with potential fun. He could hear her glorious laugh when her father said something funny, and his heart did strange things.

In the years he had been away, her beauty had matured, and she was now breathtaking. He noticed that many other men's eyes rested on her almost lustfully. A wave of jealousy washed over him. She was his, well, nearly his.

After the meal, his Uncle Charlie eventually sought him out. "Did I see you, um, embracing Mary Louise earlier?"

Charlie hated interfering, but he had to know. "One minute I was talking to you, then, poof, there was thin air next to me." He smiled at the handsome man now standing next to him.

"Yes, Uncle Charlie, Uncle Phil just gave us permission to marry, so we're engaged." Rick met his uncle's stunned look with a sly grin. With a glance over at Mary Louise, he then met his uncle's surprised look. "I'm skint, unemployed, homeless, and engaged," Rick grinned. "And I'm over the moon."

"Oh, Rick, but what about the post-wedding thing?" Charlie looked at him, suddenly realising by his nephew's embarrassed face the reality of the situation. Understanding dawned on Charlie, "Oh, that was a set-up, wasn't it? I often wondered. It was out of character for both of you. I can't believe she was in your confidence this entire time. I know she has turned down numerous marriage proposals. Phil told me he was getting exasperated. She obviously had her eyes on you the entire time."

Rick grinned in reply and nodded.

His uncle probed deeper, "I suppose you've been in contact with each other this entire time, too. That greeting would make me presume so."

Again, Rick nodded in reply, but his gaze sought out his beloved face in the crowded room. "Frequently, Uncle Charlie, but I wrote to her mid-year to say I was thinking about coming home as I would be of age when I returned. That happy event occurred last month, of course. Well, her wired reply to me was three words. 'Come. I'm waiting.' I left Ballarat that week. It takes a while to walk nearly five hundred miles. I hoped to be home by Christmas. I got a 'Kalamazoo' lift for the past fifty miles or so as I brought up Mr Campbell on a rail pushcart. Did you know they were called Kalamazoos? I didn't." Rick's eyes had not left Mary Louise's.

"Oh, Rick, my boy, I forgot you're now of age. Congratulations! Bette is still not married, you know. She has been mooning around home, missing you. She said she would stay a maiden aunt and even threatened to be a nun if your father forced her on to someone. That will be the day. It certainly wouldn't be a silent order anyway." Charlie's eyes showed his mirth, and he was biting his top lip, trying not to laugh at the thought of his never-silent niece being a nun.

Rick laughed loudly. Knowing how much his twin loved to chatter about simply everything, often music or nature. It was no wonder he'd been able to hide his discontent so well.

Finally, the afternoon's formal events drew to a close.

Phil took his daughter's hand and drew her into the sitting room on arrival at their hotel. "Poppet, I just wish to be sure about your feelings for Rick. He has not forced himself on you or anything?"

"Papa, no, he certainly has not. That was all a big set-up so he wouldn't hurt his family. We have been in regular contact using Hamish Macdonald as our go-between. We arranged the communication and our reunion before I set things in motion on that infamous day. I love him, Papa, I always have, and he loves me too. I'm going to marry him and soon, maybe even by Special Licence." Her eyes held his steadily.

Phil knew his wilful daughter well enough to know she would not change her mind no matter what he wanted. He would welcome another of Wills and Cathy's children as in-laws. The last time he had seen Rick was at his son, Alfred and Rick's sister, Goldie's wedding. Rick had always been a delightful young man, and soon he would be able to call him a son or be as good as thrilled by him. Phil smiled, remembering that he and Alice had visited Rick's parents and their newborn twins the day after they were born.

Phil thought back to the first days he met the family when he was just a boy. Rick's Uncle Ed had lived with the Evans family when a child at school in the 1830s. The two families had been close since then. Phil's uncle, Thomas Tindale, the Parramatta blacksmith, had taken on Ed Lockley as a six-year-old apprentice in 1827 and sent him to school as he grew older. Later, they went into partnership. Thomas and one of the soldiers who had befriended Ed's father had paid the school accounts for Ed as well as Tim Miller.

Phil smiled. It had taken years for Tim's father, Bill Miller, to admit that he had a double degree from Oxford University. Not only that, but he had duxed the year and won nearly every award whilst there. No wonder Tim was brilliant. Bill had been a friend of Governor Lachlan Macquarie for the short time they had been in the colony together. The governor had consulted Bill about specific points of law and the wording of essential documents. Tim had kept that quiet, too.

Phil laughed to think that he was now junior partner to Tim's meteoric rise in the firm, and that Tim was now a co-owner. He wasn't jealous, but Tim married Rick's Aunt, who was Charlie and Ed's sister, Anna Lockley, and then everyone later found out that Ed's father, Charles, was an Earl. That certainly didn't hurt Tim's career, either. Not that he ever mentioned it. He didn't need to.

Phil smiled to himself when he thought of other family connections. The mysterious soldier friend of his Uncle Thomas was Major Ned Grace. He turned out to have secrets as well. After spending some twenty years in the colony as a soldier, a doctor friend from England came looking for him to inform him that he was now the Duke of Gracemere. It was only on Ned's return to England that he discovered a previously unknown connection to Charles Lockley. They were, in fact, third cousins and never realised it. Ned found that Charles, now Lord Charles, was an

Earl and blissfully unaware of that either.

Charlie Lockley inherited the title in 1870 upon the death of Lord Charles. Charlie's brother Eddie had been named Edward, after Major Edward Grace, better known as Ned, as he was born on his birthday. His parents, not realising their son's name was the same as the Duke's, were actually Edward Lockley. So, the Evans and Lockleys families had always been close. All the children used courtesy titles, such as "aunt" or "uncle", to address all the adults. Eventually, the Evans, Miller, Ellis families, as well as the Tindales, all received such honorific titles.

Phil thought back to the last five years. First news of the Earl's passing, then months later, they found out Duke Ned had died the same week in England, but the information had taken months to reach them. The following year, his own Great Uncle Thomas, Eddie's mentor and partner, had died. All would have been seventy-five now or thereabouts. The world was a sadder place without those three men, he thought.

Phil knew that Lord Charles' wife, Aunt Sal, had thrown herself into helping anyone she could. It was how she coped with her grief.

Chapter 8   Transformation

$\mathcal{E}$arlier that evening, Charlie decided that Rick could not go looking as he was. He needed to be groomed. It turned out that Charlie was a dab hand at both shaving off beards and cutting hair. "I really wish your mother could have seen you first; she would have had a fit, you know." Charlie laughed as he took a handful of Rick's beard and hacked it off.

"Uncle Charlie, I'm in the photographs in the station with my beard," Rick smirked.

Charlie smiled at that thought and continued, "She kept you children immaculately dressed. How, I have no idea, as all six of you were tear-away terrors when you were little, you and Bette especially." He kept the chatter up while he cut and trimmed. Once the excess hair had been binned, he ordered some hot water and pulled out his cutthroat razor. He honed it on a leather strop and soon had Rick lathered up and, with his thumb under his chin, started to shave him.

Rick tried to talk while he was doing it, but Charlie kept telling him to "Shush." Then asked, "Do you want it all off, sideburns too?"

"Your call, Uncle; I don't have to look at myself, so I don't care." He relaxed under Charlie's caring prowess. Soon, his chin was being wiped, and the mirror was passed to him.

Rick's grin was Charlie's mark of satisfaction. "I'm me again, Uncle Charlie, thanks. Now for the hair!"

"I'll do it, but Gracie will need to tidy it up when we get home." His shoulder-length fair hair may have been clean, but it looked ratty. The ends were all uneven, and Charlie said. "I hate cutting curls. So we're going to wet it and just do an even cut all over. If you brush it while wet, it should not frizz too much." A hank of long hair came off in one handful. "The side part is 'in' and not too short. Okay with that?"

Rick merely nodded.

Snip, snip, and half an hour later, Charlie was satisfied with his work. "You'll do." Again, he handed Rick a mirror.

Rick looked and grinned. "An improvement if I say so myself. I'm sure Mary Lou will approve, especially the kissing bits. She said it tickled. The beard, that is."

"So, you even have a pet name for her, do you? She's always been Mary Louise to everyone else," Charlie asked.

"To everyone but me, Uncle, she's been my Mary Lou for a long, long time. Now I can claim her in real life, not just in my dreams."

"Now for some dinner clothes. You'll have to make do with that shirt; mine won't fit you, but I brought a spare dinner suit. It's a fraction too big for me, so it should do at a pinch. We're of a height, so it should nearly fit." Charlie, too, had spent much time at the anvil with his brothers and nephews.

~

Once togged up, Rick decided to seek Mary Lou's reaction and test the kissing bits again. Rick grinned in anticipation. He couldn't wait until dinnertime. He knew what she'd do if she saw him like this, and he could not risk that in public again. Uncle Charlie said he'd go immediately and see Phil.

Charlie knocked and joined Phil and Mary Louise in the sitting room. "I believe congratulations are in order, Mary Louise. You both had us completely fooled, naughty puss." He gave her a congratulatory kiss on the cheek.

"Thank you, Uncle Charlie. We didn't want to hurt Uncle Wills and Aunt Cathy. This way, it stayed with us alone. Ricky's always been the only one for me, Uncle Charlie," she admitted bashfully. "But it was my idea. I didn't even tell him what I intended to do. Hence, a genuine look of shock was on his face. I had to make it look real."

"As I said before, naughty puss, but as you were only sixteen, so I suppose I can forgive you." Charlie had asked Rick to join them before his brother-in-law, Tim, arrived.

Now dressed appropriately, Rick walked down the hotel corridor to Phil's room and knocked gently.

When the door opened, Phil stood looking at him. "Well, that's certainly a major transformation." He walked around him and gave his nod of approval. "Charlie did this? And you fit into his suit? You go up in my estimation more and more. Charlie, you're a man of many talents."

Rick stood still while being inspected and replied, "Sir, I was wondering if Mary Lou could see me before dinner so there will be no more repeat 'public displays of affection' that might embarrass you all."

"Yes, come in, lad, she's here in my sitting room. Go in and surprise her." Phil ushered him in and watched her reaction when the door opened to Rick.

Rick knocked and entered the private sitting room. He walked directly to her side and took her hand.

"Oh, Ricky! Oh, Rick, it's really you. I mean, not that you weren't before, but oh, you know what I mean," she said breathlessly. She blushed delightfully.

"It's me, my sweet, back to my old self." He held her hands, and they gazed lovingly at each other.

Phil smiled. "Oh, for goodness' sake, kiss the boy and get it over and done with, Mary Louise."

"Oh, may I, Papa?" She giggled.

"You may, you are, after all, engaged, remember, but I shall turn my back again. I am going to have to get used to this, so you may as well start now," Phil said in a matter-of-fact voice but with a smile on his lips. He was wondering if she would ever marry. Phil had told that Rick would be allowed to kiss her again, in private, with chaperones, and that time had come. "We'll be listening but not watching, Rick," Phil said as he and Charlie walked to the windows and looked outside.

A soft chuckle was heard, then silence…

Rick waited until their backs were turned, and then he drew her gently to him.

She slid her hand over his newly shaved cheek. "I love you no matter how you look, scruffy or smooth, or how much money you have or don't have. Just don't leave me again, Ricky."

"I won't; if I get the wandering bug again, you'll come too." With that, he lowered his head and silenced her. The feelings that she stirred in him were new and almost overwhelming for him. Her kisses were sweet and innocent yet full of the promise of her unbridled desire for him, too. He raised his head a little and whispered, "I missed you so very much." She had no idea how she made him feel. He kissed her again.

After some minutes, Rick pushed her away from him. "Oh, Mary Lou, please don't make us have a huge palaver of a wedding, will you? I want you in my life, and soon." He was fighting for control.

"Me too, Ricky, it's about the marriage, not the wedding; that's just one day." She silenced him with another heart-melting kiss. "… But I don't want a 'quickie' wedding with no one there. I want to get married in a church. I don't mean not a Special Licence one, but not one of those where the family don't get to come. I remember Uncle John's wedding to Aunt Colleen. It happened after church, and we were all there. I love that, simple and sincere." She kissed him again.

When they came up for air, again she continued, "...They had a Special Licence. Oh, did you know they had a surprise sixth baby last year? They named her Cara." She reached for him again and whispered. "Ricky dearest, I have the dress already. Is that naughty? You did keep inferring, and I had hoped you wouldn't want to wait long." She had a coy look about her.

"I don't care about the dress, or the hair, or the party. I, too, would like a church wedding with all the family, but there's no need to fuss over a huge party. Like you, I'd like the family there. I wonder if there are any family do's planned, and we can tie it into that. What do you think?"

"That's heavenly, Ricky; there's always Christmas; we're all going to Parramatta for Christmas this year. Neddie and Miriam are having their sixth child about then, and Mama wants to be there. We can tie the family reunion into the day after Christmas, as Uncle Ned and Aunt Christina did. Only their wedding was a secret; this time, everyone could stay. We could even do it in the morning service as it's no secret, but I don't think that would be allowed."

"Sounds perfect, my darling love. Christmas it is, unless there is something on beforehand. We'll get the banns done as soon as possible, and then, if everyone is together, we'll get married. Seven weeks maximum." He drew his breath, releasing a huge sigh. Seven weeks until she would be his. At that time, he had to find a job, a house, and sort out his family.

She rested her head on his shoulder. "No longer, I promise."

"Done yet?" Phil asked when he heard them talking.

"For the moment, sir, thank you," Rick answered. He had not yet released her; she stood comfortably still, wrapped in his arms.

Phil motioned for them to sit down. "Did I hear you talking about dates? Or have you been too busy for that?" His eyes were smiling, and Rick caught his twinkle.

"We were, sir, we were thinking Christmas Day as all the family will be together. I have no idea who the current clergyman is at St John's, but is Reverend Clarke still alive?"

"I believe he is, son," Phil said.

"Do you think he would be up to doing our service? I'd love to have that link. He married my parents and knew Grandfather and Uncle Ned well. I know Father would love it if Reverend William could also perform our wedding. He's one of the last of that generation. Did you know he is even older than Grandfather and Uncle Ned, as well as Uncle Thomas Tindale? His trekking around the country certainly toughened him up. I feel somewhat closer to him now. I understand the draw of the wide-open spaces." Rick had now released Mary, and they had sat down on the settee; she sat snuggled under his arm.

There was a gentle knock at the door, and Phil answered it. Charlie's brother-in-law, Tim Miller, stood there; Phil ushered him in.

Rick stood on their entry. "Hello, Uncle Tim; good to see you again. How is Aunt Anna?"

"She's well. Now, what's this I hear? Engaged?" Tim looked at the lovely young lady on the settee.

Mary Louise nodded. "Yes, Uncle Tim, we are. Oh, and this will mean that you will be my real Uncle by Christmas. No more unofficial 'Uncle' stuff." Her smile brightened the room.

"Oh, by gosh, so you will. That's good news, love, no more honorary titles anymore." Tim grinned.

"Father doesn't know yet," Rick admitted.

The four men seated themselves, and although Rick didn't put his arm around her, he sat close and took her hand.

"So, you'll return to Sydney with us tomorrow?" Tim inquired.

"Yes, sir, I'm back for good. No money, no job and no home, but I'm back."

"I daresay your grandparents' cottage or even Ned's Gracemere Cottage is available if you want it," Tim suggested.

Rick's eyes flew to his Uncle Charlie's in fear.

Charlie was quick to realise his anxiety. "No, no, lad, your grandmother is alive and well, but she's finally moved in with Eddie. Aunt Jenna finally persuaded her that, as the family grew, the cottages were needed for others. With the facilities at Ed's, she is content, as are the rest of us. Our place is too noisy with the inn, so she opted for Ned's room at Eddie's house. Tim and Anna are always on the move. And Liza is always at one or another of her children's places."

Rick heaved a sigh of relief. "Oh, thank goodness. You had me worried for a bit."

"No, she's fine, but hard to believe she's seventy-five, but she's fighting fit and as active as ever," Charlie explained. "As you can imagine, she misses Father greatly."

Rick nodded, but Mary Lou teared up, "We all do, Uncle Charlie."

~

The dinner was a success, and after a night in a comfortable bed, everyone was up early to catch the first official Sydney train from Gunning.

They were all placed in a first-class carriage with the Governor and his contingent. The carriages consisted of compartments with opposing seats. As the Governor was on board, a butler brought around food and drinks from the dining carriage. They, however, went to the dining car for their luncheon. Charlie went to the Governor's huge compartment to check all was well. It was, and Sir Hercules said he would have a nap, so he dismissed Charlie and told him to stay with his family.

Charlie was relieved that he could now be off duty, so he settled down and relaxed in their compartment. If Mary Louise had not been with them, all their feet would be up on the seat opposite.

Rick sat either cuddling Mary Louise or holding her hand. She fell asleep, cradled against his chest. Her rhythmic breathing against him made him feel so protective of her.

Charlie sat watching his face as the emotions flickered across it. Charlie knew them well, as he still felt the same way about his Gracie, after thirty-four years of marriage. She was his rock. They had both been thrown into the role of Viscount and Viscountess the year after they had married. Neither had much formal education nor any specific training. Things went pear-shaped in his life when he was abused as a small child; it was to Gracie he turned as he grew older, and together they worked through it.

The train's clickety-clacking sounds and the rocking, rolling movement of the train lulled them all to doze for a while. The trip was about six hours long, with frequent stops for filling the engine's water tanks. The waiters took these opportunities to serve them all with hot beverages. Charlie ensured that the governor and his entourage were well-fed and had sufficient food and drink.

Rick thought back to his time train-hopping with Jack. Sydney drew closer, and Rick relaxed as they drew closer. He spent time in silent prayer, praising God for his safety during the years he had spent on the road. His first trip was where he'd met Jack, and his exhaustion had caused Jack to be concerned for his welfare. What a blessing he'd turned out to be. As he thought about Jack, he realised he had not mentioned him to Charlie. Rick knew he'd invited him to come and visit, if not live with them, but, as yet, they had nowhere to stay. He'd not renege on his invitation, but he had nowhere to offer him a bed.

"Love?" Mary Louise said. "I felt you tense."

"I have to tell you about Jack, sweetie, Uncle Charlie, and you, too. I must tell you all, actually. You see, I have asked him to come, and he said he will in a year or so." Rick looked at her reaction.

"Tell me about him, Rick," Mary Louise asked gently. His mentions of this enigmatic man piqued her interest.

Rick spent over an hour telling them about Jack. He also spoke about Dylan, Mr Tyzzer, Mr Swallow and his homestead, and the incident with Mr Turner's horse and cart. Then, of course, Mac and Mary Wallace were not to be left out.

The retelling of the past years was very cathartic for Rick. It settled him into the future that was potentially before him.

~

On arrival in Sydney, the train pulled into the new Central Station.

Rick looked around him, admiring the beautiful new building. He had time to hand over the film to the man waiting for it. He had eventually appeared from the stationmaster's office. Clive Johnson was an extremely tall man with a beaming smile; he had round wire-rimmed spectacles and a pocket full of assorted pens and pencils. One had obviously leaked, and he was oblivious to the fact.

Rick pointed out the ink spill to him. "You'll need to soak that in milk, sir."

The man just looked down at his pocket, then at Rick and nodded. His wife would not be happy with him again. He'd forgotten to cap his pen once more.

Once that job was done, Rick was able to relax fully.

The Governor insisted that they take one of the Government Town Carriages awaiting him and deliver them to their various destinations. He thanked Charlie for his assistance and for accompanying him. Tim would return to Anna in their home on George Street in Sydney. Once Tim was dropped off, the remaining four chatted before Phil and Mary Louise were taken to their house on Pitt Street. Charlie and Rick were to stay at The King's Arms Hotel.

Mary Louise had already invited them to come for dinner.

Rick was thrilled.

Phil and Charlie realised she had something on her mind. The absolute innocence on her face belied a mischievous glint.

The look they gave each other made Rick chuckle. They had yet to tell her mother, Alice, of the engagement. Mary Louise whispered to Rick that she already knew.

Phil made a face, then rolled his eyes in reply to Charlie's grimace.

"Glad it's you, mate," Charlie said, trying hard not to laugh.

"Oh, Papa, Mama has already guessed. It's only you men who are so blind. She's known of my attachment to Rick for... hmm, about three years, maybe more." Mary Lou blushed as she spoke.

"She guessed, or you told her?" Phil asked.

Mary Lou looked at her father innocently, "A bit of both, Papa. She realised I was much too upset over the occurrence after Alfred and Goldie's wedding. Far more than a simple incident should have been created. I confessed all to her. Rick will tell you that it was Mother's inappropriate comments that caused the issue in the first place, so when I say I confessed everything, I also told her she was responsible. Papa, why do you think she allowed me to come with you on this trip? She knew she had to make amends." She looked at Rick and mouthed, "Sorry."

He gave her a quick peck to show she was forgiven.

Phil looked at her, then at Rick and Charlie. "You live with a woman for thirty years and think you know how she ticks. Nah! Wrong every time. How did I miss that?" He smiled lovingly at his daughter. "Okay, miss, answer me this: how did you know Rick would be there at that time?" Phil now had his arms folded and looked stern.

"I didn't exactly know the date, Papa, but Rick said in his last letter from somewhere south of Yass that he'd make for the railways as soon as he could. He said he had heard the Gunning line was about to open. If he had not turned up, then I would have twisted my ankle or something similar. Trust me – I would not have moved until he came home." Mary Louise's butter wouldn't melt in my mouth. Rick's smile was one of absolute innocence.

The three men all threw back their heads and laughed.

The carriage pulled up at the Evans' new house, a few doors up from his parents' house.

"Oh, a new house, Uncle Phil?" Rick asked.

"Yes, John and Colleen finally bought out Father and Mother on condition that they stayed living with them. It meant our parents could hand on our inheritance before they passed on, which thankfully neither has; hence, Stevie and I have moved closer to them. Funny, eh? You spend your formative years planning to leave home, then when you can, you wish you were back there again," Phil mused. He opened the door for Mary Louise. "It's nice, though. Wait, and we'll show you through tonight." He sighed. "Now to face the missus."

Mary stole a quick kiss while her father's back was turned. "See you later, Ricky," she whispered.

Grinning broadly, he said, "You bet, love."

Charlie sat chuckling, watching the young people's antics.

Rick swapped seats with the forward-facing one next to his uncle, and the carriage took them to the hotel, just a block or two away. As they walked into the foyer, Charlie called over the manager. "Evening, Mr Stewart; any chance you can produce a full dinner outfit with all the trimmings and a morning attire, too, for our wandering Rick?"

"Yes, my Lord," he smiled and nodded at Rick. "There are a few who will be able to supply your needs, Thomson & Giles in Denison House and also J & E Dawson. Both are only on George Street." He smiled at the Earl. He then turned his attention to Rick. "Mr Richard, welcome back from your travels. I wouldn't have, err, recognised you, sir." Mr Stewart clapped his white-gloved hands. A footman appeared, and the manager gave him instructions for a merchant from both stores to attend as soon as possible.

Rick smiled at the manager. "Thank you, Mr Stewart; you should have seen me a few days ago." By the time Rick's dirty swag was unpacked and placed on the floor of his luxurious room that had a harbour view, two overdressed gentlemen were arguing and vying for his attention.

Charlie came in, hearing their noise, and order soon returned. He gave them instructions that both were to supply day clothing outfits, and each was to provide a set of evening attire immediately. "We need the full evening attire within an hour. One full set from each of you, please."

They decided to work together to take Rick's measurements due to the time constraint, and now knew that each was getting the same order. Once done, they hurried away, but Charlie asked them to wait outside for him. He didn't keep them long; he asked them to each supply six complete sets of attire for all times of day and night, right down to the skin, and new sleeping attire as well. He had caught sight of Rick's lack of decent underclothing and smalls. For him to return home, he needed some suitable clothing. One of the perks of being an Earl was that things would be done quickly.

Charlie also knew that only the best quality would be delivered. He knew that if Rick complained, he'd talk it over with his little brother. He could call it delayed payback for building him a house many years before. They still lived at Willow Grove and loved it. Ed was down the street a bit, and Luke was on the corner a few blocks down. Wills was the only Lockley brother not living nearby, as his primary residence was in Emu Plains. He owned *Roseneath* in Parramatta, as well as another in Sydney. Hopefully, Rick would be staying in Parramatta. Time would tell.

"Lad, your new wardrobe will be here within the hour." Rick opened his mouth to say something, but Charlie butted in. "It's payback to Wills; you're just the beneficiary. Call it an engagement gift if you must. Alice will require you to be properly attired tonight. As she will be your mother-in-law, trust me, you do not wish to offend her. Let's see what their off-the-rack clothing is like. I wonder if they will bring shoes?"

"Yes, they measured my feet too. Thank you, Uncle Charlie; I will accept with pleasure. You should have seen what I looked like before Mr Campbell togged me out." He grimaced. "I can still smell my clothing from here. I'm sure they walked into my swag themselves."

Charlie left Rick to settle into his room, then went to prepare for the evening himself. He rang for tea, and as he sat watching the boats on the harbour while drinking his tea, his mind thought back to his childhood. Charlie chuckled, remembering when his clothes were like that when he and Eddie were children.

They had wonderful times fishing and swimming in the tidal river, playing with their friends and the local Aboriginal children, and learning a great deal from them. He still missed those carefree years. They were his formative years; he'd spent his first twenty-one years as a convict's son playing with the local indigenous children. He had been horrified to learn his father was an Earl, and then discovered what that entailed for him as the eldest son. From then on, life had been one awkward situation after another. It was even worse when his father became the Viceroy for the area. After some years, he handed that job over to him. For years, he'd panicked over inheriting the title. Thanks to his friend Jim Leslie, he'd finally talked over his feelings with his father. When that awful situation had occurred five years ago, when they had found his father dead, he found his life little changed. He still lived next to the Jolly Sailor Inn with Gracie, only now they owned it, not just the inn lease. Their eldest son, Teddy, the future Earl, lived in England with his wife and seven children. Teddy, now Viscount Edward Lockley, ran the family walnut farm and orchard in Kent. Charlie smiled to himself that his father and Uncle Ned had purchased it for the Earldom, and his father called himself the Earl of Nuts. He only got to visit the farm in Kent once. Charlie had been over a few times now and planned to go again soon. His second son, John, Ted's twin, was now assistant Viceroy, so Charlie and Gracie could travel when they wished. John's wife was his friend Harry's daughter, and Harry himself was the son of an English Viscount. So, it was a role John and his wife, Sarah Joy, were ideal for. He thought to himself that the family now had more titles than many in the English Aristocracy. Who knew the Lockleys *en masse* could claim Dukes, Earls, and Viscounts as Ed's daughter, Tina, had married Uncle Ned's son, Chip, who was now the 11th Duke of Gracemere. Their son CJ was just fifteen, but he would use the title of Marquess when he turned twenty-one.

Charlie chuckled again at the thoughts, then he put his head back, closed his eyes and rested before dinner.

On the way out to Phil Evans' place for dinner, Charlie handed the manager some telegrams and a note. He managed to do this without Rick knowing. "Can you send these tonight, please?"

"Certainly, my Lord." Mr Stewart took the messages from him.

Charlie nodded thanks. He could innocently say that it was just a message to Gracie. It was, however, that he had added words to the bottom. It read, "Home tomorrow @10 with Rick, tells Wills, etc."

Chapter 9 Meeting the Family Again

$\mathcal{R}$ick greeted Phil with a firm handshake. "Mary Louise wasn't joking when she said Alice knew. She'll be all over you, lad, so prepare for some kisses from her." He groaned, "And Phillipa is here too. Seems I'm blind to the ways of women."

Charlie laughed heartily. "So, what's new, Phil? If you ever discover how they work, write a book as it's sure to be a best seller."

Rick looked puzzled at his uncle's comment. He started to say something, "But, Uncle Charlie...."

Charlie looked at the newly engaged young man. "Give it time, Rick, and you will discover what I mean. When you think you have her worked out, she'll surprise you by doing exactly the opposite. Women! Got to have them, certainly love them, but you will never figure them out."

Charlie and Phil chuckled in unison.

Mary Louise entered, followed by her mother and her older sister, Phillipa, and went straight to Rick's side, took his hand, and stayed next to him.

Alice came and welcomed him with a kiss. An obviously expectant Phillipa smiled and said, "Hello, Richard."

"Hello, Aunty Alice, Phillipa, hello sweetheart." He bent and gave Mary Louise an all too brief welcome kiss.

"Well, aren't you two a bit clever?" Alice said with a smirk. "All that palaver about having a fight in front of everyone, just to scarper off for years and see the world, eh."

Alice smiled at Rick's embarrassed face. "Oh, Ricky, I picked it straight away. Well, soon after anyway. Okay, I knew that when she cried for three days, there was way more to the story. Mind you, I had my suspicions on the ferry; Mary Louise had to let on eventually." Alice saw her daughter frown at her comments. "When she refused however many proposals, I knew she was pining for someone, you were the only one I could think of. Oh, I know it was my words that set things off, and I suppose I should say sorry, but, Rick, however, this is my dream. You were made for each other."

She continued in this vein for some time. Eventually, Mary Louise stomped her foot angrily and said, "Mother, really?" Mary Louise looked totally embarrassed. She hid her forehead on Rick's shoulder.

Alice bit back, "Yes, Mary Louise, really! Anyway, now that you are back, Richard, I believe we have a wedding to plan. I suppose you don't know, but Phillipa got married last year, and her husband, Mark, is currently in Melbourne; otherwise, she wouldn't be here. I would not let her stay alone in her advanced condition. It also means that you two don't have to wait until she's married, oldest daughter and all that."

Alice prattled on again for some considerable time. Rick met Phil's eye, and both smiled.

Rick did manage to say, "Thank you, Aunt Alice." Rick got the gist of what she meant, but if they could marry soon, he wasn't worried. "I believe she has got most things ready. She knew I would not want to wait long when I returned."

He thought, thank goodness they didn't have to live with Aunt Alice! Bette was talkative enough, but she also sang, and she did it nicely. Bette was also a brilliant pianist, and her singing was often heard when she played. He saw Uncle Phil roll his eyes and bit back a chuckle. He realised his future mother-in-law was still talking and tuned into her words.

"Ahh, yes, I believe you've been in regular contact over the years. Hamish?" Alice enquired.

Rick nodded. "Err, yes, sorry, but we knew he would pass on our letters with a minimum of fuss. He loves a good romance. Has been doing so since he secretly married Effy."

Charlie laughed at that comment. He had come over to rescue Rick.

Hamish had covertly married the Evans ex-convict maid some seventeen years ago. Effy had only been ten when she was assigned to them as a convict girl. Phil, Stevie, and John adored her almost like an older sister, as did Ed and Tim when they lived with them. Although Effy had been a convict placement, she had never left. Almost literally, as Hamish and she lived next to the Evans' seniors, who were both in their late seventies.

Although Hamish and Effy had both been in their forties when they married and now had two children, it came as a huge surprise to both of them.

Charlie eventually said, "I think it's hard to believe they have two teenagers now. Ferdie is what, sixteen and Elspeth fifteen? Where have those years flown to? Rick, Hamish's brother, and Fergus and his wife, Katy, lived with them for some years until they eventually moved his English cousin, James Styles, into the house in Glebe. It was called *Rock Cottage* or the stone house behind it, actually. The old tenant, Major Tom Turner, had died after many years as caretaker." Charlie remembered that one of his nephews had lived there for some time until he, too, left. Charlie continued, "Fergus' cousin, Danny, had offered him the house for a peppercorn rent of a shilling a year, as he wanted someone to live in it. Fergus accepted the offer and moved his small family to *Rock Cottage* for five years. They are about to move into a house only two doors up from Hamish and Effy. They had bought the two-bedroom, two-story house and are having extensions completed. These were, in addition, three more bedrooms, electricity installed, and an inside bathroom and privy. So, they are still frequent visitors. When they leave *Rock Cottage*, another cousin, James Corbett Garney from England, will move in. He wrote recently to say he's arriving soon."

The family dinner was a success.

They were all just walking into the sitting room after dinner when a knock was heard.

"Expecting anyone, love?" Phil asked.

"No, Phillip," Alice replied.

The maid had opened the door to the unexpected visitors, who entered the room without knocking.

Alfred and Goldie entered first, followed by Alfred and Mary Louise's brother, George and his wife, Annmarie.

Goldie breezed in, "Hello, everyone, we were at Uncle Tim's when he arrived home. We heard my Ricky was back, and so we came to say hello before we went home." Goldie bowled into the room as she was wont to do. She waltzed over to her little brother, who was now standing by the window, but who now towered over her.

Rick smiled at his boisterous sister's entrance.

"My, my, you've put on some muscles, haven't you, baby brother?" She squeezed his biceps. "And working hard too," she reached up and kissed his cheek.

"Hi, Goldie, nice to see you too. As to the arms... I've been on a blacksmith's hammer off and on since I left." He gave her a big hug and swung her around with ease. She squealed with glee and made everyone laugh.

Alfred shook his hand in congratulations, "And if ML's hand now clutching your arm means anything, I'm guessing congratulations are in order?"

Rick looked down at Mary Louise, who was nodding to her big brother.

"But what about that hoodoo the day after the wedding? I suppose that was a setup, too?" George asked.

The guilty look on both Rick's and Mary Louise's faces was enough of an answer for him. Both nodded, smiling.

George and Annmarie were more sedate in their welcome.

Mary Louise replied sweetly, "Sorry, but yes, it's a long story, but certain comments were made in our hearing," she glared at her mother, "And, without really thinking it through, I came up with that idea. I didn't even tell Ricky what I was going to do." Mary Louise reached up and kissed his cheek. "Sorry, love," she said. His answer was to slide his arm around her and draw her to him.

She wrapped her arms around his waist.

They stood hugging each other with wide grins, showing no embarrassment at all.

Both her brothers congratulated her and commiserated with Rick. "You do know what you're taking on, don't you? She's a termagant," said George.

Rick gazed adoringly at his fiancée, "I know, and I love it. Mary Lou may have to live in a tent and hump a swag if she marries me, so she will need to be. I don't have a bean, George!" Rick teased.

"I'm ready to do it if we have nowhere to go, Ricky. As long as you're there." She chortled, much to her mother's horror.

"Oh no, you're not, my girl. Papa can talk to his father. You are not living on the streets like a… like a…"

"…Swagman, Aunt Alice?" Rick finished with a mischievous smile on his lips.

He heard Mary Louise chuckle.

"Yes, like one of them. Hopefully, Richard, you have this out of your system," she stated solemnly.

Rick replied meekly, "Yes, Aunt Alice, it is."

He felt Mary Louise poke him. "Ouch, love, what was that for?" he said jokingly and a little too loudly.

"Well said, Rick," said Alfred, "Tell Mother that living on the street would tame ML a little. Go on, Rick, make her do it."

The conversation for the evening was very jovial, but eventually, it came to an end.

Phil asked Rick and Mary Louise to follow him; he had something to say to them.

They followed him into his office.

Phil then walked to the window and flipped his hand. "Just an excuse so you can kiss her goodbye. Alice and I will come out to Parramatta on the weekend and stay with Ed. So, make sure you're back there again after visiting your parents. I'll try to see Reverend William Clarke before then. So now ... say good night while my back is turned. Rick, are you really sure you want to take her on?" Phil wished to ascertain that he was aware of what he was taking on.

"Yes, absolutely, sir, and thank you, sir," Rick said affirmatively.

"Okay, then I'll place an announcement in the paper tomorrow just to make it official. Is that all right?" Phil said just before he turned around.

"Yes, sir! Thank you. But can you hold off one day so I can tell my parents and family first?" Rick asked.

Phil nodded, then turned his back to the couple.

Rick opened his arms wide. He was still not accustomed to holding his beloved, let alone kissing her, with her father's permission and in his presence.

Without a word, she lifted her lips to him.

He bent and brushed his over hers. Her soft moan made him draw her close, and he deepened his kiss. When she opened her mouth to his, his emotions ran wild. He had to remember that her father stood listening. As much as he wanted to respond to her unvoiced invitation, he gently pushed her away from him. "Soon, my darling, soon," he whispered so only she could hear.

"Very soon," she said naughtily.

He was somewhat surprised at her innuendo. "No! We'll wait, love. It's only a few weeks, then you will be mine, guilt-free, my sweetheart," he mouthed into her ear. "And then..." he retook possession of her lips with such force and passion she sighed when he again lifted his head, "...Then I will take all you offer."

"It can't come fast enough," she eventually replied in a whisper.

"For me either, but we won't have a real honeymoon as I have no money. I really am skint, love." Rick admitted.

"And Ricky, I don't care as long as I have you. I meant it when I said I'll go on the road with you if I have to." She pulled his head back down to hers again. "This one has to last until Friday. So, make it a good one."

When he kissed her, she ran her tongue over his teeth and sent his emotions through the roof. When her tongue touched his, he wished they were already married. Against his will, he again pushed her away instead. The pain on his face hurt her.

"Sorry, Ricky," she murmured. She watched his heavy breathing and observed him battling for control. "Are you okay?"

He nodded. "Just no more kisses like that until we're married, please. Then... lots more," he grinned.

Phil had heard nothing of their whispered conversations. He figured he had given them enough time to say goodnight. "Are you two done yet?" he asked before turning.

"Not really, Papa, but I know he has to go." She took Rick's hand and kissed his palm, then held it to her cheek.

Rick stood with his back to Phil, waiting for his control to return. His tight trousers were well stretched at the front.

"Are you okay?" she whispered.

He gave a minute nod. Taking a deep breath, he released it slowly.

Phil knew the battle he was having and ushered Mary Louise outside, leaving him alone in the room. He squeezed the lad's shoulder as he passed his future son-in-law.

Rick, willing his body to behave, left the room a few minutes later.

Charlie and Rick said their farewells to the family.

Rick gave Mary Louise another quick kiss and said that they'd meet again on Friday at Parramatta. She clung to his hand as long as possible.

When the door closed behind him, she was bouncing on the spot. "Isn't he wonderful?" she said to her sister.

Phillipa grinned. "Now you will understand how I feel about Mark." She slung her loving arm around her little sister's shoulder. "Rick's certainly easy on the eyes now he's grown up."

"Hands off, he's all mine." Mary Lou giggled.

Charlie and Rick decided to walk down the hill to the King's Arms Hotel. Charlie knew it would take some time to ease his raging emotions, and this was best done in the darkness.

"Oh, Uncle Charlie, I didn't know emotions could be so strong. I thought that what I felt before was amazing." Rick was battling with how he was unable to cope with his bodily reactions.

"Rick, have you ever heard of 'the joys of marriage'?"

"I've heard the term; I think I'm beginning to understand it. I had no idea how strong the, um, desires can be. Tonight, well, I'm pleased Uncle Phil didn't leave us alone," Rick admitted.

"Son, it's tough but worth the wait, believe me. Just make sure you don't allow yourselves ever to be alone, and now you know why." Charlie knew the temptations before him.

"Thanks, Uncle Charlie, yes, I know. I most certainly won't. I don't trust myself, and that surprises me. It was like I lost my head for a moment. I've never felt like that before." Rick fell quiet.

Charlie patted his shoulder in sympathy. "It's nice, isn't it?"

They walked on in silence for a while. "Uncle Charlie, tell me about Father and Mother. Were they really upset? I have not dared to ask, but I needed to go," Rick asked hesitantly.

"Rick, your mother saw through the ruse before you had even

gone. She sent messages to Ed and me. Wills wasn't so sure; it took him a while to understand until Ed put him in his place on his way home. Your letter made him stop and think. He did the same to Ed and me. Wills called in to tell Ed, and he apologised for the way he had treated him so many years before. When you wrote to Ed instead of your father from Goulburn, it hurt him, and that gave me a chance to point out that he had done exactly the same to me when he had run away. Once Ed and I took him to task for his behaviour toward us, he settled down. Rick, you are so like him, you know. Your older brothers were part of the business's development, but you came along a bit later and missed out on all that. Wills just presumed you would follow the older boys. Again, I took him to task and told him to offer you a job rather than presume you would just do it. Rick, talk to him; he will listen now, trust me in this. His business is now so huge that whatever you want to do, I'm sure there will be a role for you somewhere. From a labourer's apprentice to management, he'll find something for you." Charlie knew that his talk to Wills had made an enormous difference to his attitude.

"Thanks, Uncle Charlie, it's why I didn't want to go in the first place. It's also why Mary Louise did what she did. She knew I would not have gone otherwise." Rick sounded remorseful.

"Lad, think positively. You now have a wonderful fiancé. Your father will sort something for you job-wise, and I have control of the cottages, so you can have either of them if you take a job in Parramatta. So, rest easy, young man. If you still believe in God, then trust Him, lad. It's all in control."

"Really, Uncle Charlie? Sometimes, I wonder if I did the right thing. How can running away be God's will?" Rick questioned.

"Growing up in the limelight doesn't help. Ricky, my boy, think back to your father. When he ran away, he thought the same thing. I won't elaborate here," people were walking past them, "but look at what happened to him back then and look at what he did with it for the community. This entire colony owes much of what it is now, in essence, because he ran away. If he had not gone, think of what we would all be like now. The gold would still have been found, and the place would have been in turmoil. You would not know of his wealth by looking at him. In a way, this has been good for him because, for once, it didn't go how he planned. He is far too organised for his own good sometimes." Charlie smiled, "Until you left, the world had fallen at his feet. Yes, he found it hard to swallow, but he's fine now."

"Sure? I love him so much, Uncle Charlie. I knew that when I went, it would hurt them both, but I was torn. Now I'm back; I have bridges to build and apologies to make." Rick knew the next few days could be difficult but worthwhile. He always had Mary Louise to come back to.

"I've kept in contact with them, you know, and filled them in on what I've been doing. I've learnt a lot about myself these last few years."

Charlie nodded, sure that was true.

They arrived back at the hotel, and Charlie informed him that the ferry would leave at nine the following day. He did not tell him he'd basically telegrammed his father already.

Tomorrow would be interesting, as someone else had also received a telegram.

Chapter 10 Like Father, Like Son

$\mathcal{R}$ick slept the deep sleep of youth. He was awoken the next morning by a chambermaid drawing back his curtains and placing some hot chocolate on the table. After the past years on the road, he woke with a start. "Morning, sir, his Lordship asked me to wake you as it's past seven o'clock. He said a Reverend gentleman was coming at eight, and apparently, you needed to see him. Your chocolate is on the tray and is getting cold, sir." She flicked open the last curtain, bobbed a curtsy and departed. Rick rolled onto his back and yawned. He lay in bed and gave thanks to God for a soft, warm bed. His window looked over the harbour, and as he sat up, he remembered he was naked. He'd had no clothing to put on except the ones Iain Campbell had given him. He went and grabbed his chocolate and sat back on the bed to drink it, having flicked a sheet over him. As he did so, there was another knock at the door. This time, he quickly got into bed and hid under the covers. He cleared his throat. "Enter," he called huskily.

Charlie stood there with four men behind him. "Ready to become a clothes horse, lad? Here, put these on and come and try on some togs." He smiled, knowing he'd had to sleep in the altogether. He had brought a pair of his own clean smalls. The four other men went into the adjoining sitting room and, with some little argument, finally called for him to enter. Charlie had also thrown him the dressing gown that was provided in each room. So, now partially covered, Rick followed his uncle into the other room.

Half an hour later, Rick emerged clad in a new outfit. The shoes pinched a little, but no more than new shoes usually did. The men's measurements were excellent, and rather than disappoint either store, he wore a mix-and-matched outfit assembled from both stores. Now suitably attired, he went to meet the clergyman with his uncle. Charlie gave instructions for everything else to be packed and sent to his house in Parramatta, including the accounts. All outfits fitted perfectly, and Charlie was pleased with the outcome.

In the foyer, a bent and weary-looking gentleman was ushered in. He was accompanied by his ever-loving shadow, Maria. The Reverend William Branwhite Clarke was a well-known man about town. He was now bent over, white-bearded and with a frizz of longish white hair. His smile and beady blue eyes belied the aged look. His mind was still as sharp as a tack, but he frequently complained that his body was letting him down far too often. Maria, although much the same age, stood firmly beside him. True to her word of years ago, she'd not left his side willingly since her sojourn in England for over fifteen years. That was now nineteen years ago. She had travelled back from England with her children and Rick's grandparents. Their children had now all married, and she'd stayed with her beloved William in North Sydney Parish. They rattled around the large rectory, missing their family. Every visit he'd made to their home since she had been with him. Rick adored the elderly couple, who were like grandparents to him. He had visited his parents the day after he and his twin sister were born. The choice for a minister to marry them was an obvious one. It would be William by choice, no matter where or when they married. Rick greeted the couple with a hug and a kiss for Maria. Very early on, they had been adopted as honorary family members. There was a connection, but it was so tenuous that it should not be counted; however, for them, it was significant. Two fourth cousins married Maria's nieces. For without this reverend gentleman, Wills' gold find would not have occurred, and the Bathurst boom would not have happened. William Clarke was the epitome of loving generosity. He had found the first traces of gold, and although he officially reported it to the Governor, he then told Wills Lockley. At eighteen, Wills ran away, found the mother-load of reef gold, then more at Bathurst. He and his six English friends came home and prepared the colony for a gold boom. Then, they worked with the family to do what they could before the word leaked out. By the time gold hit the news, all was in readiness. Gold stores were built, roads made, and stores readied to buy goods. Even policemen are in a position to deal with the influx of greedy miners. William held his arms open to the young man. "Ricky, my boy, you've grown so much. So, you're home to stay?"

"Yes, sir, hello, Aunt Maria." He looked puzzled. "How did you know I was here?"

A voice from behind him answered. "Ahh, well, that would be me." His Uncle Charlie entered quietly. "I figured that if we had all the details arranged for Christmas Day before we got home, there would be less fuss over it." Charlie finally greeted the elderly couple. "Hello William, Maria, are you both well? I didn't expect you to both come; I thought you would send a note." He shook William's hand and kissed the old lady's cheek. "I presume you are both coming for Christmas lunch as normal. If so, Rick has a favour to ask you, William. Fire away, lad." Charlie motioned for the older couple to take a seat. He then sat and watched Rick.

"Oh! Gosh, thanks, Uncle Charlie; yes, that would be great." Rick took a deep breath. "Uncle William, if you come on Christmas Day, will you marry me?"

William's eyes twinkled with mischief. "Ohh, Maria wouldn't like that, would you, dear? She said she would never leave me again." He chuckled mischievously. He saw the confusion on Rick's face.

"Oh, William, behave." Maria smiled knowingly. She had heard William's joke hundreds of times over the years. She ignored him. He was right; her fifteen-year absence in England had been far too long.

"Oh, lad, I'd be honoured. Christmas Day, you say. Well, we'll be out there, of course, as we normally are. What a wonderful way to celebrate! I should ask, do I know the young lady?"

"Um, yes, sir, it is Mary Louise Evans," Rick said, grinning from ear to ear.

"Oh, congratulations, Ricky," Maria added. "I wondered about the stories I heard, not like either of you. So, I'm guessing a set-up?" She looked at him with a twinkle in her eyes and one raised eyebrow.

Rick nodded and returned her smile. She was always on the ball. He was thrilled Reverend William, aka Uncle William, would do the honours. He thanked them profusely. Sadly, they had to catch the ferry to Parramatta, so they could not stay talking long. Mr Stewart already had a carriage at the door for the four guests, and it would deliver them all to the Phoenix wharf at Circular Quay. He had sent down a footman to hold the ferries for both Parramatta and North Sydney. Charlie had made arrangements for the luggage to be sent by road. Being an Earl certainly had some benefits. Charlie and Rick thanked the Clarkes for making the trip over from North Sydney. They hugged Maria again before they waved each other farewell.

"I sent your luggage on to my place, Rick. Your swag, too, was 'high'. You weren't wrong about its odour. It was pungent," Charlie noted with a grimace.

Rick chuckled, "If you think that's bad, you should have smelt Jack and me after we'd been cutting bootlaces and mattress straps for three months in Melbourne. We stank of tanning solution, stale urine, and dog faeces. I have no idea how Uncle Bertie doesn't smell like that; I must ask him, as I'll send the information to Mr Tyzzer. Oh, Uncle Charlie, it took months and many, many washes to get the stench out of our clothing. Our hands were stained too. Even the bushrangers would not let us sleep in camp." He slapped his hand over his mouth. "Oh, please don't tell mother about that, will you?"

"Oh, Bertie uses bi-carbonate of soda, soap and vinegar. I buy it in bulk for him. Also, he does not use doggie poop to condition the hides.

Now, spill about the bushrangers, lad. This will be interesting." Charlie's eyes grew wide as Rick unfolded the story of the bushranger encounter and feeding a group of wanted outlaws roast ducks.

This character, Jack, also intrigued Charlie. "Rick, before we arrive home, I would like to say something to you. I believe that your friend Jack will arrive at some point, as you expect. I want you to know that he will always have a room with us. Jim's old room under the house is empty, and we can convert it into a special room for him. He won't be far from you if you are in the cottages. I was thinking of turning it into a sort of bedroom-cum-sitting room anyway. If we enlarged that small window and added an inside toilet, he could be quite comfortable there. We've already added a small brazier and dug out the embankment some more, so it's now larger. He seems to be important to your story." Charlie watched for the young man's reaction.

"Really, Uncle Charlie? You would do that for him? He became like my guardian angel. I met him for the first time on the day I left and again on the day I left Dylan. My years away would have been very different years without him looking after me. If I had a house, he would get our best room. He never told me his full story, and I know he has one. However, I can tell you he's married, and his wife cheated on him. She's still alive. No matter how I tried, I never found out his surname. He's an enigma, but I love him so. He's seventy-five, the same age grandfather would have been, but like Uncle William, he's spry. Oh, I know he's also from Kent, and his best friend was someone named Paul."

"If you ask him, will he come? If he knows we have a room for him?" Charlie asked in earnest.

Rick shrugged. "I did already; he said he'll come in a couple of years, or at least when we have a child. By the way, I promised I'd name a son after him. I presume Jack is John, so our first son will probably be called John. Jack let it slip that he was born on St John's Day, and he was named after that. So, I know his birthday is June 24."

Charlie kept him talking for most of the trip, mainly to keep his mind off what was before him. He hoped that Wills had received Gracie's message and would be there to meet them. Only time would tell. They rounded the final bend of the river and came in sight of the wharf. A huge crowd was gathered at the wharf, and two carried a banner that read, "Welcome Home, Rick." Charlie stood grinning. "Oh, I love my family," he thought.

"Whaaat? How did they know? Uncle Charlie, did you send through a message?" Rick was stunned.

"Um," Charlie grinned at his nephew. "I might have sent a note to Gracie to say I was coming home on this ferry with someone who may need a room for the night." He had a twinkle in his eye and a smile on his face. "I'm not quite sure who she told." He said it with all honesty. Well, it was the truth.

Rick turned to him and took his hands. "Thank you, Uncle Charlie, thank you so much." Rick waved to all the familiar faces as the ferry drew closer. Two, in particular, stood at the front of the group. A lump caught in his throat as he saw his mother almost jumping on the spot. His father waved both arms above his head. He knew he had been forgiven even before they docked. When the ferry pulled in close, he jumped ashore—not even waiting for the walkway to be put in place. He was in his mother's arms a moment later. His father soon joined them, and the three embraced, all forgiven. The healing could now start.

Cathy pulled away first, "Go greet everyone else, son. Then you're mine." She reached up and stroked his cheek, then kissed him again. He smiled. Trust his mother to think of everyone before herself. He pulled out of her arms and turned to greet the rest of his vast family and school friends. He stood stunned at the love that was being shown to him. He felt he'd betrayed them all, and here he was being welcomed like a king instead of grovelling like the prodigal son. He wiped away a tear. An action his father saw. "Son, I know that feeling; I'm sorry you felt you couldn't come to me. I was so engrossed in the business that I forgot about my family. Will you ever forgive me?"

Rick was stunned. "Are you kidding? I was never angry with you. You're the best father ever, but I was young and too silly to see it. It took me to leave to understand it. I'm the one who should be begging forgiveness, and I am." They hugged again.

"Let's call it equal and come and celebrate. Charlie said you have something to tell us. Can it wait?" Wills asked his son as they walked side by side to Charlie's house near the inn.

"Um, no, it can't." He beckoned his mother. "You see. I'm engaged. It's going to be in tomorrow's paper, so you'll find out anyway."

Cathy grinned, "I bet it is to Mary Louise, isn't it?"

Rick was stunned. "But how...?" He left the question unfinished and just grinned and nodded. "Yes, we're being married on Christmas Day here at St John's, and Reverend William is going to do the deed." His grin showed them his happiness.

Cathy gave her husband a loving shove. "See, I told you it was all a set-up." She giggled as she caught her son's eyes on her.

Rick just smiled and shook his head knowingly. The family welcome was all Rick could have dreamed. His twin, Bette, welcomed him demurely, then got cranky with him for clearing out without a word or a letter the entire time. At least she was mentioned in the few letters to his parents. Rick was duly repentant. "I couldn't, Bette; I felt horrible leaving anyway." Soon, she linked her arm with her brother's as they walked up the hill. As different as the two were, they had always been close. Rick was quiet; she was far from it, chatting nonstop. Another family member Rick needed to spend some time with later was his Uncle Ed. He wanted to thank him for what he'd sent to both Dylan and Mac. The differences these deliveries made to their businesses were terrific. Time for that later. Wills and Cathy decided to stay in Parramatta until at least Monday the following week. Wills explained after he told them about his engagement. He had some work to do at the Parramatta warehouse, but he wanted to spend quality time with Rick. He was content to stay for a few days. If he went back to Emu Plains, he would get busy with work. He needed to dedicate some special time to Rick. Gracie had arranged a luncheon at their house, after which Wills and his family left with Rick for *Roseneath*. His luggage had arrived at Charlie's house. Charlie sorted Rick's new clothing from his own, as he had packed them in the same case. He told Wills he had supplied his nephew with an entire wardrobe of clothes. He then added, "And Wills, bite it, as to repaying the costs." Charlie grinned at Wills's reaction.

Wills had started to argue, but then he saw the glint in his oldest brother's face. "Thanks, big bro. Much appreciated," Wills smiled, knowing that Charlie was happy. Wills still felt somewhat guilty that the three younger Lockley brothers were rolling in wealth, and Charlie had little. Admittedly, he was now on an excellent annual allowance as Viceroy, a form of compensation. The title brought in little if anything; however, now his son insisted on giving him a percentage of the farm profits. The income was still a mere pittance compared to what Ed, Wills, and Luke each earned per month. None flaunted their wealth, and each ensured that their extended families lacked for nothing. Much of their expenditure was spent in the community and often done secretly, without even telling their siblings. Charlie had the title of Earl but little else. He was content. He felt guilty because he had the title, and his oldest son, Teddy, would inherit that. He had a loving and supportive wife and a close family. Their oldest son, Teddy, admittedly lived in England with his wife and family, but they only resided in the cottage where his grandfather had been born. They had enough for their needs.

Ed invited the whole family for dinner at his house. His housekeeper, Cara Connor, was still in the kitchen there, but she now had two full-time paid assistants. Her husband, Paddy, still plotted around the garden, but as they were both nearing seventy, they could no longer work a full day. Each had been offered retirement, but as life convicts, Paddy said, they would keep working to earn their keep. Ed had built them a small two-bedroom, self-contained cottage in the back corner of his large yard, but they preferred to stay in the simple quarters attached to the stables. The new maids, Janet and Fizzy, whose real name was Felicity, were currently in the cottage with their brother Bertram. They were an orphaned trio that the family had found and employed all at once. Bertram was now head gardener. He had enhanced the front gardens, to Paddy's delight. Paddy had trained him and then handed the bulk of the garden over to his care. Paddy still tended his spuds and would let no one else touch them. Ed had made him a kneeling frame, so he had handles to assist him in standing up and a soft pad to kneel on.

Dinner time came, and the family *en masse* descended on Ed's house. After dinner, Rick held the floor for most of the post-meal chatter. With everyone listening in rapt attention, he retold some of his adventures from the past years. Even the children sat in awe of their cousin. He initially left out the bushranger story until Charlie brought it up in his conversation, and Rick was forced to retell it. He moved to his mother's side as he did so. "I was in no danger once I knew who he was, mother. I knew him to like his tucker, and also, we still stank."

Wills and Cathy sat listening in wonderment as he retold some of his saga. Wills looked around at his mother and the older siblings. Addressing his mother, he said, "Mother, you know I ran away when you were in England with Father, well, I was only a teenager too. Upon my return, I promised myself that I would give my children a significant voice in their future. I have not done this for Rick. I had his future plotted for him from the day of his birth, never questioning if it was what he wanted." He turned to his son. "I'm sorry, son." Wills looked contrite. "I look forward to sitting down with you tomorrow and listening to what you have to say. My mind and heart are wide open. Whatever you want will be fine with us." Cathy took his hand, knowing how thrilled Wills was when word came that Rick was back. He had dropped everything, cancelled numerous appointments, and came. Wills looked somewhat crestfallen and penitent.

Rick, still standing, said, "Father, you may well be surprised by what I'm about to say, but I'd be thrilled if your original offer is open at any stage. I find I know the job well and now know how I can assist many of the smaller blacksmiths in the smaller towns, having set both Dylan and Mac up with a mail-order system. That will be something I'm interested in developing, as well as producing a printed catalogue of the items we stock. It could be posted to every blacksmith, in every town, in the land. The warehouse and Uncle Ed's forge can supply the goods, and Uncle Luke's wagons can deliver the orders."

Wills' face looked stunned. "You mean it, son? You'll come back?" His eyes glazed with happiness. Before Rick had a chance to reply, he was enfolded in his father's arms again.

Before the evening drew to a close, he finally told everyone about his engagement to Mary Louise. The announcement would be in the paper the next day, and he wanted everyone to hear it from him in person.

Knowing that everyone there had witnessed the incident after church, he was soon inundated with questions. He confessed his dissatisfaction with having his life ordered for him and how it had irked him, but it was a stray comment heard about arranging his marriage by a non-member of the family that, as he put it, was the straw that broke the camel's back. He and Mary Louise discussed how to leave. "Let's just say the rest is history." There was no way he would say she had not told him what she intended to do. They shared that responsibility equally. As the family drove back to *Roseneath*, Rick again apologised for the angst he had caused.

Cathy squeezed his hand, and Wills gave him another hug. Bette just sat grinning at her brother. "Let's see what the morrow brings, son. Sleep well, and we'll see you in the morning." Wills cupped his son's face in his hands. "I missed you so much, son." He drew him into his arms, hugged him, and then sent him to bed. He would always be her baby.

~

Rick awoke at dawn and wondered where he was. The ticking of the hallway clock sounded familiar, and he also recognised the room. The slow recognition of his surroundings brought a smile to his lips. He was in his own bed in his family's 'Parra home' as they called it. Their real home was in Emu Plains, but his father had bought this house from Uncle Harry Harlow before he was born. He was equally at home in either. He loved it and was content there, just as he was anywhere. His room contained every possible comfort, and the house even had a new indoor bathroom. His father had sacrificed a small back storeroom to install a septic toilet and washroom inside the home. He had done this too for both cottages years before, building extensions out the back, and Uncle Luke had also installed one when he bought his house. This recollection brought a smile to his lips as he remembered using Dylan's privy for the first time. He had forgotten to check for red-back spiders under the toilet seat and was very lucky not to have been bitten by the big mama one that crawled out just after he'd stood up. The big, red slash on their backs was like a warning beacon. Rick knew it would take him a while to settle back into the routine at home. He was no longer his own boss and once more must fit into a family and its demands. He sighed contentedly. After his reception yesterday, he was no longer anxious about today's meeting with his father. He heard a gentle tap at his door, and he called, "Enter."

His mother arrived with a tray of hot chocolate and toast. "Don't get used to this, son, but this is my way of saying welcome home." She bent and kissed his cheek. "All good, son? Sleep well?"

His beaming smile was her answer; she left the room happy. "Thanks, Mum." She just stroked his cheek and left him to enjoy his hot chocolate.

Chapter 11 A New Beginning

Once Rick was up and dressed, he knew his father was waiting to see him. Rick had no idea what he wanted to do with his life and had no plans other than to marry Mary Lou and hopefully work for his father. He felt at peace, which surprised him. He didn't care if it was only as a labourer.

Three hours later, the two men emerged from the small office with a mutually approved future plan.

Wills had his arm along Rick's shoulder, and they headed to the kitchen for a mug of tea. Rick's head was still reeling; he was to take over complete management of the warehouse in town and put his planned mail-order business into action.

The looks on the faces of Ed, Luke, and Wills last night when Rick had pointed out the benefits of a mail-order business for small towns took his breath away. It had obviously been on his father's mind all night as well.

Wills pumped Rick for more information about his idea as soon as he sat down. As the thought had only come to mind moments before he voiced it, he just said it was a work in progress. What also stunned Rick was that his father offered him the full use of *Roseneath* to live in after he married. Brodie and Shauna Murphy would stay in their accommodation at the back of the stables with their children. The two maids would also be kept at the house. To top it off, Rick would not only have a job but also a regular salary. He would also receive half of the profit from any mail-order sales. He would have free rein over what to stock in the warehouse. If orders were for regular stock items and an Emporium was nearby, then orders could be collected free of charge from there.

Rick would be given a budget for the mail order catalogue, and special item orders were also available. To say he was stunned was a vast understatement. He couldn't believe it, and he was extremely thankful. He couldn't wait to let Mary Lou know on Friday when they arrived for the weekend. Hopefully, by then, he would have a list of things to be included.

Rick's mind was already tossing up ideas; he thought of setting a limit of two hundred items in the initial illustrated catalogue, with an unillustrated list of more items available on request. He could change these in the catalogue for each reprint. Dead stock could now be discounted and moved quickly. They would be sold on a first-come basis. He spent the next day familiarising himself with the items in stock. Most were the same as when he left. He had shortlisted some things for the catalogue and needed forty more. Wills suggested adding a specials page with sale items available in each catalogue; these were overstock or dead stock items. That only left twenty to add. The idea of swaggie kits came to mind, and so he added that to his list. As there was no urgency, he left the rest until later to sort out. Next, he needed drawings of each chosen item. So, he set about quickly marking which items to sketch. He knew that they would only be simple line drawings, as that's all they could print. He knew this would take an immense amount of time to complete and something he could do at home; he set this work aside until the evenings.

~

By Friday morning, Rick was yearning for Mary Louise to arrive. She was coming with her parents on the last ferry of the day. Ed had offered them rooms. The ferry was on time and brought the Evanses. Only Phil, Alice, and Mary Louise arrived, as Mark arrived early from Melbourne, and Phillipa returned home. This suited Rick as it meant that he did not have to sit and entertain her. He knew Phil would allow him to be with Mary Lou, which he was looking forward to.

Rick greeted Mary Louise with a gentle kiss on her cheek. "Wait until later, sweetheart," he whispered.

The beaming smile she gave him made his heart skip a beat. The promise of her sweet kisses sent a surge of blood to his lower regions. He groaned softly, but not softly enough; she had heard and giggled.

He ignored her as best he could, considering she was clinging to his arm. "Uncle Phil, the first thing we have to do tomorrow is go up to the church and see the minister. Reverend William Clarke is fine to do the service as he'll be here for Christmas anyway, but Reverend Gunther wishes to meet us all together," Rick explained. "Is that okay? You're still happy that we go ahead with a Christmas wedding?"

"Yes, lad, we are." Phil looked at his wife, who was nodding.

Wills hadn't heard Rick's conversation and said to Phil, "Hey Phil, I have even made enquiries of Reverend Gunther. He's expecting us all at ten tomorrow morning. I've told him Reverend William would do the honours, and knowing our history, he's happy for that to occur. You only must decide if you want it in the early morning service or just afterwards. As the morning service is at 8, I would suggest 10 would be good. That would give everyone time to dress. If you two didn't wish to go to church in the morning, then we could do a Communion Service for the wedding."

Rick and Mary Louise put their heads together and discussed the time of their wedding as they walked.

"Father, I think we'd like to have it after the morning service at about eight or soon afterwards, if that's suitable," Rick said just before they reached Ed's house. Rick was looking forward to greeting her properly.

Phil gave them the opportunity as soon as they arrived. Alice visited the bathroom, and the two fathers sat in the kitchen with Jenna and Cara. Ed was still at work.

Rick escorted Mary Lou into the sitting room and closed the door behind him. She turned and stepped into his arms, wrapping hers around his neck. He stood still for a moment, almost devouring her face with his eyes, then, with a slight groan of desire, hungrily kissed her.

She returned his passion, their kisses heating them both with unfulfilled yearning. "Oh, these weeks can't go fast enough for my liking." He kissed her again before telling her of the week's happenings. "We've been given *Roseneath* to live in, sweetheart."

"What? So, no cottage or tent? Do you mean the entire house? Oh, Ricky, that's amazing! It's even got staff and, well, everything hasn't it? Brodie and Shauna still live there, too, don't they?" She was jigging up and down with excitement.

"Yes, to all of the above, and it gets better. My father has handed the big warehouse over to me to run, and I'm to proceed with a mail-order catalogue. We will receive half of the profit from the sales. With no rent to pay, sweetheart, we'll be secure and...."

"...And able to start a family as soon as we can," she said quietly and watched him blush.

"Yes, but until that happens, we can practice." He silenced her for a bit. "After our wedding, of course."

She willingly responded to his attentions.

Rick knew there was one subject he should mention to her, "Mary Lou, it also means that if, or should I say, when Jack comes, we'll have room for him, do you mind?"

"Oh no, sweeting, I would love to meet him. If he's that special to you, then he must be some amazing man." She had a flash of concern cross her face.

He explained, "He is, my darling. I know there is something in his background he didn't tell me, well, much actually, as I don't know much about him except that he comes from Kent, too. His name is really John, and his birthday is St John's Day. I don't even know his surname, but Mary Lou, I trusted him with my life and still do. He jokingly called himself a 'Prince among men', so it could be some play on his name. I feel he knows Uncle Ned's family, as he thought I looked like a friend of his named Paul. Having seen Uncle David's young portrait at Gracemere and met Uncle

Paul, I know of my similarity to him. Uncle Ned said I looked a lot like Paul when he was younger, as did grandfather."

~

The next six weeks flew by. Rick spent weekends at his father's Sydney house so he could see Mary Louise. Christmas week arrived, as did the family, again *en masse* from all over the area. Most were from Emu Plains. Rick was allowed to walk with Mary Louise along the riverbank as it was close to the family homes and within public view. They were very circumspect after one situation where they had found themselves alone for some length of time, and as Rick said to her later when he apologised, his intentions had nearly come undone. She seemed equally keen to touch his body as Rick was with hers. Her moans of passion had finally brought him back to reality, and he gently pushed her away from him. Her eyes hooded with the heat of unquenched desire. Both were struggling to regain control through heavy breathing.

They discussed where to go for the honeymoon. Rick suggested that they should sit and talk, as he dared not touch her again for a while. Eventually, they settled on a week at the King's Arms Hotel in Sydney. Other family members had stayed there for their honeymoons and loved it. The additional benefit was that the hotel offered room service, and the main suite Rick had booked featured a sitting room and *en-suite facilities* with a double bath and a private bathroom. If they wished to go out, there was a lot to do in town.

~

Christmas week finally arrived, as did the first of the wedding guests.

Reverend William and Maria Clarke were to stay at *Roseneath* with Wills and the family until the wedding; then, they had to leave and travel to their son's house. He was able to have long talks with both Wills and Rick. Rick's room now held a new double bed and had been refurbished for a couple.

Another conversation that took place was between Wills and Rick the night before the wedding. As there was no cellar in that house, Wills took Rick out to their barn, and in the darkness, they sat and discussed marriage and all that it entailed. After giving Rick the full facts of what marriage involved and that the enjoyable act of procreation was just one delightful side of it, he told Rick of the necessity not to use soap down there, as it burns the girls. "Rick lad, this is important; even though the soaps nowadays are not as caustic as when my Father married, it's true, they still burn and… her, um, desires for you are somewhat quenched due to her discomfort. So, it's for your benefit; remember not to use it."

Rick could tell his father was embarrassed, but he listened hard. His father warned him that the first time would be somewhat painful for her, but their unions after that would be pleasurable for both and frequent too if he took the time and pleasured her.

Rick was both astonished and delighted. "First time? More than once, Father?" Rick stammered.

Wills chuckled. "Oh yes, son, frequently and the more pleasurable you make it for her, the more often it will occur, often in one night too. For that to occur, hold back as long as you can, and you will find out why. Ask if it's all right to touch her; do not presume."

"Oh, wow, seriously? I thought maybe once a week if I was lucky." Rick was flabbergasted with the information he'd heard.

Wills explained more hints about marriage, other than the physical side. "Do you remember Grandpa always used to bring in a flower or a pretty leaf for Grandmother? It showed that he cared and thought about her. You, of course, remember his snake bite? It's what he was doing when it occurred, picking her a flower. Ricky, my boy, it's the little things in marriage that mean so much to a lady. As you know, we have more money than we can possibly spend, but your mother didn't think I had a penny to my name when I proposed. Cathy is like Mary Louise; she loves me for who I am. Not for the money or wealth of trappings that brings. Rick, it's the caresses, the signs and affection, the little things you do for her, that you show her your love for her. That will mean more to her than any diamonds you could ever buy her."

"I know about Grandfather and his flowers because of his snake bite incident. I found out about what he did then, but Father, I never ever understood the importance of it." Rick fell to thinking. "I never really comprehended how vastly beneficial this was to a marriage, Father."

"Rick, eventually, you will need to find your own place, and you will become independent. After I go, there will be ample funds to support all six of you, but, son, I need you to keep an eye on your twin sister. She's never fully settled nor found her life partner. I'll never force her to marry if she doesn't want to. Mind you, I have no intention of dying for a long, long time, so you will have to make do until I shuffle off this mortal coil. Will you promise me that you will care for Bette? I know it should be your eldest brother, Lukie, or even Pip, but I'll leave her in your care, Rick."

"Of course, Father, as you only turn fifty this coming year, you have decades left, but I promise I will look after her. You have my word on that." Rick was honoured. He adored his twin sister; he would always watch out for her.

~

Christmas Day dawned as a glorious morning. It was crisp and clear; the cicadas were in full voice, with no fires around to darken the mood, and the weather was mild for a Parramatta summer.

Wills was far more nervous than Rick was when the family left for the church.

Over at Ed's house, Phil had to get Alice to wake Mary Louise, as she had slept in. When she awoke, she muttered sleepily to her mother, "I'm getting married today, Mother." She stretched and grinned. Alice had come into her room just before they retired and had the obligatory mother/daughter pre-marriage talk. As usual, Alice was hard to keep quiet; this conversation left Mary-Louise speechless for long periods. Then Mary Louise asked all sorts of embarrassing questions to the point that Alice eventually just answered, "Rick will be gentle, I'm sure. Just know that whatever he does to you is what marriage is about. As that side is known as the 'joys of marriage', it's supposed to be enjoyable. If you respond, it is, and dear, it is meant to be. I will not say any more." As she was beetroot red, she kissed her daughter and left before she asked any more embarrassing questions.

Phil was more impatient to get everyone up and ready than Mary Louise was. However, she was prepared before her mother, and she had to wait downstairs for them before they all had a quick breakfast. All had decided only to have toast, as the Christmas feast cum Wedding Breakfast would be vast. As fast as Cara and the girls could cook the toast on the stove's hot plate, it was devoured.

Finally, all left for the church in two carriages. Charlie's carriage joined them in a procession up the hill. Phil and family had come by carriage to Parramatta as they had good clothing and lots of Mary Louise's luggage to bring.

The Christmas service was about to start, and the family only had minutes to get seated. Phil and Mary Louise sat in the shade outside the vestibule and came in after everyone was seated. As they were seated at the back and wore a wrap, she decided not to take Holy Communion as Rick would see her.

The Christmas service was over, and Reverend William invited everyone to stay for the wedding if they wished. No one moved, so he started the marriage service immediately.

Mary Louise stood, knowing that it was finally time to be married. Phil had taken her back outside again. Taking a deep breath, she squeezed her father's arm as she took it.

Phil bent and gave her a brief kiss. "Let's do this, pumpkin."

Mary Louise nodded, knowing she was looking her best. Her gown was white and made of superfine silk. It shimmered as she moved. She wore her mother's lace-edged net veil over her small poke bonnet, and Phil pulled a small veil over her face. She had intended to have no bridesmaids, but when she arrived the day before, she asked Bette if she'd stand up with her. She would not walk down the aisle but would be waiting for her at the front to hold her flowers.

Bette was thrilled and had been overjoyed to be part of her twin's marriage.

Rick asked Mary Louise's cousin, Jonty Evans, to stand with him. The two boys were only ten months apart in age and had always been close friends, closer than even his brother was.

Bette and Jonty would also witness their signatures.

When Mary Lou stood at the church door, an audible gasp was heard throughout the church.

Rick had noticed the light that suddenly filled the building and turned to watch her as she came down the aisle. Having discarded her wrap, her gown caught the morning sun, and the reflection filled the church with shimmering light. Unlike the congregation, Rick didn't gasp, but he did have tears in his eyes. One trickled down his cheek unchecked. She looked glorious.

Her smile lit up the church even more than her gown did. Her eyes were fixed on his. Rick chuckled, as, rather than a sedate glide down the aisle, she was almost tugging her father to hurry. She could not get to Rick's side fast enough. Once there, she hastily dropped her father's arm and grabbed Rick's hand.

Reverend William Clarke stood waiting for them to reach him and, in front of everyone, said the magic words that bound them together for life—musical words to both their ears and blessed by God.

When he asked who would give the bride away, Phil willingly gave his permission and leaned over to Rick, whispering, "No returns, remember," and chuckling.

"Not likely!" Rick said, grinning from ear to ear.

Reverend William pronounced them man and wife and said that he may now kiss his wife.

Rick had intended only to give her a quick peck on the lips as was proper. Mary Louise had different thoughts. She was now allowed to kiss him as she wished, and she wanted to right now, and that's just what she intended to do. Rick raised her veil from her face. She lifted her hand and set it on his chest. As he bent his head to brush her lips gently, she slid her arm around his neck.

His gentle peck turned into a burning, hot, passionate kiss that rocked him with its intensity.

William coughed twice before she let Rick go.

She gazed at Rick's embarrassed face lovingly and then innocently turned back to the two ministers.

It was time for them to sign the register.

A nuptial Holy Communion followed that for just the pair of them, as she had missed out earlier.

Reverend William presented them as man and wife. After the

service, they preceded everyone out of the church. Rick drew her under a tree to wait in the shade for the family to join them.

She occupied him by repeating the fiery kisses she had given him in church.

Rick gently pushed her from him, "Cor, Mary Lou, if that's what you can do to me with your kisses… We'd better stop, or you might regret it. I might have to race you up home, and we'll be late for our party."

She whispered back, "Wishful thinking, my husband, but certainly an idea; a good one too. Everyone else will be heading down to Ed's straight away. Could we have some time together first? It's only nine now, and lunch isn't until noon."

He saw she was in earnest. "I don't want the first time to be hurried, love."

"Who says it will only be once?" she said provocatively. "Think of an excuse and quickly, husband dear. I want you."

He looked at her enticing grin and said, "We'll see."

Everyone was soon milling around them. Rick decided to take her up on her suggestion. His breeches could not hide his desire for her all day, and she was willing. They could have a few hours to themselves before lunch. They were to stay at *Roseneath* that first night, as no ferries were running on Christmas afternoon.

The rest of the family returned to Ed's place for the usual Christmas luncheon in his backyard and to stay the night there.

Wills and Cathy came and spoke to them before they left for the luncheon. Wills let Rick know they had a few hours before they needed to appear and face the fuss. He suggested they use the gig. Then he smiled at his son and congratulated him.

Cathy hugged her new daughter-in-law.

Half an hour later, Rick made excuses and said they had something to collect from the house; he had genuinely forgotten to bring her engagement ring. Mary Louise had chosen the ring the weekend she had come for a visit six weeks earlier; it had needed resizing. Rick had only collected it two days earlier. He should have let Jonty make it, as he would have been quicker than the jeweller in town. He was halfway through his jeweller's apprenticeship, and his work was wonderful. Collecting the engagement ring would be an adequate excuse for their departure and absence. They borrowed his father's gig and went back to *Roseneath* to collect his gift.

Mary Louise was nearly laughing aloud as they left.

"Shhh, you'll give the game away, love." Rick tried to shush her, but by the time they drew the gig into the backyard of the house some five minutes later, he was in such a state of mirth himself that he nearly dropped her as he lifted her from the gig after flicking the reins to a hitching post. He then carried her inside through the kitchen and directly into his, or now their, bedroom. He barely had time to close the door before she was in front of him and busily unbuttoning his clothing while sending his desires spiralling with her deep, passionate kisses. A trail of apparel soon covered the floor, and once unclad, he gently lifted her onto their new bed.

Rick drew back slightly to admire the view. His fingers nervously reached out and touched her stomach. More, he dared not do yet. "May I?"

Mary Lou nodded and giggled, somewhat embarrassed at being in bed with a man, even though he was now her husband. "Ricky, Mother said the first time will hurt me a bit, but I don't care; I need you now." She drew him down to her.

Initially, he was beside her, and he again put out his hand to touch her soft, glowing skin. Her breasts were as soft and smooth as he had imagined them to be. Her body was exquisite, white and smooth like the silk gown he had recently removed from her.

A guttural groan of desire broke from him, and he gathered her into his arms.

Her kisses outside the church were nothing compared to what she was doing to him now. Her hunger for his body was as needy as he was for hers.

Their marriage was consummated, much to the utter delight of both. As both were innocent in the ways of marriage, Rick tried to take his time; at least he had intended to.

The momentary pain she hardly noticed as she pulled him into her. Instinct took over and guided them far more than any talks or instructions.

They lay back, temporarily exhausted.

He reached out and started gently caressing her breasts, still unbelieving that he now had the right to look, touch and adore this view. He certainly admired what he saw before him—softly running his hand over her flat stomach and sending thrills through her body. He had never seen a woman unclad before, and the sight was delightful.

She, too, discovered the joys of a strong, healthy husband's body. Having never seen a male unclothed before either, she investigated the differences. Her gentle touch to his nether regions sent electric shock waves through him. Another groan emanated from him.

When she reached for him only minutes later, he was far more than stunned, but he was ready for her, and she could tell. She drew him on top of her, and she wrapped her legs tightly around his torso, trapping him to her.

He was amazed and delighted at her suppleness. He was more than happy to obey her request, and this time, they took the time to enjoy the delights of their new marriage.

Neither had known nor understood the joys that had awaited them.

Rick remembered that his father had told him to hold back for as long as he could. This time, he did and discovered that her rapturous release equalled his own.

She arched against him and gasped with delight. "Oh, Ricky! Oh, my goodness, Ricky, I was taken to the stars and back again," she murmured against his neck when he finally released.

He moved beside her and drew her into his arms.

They looked forward to the week before them.

They were temporarily sated and dozed, enfolded in each other's arms.

~

The clock in the hallway struck eleven, waking them from their slumber.

Rick realised that they must dress and join the family. As it was, they would be cutting it fine to return by noon. He suddenly remembered the engagement ring that was their excuse for heading home. Whilst still naked, he grabbed it from his bedside drawer and slid it onto her finger.

Rick had never dressed a lady before, and he soon discovered how distracting an activity it was. She had a very desirable body hidden under her garments. He managed to draw on his shirt before she, still only partially clad, needed assistance doing up the back of her gown.

It took another fifteen minutes before they managed to find their shed clothing and dress as neatly as they had been before.

She needed to fix her hair as some of the pins had come adrift.

Eventually, they were presentable enough to face their families. Both were fearful they would be embarrassed when they entered. However, neither really cared; they were, after all, married.

The large blue sapphire sparkled on her hand. She would make sure everyone admired it.

Chapter 12 The Surprise Visitor
Two years later

$\mathcal{R}$ick and Mary Lou were celebrating their second wedding anniversary at Ed's place. Once again, the family gathered for Christmas Day luncheon when a black-hatted hobbling figure caught Rick's eye.

Abandoning everyone, he cried, "Jack, you came!" Rick left his wife and daughter's side and crossed the yard to meet the old man.

The two embraced in a loving bear hug, then Rick reached across and took the old man's swag.

Introductions were soon made to everyone. Mary Louise was, of course, first to issue him a welcome after Rick. The rest of the family followed once they realised who this old man was. Wills made a beeline for Jack's side and thanked him profusely for looking out for Rick. Cathy was called over and introduced.

When Jack was later shown the bathroom, he relished the running water and the flushing toilet—luxuries he had not seen before. Rick laughed, and he heard his exclamations. Then, he showed him how it all worked. "Excellent, lad! Such wondrous inventions they have these days. How clever were the people who thought them out?" He thoroughly washed his face and hands, and Rick escorted him outside to join the family luncheon. "I'm sad I missed the ferry yesterday; I would have liked to have been at church with you today, lad. I'll be able to come with you on Sunday, son, and that will be a blessing for an old man's heart." Jack smiled. He stood looking at the family members who surrounded him. "Oh, Rick, my boy, you do all look alike and so like my friend Paul that I figured you must have been related."

This was the first time Jack had made such a blatant comment that gave Rick an 'in' to ask more. "Jack, was Paul related to a duke in Kent?"

Jack froze; his stare and a slight nod were an affirmation of Rick's enquiry. "Yes, a son and later, his brother," he finally managed to say softly.

Rick explained that Ed's daughter, Tina, was now married to Paul's nephew, who was Ned's son, Charles, or Chip as he was known, was now the Duke, and therefore she was the current Duchess.

"I know about David and Ned, lad." Jack would say no more. The gasp and look on Jack's face almost frightened Rick. "I wondered, lad, the look of you and the name. I so wondered. I can't tell you now; my story will have to wait a while, lad." Jack was choked up, so Rick didn't push him.

Ellen and Luke were walking up to talk to him. Jack looked around in awe at the numerous family members surrounding him. Many, if not most, were fair-haired and blue-eyed and looked amazingly alike, no matter what age. There was a smattering of brunettes, like Mary Louise, or mousey-brown-haired folk, like Jenna. For the first time in many a year, Jack felt at home and thoroughly welcomed. The reception he had received from every single one of them was a joy to his lonely heart. He had had enough of wandering, and he had come to spend his last years with Rick and his family. Home, he had not had one of those for a long time.

Rick saw him wipe away a tear. An apologetic half-smile crossed Jack's face briefly, and Rick went to his side. "Jack, are you all right? Is it too much for you? When we all get together, we are a mighty number, and Christmas Day is when all the hanger-owners join in. So, all the rest of Mary Louise's family is here, as are the rest of Turner's. That is Mother's and Aunt Jenna's family, and her other sister, Vicky and her brothers. Mother, Aunt Jenna and Aunt Vicky are sisters; they are the older couple with my grandmother. Would you like to meet them?"

Jack nodded, "I'm fine, lad." Then he replied to Rick's question, "Yes, I'd be delighted to meet them."

Rick escorted him to the three older folks sitting on an exquisitely made, painted, wrought-iron garden setting.

Once introduced, Rick's grandmother invited him to join them. He was thankful he had taken the time to source some clean clothes and have a good scrub. For a man who had lived the past thirty or more years on the streets and bush, he had scrubbed up quite well.

Sal Lockley invited him to sit next to her. At seventy-seven, she held her age well and still looked beautiful. Though her hair was now white, her blue eyes danced with laughter. She had heard Rick's full story about Jack often over the past two years. Now, she met him; a vague familiarity made her frown. She shook her head, trying to clear her thoughts.

Jack saw her confusion and stayed mute.

"Have we met before, sir?" Sal asked quietly.

"Ma'am, unless you have frequented many fallen logs in the Australian bushland, who knows?" Jack was exquisitely polite, and his comment was not at all rude. He didn't actually deny the meeting.

"You remind me of a wonderfully kind gentleman I met many years ago in England. He was the friend of our cousin's friend."

"I wish it were so, ma'am, but any past that I may have lived before is long gone from my memory. My life is what you see: a simple man who has lived from day to day, seeking no more fulfilment than peace with my Maker. Rick's presence in my life was a blessing from above. He came to me in my hour of loneliness and has been a constant blessing ever since. Even when he left me, he sent letters of encouragement. For the first time in a long time, I felt needed. That, ma'am, is an extraordinary gift to give a lonely soul." Jack spoke in earnest.

Sal looked deeply into the old man's eyes. "Are you sure, sir? For I do feel I know you," Sal inquired again. Sal knew it was him, and for some reason, he didn't exactly deny their meeting; he just ignored her question. She didn't push it. She even recognised his voice and his piercing blue eyes. Jack knew he would not lie, so he just smiled, leaving her question hanging. He thought it was best she be left wondering than to know his story. It was not yet time for that to be revealed. One day, he would confess the truth.

~

Jack settled into the back bedroom at *Roseneath*, next to the bathroom, and made himself useful around the house. Brodie learnt to leave some jobs for Jack to potter away at, as Jack hated being useless. Polishing the tack was a job he adored. The smell of neatsfoot oil permeated the tack room and accompanied him as he came inside; Jack's hands were often stained with the substance.

Jack had been with Rick for six months and had befriended a regular visitor, Reverend William Clarke. He even occasionally made what he termed the perilous trip on the ferry to visit his ageing friend in North Sydney each week.

One Monday in June, Jack returned home before luncheon, much saddened. Reverend William Branwhite Clarke was dead. He had been failing for some time, and Jack had visited him every Monday for the past two months. Now, he was gone.

Jack's early return and his silence at luncheon worried Rick. Jack waited until the children were asleep for a nap before he told Rick the sad news. They sent a message to Wills and Cathy, letting them know the tragic tidings, then went and told his Uncle Luke. This was a special funeral that the entire family was not prepared to miss.

It was held in North Sydney two days later. William had been such an important figure in all their lives that they would be there to honour him and support Maria and the family.

After the family returned from the funeral, Jack asked Sal to go for a walk along the riverbank. Reverend Clarke had almost been family, and Sal was feeling his loss intensely. Each member was feeling his passing, but Sal had no one to turn to but Jack. He was there for her as she was for him.

Jack's adoration of little Mary Kathleen, whom he called Kitten, was something to behold. The small child would crawl up onto his lap and hug him. "You need a hug, Just Jack." She had her mother's dark hair and her father's blue eyes. She adored him, and they were often seen walking hand in hand around the extensive gardens. He would pick a flower for her or would spend hours with her on the various swings he had made for her in the large trees in the garden.

~

The time came for Mary Louise to deliver her second child, and when Jack William was born the Easter after Jack had arrived, he thought he had died and gone to Heaven. "Rick, my boy, I didn't mean it when I said to name him Jack. Call him John, as I believe it's a family name."

Rick placed the tiny sleeping child in Jack's arms. "No, his name will be 'Jack' after you, not anyone in my family. Yes, yes, I know you are really John too; you told me that in Ballarat, but you are just Jack to me. 'Nothing more, nothing less,' remember. Do you not realise that without you looking out for me and eventually sending me home, he would not exist? He will be a daily reminder of what we all owe you. Not to mention the fact that we also adore you to bits."

Rick saw the tears form in the old man's eyes. "Oh, son, I'm so honoured. I truly am." Jack hugged Rick and turned to admire the tiny dark-haired baby. "He's beautiful, lad."

"Jack, would you consider being his Godfather too?" Rick asked, knowing that if he did, they would find out his real name.

"No, I'm too old, lad, but I'll willingly become his foster grandfather. That is a role I would love to have. As Kitten calls me, I'm 'Just Jack'." Jack looked down at the tiny babe, now asleep in his arms. His rough, gnarled finger stroked his velvety cheek gently. "He will be my foster grandson, Rick. The one I always wanted." One of Jack's happy tears fell onto the sleeping child's cheek, and the babe smiled in his sleep, his dimples popping as he did so. Jack chuckled. "He's got your dimples, lad."

Rick nodded, and his dimples popped, too, as he smiled.

Jack celebrated his seventy-eighth birthday only weeks after young Jack was born.

~

By the time of his next birthday, Jack was often found not walking around the gardens as he had previously loved to do, but sitting in an oversized cane chair with both small children cuddled in his arms. He would be telling them stories of his time on the road and others he had made up or read to them. By the time young Jack was up and running around, old Jack was fading fast.

Both children called him Just Jack, for that was how he referred to himself: 'Just Jack, nothing more, nothing less.'

The two cherubs would sit still for hours, absorbing the love he exuded for them. One or the other would often stroke his bewhiskered cheek. He was the grandfather they had missed out on, with Wills' father, Charles, having died some eight years before.

Jack was content, as were Rick and Mary Louise, with him spending time with their children. They adored having him live with them. He was loved, and he was family and introduced as such: "Jack, our children's foster grandfather, nothing more, nothing less."

~

Rick's mail-order catalogue business had not only been a good idea but also a roaring success. Consequently, this had picked up business for both his Uncle Luke's delivery firm, Lockley's Logistics, and for Wills, other Emporiums, and Ed's foundry and smithy. Wills now had approximately forty stores statewide, and delivery times for orders were significantly reduced. Many towns were now on the wireless lines, and orders could be placed by catalogue number and quantity. The warehouse could now restock quickly, as Wills had made arrangements with his nephew, Teddy Lockley, in England to source and send stock. Wills had planned for this to occur when the Overland Telegraph opened six years earlier, in 1872. It had occurred a week or so before Rick had left. Messages were sent via Adelaide, and within a few days, London received them, and they were delivered as telegrams. Or directly to the local post offices in the nearest towns. Teddy was paid a commission, which allowed him to assist his family at home. Once Teddy purchased the items, they were sent via the new Suez Canal passage. The orders could be in the warehouse within less than four months from the day of placing the order, but more often, much less time if they could be loaded onto a steamship. Sometimes, the turnaround can be as short as eight weeks. A week for the message to arrive, another week for Teddy to find the stock and six weeks for the return trip. No one else could turn around orders as fast, and it brought in much custom for the extended Lockley family businesses. Wills had been one of the first to send a message when it had opened six years earlier. He had heard that it was soon to be completed, and he had written to Teddy, asking him to be prepared when it finally happened.

Within a month of the first messages being sent, Wills placed his first order to England.

When Rick heard about this, he realised the benefit for the family businesses. Mac had told him of the connection of Ballarat to the telegraph wire, and he knew messages could be sent quickly from Ballarat to Parramatta, as he had done that himself from the post office. Rick even took himself into the new telegraph office and watched the messages sent via long and short taps on a clicky machine, and they were received on another. Rick knew that private lines would soon be available, and it was something else that he would be able to offer from the warehouse. Messaging directly to the major towns in his state would be a boon. When Rick investigated, he found that it was not as simple as it should have been. When he decided to learn Morse Code, he discovered that there were three versions of the code he could learn. There was the original American code, a Continental code, and the newer International code. He decided to throw himself into learning the International one, as it was only two sounds, short and long. When he told his uncles what he wanted to do, they all looked surprised.

However, his Uncle Luke said, "Hold that thought, lad, I have something at home you can have. Call in on your way home tonight."

Rick did call into Glenmere on the way home and collected what his Uncle Luke had promised him.

"I had this made up for a class I was teaching about the Australian Overland Telegraph when it was officially opened six years ago. The boys couldn't understand how the system worked. Uncle Ed and I put our heads together and knocked this up. It doesn't work, of course, but you can practise on it. Otherwise, you have to tap your finger on a desk. This is much better." Luke handed him the odd-looking contraption.

It consisted of a block of wood, a flat metal bar, and a knob on the end with a spring attached to the hinge. Rick accepted the contraption willingly and thanked him profusely.

Within weeks, Rick became quite proficient at it and soon reached a rate of about thirty words a minute. He had read that the most proficient operators were forty words a minute, so he was pleased with his skill.

Jack would sit and read something to Rick, waiting for him to tap out the words. Jack kept time and encouraged Rick to keep practising. When Rick beat his own time, he was never sure if either he or Jack was happier.

One day, Jack arrived at their session, having made an exact replica of a Morse code tapper and even added wires so that the two could be connected. He had also added a very primitive battery, using a giant potato. Rick had never seen anything like this before.

"Just something I was tinkering with, lad," he told Rick. He'd learned the code too, and unbeknownst to Rick, he'd been practising. He was fast enough to send a message to Rick, and Rick received it. "It is no use just tapping out the messages if you can't read them, too." They sat, playing with Jack's new toy for ages, sending and receiving jokes and random messages.

Rick was thrilled and thanked Jack profusely.

Wills decided to build a telegraph room onto the warehouse and set it up so that, once the line was connected, they could connect directly into the line rather than having telegrams sent to the post office.

Business in the mail-order section of work was now brisk. The stock was moving faster than even from the Emporiums, and Wills found it hard to keep enough merchandise in the warehouse for regular business. Consequently, Ed's forge and his new foundry grew, as did Luke's Logistics company. Ed had at long last fulfilled his dream of building a complete foundry. Until now, he'd only had a small affair, but with the uptake in business, he expanded to a fully functioning foundry.

Jack celebrated another birthday with Rick. Seventy-nine was a good age. He sat gazing at Rick, "I love you; I hope you know that, son. You brought me joy that I could not have imagined."

One thing Jack loved to do was to go to work with Rick. He was well-versed in blacksmithing and the tools it required. Jack often worked with Mac, so he suggested to Rick one day, "Why don't you open the mail order side up to anyone who wishes to purchase things when they can't get to a store? You know general items like clothes, shoes, and even some bulk food items. Rick, even stock feed could be delivered." He suggested that each store outside the big towns be sent an essential items catalogue and that anyone could place orders. Luke's company could do cash on delivery, and for the tiny towns without blacksmiths, this would be a boon. This idea was soon put into practice as well. A new catalogue was produced. Businesses that stocked general store supply items were encouraged to advertise in the new catalogue. Everything from dried food products, tinned food, preserves, clothing, riding boots and all sorts of leather goods and saddles, particularly from Bertie's saddlery and leather goods store. If it could be transported, it was added. Most of this was unillustrated, but as time passed, the catalogue grew fatter.

Jack beamed that an idea of his was so successful.

Just before Easter, Jack asked if they could have another campfire dinner. Everyone loved these, and all the extended family tried to come. Even some of the Evans family arrived from Sydney. Jonty was staying with Ed, so he came too, as he was courting Uncle Luke's daughter, Lottie.

~

It was not long after this that old Jack didn't appear at the breakfast table. It was just after Easter in 1880. Rick knocked and received no answer. When he entered, he saw Jack still in bed. His eyes followed Rick, but obviously, something was seriously wrong. He was unable to move, and his face had dropped on one side. Rick knew immediately that Jack would not be with them for much longer. He called the doctor.

When Doctor Pringle arrived, he gave Rick the dismal prognosis of apoplexy and said it was unlikely Jack would see out the day, let alone the week. Rick knew his time with his old friend had drawn to a close. To make matters worse, it was close to the tenth anniversary of his grandfather's passing.

Jack couldn't speak but could point and make the motion of writing. Mary Lou went and brought a pencil and a blank journal. Holding it steady, Jack started writing his side of the conversation. "Rick, rejoice with me, for soon I will be with our Lord in Heaven. Thanks to you, my last years have been wonderful." Jack wrote in a shaky hand.

Rick replied, "Jack, to me, you are so special. Never underestimate yourself, dear man. I love you so much."

He wrote, "Get my billy can. The contents will explain much. Not to open it until I've gone. Promise me?" Jack looked at Rick, and a tear dribbled down Jack's cheek.

Rick replied with a nod and went to retrieve the old, blackened, dented billy can from where Jack had stored it. It was much heavier than he expected, but as he promised Jack, he did not open the lid. He knew it well, as they had shared many a meal from it. Rick returned to the room and placed the blackened billy can close to Jack.

The old man gave a smile as best as he could; only half of his face moved. He reached out and took Rick's hand. He had written quite a bit during Rick's short absence and then resumed writing. "I leave everything I possess to you, Rick; it's all here in this billy. Value it and use it wisely. I do this because you loved me as I am. Remember, nothing more, nothing less: no expectations but real unconditional love. You don't realise how much I valued that, lad. Then you and your lovely lady opened your home to me and made my final years the best ever." Tears were now flowing freely down both his cheeks as he wrote.

Rick, too, knew that he could not trust his voice not to break. His heart certainly felt as though it was. Tears did more than well in his eyes. He brushed them away, not wanting to waste a moment with his friend.

"Lock it up safely until after my funeral, lad. Read only the top letter beforehand, as I'd like to be buried under my own name. Then open it with your grandmother and Charlie, as well as your Mary Lou. Please tell Sal I'm sorry for denying our meeting. I could not risk her finding out who I was. You will realise why when you read the top letter."

Rick did just as he asked.

Sal and many of the family came and said their goodbyes.

Sal spent an hour with him and came out in tears. She would not speak to anyone and went home to her cottage alone. She clutched the sheets from Jack's side of their conversation. She was freely weeping.

Rick had snatched an hour's sleep here and there; otherwise, he barely left Jack's side.

Reverend Gunther came daily and prayed with the dear old man. He, too, left with a sheaf of papers from their conversation.

~

Three days later, Jack passed away in his sleep with a smile on his face. Rick had stayed with him almost the entire time, except when other family members were with him. Exhausted, Rick had finally fallen asleep while holding Jack's hand. They had prayed together the night before. Rick had his head on the edge of the bed and dozed. He knew Jack had gone when he heard a gurgle, then silence. The noise had woken him.

Jack's eyes were open as though looking at him.

Rick gently closed them and placed his hands on his chest, then covered him with a sheet.

Mary Lou heard Rick scrape back his chair and was at the door by the time he stood up to leave the room. He walked into her waiting arms and sobbed.

He didn't need to tell her he'd gone. Jack had become a part of the family and was beloved by all. It was two o'clock in the morning on April 7th, a day Rick would never forget. A mere ten days shy of ten years since his grandfather had died. He knew he would not sleep again that night and thought that he would read the top letter in the Billy Can. He promised Jack he would not look deeper until after the funeral. His grandmother and Uncle Charlie were to join Mary Lou and him after the service, and the billy can was to be opened to reveal its secrets..

Rick took the top letter from the billy and replaced the lid; he took it into the sitting room and slipped the letter from the envelope. He had seen Jack's writing many times and admired the lovely, flowing script. He knew there was so much more to Jack than he had ever told Rick, but what he read took his breath away.

Parramatta
December 1879

My dear Rick,

I am writing to you about what I could not say in all the years we've been together. My real name is Sir John William Princhester. My next-door neighbour in Kent was Jimmy Westaweller, better known to you all as Viscount Pittford and Amelia's brother. His house is where your grandmother met me many, many years ago. I will explain more after the funeral (another letter), filling you in on all the gory details. However, I would like to be buried under my real name. I have no family left, so I leave all my worldly goods to you, lad. The other contents of the Billy are all I possess, and they are now yours. Do with them as you will, as I have no one else to bequeath them to.

Go and bury my mortal remains and afterwards make a billy full of tea in your can and open my billy . . .

Be happy, my boy. You gave me heart and became my friend. Love Mary Louise forever, son, for she is a treasure beyond price. Kiss your ragamuffins for me and tell them I love them so much. Keep your love for the good Lord as the centre of your life, and you won't go wrong.

Your loving friend

Just Jack

Sir John William Princhester was buried the next day at St John's Cemetery. Reverend Gunther did the service. Jack had confessed much to him some months ago and swore him to secrecy. He told the minister what he wanted to say at his funeral. Jack had arranged everything with the minister and even chosen the hymns. They were happy, joyous hymns, unlike the ones usually played at a funeral. He had chosen 'Praise my Soul', the 'King of Heaven', 'Amazing Grace', and 'And Can it Be'.

Rick could not sing these wonderful hymns as when he closed his eyes, he could hear Jack's mighty voice belting them out around a campfire under the glorious stars. He called it, 'Speaking to the sky.' He deep breathed through them and sat, clenching Mary Louise's hand. Each had a child on their lap. Rick buried his face in young Jack's back.

When Reverend Gunther gave the sermon, you could have heard a pin drop in the church, as no one knew anything about Jack, including Rick. The eulogy they listened to spoke of a man who was disillusioned by life until God brought a runaway boy into his life. Rick swallowed and went sheet white, remembering the day of his train trip, waking to find a hand in his shirt. Later, their second meeting occurred on the bank of the billabong in Goulburn. Both lives had changed when they joined forces.

At the end of the sermon, Reverend Gunther said, "Richard, Sir John asked me to say this to you, 'Inasmuch as ye have done it unto one of the least of these my brethren, ye have done it unto me.' This is taken from Matthew 25 verse 40. He asked me to say, 'Thank you, for you accepted me just as I was, nothing more, nothing less'." Reverend Gunther looked directly at Rick. "Rick, he could never thank you enough. He was also sorry that he could never tell you to your face who he was." With that, the minister sat down.

The church stayed hushed and still for some minutes. No one even wiggled in their seats. Rick was dizzy and white in shock, hardly able to breathe. Mary Lou sat clutching his hand, her eyes fixed on his face; she was sick with worry. Rick felt his nose tingling; he was trying hard not to weep. He could hardly catch his breath, though.

Rick vaguely remembered the end of the service. Then, they all left the church immediately after the service for the burial at the cemetery on the hill.

How Rick got through that, he had no idea.

Wills stood by him in case he was needed. Cathy, too, was worried for her son. Mary Louise didn't leave his side.

They knew the bond between these two men went beyond mere friendship. After the burial, Ed took Rick's children to his home when he dropped off his mother at *Roseneath*. He knew Charlie would bring her back. They all realised that Rick and Mary Louise would need some time together before the children were returned. How right he was. Wills and Cathy could bring them home later that afternoon.

Rick and Mary Lou went directly home after the funeral, not stopping to chat with anyone. He just walked out the gates and left with Mary Lou. On arrival home, Rick immediately retrieved the billy can and set it on the sitting-room table. As instructed, he made some tea, but in his own billy. It was this simple act that finally brought Rick undone. He had kept his emotions under control throughout the funeral and burial, but the simple act of making a billy full of tea was the last straw. How well Jack knew him. It had been the symbol of "talk time."

Mary Louise found him sitting on the kitchen floor, sobbing. When she sat and joined him, he turned to her and wept for his lost friend. He had trusted Jack with his life... often. He, too, had saved Jack.

To Rick, Jack was family.

When they heard Charlie arrive, he stood up. While Mary Lou went to greet him, Rick sniffed back his tears, washed his face and finished making the billy tea as he had promised. Strong, black and sweet. He poured the four mugs and took them into the front room.

The old black Billy sat on the low-sitting-room table.

Rick brought in the four mugs of billy tea and handed them to his wife, grandmother, and uncle. Rick took off the lid, and they could see a calico bag tied with a string. He unpacked the billy, and under the calico bag was another letter. Rick made a toast, "To Jack." Unable to say what he wanted to, he sat down and picked up the letter.

Roseneath,
Parramatta
Christmas 1879

My dear Rick (to be read aloud)

Oh, where do I start? By now, the funeral will be over, and if you have done as I asked, you will be enjoying a mug of sweet black billy tea, just how I like it.

I need to apologise for never getting around to telling you my story. I just couldn't, Rick. But I will now...

I'll start in 1843 when Ned returned as the duke, and he was married to

Christina. David's wife, then the Dowager Duchess, Elouise Wickham, as she was before marriage, fled to her home. Elouise didn't stay there long, and I met her in London later that year. Even though I knew David had died two years before, she played the grieving widow, and I fell for it. Sadly, I had been one of her London conquests and married her in secret a few months later (her wish). I have regretted this every day since the honeymoon was over. We had been married less than a month when I arrived home early from a meeting to discover her in bed with one of our groomsmen. (I did tell you that much). I sacked him on the spot, then packed and left home that afternoon. I moved to my London house and gave a swathe of instructions to my Lawyer. I had not believed Paul when he told me of her shrewish ways; I should have. She was a pretty alley cat with morals the same. One of the instructions I gave was that she would never file for divorce or move from the house. I contacted my Lawyer yearly and acknowledged my earthly existence so she could not have me declared dead either. I also gave her an allowance while I lived, so she couldn't say she was a 'deserted' wife. I have left her £1 in my Will as she deserves no more. I have all the Estate accounts paid by the Lawyer's office. Mr Couchman has all that under control. Why do I share all this with you? Because all is now yours, Rick.

The houses; that's the entire Princhester Estate; Princhester Court in Kent, next door to Pittford Manor; the London house in Piccadilly, Princhester House; and lastly, the Hunting Box in Essex, they are for you. The London house is just down the road from 'Gracemere House', so it will be convenient for your family.

Rick, you restored my faith in humanity. You accepted me as I was and never asked for more. Every day, I waited for you to ask, but you never did. If you had, I'm not sure how much I would have told you. Then, when I came to live with you again, you never pushed me for more than I was prepared to give. Except for wanting me to be Jack's godfather, I knew your reason was that you hoped I would say yes so you could learn my identity, but he needed someone younger.

Dearest Sal, will you forgive me? I dared not admit to who I was. I was still so desperately ashamed that I, too, had been duped by the shrew. I have loved getting to know you over the past few years and have valued your friendship way beyond reason. Again, knowing I was accepted for just being me, just being just Jack, was healing my hurts and soul. Rick may tell you of the day beside the billabong in Goulburn. Ask him. I'm sure he remembers what I said that day. Sal,

I have a feeling you may have eventually guessed my secret. Thank you for keeping that knowledge quiet.

Lastly, Charlie, I know the Earldom does not sit easily on your shoulders. The responsibility of such a role comes with many strings attached. As a Baron, I had them too, but not to the same extent. But be assured, you are doing a mighty fine job. I wanted you here this morning because your son Teddy may find the use of my houses most beneficial. It's ultimately up to Rick to decide whether he will keep them and how he will use them. I leave no instructions or directions for their usage. Rick, if you wish to use them this way, know you have my blessing. Please be aware that Elouise will leave once the word is received about my demise, as she will then be free to go. Through the Lawyer, I have provided enough for her to leave. Trust me, she will scarper.

Charlie, in my Billy, is a letter I need you to post to my lawyer. Take it from Rick now; before he's tempted to open it, it is not for him. Post it, and my Lawyer will start the ball rolling. This is merely a notification of my death, no more than that. I have already sent him instructions for Elouise's removal. All he needs is the date of my demise. On the back of the letter, please write the date of my passing before you post the letter.

Now, Rick, I spoke to your Uncle Tim a few times over the past years; I was in contact with him even before I arrived, as you let slip his direction once. He did not know my real identity as I confided little to him. He, too, has instructions to assist you at this time and will ensure that my Will is executed according to my wishes. He also has a box, and its contents are for you and you alone (other than Mary Lou, of course).

Now that you have read this lengthy screed, live your life to the best of your ability. Never forget our times swagging our matildas through the countryside. Remember the myriad of stars that our Lord placed in the Heavens and the nights we lay admiring them in song and prayer. Remember the campfires and speaking to the sky in song, and think of me often.

On the anniversary of my passing, have a mug of billy tea for me. Goodbye, dear boy. You are the son I wished for and never had. I love you always.

Jack

Rick was stunned. Finding himself almost unable to breathe, he looked at the three in the room with him. "What do we do next?" he finally managed to ask.

"Well, the first thing is you give me the letter for his lawyer in

London. I'll deal with that. Then I dare say we contact Tim. I'm surprised he hasn't already come to visit if that was his instructions. I presume Jack told him to come. He was certainly at the funeral." Charlie reached for the bag and carefully untied it. "Cor, this is heavy; what's he got in it?" He untied the string and then pushed the bag to Rick.

Rick shrugged. "I have no idea, Uncle Charlie."

When he opened the bag, it contained another bag tied the same way and more letters. One was addressed to Sal, and Charlie handed it to her. Another was the one for his London lawyer, Jones and Couchman and a third letter for Tim.

Charlie took only the letters and handed the other bag to Rick. One letter Charlie gave to his mother. Then he said, "This tag has your name on it, lad." Tied to the neck of the inside bag was a swing tag with a note for Rick.

Dear Rick,

Mac gave me the day off one day, and I tripped over. Your Uncle Tim has something in his keeping, and it is for you. Later, I tried my hand at panning in a nearby creek that I found. This is from a few weekends panning; good, eh? Mac and I had a bit of luck; this is my share. They are retiring on his share. I bought a sea fare to Sydney with some of mine so I could come to you. Spoil Mary Lou and then take her to England to see the houses. Don't decide anything until you have seen them for yourselves. Use this to get there.

Jack

The puzzling note gave Rick little information, so he untied the string wrapped around the second calico bag. "It must contain a hammerhead or something because it is heavy. Surely it can't be gold as he infers."

The string fell on the floor; all saw Rick's face when he looked in the bag. "Cor blimey, it is alluvial gold. Look." He dipped his fingers into the bag, and as he lifted his hand, the sun rays caught the sparkly powdered gold as it fell in a shower of shiny dust. "Wow, there must be over ten pounds or more of gold dust in here, and at £10 per pound, that is over £1500. That's a fortune! No wonder Mac has retired."

None had noticed Sal's silence.

She had quietly opened her letter, read it and folded it again. Jack, of course, had again apologised profusely for denying he knew her. He revealed all to her when she visited that last time, then asked her to burn their conversation. But her letter contained much more than that. Over the past few years, he'd counselled her to keep being strong for her family. The paragraph that started with an affectionate term caught her eye. Jack could see that she still wanted to fold under her grief from the loss of Charles.

. . . My very dearest Sal, they need your strength as the matriarch.

Sal, now is the time to build up your children, especially Charlie. He needs you so much. I suggest rotating through each house for a while and living with each of your other children for a few months. The girls especially feel somewhat neglected. I see them both looking at the four boys, their faces filled with sadness.

My dear, dear and gracious lady, know that I have valued your friendship more than I can ever express. I would dearly have loved to have kissed you, but I am married, and when I said my vows, I meant them, even if she did not. I wish to know that, and I will leave it at that.

Jack

The four sat reeling at the revelations in the letters they held.

Charlie looked at Rick, Rick at Mary Lou, and Mary Lou at Sal, who had barely lifted her eyes from her hands that were still clutching the valued letter. None was game to speak or voice their questions.

They were all startled from their reveries by a knock at the door. No one had heard a carriage. Knowing that the staff were all down at Ed's, Rick answered the door himself. He released his held breath when he saw who it was. "Oh, Uncle Tim, thank goodness."

Tim looked confused. "My condolence's lad. I know his passing is sad, but trust me, he's not done yet; he is going to lead us all a merry dance. He left me something to give to you. I must go and get it, and as I can't carry it by myself, you'll have to come and help. I have no idea what's in the box, but it's heavy and nailed shut. All he said is that he found this on his trip."

Rick froze. "How heavy is this box, Uncle?"

"Very Rick, why? Come and help me. It nearly broke the springs in my carriage; we couldn't lift it into the gig. It was too high. Phil, Stevie, and a couple of others from the office helped me lift it in. It's why we came by road this trip."

The two men walked to the driveway where he had tethered his horses and carriage. "The old swaggie sent it on a homemade cart with wheels. Now I know why. He also gave me a letter to be opened with you today and another with instructions for me to be opened in your presence, but not read aloud. I gather Charlie and your grandmother are still here. He told me they would be."

"Yes, Uncle Tim," Rick said.

The two men had arrived at the carriage, and Rick opened one door while Tim went around the other side.

Tim sat on the seat and pushed it towards Rick with his boots while Rick tugged at the rope handle from the other side. Inch by inch, they dragged it to the door.

"We're going to need Charlie; bring him out, lad," Tim muttered, exhausted.

Rick hastened inside and asked Charlie to join them. The three men managed to set the large crate down with a thud, and from there, they were able to drag it inside. They had to stop twice and take a break.

"Cor, what's in it? You would think he found the mother load, Rick," Charlie muttered.

"Eh, mother-load? Of what?" Tim puffed.

"Wait until you see what the old codger left the lad Tim. I gather you have not opened the letter he left for you?" Charlie said while taking a breather. "Okay, on three, up to one step."

"No, I haven't, Charlie, that wasn't his instructions." It took another three heaves, but they finally managed to get it inside. "Do you mind if we drag it along the carpet, Rick?" Tim asked. "I'm pooped." He mopped the sweat from his brow.

Tim and Charlie pulled the rear handle while Rick took the front one and dragged it. Mary Lou held the sitting room door for him, and the three of them moved the crate into the centre of the room. Sal looked up at the happenings occurring in the corridor; she seemed to have recovered again.

"I'll get a jemmy," Rick said as they finally got it into the room. He walked out. He returned shortly with a small crowbar and prized open the crate. No one expected what they saw. The crate was lined in hessian, and on top of it was another letter.

Ballarat
September 1875

Dear Rick,

You told me that God works in mysterious ways, even to the point of tripping over. So one day, I did just that, by accident, not long after you had left. I tripped over a tree root in Bulldog Gully, and instead of standing right up, I noticed a tiny sparkle near my nose. I wiped my hand over it, and lo and behold, more appeared. Rick, this is for you. I have told no one about this, not even Mac. There is no record of it being found, but it was on the same knoll as they found the 'Welcome Stranger' in '69. That weighed in at approximately 240 pounds net. I believe this must be nearly that weight. I think that there may be almost two hundred pounds of gold in this if my estimations are correct, and this one doesn't seem to have much quartz in it. It took me over a week to dig it up. I pitched my tent over the tree it was under and slept on the darned thing. The little ones were packed around it, so I took them too, of course. Then I had to borrow a mule to drag the sled, which I had made, back to the forge. I had to wait until Mac took Mary shopping, then I hid it under my bed. I made the crate and shipped it to your Uncle Tim, whom you told me was a Lawyer. I have written him a letter, and he's to read it to you sight unseen as you get this. Hopefully, he's followed my instructions and delivered it personally after I'm gone. He said he would when I asked him if it had arrived safely. There will be other instructions awaiting him at his office on his return, and more in London for my Lawyer there. Tim will deal with all that.

Smile, lad, remember that verse from Matthew chapter 25.

Jack

They folded back the hessian, and what they beheld filled them all with awe. The crate held not only the largest gold nugget they had ever seen but also many smaller ones packed around it.

"Blooming heck! Oh, sorry, Grandmother and Mary Lou, but truly, wow." Rick nearly said an expletive, but stopped in time.

"You're not wrong there, lad," Charlie said. "I'm guessing he said nothing to you about this either?"

Rick was speechless, looking at the colossal gold rock sitting in his sitting room. He shook his head. "Nothing at all, but by the date, he found it just after I had left."

Tim tore open his letter. "Well, he's got more surprises for you. Has he apparently mentioned to you some property in England? Did you know that there are over 500 acres of prime land attached to the Kent Estate, including a London house and a hunting lodge in Essex? The solicitor in London will fill you in when you get there. He has left instructions on how to contact them. Charlie, I gather you have a letter to be posted." Charlie nodded. Tim continued. "Mary Louise, he's also left you personally the Princhester family jewels. He hopes the gems will not be sold, but he says you can give some to your family if you wish. Kitten is to have the sapphire set for her twenty-first birthday. He wants future children to be given a share; Jack is to have his mother's diamond ring for his future wife if he wants it. Other children are each to have something of value from this hoard, and Mary Lou is to choose what they will be. They are with his lawyer in London. Apparently, he had meant to give them to his wife after their honeymoon, but something happened, and she never received them."

Rick looked at Mary Louise and smiled. She married him with nothing to his name, no job, and at the time, she accepted his proposal; he did not even have a roof over his head. She was prepared to be homeless with him; now, she was wealthy beyond comprehension. She wasn't sure she wanted it; she loved Rick as he was. The one gold nugget alone would be valued at the best part of £34,000 or more, and that was without knowing the weight of other smaller nuggets and dust. The crate must weigh on the best side of two hundred and fifty pounds if their struggle was anything to go by. Rick was still squatting next to the box. He fell back onto his butt and laughed until his sides hurt. Mary Lou sat giggling, but Rick could see she was in shock. He crawled to her on his knees and took her in his arms. "Thank you, love, for taking him in." Life would change for them all, including the Earldom. The aftermath of the revelations left him reeling. Rick was totally out of his depth and turned to his Uncle Charlie for his wisdom.

~

Charlie decided that his three brothers needed to know, as they would all be required to deal with the consequences, as he put it. He had not only posted the letter but wired the lawyers in London, too, so they could get things moving quickly. He had already received a reply but had not told Rick. Elouise had already gone. The house was empty.

Ed's foundry would smelt the gold, for they knew what would happen if word spread of its find, and Wills needed to support Rick and Mary Lou in their future endeavours, as now they wouldn't be confined to the warehouse. Luke's Logistics business was just part of the whole plan, and Charlie didn't want him left out. Charlie knew that Luke wanted to take his two youngest to London, so this would work out well. Lottie was not happy with her father, as just before Christmas, he had refused Jonty's request for her hand in marriage. Jonty had then set off for Africa, but few knew where he had gone. Rick was one of the few who had noted his absence.

Luke was given more instructions about Jack's wishes, especially concerning the house. Charlie let him read the letters and filled him in on Jack's wishes. Tim was married to their younger sister, Anna, which left Liza, their older sister, to be included somehow, but probably later. Liza and Bertie were already benefitting from the increased business with Jack's store catalogues. Charlie would push that more, especially the saddles and leather goods. Bertie still had a Royal Warrant to make Queen Victoria's personal saddles, and Rick ensured everyone knew about that. It was even mentioned on the front cover of the catalogue.

Rick had already decided that all of them would benefit, but he wasn't sure how just yet. It was all too new. Everyone had accepted Jack for who he was, not just Mary Louise and him. Each had known he probably had a backstory, and not one of them had asked, so Rick felt that all should benefit. One thing he knew was that they had to go to England.

Chapter 13 England

Charlie and Luke took over the arrangements for their departure to England, and within weeks, they were bound for London on the *Kosciusko*, a massive ship with a Captain Smith at the helm.

When the extended family heard that they would be going to England, some of the young ones wished to join them. Rick's cousin Lottie and her twin brother, Charles, or as he was known in the family, Carlo, had obviously pleaded with their father for them to be allowed to go and be presented.

Luke relented, and he and Ellen joined Rick and Mary Louise on the passenger list. Lottie had initially not wished to leave, but as her father refused to allow her to marry Jonty Evans unless she had been presented, she went. Jonty had already left for Africa, so pining for him in England was much the same as in Parramatta. She would do everything her father wished, then insist that she be allowed to marry Jonty upon her return. She couldn't write to him as she didn't know where he was. She had received only one letter from him, telling her he had arrived in Cape Town. That had been in January. He didn't even know Jack was dead. With a shrug, she may as well enjoy herself. She knew he would wait for her... she then frowned. She hoped he would wait. She released a sigh of resignation. There was not much she could do anyway.

As Jack suggested, Rick decided to smelt, then sell, the alluvial gold, and this gave him the ready cash he needed to travel in some style. Something neither he nor Mary Louise had ever done before as a couple. Mary Louise had been to Auckland in New Zealand with her parents years before, but she hadn't been back since.

Charlie had wired their cousin in England. Duke Charles, or Chip as the family called him, was in Kent, and Charlie arranged for him to meet Rick in London when the ship docked. Hopefully, Chip would know where to find Jones and Couchman Lawyers. Rick could make no plans until they had been visited. Charlie also asked that Teddy be involved in everything. Bella, too, but didn't say why.

Sal suggested that they only buy the minimum amount of clothing to wear, as fashions here were vastly outdated compared to what was available over there. She also suggested that they take lots to keep occupied on board. Jenna supplied a suitcase full of fabric, some of which was leftover from previous trips. Ellen and Mary Louise found that it also contained all the notions to finish a wide selection of garments, from men's shirts to gowns, as well as some baby clothing fabrics and minute shell buttons. This case was added to their growing pile.

Rick confessed to his father his fears of travelling to London and facing what was before them.

Wills wished he could go too, but someone had to stay to run the now hugely successful mail-order side of the business that Rick had started. Neither of his two older sons understood the new side of the business. Lukie and Pip each had control of some twenty of the other stores. Wills oversaw the overall business.

Over the past four years, the mail-order side had grown to such an extent that Wills had built a new office off the warehouse for the staff employed to process orders. He had not only got the blacksmithing side going, but now the general store catalogue was even more popular. These were now sent out monthly to a regular mailing list. The advertising entirely covered the cost of all this. The warehouse now had its own telegraph receiving area set up, and five were employed just to run that new side of the business. A new storeroom next door was built to stock the essential items that were in high demand.

Rick's profits from the sales astounded him. Most items in-store had about a 50% markup from cost price; his 50% share of sales profit netted him an amount that stupefied him. The blacksmith catalogue had grown from the original two hundred items to over one thousand. It was only sent out every six months as it was so large, and it changed little. The specials page with the advertising was still posted monthly. Jack's general store catalogue had reached three hundred items, ranging from shoes to saddles, fishing poles, and empty hessian bags. If someone asked for a special order, it was likely that it could be supplied. Each month, a special page was added to both catalogues.

About a year ago, Mary Lou suggested that some companies would like to advertise in the blacksmith's catalogue. The costs the businesses had to pay subsidised the printing and postage costs. A small section was added to each page, and this was available for advertising. Within six months, advertising was totally offsetting the total cost of publication and postage.

Rick grinned when he told Mary Lou that they had achieved this milestone.

Wills knew that he had to stay home and keep this side of the business chuffing along smoothly. He was determined to train his two older boys in this, as it would free him from what Wills thought would be at least an eighteen-month trip, if not longer. That's presuming they came back at all.

The travelling group had grown as quite a few of the younger family members wished to come. Luke said he had arranged to have some of the girls in the extended family presented at the 1881 Queen's Drawing Room. The boys were also to have their day of festivities at a Levée. All would be presented to Queen Victoria or the Crown Prince. A general invitation had been issued to various branches of the family in Sydney and in Emu Plains. Three younger members joined the passenger list. During a recent trip to England, a long-term friend in Bathurst, a widow named Mattie Saunders, was discovered to be a cousin of the Lockleys. Other family members had wished to come but had to renege at the last minute. Mattie's children were delighted to be invited. Mattie had come out as a young convict child and married Jim Saunders, the son of the local storekeeper from the Hawkesbury River area. He was later shot by the bushranger Gilbert when they were travelling to Bathurst to open a store. Their youngest child, Molly, had only been a tiny baby. Now Mattie's children were grown, the Lockley family had taken her under their wing, so to speak. Wills sponsored their trip, knowing that she'd not accept anything for herself but would for her children. All were amazed that Mattie never remarried, but she never loved anyone as much as she loved her Jim.

The final group consisted of Mary Louise, Rick, and their two small children; Rick's sister, Bette; Luke and Ellen, and their two youngest children, Carlo and Lottie; and finally, Mattie's three children, James, known as Jem, Margaret, and Molly, rounded out the group. Jem and Carlo were nearly the same age. Margaret, Molly, and Lottie were all good friends of long standing from Wills' many trips to Bathurst.

Luke and Ellen took them all in hand. He had made the trip before.

At twenty-five, Bette was indignant that she still needed to have a man in charge of her. When Wills had told her of his decision, she said, "Father, I'm an independent woman, and I can look after myself," she said somewhat sulkily to her father as he said farewell.

Wills explained. "Trust me, dear Bette, sometimes it's nice to have someone take responsibility for things. Rick is merely being given legal authority over you. I know you trust each other implicitly, but if you so wish, I could make it Uncle Luke, but he would hold your reins much tighter. England required this, my darling daughter."

She looked horrified. As much as she loved her Uncle Luke, he was the epitome of a strict schoolmaster. She shivered, then nodded. Huffing, she saw the wisdom in his actions. "So what authority exactly does this give him, eh?" Her pert question made her father raise one eyebrow. Her attitude was rude, and he told her so.

However, Wills stroked her cheek lovingly. "Well, firstly, mind your behaviour, miss. If you find your prince charming, your brother has my authority to approve the match if he likes the fellow. Secondly, it also works in reverse; if you want him to get rid of someone, he also has the authority to keep them away."

"Oh, all right, Father, but only in that case. Please make sure he knows the limitations of his authority." She smiled mischievously, having no intention of utilising either, especially in the former situation. She had no intention of getting married. No one would have her anyway; she knew she talked far too much and was somewhat wild. Her father often called her a musical flibbertigibbet as she was always singing, and she loved music.

Her mother often said to her, "Darling girl, you could sing underwater if it were possible."

Bette was sure she was correct. She loved life so much, and there was so much to be thankful for; why not sing about it?

~

The day of embarkation arrived, and three of the young folk on board were ecstatic that they were able to leave their mother, Mattie, and work behind. Luke had Margaret, aged twenty, Molly, aged sixteen, but she would be seventeen by the time of the presentation, and their eighteen-year-old brother, Jem, was near them. Adventure awaited, and they were to meet family members they didn't know existed.

Luke and Ellen's two youngest children, twins Carlo and Lottie, were bouncing with excitement beside their cousins. The five looked amazingly similar. None had realised the closeness of the two families for the many years they had all been friends. The revelation had only occurred a few years ago when the connection eventually came to light through their mutual cousin, John Saunders. He was the son of their grandmother's brother-in-law. Therefore, Mattie was his first cousin.

Ellen was sad to leave, as both their married daughters, Mary May and Sally, were due to give birth to their first children. Being twins, it was not surprising that they were expecting at the same time. Mary May had married Marcus Harlow a few years before her twin. She had not fallen with child straight away. Her twin, Sally, had married Marcus's younger brother, Jimmy Ant, in 1877. At least she got to spend a little time with their son's new son. Their first grandson, Henry Lucas, whom Luke had already nicknamed Hal, was eight months old, and Ellen knew she would miss him walking and so many other milestones. However, she had made up her mind to enjoy this trip, and she would. She sighed as she leaned against her husband. Their arms grew tired of waving.

From somewhere, one of the younger family members produced a bag of coloured streamers, and as the ship left the dock, they threw them to the waving family. Clasping the other end of them, they held them fast until the distance broke them apart. Cheers went up, and the joy of the trip ahead was apparent to all the rest of the passengers. The remains of the colourful ribbons of paper were tied to the railing at the stern, and when they got underway, they were visible as a rainbow tail behind the departing ship.

Rick and Mary Lou were holding their small children tightly. Before they reached the heads of the huge bay, Mary Louise stood with Kitten in her arms and smiled lovingly at her husband. "Ricky, dearest darling, I should have told you before, but I thought you should know that when we arrive, if we're on time, we may need a maid of sorts to care for the children."

He looked down at her sweet face with a puzzled look. "Why love?" The only time she had not done this herself was when she was expecting. Suddenly, it dawned on him she was expecting again. "Are you kidding? Why didn't you tell me before? We could have postponed the trip. Oh, sweetheart, it is brilliant news, but we're on board a ship and will be for some months."

"I know, Ricky love, that's why. We need to go to England, and it will be far easier to travel while expecting than with a tiny baby. No napkins to wash on board. I just hope we reach London before it's born, as I didn't pack much." Mary Louise grinned guiltily. "Aunt Jenna did put in some baby fabrics in the case she gave us. She guessed, as she always does."

"Mary Lou, you could have given me some warning." He chuckled and bent down to kiss her. Both children giggled as they got somewhat squashed.

Kitten giggled. "Jackie, Mama is having a baby."

The little boy's eyes grew big, and he sucked his thumb harder.

Luke, who was standing next to Rick, heard his exclamation. "What's up, lad? All okay?"

Rick still looked somewhat stunned. "Um, yes, Uncle Luke, Mary Lou just dropped on me that we're having another child. She's due soon after we reach London."

Ellen came and joined them, "Did I hear correctly, pet? Are you 'interesting'?" Ellen asked discreetly.

"Yes, Aunty Ellen, I didn't want to say anything earlier as I knew Rick would postpone the trip. I hope it will be easier to travel while expecting a child than with a tiny baby. My only problem is that I've been so sick. Thankfully, Ricky has been leaving for work early each morning, so I've been able to hide it from him for some months."

Ellen looked at Luke with horror written across her face. She knew what extensive morning sickness was like; she had two confinements, the first, she produced triplets and the second, twins. "Err, when do you think you are due, Mary Louise?" she asked apprehensively.

"Oh, probably about November, so we have plenty of time unless we get stuck somewhere," Mary Lou said cheerfully. "I brought a few things with me, but I figured that I would only really need some flannels and wraps if I really got stuck." Her chirpiness belied the anxious look now on her face.

Luke saw a strange look on his wife's face. He was not surprised when he heard her next comment.

"Excuse me, gentlemen, we need to have a little chat." Ellen took little Jack from Mary Lou's arms, passed him to Luke, and led her niece to a sheltered spot on the deck. "Mary Louise, you do know of the, err, family condition, don't you?" Ellen asked tentatively. "Rick's a twin himself, you know that."

"Yes, why Aunty Ellen?" she replied, somewhat puzzled. Then, suddenly, horror showed; she had realised why Ellen had asked. "You don't think I'm having twins, do you? I know I'm much sicker with this confinement than the last two, but I just put it down to nerves about the trip. And I'm showing a bit more than the last two at this stage. Yes, Rick's one... I just never thought." She grinned but was afraid. "What made you realise?"

Ellen smiled. "The length of time you've been sick, dear. It happened to me both times. Oh, Mary Lou dear, I do wish we had known. You see, twins often come early, too. Well, not *often*, more like *usually*. I don't even know what the doctor on board is like. Thank goodness you're not travelling alone, though. Mama Sal taught me to assist her with births, and so I've helped deliver a child before, but not twins. But this will certainly make the trip interesting."

Luke called them. "Ellen, we're just about to leave the heads. The seas will get a bit rough, so we're taking the children inside." He held out his hand for her to come, too. He'd already ushered the rest of the young people into their cabins to settle in. Jem and Carlo shared one cabin, and the three young ladies in the other. Bette had her own, and the children were in a room between her cabin and their parents.

The deck was already unsteady, and Rick followed, holding Mary Lou's hand. He had Kitten in his arms. Luke still had Jack.

"Our cabin, Rick, now please, Luke, you too," Ellen said as they made it inside.

Rick looked shocked at her tone, but followed her to their cabin. Luke was hard on their heels, and he, too, wondered what had occurred. Ellen held the door open for them and asked them all to take a seat. She called in her daughter and asked her to care for the little ones in their room. Lottie, Molly, and Margaret took the little ones out and left the adults alone.

Ellen waited until they were alone. "Now, Mary Louise, first congratulations to you both, but Rick, Luke, we may possibly have a complication; Mary Lou is still morning sick," Ellen said simply and raised one eyebrow at her husband.

Luke grasped her meaning immediately. "Nooo!" he said and then chuckled. He looked at Mary, grinned and blushed. "Sorry," he said, smiling.

Rick just looked very confused. "What? Have I missed something, Uncle Luke?"

"Rick, my dear boy, how many children do we have?" his Aunt asked.

"Five, Aunt Ellen ... but ..."

"And how many confinements have I had?" she asked with a raised eyebrow.

"Um, two." It suddenly dawned on him. "Oh nooo! Mary Lou, are you having twins?"

Mary Louise's eyes were wide with excitement. "I don't know, love, but as I'm five months along and still feeling sick most mornings, and well, I'm bigger than I was with the first two, I suppose it's possible." She looked stunned. "Twins, wow, I never thought..." She was unable to finish as she was giggling.

The look on both their faces made Luke laugh. "Now you both know how we felt. Mind you, we didn't know we were having triplets until the third one was born on the day. Trust me, we know about shocks. When the twins came a few years later, we were relieved there were only two. Ellen never fell again. We were almost thankful for that. We were utterly exhausted. Five children under three made life, well, interesting, to say the least." Luke smiled lovingly at his wonderful wife. Thankfully, her parents moved in with them soon after finding out she was expecting and were on hand to assist. Now, it was Ellen's turn to help Mary Louise. How they would have coped if all the family had not stepped in and helped, they didn't know.

Bette had intended to take charge of Kitten and Jack soon after she boarded, but she succumbed to seasickness before they had reached the heads. She had even hoped that they would sleep in her cabin occasionally. However, apparently, Bette was not a good sailor; this may have been because she had a head cold, but she refused access to anyone but the ship's maid. It took a month before she got her sea legs and began to sit in the sunshine.

~

The months at sea passed slowly. Mary Louise grew bigger by the day, and after six weeks, she could definitely feel movement in two places at the same time. They were still five or more weeks away from London.

After the first four weeks at sea, just before they rounded Cape Horn, Captain Smith had been informed of Mary Louise's situation when Luke saw him eyeing her frowning one day. Luke confirmed she was expecting and possibly having twins, which, he explained, invariably came early. The captain became quite concerned, as they had no proper doctor on board, only a medic, given the small number of passengers. It never occurred to him that there could be the possibility of having a birth while at sea. He mainly transported the wool clip and the occasional passengers. The medic was primarily for the crew, his skills basic at best. With a deep sigh, he hoisted every sail he could on the clipper ship, and once they rounded the Cape, he mustered every ounce of speed possible. He did not want any babies born on the voyage, let alone twins. Two screaming infants were not conducive to a peaceful voyage. His clipper ship had previously made the trip in eighty-six days, but as he'd already lost four weeks on this first long leg, he now had to muster every possible resource known. Stopping time would be kept to a minimum, and sailors would be promised a reward if they roused themselves to make his ship fly. The heavy cargo didn't add to their speed. These eighteen passengers would reach their destination early if it were the last thing he did.

There were two other married couples, a minister, and a single gentleman travelling with them, as well as the twelve members of the Lockley family.

Carlo and Jem were fascinated with the volume of sails now hoisted. They counted seventeen square sails on three masts, three triangular sails on the bow, and numerous others. They caught every breath of the stiff breeze in something a sailor called handkerchief sails from the sides of the square rig sails. They were not often deployed on a cargo run, but Captain Smith even dug out spare sails and hoisted them, too. The boys felt like the ship was flying. They were often seen standing on the bow with their arms outstretched, as if they were flying. The feeling was exhilarating.

With the unseasonal breeze behind them, the captain was thrilled to head straight up the South American coast. The ship turned and headed northeast after some two weeks of sailing. They were due in London around mid-October. Hopefully, he could make it before then. He kept his eye on the expectant passenger, and by mid-September, he was sure she was almost ready to deliver. He knew he couldn't be far away from his destination.

When the cliffs of Dover came into sight on the last days of September, he cheered. If she could now just hold on for a few more days…

Chapter 14 Just in Time

$\mathcal{T}$he first day of October saw them being pushed by steam tugs alongside the wharf in London. They had made it. Captain Smith gave an air punch as they were tied up to the quay. Now, to unload both passengers and cargo, and he'd be happy. The crew would get a bonus, and he could be home for a couple of extra weeks. As the family disembarked, they were met by their cousin Chip and his wife, Tina, and all their six children, as well as Teddy and his wife, Bella, and their brood of seven.

Ellen and Luke were greeted warmly by his niece and nephew and their spouses. Rick introduced Mary Louise to them, and when they worked out that she was Uncle Phil Evan's daughter, all fell into place. Chip and Teddy took Rick's small children. Rick assisted his very expectant wife.

Luke and Ellen sorted the rest of the family. Thankfully, Chip had brought a convoy of carriages. Somehow, they piled in and left the quay. "I do hope you don't mind, but we're all staying at *Gracemere House* tonight and maybe for a few more nights by the look of things." Chip smiled at Mary Louise's advanced condition. He could tell by the size of her that she was having twins at least. "It's a bit scary, Mary and Rick, but you'll both survive. We've had two sets of twins, and at least here, there are masses of help in both the house and at the castle." Chip was thirteen years older than his cousin Rick and knew the anxiety that was before him. Rick's memories of both Chip and Teddy came from his previous visits to London with his parents, rather than from home, as both were somewhat older than he was. Both were as easy-going as the rest of the family.

Once loaded up, they set off. Soon, a line of carriages was arriving at *Gracemere House* in Piccadilly. Tina had been in the front carriage and met them at the door. Without asking, Tina escorted Mary Louise into the privy. "I've carried two sets of twins, dear. Trust me, I know what it's like. Aunt Ellen knows too, so I'm glad she was with you."

Mary Louise nearly threw her arms around the Duchess's neck.

Chip suggested that they take a week to settle in before they adventure out to any functions or appointments. Luke, Chip, and Rick did, however, make an appointment to see the lawyer at Jones and Couchman in London. Armed with another letter Jack had left with Tim, Rick entered the office, having no idea what the day would bring. He was just about to sit down and start his discussion when an urgent knock was heard at the door.

Mr Couchman called, "Enter," and a flummoxed-looking secretary entered, telling Rick that his wife needed him at home as soon as he could make it.

Rick apologised and told the man he'd have to reschedule. "My wife is having twins, and I am needed." Without asking or waiting, Rick walked out of the office. No house, jewels or money was worth missing the birth. Chip, Rick and Luke hot-footed it back to *Gracemere House*. Teddy, Chip, and Luke all insisted that Rick attend this birth. Rick was horrified but bowed to his older cousins' and Uncle's encouragement.

His Uncle Luke gave him instructions on what to wear and then sent him to use the privy and scrub his hands. Luke doused them with gin on his return. "No, you can't drink it, lad. I can't believe Dr Pringle didn't allow you to stay for the first two."

"Oh, trust me, he tried. I cleared out. Father said I was missing something amazing. Looks like I can't squib here," Rick said somewhat mournfully. "I'm not into blood, Uncle Luke. I drop like a stone," he admitted sheepishly.

Teddy, who was relaxing in a chair in the sitting room where they had been listening to the conversation, said, "Nope, we get them into this, Rick, it's your duty to see them through it." He was chuckling and inspected his fingernails. "Sorry, cous, I've been sorting walnuts, and they make my hands go a horrible colour. My nails especially get stained." He smiled and continued cleaning his nails.

Rick shook his head in disbelief; he would not be able to avoid the coming ordeal. He took a deep breath and followed his uncle across the corridor to the birthing room door.

Luke turned at the door and pushed him inside. "We'll be all out here praying for you both, lad. Yell if you need us. Dr Fynn Wilson has done this all before. He delivered Charlotte's quads at home with Uncle Gerry, so delivering twins will be a breeze." He chuckled as he closed the door behind Rick. Rick stood just inside the door, trying as hard as possible to be invisible. He felt positively ill with nerves. Aunt Ellen, his cousins, Tina and Bella, were there with a bevy of staff and the doctor he had met earlier. Then he saw Mary Louise; she was in agony. Suddenly, he knew what he had to do. He went to her side and brushed her face, caressing it lovingly and encouraging her as she groaned through the pain.

"Ricky, it's too early. They are too early." Mary Louise was in tears.

Not knowing what to reply, Rick looked at the man at the end of the bed. He introduced himself. "Hello Richard, I'm Fynn; we met before at the castle on your last visit. I'm now the family doctor and, of course, a friend too." His voice was calm and not stressed at all. "Mary dear, listen to me; the babies are well. Twins often come early by a month or so; these two are only a week or two early, so you've done well. They will be fine, you'll see. If you stress and panic, it won't help them. I need you to keep calm, and we'll have them out and in your arms as soon as we can." His gentle, calm voice gave her the assurance she needed.

The doctor continued to give his soothing instructions, "Deep breaths, Mary! In... out... that's the girl. Keep it up. Remember to breathe through the pain. Listen to Ellen; she'll assist with that."

Rick's presence gave her the comfort and strength she needed. "Come on, love, this is not your first birth. We have some babies to welcome." As he said this, she had another contraction. His eyes nearly popped with the strength of the grip on his hand. He tried hard not to grimace. At least he couldn't see much from where he was sitting.

Fynn's voice was calm and soothing. "Good, they are now only five minutes apart. We'll get you in position soon. I learned that there are many different positions to deliver. How did you have your first two? Lying flat or squatting?" Dr Fynn asked.

"Um, lying," she said with another groan. "And it hurt like hell."

"Mary!" Rick said, astounded at her language.

"Well, you damned well try laying a pumpkin, Richard Lockley. It hurts." She breathed through another contraction.

"We're nearly ready; you're fully dilated, Mary." Fynn smiled comfortingly, "Not long now, dear."

"Basin, quick," Mary Lou called. Tina was standing waiting.

Rick nearly needed one himself. He was pleased he could not see what was happening at the business end of the bed.

"Ricky, we're going to be parents all over again, double the family in an instant. Ready?" Mary Lou said while looking lovingly at him. Her brow was wet with perspiration, and her face was white from the effort.

"No, love, but we'll cope." Rick couldn't trust his voice to say much more.

"Okay, here comes the first one." She took a deep breath and pushed, then another. On the second push, Fynn made a grab for the tiny infant she'd just delivered.

"Rick, Mary, you have a son. And what a fine specimen of manhood he is. For a twin, he must be close to a six-pounder." Fynn had the child safely in his hands.

Rick watched the babe change colour as he breathed, the cord pumping the blood into him.

Fynn said, "Look, Rick, he'll go from bluish to pink in a minute." They all watched the miracle of life before them.

The babe let out a scream. "Hey, he's got good lungs." Bella giggled. "I bet he'll keep you awake at night."

Soon, Fynn was ready to cut the cord. "Rick, see, the cord has now gone flat? That means it's empty. I can cut it now, and he'll be fine." The doctor got busy and handed the baby over to the waiting hands.

Tina took the child and handed him to his parents. Rick felt ill. He shivered; he hated blood. Rick hid his face against Mary's neck. At least they'd wiped it from the baby's face. He looked up and saw the baby. The child was red and wiggled; he shuddered. Rick thought, "Another son, Jack, would have loved that. He would have adored twins."

Mary Louise gazed lovingly at the little boy. His eyes opened, and he frowned. Then he pulled a grin, and she exclaimed, "He'd got your dimples, Ricky, look."

"Neither of the other two has them, do they?" Tina said.

"Jack does love," Rick said. "He hates them as I do. Old Jack said the same when he was born."

"Sorry to cut things short, but Tina, can you take the babe? Please, we have to get Mary up and walking for a bit," Fynn said.

Rick was aghast. "But she's just had a baby. She can't."

"She has too, Rick," Tina said; the other baby needed to turn. "Trust me, she'll be fine. I don't really know why women are advised to stay in bed after delivery, except to rest. I'm normally up walking a few hours after each birth, and I've had six myself."

Fynn explained that the second twin needed to be in a head-down position to facilitate easy delivery.

Mary Lou comforted him with, "I'm fine, love. He was so much easier than the other two. They were both over eight pounds each and really hurt. I'm surprised I didn't tear with Jack. Don't get me wrong, this is no walk in the park, but it's easier than last time. Jack was just shy of nine pounds."

"If that's easy, I'll eat my new top hat." Rick was giddy himself. He'd hate to know how Mary felt.

Mary Louise was now sitting on the edge of the bed. "It's the afterbirths that hurt love. It's a totally different sort of pain. It feels like your insides are being ripped out, which I suppose in reality they are." She was chatting as she stood up.

Rick was in awe of her strength. They walked around the room for some fifteen minutes before Fynn asked to feel if the baby had moved. She half lay back into Rick's lap; as she did so, the first contraction hit. "Ouch, that was a hard one, first up," she exclaimed.

Tina said, "Yes, Mary Lou, the second one is already halfway done, so I found they started hard."

"Me too, Mary, they get hard, fast. So be prepared," Bella said.

Rick was again feeling quite ill. How they were all so chirpy astounded him. At least they had removed the bloody cloths from the bed.

Fynn had a feel of her stomach. "Yes, it's turned. We're all set."

Mary Louise groaned as another one hit. "Cor, Bella, you're not wrong. That one was strong."

"Not far apart either, only five minutes already." Fynn was checking his watch. "Mary, would you like to try this one squatting? The girls tell me it's much easier."

"I'll try anything if it makes it easier," she muttered through clenched teeth.

"Remember your breathing, Mary. In... Out..., deep, even breaths, and mouth open so you get the air in." Ellen said from near the bedhead.

She had another contraction. Rick's hand already felt like jelly. He was sure every bone was crushed.

Before she sat up, Fynn checked her. "Whoa, you're crowning already. You're nearly ready, Mary. So places everyone." Fynn showed Rick how to sit so Mary could squat between his legs. He was to wrap his arms around her, and she could rest her head on his chest. By the time they got themselves into position, she was ready to deliver the next baby. The squatting position made the delivery very quick and was certainly easier on the mother.

Rick felt her fingernails bite into his thighs, but stayed silent. He had no idea what women went through to give birth. He had done this to her, and she kept saying she wanted more; he was astounded. The other two girls had thirteen between them; each had two sets of twins. Being a twin himself, he should have discussed this with Mary Lou earlier, but it had simply not occurred to him. She knew the family well enough to recognise the high incidence of multiple births. He shook his head to clear his thoughts; baby number two was about to arrive. He felt her fingernails bite again and then the whimper of a new voice, nowhere near as strong as its brother. Thankfully, he still couldn't see much. The bloodied child was hanging by its feet in the doctor's hands. He gagged. Blood and the gooey cord turned his stomach.

Fynn heard Rick's gag; he caught his eye and frowned. "Bottle it, lad." Rick nodded and swallowed his bile. Soon, Fynn lay it down; again, they watched the life-giving blood pump into the baby from the cord. The baby turned pink and gave a small whimper again. Fynn turned it over and smacked its bottom. It took a deep breath and howled. "Oh, that's better." Fynn saw Rick's shocked face. "Sometimes, they don't fill their lungs fully. A smack shocks them into taking that first important full breath. I don't have to do it often, but it's the easiest way to make a baby breathe." He smiled at the screaming child in his hands. "Oh, and you have a daughter. Same as you, Rick, I believe?" He waited, then tied and cut the second cord.

"Yes, Bette, and she's here with us. She'll be waiting outside somewhere close by and praying if I know her." Rick smiled, and he then bent and kissed Mary Lou's neck. "Congratulations, love."

"It's not over yet, Rick; the bad bit is yet to happen. I'm just going to stand and stretch my legs." She stood up with Rick's help. She stood with her back leaning against him. "Ricky love, this really hurts, and I'll probably scream enough to make the windows rattle, and with these two, I'll have two to deliver. Just so you know." Mary Lou relaxed against him, and he cuddled her from behind. "And Ricky, love, there will be lots of blood, so don't look."

Rick had no idea what to expect when he entered the room, but his Mary Lou was so strong. "I'm here for you, love. You'll never have to do this alone again."

She wasn't wrong when she said that she would scream enough to make the windows rattle. Her blood-curdling screams ripped through him. "One down, Rick. I'm so darned tired. When Kitten was born, the blooming doctor tugged at the cord, and it hurt so much. Thankfully, your grandmother stopped him quickly. I never want to have pain again like that. It's why I insisted on Doctor Pringle for Jack's birth. He was away for Kitten."

"I remember he got called away halfway through for some axe injury; his assistant delivered her, didn't he?" Mary nodded.

"Mary Louise, the second afterbirth is not coming away as it should," Fynn said.

"Oh, okay, give me the girl, baby; I'll give her a bit of a feed. I don't know if I have much, but it should do the trick." Mary felt her breasts. She had insisted on feeding her own children and not using a wet nurse, so she was familiar with the routine.

Fynn turned his back while she fed the little baby.

Rick thought this was funny as he'd just had his hands on her private parts, but he stayed quiet, smiling at his private joke.

"Ouchh! Quick, take her," Mary said.

Tina grabbed the baby as Mary groaned and then gave an almighty scream. The second afterbirth came away, and she passed out while still squatting in Rick's arms. He took her full weight.

Fynn acted quickly. "Quick, lay her down. Lift her legs, and Bella, get a cold towel from that tub of ice water and use it as a compress. Place it on her stomach. I know it sounds strange, but put both babies on the breast. It's her best chance." Fynn moved like lightning. His voice sounded panicked. The others realised the situation was dire.

Rick still had not understood what had occurred, "Chance of what, doctor? What's happening? Why did she pass out? What's wrong?" Rick's questions were tripping off his tongue, and no one was giving him answers. Mary Lou was still unresponsive, and there was blood everywhere.

"Rick, just hold her." Tina tore open her nightgown, then she and Bella each held a baby onto her breasts. Ellen was gently slapping Mary's cheeks to rouse her. There was no response.

Fynn was holding a cold, wet towel on her exposed stomach and another on her private parts, trying to stem the bleeding.

Rick now saw the fear on the doctor's face.

"Damn it, come on, babies. Suck," Fynn said now with fear in his voice. Both babies latched on and sucked hard. Soon, the bleeding lessened.

Mary Lou was very pale and weak, but she eventually roused a little. Rick could hardly breathe when she murmured; he wept but spoke encouragingly to her. "Come on, love, fight hard." Her violet-grey eyes opened but were vacant.

Fynn looked worried. "Rick, I have some ergot here, and I can use it, but I'm hoping that the babies will do the trick. It's sometimes more dangerous than doing nothing. I can see the bleeding is slowing already." Fynn checked her and grinned. "Yes, it's working. Leave the babies on as long as you can. Even if they don't get any milk, the action is contracting the uterus."

They all stayed silent, watching her, waiting and praying hard. Finally, Fynn said that they could remove the children. Rick covered his wife's breasts as best as he could with her torn gown. He gently covered her lower area with the bloodied sheet.

Tina handed the baby she was carrying to one of the hovering staff members. She found a clean sheet and covered Mary Louise properly.

Fynn said to Rick, "I'm going to have to 'pack' her, Rick, to stop more bleeding. It's easing, but we have to keep her as still as we can. We'll put the babies back on in about fifteen minutes. It should cause more contraction of the uterus."

Rick just nodded. His eyes were fixed on his wife's white face. He stroked her cheek and kept whispering to her. "Fight love, don't leave me, sweetheart."

After some time, she stirred again. "Ricky, I'm so cold."

Fynn nodded to the staff, asking them to bring blankets and cover her. "Rick, lie beside her and cuddle her. Your body heat will warm her best," Fynn said.

Rick was beside her in an instant, drawing her into his arms and snuggling close. He could not believe how fast the joy of the twins' birth evaporated. The prospect of a life without her shattered him. He angrily wiped away tears that streamed down his cheeks. He kept saying, "Fight love, come back to me. You must fight. I love you." He could not hold back his sobs as she lay so still and pale in his arms.

After some ten minutes, Fynn said, "Rick, we'll put the babies back on the breast again, and hopefully, this will do the trick. It certainly worked before, and the bleeding is now nearly at a more normal flow." He motioned for both babies to be brought back, and Rick gently folded back the sheet and blankets so the babies could feed. Some minutes after they were put to the breast, Mary Lou lifted her hand and touched the babies. "Ricky…"

He was still cuddled to her under the blanket. "I'm here, sweetheart; you've got to keep fighting."

She rubbed her hand on his cheek; she felt it was wet. "You've been weeping, Ricky, why?"

"We nearly lost you, love. You're not out of the woods yet, but feeding the babies is helping. The girls are holding them, so you don't have to do anything but lie there." He looked to Fynn, who nodded encouragingly.

The doctor mouthed, "Keep her talking."

Rick nodded, wracking his brain as to what to say. "Sweetheart, we have to name them. Any ideas?"

"I know we've talked about family names, Rick, but I'm getting so confused with so many of the same names." She paused, taking some deep breaths. Rick glanced at Fynn again, who had nodded.

"Ricky, how about Ian for the boy? And I've always liked Clara, Daniela, or Deborah for a girl. You can choose one and the middle names." She relaxed, but she was very tired. She closed her eyes.

"Sounds lovely, sweeting, don't sleep yet, we haven't finished. How about we spell Ian the Scottish way, the same as Iain Campbell, who reunited us? So, Iain, you know it means John, don't you? So it's sort of a family name and a nod to Jack, too. I can't choose the girl, though. I'd like to keep Daniel as Iain's middle name; I like that. I like Clara too. It means 'bright'."

"Whatever you want." Mary Lou's weak agreement brought a worried look to Rick again.

"Come on, love, stay with me. Concentrate a little longer. Clara's middle name can be Deborah; what do you think?" Rick prompted her.

"Yes, Ricky love, whatever you want, I'm so tired. I need to sleep," she murmured. He felt that she was now warm and no longer shivering.

Fynn motioned for him to keep her talking.

Cor, what to say, Rick thought. "Love, what about Godparents? Who would you like for them?"

"Ricky, do we have to talk about this now? Can't I sleep a bit, please?" she asked plaintively.

"No, love, you have to stay awake for a bit. The doctor needs you to stay with us and to talk." Rick's eyes again went to Fynn's.

Fynn checked her bleeding and said softly, "It's nearly stopped. She should be fine now, Rick. Let her sleep."

Rick dropped his head to her forehead. "It's okay, sweetheart. I'll be here. Sleep now, and we'll talk later." He kissed her forehead.

"Okay, Ricky, I love you." Her voice tapered off in volume as she spoke. "So tired." She was asleep within moments. Drained and absolutely exhausted. The babes were still feeding. Tina and Bella had cradled them in pillows, and each took turns ensuring they were secure.

Fynn let them have a full fifteen minutes, then removed them and let Mary Louise sleep deeply. He called Rick to him, and reluctantly, Rick left her side and followed the doctor outside.

Teddy had gone, and so had Bette. They were apparently downstairs praying with some of the other family.

Chip and Luke were close by and waiting for him. They stood waiting to be called.

Fynn spoke quietly to Rick as they exited the room. "Rick, that was touch and go. If she had only one baby, she might not have made it, but the combined feeding of both babies made things contract enough to stop the bleeding. She'll be tired for some days, but should be fine. When she wakes, get her to drink lots and feed her red meat and a glass of stout at least once a day. Believe it or not, there are lots of nutrients in stout."

Fynn was covered in blood. Her blood. The doctor had wiped his hands on his apron, and more was staining them. He had obviously wiped his forehead, too, as it was also smeared with a red stripe.

Rick stood stock still, then finally looked at the doctor's clothing, and his face then blanched. He mumbled, "So much blood," and crumpled to the floor.

Chip and Luke were within earshot and were with him moments after he hit the floor.

Fynn looked at the prostrated father. "Just stretch him out; he'll be okay. We nearly lost her, but she's made it through. She's tired, but she should be fine. Oh, and they have a boy and a girl, Iain and Clara, I believe." Fynn, too, was emotionally exhausted. He wished he could go and lie down, but he had to go back in. Fynn needed Rick there, too. He was vital to her recovery.

"Are the babies healthy?" Luke asked, and Fynn had only mentioned their names and not their condition.

Luke heard the tiredness in his voice. "The girl needed a smack, but she's fine now. The boy is a Lockley through and through. A six-pound twin, probably another blacksmith in the making, and the girl only slightly smaller." Fynn yawned. "Have to go back in, chaps, rouse him as soon as you can. I need him back in there."

Chip knelt beside his cousin. "Rick, wake up; Mary Lou needs you." He again gave his cousin's cheek a gentle slap to rouse him. Probably not what one should do, but he was needed.

Eventually, Luke talked to him. "Richard, your wife needs you. Wake up, lad."

Rick's eyes fluttered open. "Blood, so much blood," he groaned and rolled onto his side and gagged.

"Don't you dare get sick on the carpet, horrible mess to clean up," Chip said with a laugh of relief.

Luke put his hand out to assist him. Chip did, too, and together, they got him standing again.

"I nearly lost her, Uncle Luke; she nearly died. Doctor Fynn saved her. I promised I would be with her. I have to go back to her." Rick was sheet white and not well enough to go anywhere, let alone minister to his wife.

"Not in your condition, Rick, you need Brandy! Chip, got any close at hand?" Luke said.

Chip's face lit up. "Hang on!" Chip walked up the hall a short distance and ducked into a door across the hall. He returned moments later with a half-bottle of very expensive French Cognac and a large balloon glass.

"Whoa! That's the one-hundred-year-old stuff your father had," Luke said, looking at the bottle.

Chip smiled, "Yes, apparently, Uncle David stocked up a bit. I found a few dozen cases of it in the south cellar at home. Benefits of being a Duke, I suppose, and yes, Uncle Luke, it's the good French stuff." He poured a liberal measure and handed it to Rick. "Drink up, Rick, you need it."

Rick looked at the liberal measure, sniffed it, then swigged the glass's contents in one gulp. It burned all the way down. He coughed and uttered in a very husky voice, "Smooooth!"

Luke and Chip both laughed.

"You are supposed to sip it, Rick," said Luke.

"Not blooming likely, Uncle Luke; I need to get back in there," Rick said with determination.

"Okay, ready?" Luke asked in a tone of concern.

Rick nodded, his throat still on fire from the drink, but it had done its job. He drew a deep breath, exhaled, feeling like he was breathing fire, then opened the door and returned to his wife and new children. She was awake and smiled weakly at him. He breathed a deep sigh of relief; she would be all right.

Chapter 15 *The Second Appointment*

*T*wo weeks after the birth of his twins, Rick rescheduled the appointment with the solicitor; he apologised and explained the situation. Mr Couchman was very understanding; he explained that Jack left precise instructions. He read Rick the full Will explaining some bequests, "Sir John has left one for a friend named Dickon, another to his manager, Jonas, and a third to Mac Wallace, whom I believe you know. Mr Lockley also left a bequest to us for our work." Mr Couchman had been following Rick's life since Jack first mentioned him in his letters. It was only three years ago that Jack had told him about the family connection. Jack had written copious letters after he moved in with Rick. "I believe your grandfather, the previous Earl, made an impassioned speech in the House of Lords that started the ball rolling for the Reform Bill to pass." The man looked at the fair-haired, almost giant of a gentleman sitting across the table from him.

Rick merely nodded, not knowing what else to say. "I know about those bequests, Mr Couchman, and you deserve your share too."

Mr Couchman continued. "Sir John thought a lot of you and your family, sir. I understand he was living with you when he passed on?"

Again, Rick nodded. "Yes, Jack was with us when he died. Apoplexy, you know. He could still write, and those final three days, I sat by his side, and he replied by writing his side of the conversation."

Mr Couchman looked surprised but refrained from commenting on that. "Is it true you both lived on the street as, what do you call it, swagmen for some years?" He could not get his head around this point. The immaculately, well-groomed gentleman before him and the debonair Sir John as a hobo. The idea confounded him.

Rick nodded again. He was so embarrassed that this man was here to hand him an absolute fortune in property and worldly possessions. He knew he had not earned it. Rick finally found his voice. "Jack, or Sir John as you knew him, befriended me on the first day I left home when I was seventeen. We travelled together for nearly four years. Then he sent me home to get married. I offered him a room, still without knowing who he was, and managed to extract a promise that he would come and stay. He did a couple of years later. He came to live with us. That was Christmas Day 1877; he died in April 1880. We didn't even know until he died what his real name was. He wrote many letters and tucked some in his billy can, and others he gave to an uncle of mine."

The solicitor looked puzzled. "A billy can? What's that?"

"It's a tin with a fitted lid. Jack's billy was a large one, black and well-dinted from much use. You boil water in it on an open fire. It's an essential kit for a swagman, along with a bedroll and a frypan. The entire bundle is also sometimes referred to as a 'bluey' or a 'Matilda'. All your possessions are rolled into the bedroll. Everything has to be carried on your back, so no one owns much. At best, you can carry one change of clothing and an extra blanket. It's a life of poverty and riches all rolled into one; only the riches are freedom and nature, not money as wealth. We had no idea who he was until the day of his funeral. Jack had spoken to the minister and told him, and he left a letter for me confessing all. So, I didn't know his name until shortly before the service. Seriously, sir, I had no idea who Jack was or what he had. We just loved him as Jack. However, he wished to be buried under his own name, and he was. He is buried next to my grandfather, Lord Charles, at St John's Cemetery in Parramatta. An uncle of mine, Tim Miller, had more letters and items for me, and Uncle Tim arrived with them that afternoon. Jack told me in the letters to come and see you as soon as I could."

Mr Couchman smiled and nodded; Rick's story correlated with what Jack had written to him. "Do you know all his story now, sir?" Mr Couchman asked tentatively. "Um, about his wife?"

"Mr Couchman, we have known of Elouise Wickham for literally decades. My cousin was the 10th Duke of Gracemere and was previously engaged to her before she jilted him to marry his older brother, David. I am only telling you as it pertains to Jack. David was a friend of Jack's, and she duped them both. David's brother Paul tried to tell Jack, but he wouldn't listen. A man in love and all, you know the story. Uncle Ned was well out of the relationship, and well then, he married Aunt Christina, and she was the best person. We all adore her." Rick gave an outline of the woman.

Mr Couchman nodded, remembering the screaming interview he'd had with Elouise Princhester when he had to inform her she was now without a roof over her head and must leave the house within two days. She had lived in relative comfort for over thirty years, and although he was one of the few males allowed in her presence, he wasn't there by choice. He had managed to hand her the two £50 notes as per her husband's instructions. It was more like she snatched from his outstretched hands with her long fingernail claws. He'd not heard a woman screech like that before. Considering she was nearly eighty, he was surprised she didn't drop dead of apoplexy herself. He remembered he almost wished that she had. He swallowed and tugged at his shirt collar, shuddering. "Hmm, an unfortunate situation it was indeed, sir. She has vacated the properties, and access to all the remaining properties and funds has been denied her, pursuant to Sir John's will."

Rick nodded, sad that her evil ways would end in such a manner, alone and unwanted. No one even asked if she had anywhere to go.

Mr Couchman sat uncomfortably in his chair. Unable to meet Rick's face, he said, "Mister Lockley, I'm saddened to inform you that for the past ten years, she has refused access to the house for any repairs. We tried everything and are now attempting to set things to rights, but much has been left to ruin. Thankfully, she could not deny access to the gardens and farmland, and they are in wonderful order. The rents and returns have been excellent. The estate manager was moved out to an office in the stables, I believe, at Sir John's request, soon after he departed. Jonas has been working from there and has successfully maintained the property in good condition. The estate bank account is healthy, and Jonas O'Neill has access to the funds required via our office to keep the improvements happening over the years." Mr Couchman was surprised Rick didn't react, so he continued. "Jonas's father, Brian, was the estate manager before him, and he knows the role well. Brian still lives with him on-site and assists in a small way. The stock and crops are top grades and..." Mr Couchman kept talking.

Rick knew he should be listening, but his mind wandered. He had no idea what all this entailed. He really needed Chip or Uncle Luke with him, preferably both. He heard the word "Mulberry" a couple of times, but had lost concentration entirely, as he had absolutely no idea what the man was talking about.

"Sir," Rick interrupted. "Do you mind if we leave the particulars to another time, when I can bring in my uncle and cousins? They are both more conversant with this sort of thing than I am. I'm still floundering to think I even own a property, let alone the responsibility of an estate in England."

"Oh, yes, sir, I'm sorry, I do waffle on. I've personally overseen this estate for nigh on forty years, so I know it well." The solicitor looked embarrassed.

"Mr Couchman, I would like you to keep doing that and Mr O'Neill too, until I can get my head around things. I would also like to view the properties, starting with the London house. I understand from Jack that there is one, and the hunting box in Essex has been locked up since he left?" Jack had managed to tell him that much in the letters.

"Yes, um, that is so. Both are fully staffed, though. You see, Sir John may have returned any day. I had hoped he would. I have kept everything ready in case he did. I can take you to *Princhester House* immediately if you'd like?" Mr Couchman saw the smile on Rick's face.

"Yes, please, and can we collect my cousins and uncle on the way? I'd like them to sit in on further meetings, if possible," Rick asked as he rose from the desk.

"Before you leave, sir, I need you to sign the papers to pass the estate over to you. I have the paperwork drawn up and just need your signature. It lists everything that Sir John has left you." Mr Couchman looked at Rick in such a way that Rick was a little concerned.

"I shall take it with me and read it over first, please. I'll return it tomorrow." Rick didn't wait for an answer but picked up the paperwork and walked to the door.

"But, sir…" Mr Couchman started to say.

"Tomorrow," Rick said authoritatively, "I sign nothing without reading it through thoroughly first. Surely, the properties are not going anywhere. Jack died over six months ago. Another day is not going to matter."

Mr Couchman harrumphed, then opened a drawer in his desk and removed a large ring of keys. He shut the drawer with unnecessary force and followed Rick out of the room.

Rick and Mr Couchman drove by *Gracemere House* and collected Luke and Chip. Rick had said he'd collect them for a viewing if possible.

The town carriage with the four men arrived in front of a triple-fronted stately mansion not far down the same street. The cream and white four-story house they pulled up in front of amazed Rick. Each front window was fronted with window boxes of clipped plants; each also had small balconies. The top floor had arched windows that were recessed; a long balcony ran across the entire front of the building. The entire building was pleasing to the eye and surprisingly clean, considering some of the other dirty-looking buildings in the area. It stood between red brick buildings, shining like a beacon.

Rick smiled at its pristine beauty. Typical Jack, it was different.

As the carriage halted, a footman from the house rushed to open the carriage door for them. He was in black livery highlighted with silver buttons and braid. Rick smiled, knowing his father would have approved of the simplicity of the uniform. 'Very Jack', Rick thought. Simple and understated.

They were ushered inside the huge foyer; its vast space belied the small front of the house. It nearly took his breath away. The ceilings were nearly twenty feet high, and the overall impression one received upon entering was one of understated elegance. There was nothing glitzy, no gilt statues or knobs, just simple and elegant. Everywhere his eye fell, there was a marble carving or stunning painting. Nothing was overdone, though, and all in perfect symmetry with the rest of the house.

Mr Couchman introduced them to the waiting butler. He was grey-haired and the typical English butler, only slightly stooped with age.

Chip and Luke gasped as they entered. This was far from what they had expected. The interior of the home was filled with light and felt airy. Surprising in a London multi-storied house. They looked up to see a small glass dome that filled the room with diffused light.

Room by room, the butler, Giles Branwhite, flung open the doors, proud to be showing the house to the new owner. They had arrived unexpectedly, and all was in perfect order, as though Jack was expected to arrive any day. Everything was immaculate and had obviously been lovingly cared for over the years. Considering Jack had been gone for so long, Rick had no idea what to expect.

The comfortable library drew the four men inside; all were impressed at the extensive walls of leather-bound volumes. There was no odour of mustiness. They seated themselves in the luxurious leather armchairs.

"May we have tea in here, please, Branwhite?" the lawyer asked.

"Certainly, sir," he bowed and departed.

"As you see, Mr Lockley, we have done our best in keeping the estate in good order. The hunting box is in a similar condition; sadly, as I said, we have not had access to *Princhester Court*. In the six months since her Ladyship vacated the premises, we have completed the major repairs, including those for broken windows and similar issues, as well as the removal of an offending vine from the building. It was eating the stonework. We await further instructions." Mr Couchman continued to talk about the estate, and now, with both his cousin and uncle present, Rick felt a little more confident.

"Your Grace," Mr Couchman addressed Chip. "I suggest we make a trip to the country estate soon, as then we can continue the work needed."

Chip looked at Rick, who said, "I'm not leaving London until my wife is well enough, Chip; I am in no hurry to see the house. It's waited this long; it can wait a few more weeks."

"Well, as Richard is the owner, we'll leave the decision to him. His wife is not well. She has recently delivered twins and is in a weakened condition. She nearly didn't make it, so she is not yet well enough to travel. We will go when she's well. I expect that to be a month at least," Chip said with authority.

Mr Couchman uttered, "A month? Oh, of course, Your Grace."

"Tell me, are the stables in good repair and stocked?" Chip asked.

"Um, yes and no, sir; the building is in good repair, excellent actually, but they are all but empty. Jonas keeps the working horses in there at the moment just to use them. The carriages are in good repair but are obviously dated, sir, as they have sat unused for over thirty years. Jonas has kept them maintained, though. There are no riding or carriage horses as the previous occupant was not permitted to use them," the lawyer admitted.

"How did she get about?" Luke asked quietly so the other two couldn't hear.

"She didn't, sir; she was confined to the estate and allowed no visitors either," the lawyer responded in an equally soft tone.

Luke's eyes popped with surprise, but he said nothing.

"Good then, Ricky, my boy, we're going to buy some horseflesh and maybe even a new carriage or three. Now you have some paperwork for Richard to sign, I believe?" Chip put out his hand to Rick.

Rick passed over the paperwork. "Ted is to come too."

The four sat in silence as Chip read over it.

Rick got up and walked to the window. His window, his library, his house. After so many months, he still found it difficult to swallow. If this was small compared to his other house, then it must be immense.

Chip called him over. "Rick, this all looks in order; the only thing is that the hunting box possibly is surfeit to requirements, as none of us hunt, but that's a decision for you later." He then turned and addressed Mr Couchman. "I'll get my man to run his eyes over it, and we'll return it tomorrow."

Mr Couchman nodded. He was not prepared to contradict the Duke of Gracemere even though he was half his age. A Duke was a Duke.

At thirty-eight, Chip had settled into the role when his beloved father had passed at Easter time in 1870. When he sent the letter to inform the Australian family of his sudden death, he was stunned to receive two letters, actually; one addressed to his father, from Earl Charles himself, written some weeks before his death but to be posted afterwards. The other one was from Charlie telling him of his father's demise. He was even more shocked to learn Charles, Earl of Coxheath, his father's best friend and cousin, had died the same week as his father. In further letters, his cousin Charlie, the new Earl, and he commiserated with each other, as did the wider family. Both shouldered their new roles with great regret. Over the past ten years, Chip had learned a great deal about being a Duke. Feigning authority was one lesson his father had taught him. In reality, Chip had little understanding of the legal jargon used in the document he was holding, but did not intend for anyone to know. He smiled knowingly as he folded it again and tucked it in his pocket.

Mr Couchman pulled the bell cord, and the butler returned. "May we see through the rest of the house, please, Branwhite?" Their extensive tour took over an hour, and they viewed every room from the various attics to the mews at the back. All was in order and in pristine condition. Again, the stables in the mews were empty, but the carriages had been maintained well.

The kitchen was spotless, with not a speck of dust in sight anywhere in the main house. Rick noticed a new stove in the kitchen, and the equipment was immaculately kept, with not a cockroach in sight.

The tour done, Mr Couchman dropped the three men off at *Gracemere House.*

Rick wanted to go back to Mary Lou. She was now well enough to sit up in bed and feed the babies. That in itself was draining, but she was slowly feeling better.

The names Iain and Clara had quickly turned into Danny and Debby. Rick chuckled, but little Jack refused to say their names correctly, and Neean and Lara were the best he could manage. He coined the nicknames. Rick had liked his new names for them, so they stuck. At least no one in the family was called either.

The men had a lot to talk about. Once inside, Teddy joined them in Chip's study. Chip also called in his business associate; the four sat quietly chatting while Bartholomew Walters reviewed the documents.

Chip rang for more tea, and they waited.

Bart finally finished perusing the sheaf of paperwork and joined the others. "I believe all is in order. I was surprised to learn of Sir John's wife's name, though, sir."

"Yes, she is known to us all," Rick replied without malice, but did not elaborate. Chip and Ted looked puzzled.

"Apparently, she is to be given no pension and no accommodation allowance. She received a one-off payment of £100 cash, and she was not to be allowed a penny more. If she asked for more, she would lose the little she was given. Sir John also requested that she not be allowed any credit under any name: Elouise Wickham, Gracemere, or Princhester. Sir John only left her £1 in his will."

"That is correct, Mr Walters," Rick replied. "He explained to me why; I will follow his wishes."

Chip and Teddy looked very surprised as neither had realised who Jack had been married to. Chip breathed a quiet, "Nothing at all?"

"No, Chip, I'll explain why later," Rick replied. "So, Mr Walters, is all in order otherwise?"

"I believe so, sir; other than that clause, I see no issues." He perused that paragraph again. "She really is to get nothing?"

"No, sir, nothing at all. She has lived in the house for over thirty years, she has refused entry for repairs for the past ten, and she apparently has been uncooperative." There was no way he'd admit to this man what she'd done to Jack. Rick had no sympathy for her and did not wish even to know where she went. I am merely following Sir John's wishes, which are all in writing."

Mr Walters pointed out where Rick was to sign the paperwork and initialise each page. He then offered to return the documents to Mr Couchman, as he had to pass by his office anyway. Once he and the documents were dispatched, the four men planned a trip to Tattersalls to buy some horses. Only then did Chip question Rick about Elouise.

All Rick said was, "She cuckolded him on their honeymoon with a groom."

Chip was astonished but refrained from further comment. He said he would pay for the horses, and Rick could reimburse him when the access to the estate money was finalised. He had seen how much was sitting in the bank for Rick's use. He had felt like whistling, wishing that he had over £200,000 in his account.

At Tattersalls, Rick fell in love with a massive bay stallion with a white blaze. He knew he'd need a riding horse and chose the stunning but reasonably placid beast and named him *Red Back*. The shape of the blaze was the same shape as the red mark on the spiders found back at home.

Luke smiled when Rick told him why he had chosen the name. "Apt, though, lad," he said.

Chip and Luke insisted on inspecting some twenty other steeds, and a pair of greys were also up for sale. Luke had always loved greys, so they, too, were purchased along with a stable of other horses. Rick also wanted a tiny, gentle pony for the children. They ended up with eighteen horses of assorted sizes. And two teams for the stage changes. Most, however, were riding horses for the family's use, and there were six extra carriage horses. Most were greys or bays, as Rick said he didn't like roans. If Mr Couchman was to be believed, there were assorted vehicles in the carriage house. Chip suggested that they use the castle carriages until they viewed what was in storage at *Princhester Court*. By the time they left London, some three weeks later, they had received notice that the house was once again almost habitable.

Mary Louise and the twins were now able to travel, and Rick and the lawyer had sorted out all the legal side of everything. Rick now had access to more than sufficient funds, and he paid Chip back immediately in full for the horses and the new chaise Rick had purchased. He also addressed their lack of wardrobe, as Mary now needed new clothing, and Rick, too, had brought only minimal things. Mattie's three children were taken shopping; Chip took Jem and Carlo and had them fitted out, and Ellen and Tina took the three girls and treated them to an entire debutante's ensemble. The three girls were delighted. Never before had Margaret and Molly had store-bought clothing. To have so much given at once, they thought of themselves as fairy princesses. They were so appreciative and were an absolute delight that Tina had fun spoiling them. Ellen did the same for her daughter.

Rick made sure that they had ample funds to buy fripperies, as he called them.

The travelling chaise was one luxury purchase Rick had made, and his family utilised it for the first time on their trip to the castle. The rest of the horses had arrived at the Court already. Rick had been notified that not only had they been welcomed, but they had also settled in well. Tom Hammond, the stable manager, had taken charge of them and thanked Rick for trusting him with them.

The trip to *Gracemere Castle* was uneventful. Rick sat alone with Mary Louise and the children in their new, well-sprung carriage for the first leg of the journey. Both older children then decided they wished to change and travel with their Aunt Bette, so there was a passenger shuffle at the first stage. Both tiny babies were asleep, and Rick, Mary Louise, Luke, and Ellen could speak without anyone overhearing. "Uncle Luke, firstly, thank you for all your assistance. I'm totally floundering with all this... well, um, stuff. However, I want to run something by you while we're alone. There is always someone coming in or out, and we're not sure who's listening, so here goes." He took a deep breath. He looked at Mary Lou, "Are you sure, love?" He asked before addressing Luke again.

"Yes, Ricky darling, absolutely! Not a single doubt in the world," she said with a smile, her eyes twinkling with glee.

"Right then, Uncle Luke, we haven't even arrived at the Court yet, but we don't wish to stay in England. We need to work out a way for the family Earldom to use the houses. We have been discussing and are unsure of how to proceed. I, no, we don't just wish to give it away as we need some money exactly, and we know that the Earldom does not have finances. Grandfather told me that not long before he died." He glanced at Mary Lou, and she nodded for him to continue. "My plan is to hopefully sell the hunting box, whatever that is, and keep that money, then sort of sign over the other two with permanent access for our entire family in perpetuity." He swallowed. "This is where I'm stumped; I have no idea how to do this." Rick's eyes fixed on Luke's face.

Charlie had briefly mentioned that he hoped Rick would do this, but it was up to him. "Lad, do you know how much you're talking about? It's thousands of pounds. Like, even tens of thousands of pounds. Are you really sure?" Luke knew Rick to be generous, after all, he was Wills' son, but he wanted to be sure he knew what he was doing. Luke's eyes flicked to Ellen. She had a slight smile on her lips but remained silent.

"Yes, Uncle Luke, we're not staying. This way, we get some more money, and the Earldom gets a 'seat'. I would like to think that Grandfather would be pleased." Rick's simple comment made things fall into place for Luke.

"Rick, lad, this is a lot of money we're talking about. Are you really prepared to give that much away?" Luke asked.

"It's just money, Uncle Luke." Mary Louise said softly. She leaned over to Rick and whispered something. Whatever it was made Rick chuckle and then nod.

"Uncle Luke, you know Uncle Charlie called you all in and told you all that I was Jack's beneficiary?" Rick said.

"Yeesss, why?" Luke said slowly with a definite questioning tone in his voice.

"Well, Uncle Charlie didn't tell you everything. Uncle Ed had to know as well as Father because he's my father, but we decided not to let on exactly what Jack had left me. More than just the property, Jack left me everything he possessed. He had sent a huge crate to Uncle Tim, as he was a lawyer. It contained some gold nuggets; one had 190 pounds of gold in it. There were others stuffed around it, and some alluvial gold. Uncle Ed, Father, Uncle Charlie, and I smelted it, and the smaller nuggets, and it was close to £50,000 worth of gold, if not a bit more. I've banked most of it in small ingots, as the price will be sure to rise as the gold runs out. I cashed in about £1,000, so I have some working capital. I have no idea how much the hunting box would bring in, but together with what I already have on hand, it should be ample." He smiled at his uncle, "And then there's the bank account here."

"How much gold, lad?" Luke's jaw dropped. He felt Ellen squeeze his hand hard. He knew why.

Rick slid his arm lovingly around Mary Lou's shoulder and drew her to him. "All up, it was over two hundred pounds weight of gold, Uncle. Gold is still £10 per ounce, and there are fourteen ounces in a pound, so we are well able to afford this. We don't need the houses. Teddy does, and so does the Earldom. Uncle Luke, don't forget the money in the bank here. I know Grandfather used to laugh and call himself the Earl of Nuts. We would all laugh, but I would watch his face. He was hurting. Grandfather had nothing to leave us but his wisdom. I still have the letter he wrote for me that was in his Bible when he died. Jim gave it to me the day before our wedding. I'll value that until I die. Uncle Luke, Grandfather told me what Uncle Ed, Father and you all did with your windfalls. Uncle Ed's first Emporium set Parramatta businesses on their feet, then Father's gold finds followed, and he built his warehouse and the string of other Emporiums. Then you and your gem and diamond finds set up your Logistics business employing disabled men. It's what you have all done to help others along the way. I'm trying to do that too, but slightly differently by helping the small businesses thrive in their country towns. We all need someone who cares."

Ellen and Mary Lou looked at each other. They each knew they had agreed to marry their husbands when they did not have a penny to their names. It formed a bond between them. Each had brought up the topic more than once on the trip to England. Each of them had married without knowing of their future wealth. They had married for love and that alone. If they could help each other along the way, that would be beneficial. Each one helped in a totally different way, some by employing, some by educating, and now Rick by supplying the needs of the small country businesses in any way he could.

"Ahh, now we come to the nitty-gritty. Rick, I had exactly the same quandary. It was your father I turned to, so I suppose this is fair. You were a tiny child at that stage. I had an idea, but had no idea how to execute it. Wills gave me direction. Do you have any idea of what or how to go forward?" Luke looked from one face to the other.

Both shook their heads. "Uncle Luke, in March 1875, I had £5 in the bank; this year, in March, I had a bit more as my side of the business has taken off. When Jack died and I inherited everything, including his gold, I discovered that there was apparently a bank account with over £200,000 in it. Jack would not allow Elouise to touch a penny of it; estate costs were minimal, and crops and produce were excellent. So, funds have been growing for over thirty years. I will take some of that to start whatever I, or we, decide to do; I just have no idea what yet."

Mary Louise nodded. "And then there are the jewels, Uncle Luke. I sort of expected a small jewel case of gems; it's a full travelling case of jewellery on wheels. There must be hundreds of thousands of pounds worth in there as well. The gems have been collected over generations. And Jack asked that I not sell them but give them away to family. Aunty Gracie and Bella will get to use the tiaras. Uncle Luke, Aunt Ellen, we have more than is sufficient for our needs. The lawyer estimated the value of the gems alone is over £500,000." She heard Ellen gasp. "Seriously, we have enough, Uncle Luke, and it's not like we're just giving it away; we're keeping it in the family forever."

"Rick, I had no idea, but let's put on our thinking caps. You know what Uncle Ned used to say: wait until God opens the door. Let's see what happens, Luke said. He had no idea how he could help. He thought of the community's needs back in Parramatta; it had everything now, from the new fire station built twenty years ago to nearly every other thing they could think of. Any business ideas he or one of his brothers had thought of, they already jumped on and developed. "Pray about it too, Rick, and pray hard."

Mary Louise's comfort was paramount to Rick. They had decided to settle in at the castle for a few days before taking a trip to *Princhester Court* at Aylesford. Another few days wouldn't hurt. Everything else could wait.

Bette took the two young children in hand. She had fully recovered from her *mal de mer*. She had never suffered so severely from seasickness before. She thought that it was possibly because she embarked with a head cold, and the pain behind her eyes just became worse and worse. Even now, she still had the sniffles occasionally.

Chip joined them for the final leg of the journey. He wished to go over a few things with them in private.

It was now nearly mid-November, and the weather was cooling down. Chip was a mindful Duke and let the coachmen travel with warmth, not only in overcoats, triple driving clothes, and blankets, but would insist that they, too, took a break for every horse changeover at the stages on the trip. He remembered his father telling him of Jim Leslie's arrival on the Cobb and Co. trips, and he'd be so chilled through, he could hardly stand. He had double gloves and an old sheepskin overcoat but little else. From that day on, the Duke had been made aware of the staff's needs. They, too, were humans who deserved respect and care. The staff at *Gracemere Estates* noticed the change in the old Duke's attitude, and Chip had kept it going. As a result, the trip took an hour longer. If the coachman and other staff had fallen ill due to the cold, it would have benefited them all in the long run. The staff were also given good coaches to travel in, rather than a flatbed wagon, as some of the aristocracy demand that their staff travel this way. Chip also insisted on two two-week blocks of holidays for every staff member each year. When he had come up with this idea, they thought it was a joke. But when they discovered it was also to be fully paid with a travelling bonus, they were each delighted. Harmony at the *Gracemere Estate* was obvious. All the staff almost tripped over to assist one another.

The aged Reg Hawkins was still in the estate office with his trainee, Julien Williams. Julien was a case in point; he was Reverend Hugh Williams's second-youngest son from West Sussex.

At thirty-one, Julien was also Reg's legs. Reg was now eighty, and although still sharp as a tack, his one good leg had let him down to the point that he was now in a wheeled chair. Julien asked if he could learn the job some years before, and Reg had been training him for some ten years now. Many of the outdoor staff were obviously maimed in some way.

Rick noticed an old man with a limp, trimming hedges; he waved to Jake in recognition. Other gardeners were on crutches, and some only had one arm. They were raking the leaves. Rick knew many of their stories. He had spent many hours playing with Jake and his old dog during his last visit. He knew the dog had died long ago and was sad for his friend.

Rick wished to be able to help people like Uncle Ned had. Uncle

Ned had hired many, many injured soldiers after the various wars. His friend Sam had told him to "Focus on their ability, not their disability." Uncle Ned had told him the same thing when he was a child. Now, he was able to assist people himself; he just had to work out how to do it. First, he had to sort out what was to happen to Jack's properties.

They were trundling over the stone bridge and just about to pass the Dower House. They could see the folly in the woods and noticed that it now had walls. Rick looked at Luke. He pointed out the lay of the land to Mary Louise and what each of the buildings was.

Luke shrugged and then laughed. "Uncle Ned told me it was a waste of space, so he added some walls and set up some free accommodation and food stores for hungry people. He made something useful out of an unfinished ruin. You know what he was like. Who wants a half-built Greek temple in the garden?"

Ellen giggled.

Their first glance of *Gracemere Castle* made Mary Louise gasp. "It's quite a sight, isn't it?"

The crenellated, thick stone walls gave permanency to the fantastic building. It fronted the river on one side and open space on the other three sides, with immaculate gardens as far as the eye could see.

Chip's heart still gave a slight jump whenever he arrived home. He knew that for others, it overwhelmed them; for him, it was home. He missed the days when his arrival meant everyone would gather in the foyer, and there would be hugs all around. Now his Duchess, Tina, their six children and whatever cousins happened to be around were the only ones there, other than his mother. His brother-in-law, Kit, and sister, Charl, had moved to the Dower House some years before with their brood of children.

He chuckled when they discovered they were having another child earlier this year. Thankfully, only one child again; she had delivered quads just eight months after they married. Thea Louise Edwina was not yet three months old and was totally spoiled, with six siblings and her parents answering her every whim. The quads were now fifteen, and each easily identifiable by those who knew them well. However, the quads were two sets of identical twins, and when they were young, they often delighted in swapping places with each other.

Their father, Kit, was now the minister of the Parish. He had always intended to go home to Australia, but had become part of the furniture in the place. He found that he fitted in, and he loved it.

Kit had replaced Reverend Hugh James upon his retirement. He and his wife, Isabel, still lived on the estate and now helped Kit. Chip laughed at how things had worked out. One person who would always be there to greet them was his mother, Christina.

At seventy-eight, she was still beautiful, and her elegance and poise almost made her ageless. To her, he would always be 'Chippy'. Regardless, he was the father of six and was thirty-eight years old. He was the 11th Duke, and he'd still relished the huge hug she always had on his return from anywhere. He had refused to let his mother move to the Dower House. She certainly did not wish to leave.

Chip smiled. Kit was living there anyway, so after his father's death, she stayed on at the castle. Chip's wife, Tina, adored her, and it was reciprocated.

Today, the welcome would be warm. Only Mary Louise was new to the place, and Rick would ease her into the way of things.

Luke and Ellen had been there before, and they had the five young people. She would help to prepare them for their presentations next year.

Chip knew that other family members would join in with the presentations. His eldest children, CJ and Christie, and his twin nephews, Henry and Edward, would all be presented.

Their distant cousin, Matilda Corsairs, known as Mattie, was joining the young throng of debutantes and boys attending their Levées.

Like his father before him, he hated these sorts of official functions, but sadly, they were necessary for the young people's futures.

The carriages pulled up at the enormous front door of the castle, and his mother stood waiting to welcome them all.

A new life awaited many.

Chapter 16 Princhester Court

*T*he visit to *Princhester Court* was delayed by one to two days due to inclement weather.

When Chip finally took his cousins to visit the Court, it was nearly mid-November. Rick, Mary Lou, and Bette came, as did Luke, Ellen, Teddy and two tiny babies. They squashed into Chip's travelling chaise.

It was only about a fifteen-minute drive, and they wished to talk as they travelled.

Rick and Mary Lou were in the forward-facing seats, as they needed to see the house as they drove in. Bette and Ellen sat with them and the three men opposite.

Rick noticed a street name before they turned into the Estate, Mulberry Lane. He thought about how few streets had signs and figured that Jack must have put this one up. Its name brought back happy memories of climbing up the mulberry trees at the back of Ed's house every October when they were children. All the children ate them until their mouths were red. Aunt Jenna had always told them to pocket some green ones, and when they finished eating, to rub the green ones over their hands and mouths, which would remove the stain.

Each of the occupants in the carriage had enjoyed these messy treats at some stage. When Rick pointed out the street name, they all smiled at the memories it stirred.

The thought of these trees also made Rick chuckle at one particular memory. His grandfather delighted in having a large volume of these delicious berries every October and would spend many a day picking them. He would appear at morning teas, luncheons, and afternoon teas, usually with purple splotch stains on his hands. One morning, Grandfather Charles did not appear. All went in search of him in case something had happened. It had; his grandfather was hanging by his feet upside down in the tree. He had been like this for over half an hour. He was cranky that he had spilled the berries he had already picked, but to not waste time, he had picked every mulberry in reach. He was duly extracted, none the worse for the incident, other than some bruises and a few abrasions.

Rick was brought back to the present by the carriage coming to a stop. He looked out and saw an impressive stone gatehouse. The fancy black wrought iron estate gates were opened by a limping young gatekeeper dressed in the same livery as the ones in London.

After an almost regal bow, Rick heard the words, "Lloyd Cartwright's the name, Your Grace," the young man said. The young man recognised the carriage and crest from Chip's visits to Jimmy's manor house. "I'm from next door, a *Pittford Manor* boy, sir. Along with many of the newer staff."

Chip introduced everyone, and they proceeded up the immaculately kept macadamed driveway. The road was smooth and beautifully kept.

"Oh, Chip, this is a bit of all right, isn't it?" Rick stated the obvious.

Chip could do no more than nod in agreement. He had not expected anything as impressive as this. The estate gave the castle grounds a good run for its money, and this was only the gardens. All the carriage occupants were more in awe with every mile they travelled up the long road.

The absolute silence in the carriage spoke of their stupefaction.

From the gatehouse, the sweeping shaded road was lined on both sides with ancient oak trees far enough apart for four carriages to travel abreast. The oaks themselves were hundreds of years old. The branches above their heads were interwoven and trimmed to arch the avenue. Their girths were so impressive that all the carriage occupants could not have reached around them had they all joined hands. The expansive gardens were in pristine order. Even though it was November, the autumnal leaves were raked into neat piles, and those that had not yet fallen showed a careful placement of the trees, as the shades of leaves blended from yellows to reds. The further they progressed down the stately driveway, the more they travelled.

The carriage proceeded slowly, so that they could all take in what was around them, rather than by necessity. They travelled past a large lake with an impressive, grassed island in the middle. Again, immaculately manicured. This was outlined with rushes for half of its length. Circular ripples on the water showed the presence of fish in the expansive waters. It was connected to the bank by a gracefully arched bridge that appeared to be floating. The island had a small pavilion-like building off to the side, and two small rowing boats were pulled up on the grassy embankment.

"Oh, look, Ricky, that's one thing you're going to take me on." Mary Lou was pointing to the small rowboats. "Hey, Bette, no waves on that lake either." Mary Lou giggled.

Bette poked out her tongue in jest at her comment. She had come to babysit the children and had been the one to succumb to *mal-de-mer*.

They had been blocked from viewing the house until they swept past the end of the lake. As none had ever visited the place before, an audible gasp was heard from all.

"You own this, Rick?" his twin exclaimed; her eyes were large with excitement. Bette gasped when she first saw the edge of the enormous stately mansion. *Roseneath* was a six-bedroom house in Parramatta and was considered significant for the area. This must have had at least eighty rooms and then some.

Rick was astounded, "Cor, Jack, what have you done to me?" Rick uttered. Absolutely stunned at what his eyes beheld. "How the blooming heck could you leave this and live on the road for over thirty years?" He voiced his question to his absent friend. He swallowed. "Sorry, ladies."

None spoke; all were astonished at what they saw.

Before them stood a light-coloured stone, c-shaped, palace-like building that extended back some distance and was hidden by a veil of trees.

At the front, a fountain stood with an ancient Greek statue at its centre, surrounded by a pond. It was spraying a circle of water like an umbrella over its head. This stood in the middle of the large but immaculate circular driveway. The sunlight caught the water droplets, causing a rainbow to form; it appeared to be hovering over the arched entranceway of the house.

The house itself was three stories and had a grey slate roof. The lower floor windows featured recessed marble busts above each, and the central doorway was a covered, recessed entranceway rather than a traditional porticoed porch. Other doors were visible, and all were double French variety opening onto the immaculately kept gardens. The outside stonework showed signs of the recent removal of a vine from the pale edifice.

As the carriage drew up to the entrance staircase, a livery-clad footman hurried to assist them to alight.

Chip's own footman jumped from the carriage and assisted on the other side. His young tiger, Felix, held the reins of the carriage horses.

When the occupants were ready to go inside, the front door was flung wide open, and Rick could see the staff lined up. Three well-dressed gentlemen now awaited them at the foot of the steps, and Rick wondered who they could be.

Chip greeted them by name, "Hello Bobbie, Timmo, Edward. Nice to see you, but what are you three doing here?" he asked.

A tall, dark-haired man greeted Chip. "Ahh, well, Mr Couchman mentioned to me that you would be arriving soon, and I asked Basil Hawthorne, your butler here, Rick, to let me know the day you were coming. We're only next door. It's five minutes cross-country on horseback. As Timmo and Edward were with me, I dragged them along, too. Meg sends her love. She is looking forward to meeting you all."

Chip again did the introductions.

Rick knew the family tree and how they all fitted in, but had not met any of them for years. He knew the story of Amelia, Uncle Ned's friend, and knew that her brother Jimmy lived at *Pittford Manor*, the Estate next door. Mr Couchman had explained that Mr Jimmy's son Bobbie had undertaken to oversee the repairs inside. Bobbie was Amelia's brother, Jimmy Westaweller's oldest son and married Meg, the granddaughter of Uncle Ned's friend, Sam Garney. Tim and Edward's parents were both siblings to Jimmy and Alexe, Bobbie's parents, so the families were more than close.

The two women listened to the conversation. Bette and Mary Lou each carried a baby. The twins were now five weeks old.

Ellen relieved Bette of the child she held as she was introduced to the gentlemen.

They all filed inside the impressive entrance.

Edward stepped forward and offered Bette his arm to escort her into the house. He asked her about the children, expecting one to be hers. She explained that they were her brother's twins. She was the maiden aunt brought to look after the children.

She smirked as she caught him smiling. "They tried to marry me off at home, but no one was willing to take me on. My family say I talk too much, and I probably do, but there is so much to admire in this world, I can't hold in my appreciation of it." Her bubbly, enthusiastic comments made him smile.

"Nothing wrong with continually praising our good Lord for all He sends us," Edward said with a beaming grin at the lovely, fair-haired lady on his arm.

She caught his eye and replied, "Oh no, there is not. Nothing wrong at all, good sir. Only I do it so often that I believe it annoys my family no end. I'm doing that frequently in song and music, as there is much to praise Him for." She gave a little skip with joy. "Oh, this place is so beautiful."

Her gurgling reply reminded him of a gently flowing brook. His smile spread to his eyes. She was the epitome of all things he thought beautiful. He was going to look forward to playing escort to this delightful, untouched jewel. Her freshness was also a delight; she was no shrinking violet. At nearly thirty-eight, he had never found a lady to stir his heart. He liked ladies in general, but had no one special. He knew Rick to be twenty-five, and Miss Bette was his twin, so the same age. How could such a gem slip through the fingers of so many men in Australia? It did not take many minutes before he thought of asking Chip for an invitation to stay at the castle for a while rather than a day's drive back home to West Sussex. Edward caught himself grinning at the mere thought. This in itself surprised him as he had not before been at all interested in a lady that way. They, however, had pursued him enough to turn him off seeking any relationship with any of the milk-sops he'd been officially introduced to in London.

Many years before, Edward's dramatic entry into the world at the hands of Chip's mother, the now Dowager Duchess, had formed a bond between the two families. He had even been named after both of Chip's parents, Edward Christian. His parents had also added Ralph and Daniel to his moniker in honour of other friends. He knew he would be made welcome at the castle. His mother was the only one who had used all his names, which was when he was in trouble as a child. He looked down at the fair angel on his arm, his decision now made; Tim would return home alone from this trip. He smiled; yes, he was going to enjoy his time with the delightful lady. As an Earl's granddaughter, she had no sense of her own consequence, and he had already discovered that she was a delight to be with. He had decided all that in the few minutes he had known her. She was completely untainted by the conventions of society. She chuckled when she should have been listening and was whispering when she should have been quiet.

At the back of the group, Edward had kept Bette chatting quietly; the rest of the group had been introduced to the waiting staff. "Oh, Mr Styles, I missed all their names. Never mind, I'm sure you know them and can tell me later if you don't mind."

"I'd be delighted, Miss Lockley. You really only need to know the butler and housekeeper, Basil and Hazel Hawthorne, for the moment. Both are relatively new, having been employed by Bobbie after the previous occupant departed. The only old staff work outside." Their conversation flowed easily.

By now, the housekeeper was opening the door to a room off the spacious foyer. The light streamed in from the windows above and reflected off the white marble of the stairs in the foyer.

Bette noticed that the beautiful staircase was newly carpeted in rich golds and browns, featuring a lovely vine and pomegranate design. She noticed that a few of the paintings had been removed from the walls and others had been hung in their place. Some voids were still visible. She gave a sad "Ohh" and frowned.

The butler saw her gaze. "They have been sent away for cleaning, Miss. They's was in an awful state they was. We have been doing a few at a time; currently missing is a Reynolds, a Gainsborough, and the big one at the top of the stairs is a Turner landscape from his stay 'ere in 1798."

Bella thanked him, then smilingly, she said, "Sir, I believe your name is Basil; I shall call you so if I may. I'm not one for formality; I shall be Miss Bette."

Basil's eyebrows raised in surprise, but he said graciously, "I'd be honoured, miss."

Edward's eyebrows also raised in euphoric surprise. He smiled; yes, he was enchanted by her lack of protocol; he actually delighted in it. No other lady he had ever met would deign to call a butler by their Christian name and invite him to do likewise. Many households referred to all their male staff members as "John," as they had no wish to remember their given names.

Edward knew Basil had been one of Uncle Jimmy's boys. His Uncle Jimmy, Viscount Pittford, had, many years before, started taking in wounded soldiers who had nowhere to live. He provided them with free beds and board in return for their assistance on his farm. Once Uncle Jimmy had the farm profitable again, they were not only given back pay but a permanent job if they wished. As many of these men were terribly injured, most stayed on. Uncle Jimmy brought in many more over the previous forty years, trained them and placed them with references in good positions across the country.

Edward smiled at how all this started. This had started with Sam Garney when he became the Earl. Jimmy Westaweller's son, Bobbie, married his cousin, Margaret, and over the years, the families of the four households had drawn closer. The four were Earl Sam Garney's estate, *Meldon Hall*; Edward's own grandfather, Sir Tim Broome-Hall, at *Broome-Hall Manor*; Chip's, *Gracemere Castle* estate; and his Uncle Jimmy and Bobby Westaweller's, *Pittford Manor*.

Hundreds of injured soldiers, former streetwalkers, and orphans had passed through the gates of these four estates over the past fifty or more years, and most had gone on to bigger and better things after getting their lives back on track. It had started with another cousin, Perry and Katy White's burn victims being rescued, then Peers orphans, the illegitimate offspring of the aristocracy, followed by the wounded soldiers. It had spread to the street people of the port cities around the country.

Edward had a feeling that soon, there would be a fifth estate to join their ranks. Many, if not most, of the rescues had been taught to read and write, instructed in manners and etiquette, and then cleaned up and dressed appropriately. When they were ready to leave, all were given excellent references and assured of a home if things did not work out. Basil and Hazel had been among the last to leave. Their house in a close village had burned down, and they had nowhere to go, so they lived on the street. Lloyd, the gatekeeper, was a wounded soldier, and some of the inside maids arrived with them. All the rest of the indoor staff had come from one of these four estates. All are well-trained for their new positions and eager to begin their new lives. Hazel Hawthorne held the sitting room door open for the group and nodded to her husband. He called for tea to be brought in. She stood while the family seated themselves; she was somewhat unsure of herself and uncertain about what to do.

Bette took in her anxiety and asked her to be seated next to her. Once they were, she said, "Mrs Hawthorne, Hazel, please, we are as fearful as you. We're from the Antipodes and not accustomed to having staff who are not already friends. We do not stand on formality like other households. We're not titled, so I'm sure my brother will be Mr Rick, I, Miss Bette and my sister-in-law will be Ma'am or whatever she wishes."

Rick jumped in and followed his sister's example. "Absolutely, Bette! Mrs Hawthorne, Hazel, we're all in this together, so first names all-round, please. The duke here has filled me in on a little of your history, and all I can say is thank you to you and your husband for stepping up and assisting us. We are all having a new start and will learn together. I believe Jonas O'Neill is still here, and I hope to meet him soon, as well as the other older staff members."

Hazel's nerves were getting the better of her. "Oh, Your Grace, sirs, madam, miss," she nodded to them all. "We are not yet ready for occupation. Much is still to be done. The place was in disarray inside and may take months to get things back in order. Jonas can fill you in. I asked him to wait for you in the library if that's convenient?"

"We have a library? Oh, that's excellent; I should have presumed that we do. Bette, you shall enjoy that. Oh, and yes, and please call me Mr Rick; I'm not into the formality either, but I can cope with that." Rick grinned.

"Oh sir, we have not only the library but a magnificent chapel, the round gallery out the back, the north drawing room and a small drawing room; there is the long gallery, a marble dining room, which is the formal one, the back parlour, the orangery and conservatory, the main music room with amazing acoustics, and several other family rooms including various sitting rooms, dining rooms and such." She was now in her element. "There are still rooms I have not been into and much to discover in the attics. I'm leaving them until last, as they are filled with eons of damaged furniture. Jonas's father thinks that it may not only be repairable but valuable."

They all sat stunned; Rick and Mary Louise were alarmed at the number of rooms. Surely, the house could not contain all these rooms. "Are you kidding? And how many bedrooms?"

Bette beamed. "I look forward to seeing the music room."

"I bet you do, sis. Careful, or we might leave you there," Rick said teasingly.

Hazel smiled at their informality and said, "Sir, we have some eighty formal bedrooms, I believe; there are more if you count the staff quarters. The main sleeping floors are in the South wing. You can't see that from the front at all, as it's hidden behind the trees." Phew, she'd avoided calling him anything.

~

Over the next few hours, Rick met Jonas O'Neill while Mary Lou fed the twins, then the three staff members, Jonas, Basil, and Hazel, showed the entire family group around much of the house.

When they started the tour, one of the new maids was left in charge of the now sleeping babies.

Edward claimed possession of Bette's hand again and escorted her contentedly to the rear of the group, allowing them to chat uninterrupted. As he had often visited the house with Bobbie and Tim, he was able to describe the use of all the rooms. When they reached the music room, Bette gasped. The shiny black grand piano drew her immediately. She ran her fingers over the top as though caressing it. She leaned over and propped up the lid. She then sat on its double seat and ran her fingers over the keys in a remarkable trill, then she started to play. With her eyes closed, her fingers flew over the keys; she was soon lost in a beautiful, haunting melody that drew Edward to stand beside her. His own love of music had him lost in the tune as well. His eyes, however, were not closed but were fixed on her face. She was totally oblivious to the rest of the world as she immersed herself in the unforgettable music.

Edward had already realised that he had lost his heart. He had not even been sure he had such an appendage before today. He, too, stood totally absorbed in her melody, not even realising she had stopped playing.

She turned her divine blue eyes to him. "Oh, they are correct, Mr Styles, the acoustics in this room are quite perfect," she said with a sigh.

He shook his head, realising the music had finished. He exclaimed, "Oh, Miss Lockley, that was a delight. You are richly blessed with your talent; I am prestigiously fond of the piano, especially duets. Do you happen to know any?" he asked, expecting her to refuse politely.

To his delight, she named a few.

He asked, "Do you know *Hungarian Rhapsody Number Two* by Franz Liszt?"

"I love that. Can we try it?" she asked excitedly. "With swaps, too?"

Edward grinned at her like a schoolboy. It was hard enough to play with a new partner, let alone one who changed ends halfway through the piece. "Let's have a go, eh?" he said with a chuckle.

The smile she gave him sent shivers of delight surging through him. He had never felt this way before, ever, and he was astounded at the emotions she stirred in him in so short a time. He felt like a love-sick teenage boy. He had only met her a few short hours ago. He released a deep sigh of contentment. "Okay, ready?" he said as he sat close to her with their knees touching, her foot on the pedals.

She nodded, and together, they played the opening bars. Both were totally unaware of the audience they now had at the far end of the room.

The rest of the family and three staff members were standing almost hidden by a large harp at the other end of the room.

Rick and Tim watched their siblings, their mouths open in amazement, as neither had shown any partiality to another person before that day.

Soon, the joyous melody was echoing around the room. Rick heard his sister say, "Ready?" He watched, intrigued. Surely, they weren't going to try a swap.

Edward nodded, and at her sign, he stood while still playing and moved quickly to the treble end.

Bette threw her head back and laughed; she still didn't miss a note. She slid over, making room for him on the stool.

Mary Louise got the giggles. "They are both so good. You would never know they hadn't met before today, would you?"

Tim agreed. "Rick, I have a feeling Ed may wish to see more of your sister. Chip, do you have any room for him at that tiny house of yours?" Knowing Chip lived in a two-hundred-room crenellated castle, it was a joke between them.

"I should invite you both, but I have a feeling you might be *de trop* and playing gooseberry, Tim." Chip chortled. "You both know that your wives and children, of course, are always welcome. I may have to invite you all and make it a little less obvious for them." Chip smiled as he watched the continuing performance. He stood shaking his head, unbelieving that the staid and society-hating Edward was having such a fabulous time with a lady.

As they stood watching, the couple on the piano at the other end of the room was in stitches as they kept swapping ends. They played the entire *Rhapsody* without error and laughed so hard when they finished that Edward leaned over to kiss her cheek. Unintentionally, she turned at that moment, and she received it on her lips.

She blushed and dropped her head. Grinning naughtily, she looked up at him. "That was nice," she murmured so only he could hear.

"Hmm, it was, wasn't it? We should join the others, though, I suppose." His own reply stunned him, for he meant it.

The smile that met his gave her an elfin look.

"It may not be the only one, either, if I am permitted to call upon you." He was almost afraid to look at her.

"I'd like that, sir." Bette's heart was beating a tattoo, and not just from the musical piece they had just played. "Actually, I'd like that a lot," she uttered with her chin down.

They closed the lid of the piano.

Edward once more offered his arm and joined the others. He wanted so much to cover her hand with his own and entwine his fingers with her delicate, skilled ones, but after a mere four-hour acquaintance, that was not appropriate. He had not only fallen in love but kissed her too, albeit unintentionally, but certainly delightfully.

They found no further distractions on their tour but realised that many of the rooms were undoubtedly in a state of repair, with scaffolding and paint drop cloths in many of them. The previous occupant's rooms were completely empty, but the room still oozed a sickly sweet aroma. The paint had not even covered the lady's cloying perfume smells.

Edward had fallen silent in his commentary.

Bette was worried, "Sir, have I embarrassed you? For I did not mean to turn at that time." Bette realised her actions could be misconstrued.

"No, Miss Bette, it's just that…" he left his comment unfinished; how could he say he had fallen in love so quickly and so completely? "Um, well, I should not have kissed you at all. I apologise profusely all over again. My emotions got the better of me."

She blushed and gave him a coy glance. "Did you not enjoy it, sir? For I confess, I did."

"Oh, I did, but I should not have done it at all. It was not at all gentlemanly," Edward replied with contriteness.

"And it is not ladylike of me to confess to having enjoyed it so either." She gave him another impish grin. She dropped her voice even more and whispered, "But I did." She gave his arm a gentle press. Her dancing eyes met his. "Think no more of it unless you wish to. I'm sure Rick will not allow me to forget, not that I'm likely to." Again, she chuckled joyfully.

Edward capitulated to his desire and gently placed his other hand over hers as it rested on his arm. He returned the gentle press of her fingers; a smile settled on his lips. Their eyes met in mutual understanding.

The extended tour finally concluded far too quickly for them, and they all returned to the drawing room. Edward was left to entertain Bette with Bobbie and Tim.

Mary Louise once again had to feed the babies; Ellen went with her to assist. Jonas took Rick, Luke, Chip, and Teddy to the library and showed them the estate books.

Rick thanked Jonas profusely for keeping the estate running for Sir John and now himself.

Jonas was delighted that his years of hard work had finally paid off. He knew the ins and outs of farming and was delighted that he had had a free hand at the estate farm and stock breeding. His father, Brian, had taught him well. To have had the run of an Estate like this was a manager's dream. He did not mind having an office in the stables as long as he did not have to talk to the previous occupant. He shivered at the thought of her. With her now gone and the new staff now installed, he had been, at long last, given access to the inside. He had started the week she left, stripping out her bedroom completely. Jonas had also removed the overgrown vine growing on the front of the house as its tendrils were encroaching on the stonework and windows. Jonas had left her room empty to 'air' for some two months, as her cloying perfume had permeated everything. It still had a sickly sweet odour in the empty room. He started to restore the master suites. He had asked Mr Couchman if he could install indoor privies and washrooms throughout the Court. He was given permission and set about to drag the building into the nineteenth century. He had even investigated the installation of the electric light system throughout the house. So he also made preparations for that, installing the wires ready for connection to the power. He had heard that private homes could have it in the next year or so. They would be one step ahead, so while the house was empty, all the drilling and cabling could be done without any discomfort for the residents.

Little had been done since Sir John had inherited. Although he had discussed improvements with his father shortly before his marriage, it had never been done, so Jonas knew what he wanted; his father had taken copious notes at the meetings. Sir John had been keen to install every new-fangled thing he could. Jonas faithfully tried to achieve everything possible in the time he had. He loved lists as they made his plans easily understandable for anyone. The first thing he'd done was to create lists of everything. One for repairs, another for replacement, and a third for updating. He had them all recorded on a chalkboard in his office. As each item on the list was completed, a single line was drawn through it. He had seen this system as a child when growing up visiting *Pittford Manor*. A large easel had stood in the foyer, divided into "Inside" and "Outside" jobs; it was updated weekly until the entire estate was back on its feet. He had taken the opportunity to learn a great deal from the elderly estate manager, Mr Cuthbert Mainwaring. His severely burned son, Albert, took over after some five years, and his father taught him.

Jonas's own father, Brian, still worked when he could but found it hard to do much at seventy-three. He'd taken to cleaning the tack. Some days it was all he could manage. Jonas smiled, thanking God for the way things had worked out. He liked the new owner and would be happy working with him. He had met the Duke before, and His Grace was known to be approachable, if not outright friendly. The new owner's Uncle, Lord Luke, looked nice, as did the other cousin, whom they called Teddy. Jonas discovered that he and his family lived at Coxheath. He heard Mr Rick ask if Teddy would help him arrange the house. Jonas raised his eyebrows, but Mr Rick was the new owner and had the right to ask for assistance from whom he wished.

Jonas was astounded when, later, he discovered his cousin, Teddy, was in fact Viscount Lockley. He had no pretensions of grandeur and was interested in all he saw. Yes, Jonas liked him. He could work quite happily with him.

By the end of the afternoon, Jonas had been given permission to continue the repairs, and he was to continue submitting the accounts to Jones and Couchman for payment.

Rick had already decided it might be a good idea to include Teddy and Bella in the choice of colour themes, because even though nothing had been said, Rick knew, or at least hoped, who would eventually be living here. So, he decided to invite Teddy over to assist him as often as possible. He made sure Jonas had heard the invitation to Teddy as he issued it.

Unless there were some unknown legal problems, the estate would become the country seat of the earldom; only Teddy had no idea about that. It wasn't that far from Maidstone, the village; it would do nicely. It was only about three miles cross-country to the castle and some six or so from Coxheath. Rick knew *Bramblemere House,* as the thatched cottage was called, was too small for the family, as they had seven children. From what he could remember, it only had three or four decent-sized bedrooms. He hid his smile. Nothing could be done until the estate was back in order. He prayed God would make a way. He'd oversee that first. With the young family members to be presented around Easter next year, he knew they had time to achieve his goal of setting up the Earldom for the future.

After their tour, farewells were said, and invitations were issued. Edward handed Bette into the carriage and gave her hand a gentle squeeze. Totally inappropriate, but with what had already happened today, they were way beyond that. As the carriage departed, all were waving, but Bette's waves were directed at Edward. As she was facing backward, she saw both Tim and Bobbie giving Edward an arm punch, teasing him. She smiled, knowing that he'd also given her another kiss before they followed the family group into the foyer, before departing. Again, he intended only to kiss her cheek, and instead, she turned, and again, he got her lips. Only this time, he increased the pressure a little before pulling away. She had blushed but returned his smile. She also touched his cheek gently. Even at home, this would not be allowed. The three gentlemen stood and waved until the carriage was out of sight.

"Well, young Edward, an interesting afternoon all around, I'd say," his older brother teased.

"Leave off, Timmo; you were much the same when you met Elise. How long did it take for you two to get engaged? Three weeks, that's how long," Edward said a little sulkily. At least he had received an invitation to stay at the castle from Chip. He would take that up as soon as he possibly could. He had only travelled with Tim to Bobbie's place as he was so darned bored at home. London also held no interest for him.

"Well, I like her, Ed, and at least you know her family background," Bobbie said with a laugh. A thought suddenly occurred to him. "Oh wow, if you do marry her, that's our two families finally joined. Go for it, Ed. Hey, and I loved the duet. She's obviously got both talent and character." Bobbie's grin was as wide as Tim's.

"Oh, Ed, and the kiss, hmm, nice, we all saw it, you know. Some accident, eh?" Tim teased his younger brother.

Edward was surprised that he was getting a little antsy at them. "You only saw that one. There was another later, longer too," he said before he turned and walked inside without waiting for them to continue. He caught the faces of the two men in the hall mirror. A slow smile spread across his face as he saw their stunned looks. He decided he would go back to Bobbie's and pack, then go to the castle tomorrow. Thankfully, he had brought his horse as he had intended to stay with Bobbie for a month. He would ride across the country. It was only a few miles that way, and he could do with the exercise. He would get Bobbie to send his cases by carriage. Tim had just come for a short visit; he wanted to get back home to Elise and their children, but Edward had intended to stay. He had now changed his mind. November 13, what an auspicious day, one he'd easily remember as it was the day before his birthday. As Timmo had seen the first kiss and Ed had already admitted to another one with them both, the sooner he left, the less teasing he would receive. That was a given, yet he smiled. He knew that at his age, it shouldn't bother him, but it had. He knew that teasing about this lady in particular would cut, as this time, he was serious. He had kissed girls before, but only on the cheek. He was astounded that even the thought of her lips sent his blood racing. He smiled to himself. The drawcard of Miss Bette was enough to get him to the castle fast. Her fair hair was like sunbeams on a cloudy day, as it seemed to have streaks that were lighter than others. Her laughing eyes were blue, and she had small creases at the sides of them when she laughed. His dark hair and brown eyes were dull in comparison. He loved her chuckle, her naughty, even edgy sense of humour, and her brashness. Yet, she still did not overstep propriety far. She was so different to the stuffy English misses that were constantly thrown in his path; her lack of protocol was a delight. He had stopped going to London, as twice now, some underdeveloped miss had nearly managed to find herself alone with him. Both times, he had reapplied his dire situation before their designing mamas had achieved their goal. He had fled. Bette, even her name was different. He knew it was really Elizabeth. He knew her history, that the twins were born soon after the death of their great-grandmother and step-great-grandfather. They were named after them, Richard and Elizabeth Childs. With Bette still in his thoughts, he walked back to the music room and sat again at the grand piano. He played softly so the others would not hear him. He tried to remember what she had played at first and tried to pick out the tune. It was haunting and so lovely, just like her.

In the carriage, Rick, Luke, and Ellen noticed Bette's silence. She was sitting quietly in the carriage with her chin in her hand while looking out the window. "Bette, are you all right, sis?" Rick had leaned over and touched her knee.

"Yes, Ricky," she smiled. "Yes, I am. Just a lot to think about." She smiled at him in such a way that he knew she wished to talk to him later. Her quick, subtle lift of one eyebrow spoke volumes to him. They had always been close; he supposed it was a twin thing. Each knew when the other was upset, hurt, or even happy. However, this time, Rick could not read her.

"Sure?" he asked again.

"Sure, Ricky." She turned and looked out the window. Edward's second kiss had melted her resolve to keep all men at arm's length. That was not where she wanted him. A smile settled on her lips.

The rest of the trip from Aylesford to Maidstone, they chatted about the amazing house Rick had inherited.

"Isn't Jonas pure gold?" Teddy said. "Rick, are you really sure you wish me to assist you in the restorations? Jonas is much wiser."

"That's as maybe, Ted, but he's not family, you are. You don't have to tend to the orchard as it's wintertime, and well, I'd like to get to know you better. So, spending time there would be great." Rick had already thought out a reason why he wanted Teddy there. He had managed to have a quick word with Chip a few days before, so he was not surprised at the request.

"Go for it, Ted. It will give you two a chance to reconnect. I have a few things I must deal with, and I've asked Uncle Luke to assist me, so you two will be left to entertain yourselves anyway. The carriages are at your disposal."

Ted was thrilled and agreed willingly.

Chapter 17 Debutante Practice

*T*he cold weeks of winter passed with Edward Styles staying at the Castle. After only three weeks, he had asked Rick's permission to pay his address to Bette. Rick was delighted but said he would have to wait some hours before he could give a reply. He knew what Bette's answer would be, as she had confided in him about her delight in Edward's company. When she had heard Ed would stay for Christmas, Rick had seen the smile that stayed on her face for some hours.

No, it was his Uncle Luke's wisdom he needed. He wondered if it should have been to Luke that Edward applied for her hand, but as his father had given her into his care, he wanted to take the responsibility himself.

The discussion with Luke was a formality. He just needed his uncle to tell him he was doing the right thing in allowing Bette to marry an Englishman and stay there. He presumed that was where they would live. It was something else he'd have to ask Edward.

The result of the discussion with Luke was that Rick was longer than the few hours he had promised Edward. The wait was worth it, though. After an extensive interview with Luke, he had a list of things he needed to ask Edward. Something that he knew his father would have asked. What income did he have? Where would they live? Could he support her? Considering his nerves, he was, in essence, giving his twin away, and he was also hurting. Happy for her, but still breaking his own heart. He had hoped that she would always live close to him. She had moved in with them after Jack had died. She filled the sad hole that Jack's death had left. Now, he was giving permission for her to live on the other side of the world. He may not see her again once they went home.

Rick had learned to respect Edward. He had not overstepped the bounds of decency after that first day. At least not that he knew about. He still didn't know about the second kiss at *Princhester Court*, nor about another one in the music room at the castle, only the day before. This one had occurred after another duet. Edward, this time, drew her into his arms and asked her permission to kiss her properly. She willingly consented, sinking into his arms while still seated on the piano stool. It had, in reality, been a series of kisses. Long and drawn out, yet deeply passionate. Bette didn't know one's stomach could feel like that. Her blush of desire and the small groan she emitted were enough to bring Edward to his senses.

"Oh, Bette, my love, again, I did not mean for this to occur. I find I cannot resist you." He bent and intended to give her another quick kiss before they left the room. When she opened her lips to his and responded to his passion with her own, their kisses lasted much longer than he had intended. Her arms had slipped around his neck, and she was almost crushed in his strong arms.

"Ed, you may not have intended for this to occur, but as you have left me alone for the last week, I was wondering if I have offended you." She didn't flirt, but her look at him from under her long lashes made his heart skip.

"No, dear heart, I just do not trust myself not to touch you. Being so close and having no claim on you is so hard. Your father is not here to ask for your hand." He gently sat her up.

"Ed, my father, isn't, but my brother is. I was placed in his care for this trip, and as he is of age, you could, if you wished, ask him." Suddenly realising what she'd said, she blushed again.

"Truly? This is so? Could he give permission? I have drafted a letter that I was intending to post to your father." He cupped her face in his hands. "I'm hoping for an answer in the affirmative if the question were asked?" He lifted her scarlet face to his and looked lovingly.

A tiny nod was his reply.

His heart sang. When he spoke to Rick, he was hoping for an immediate reply. He was asked to wait for a few hours. He went for a long walk in the extensive gardens to cool both his heels and his ardour. He would have liked to ask Bette to accompany him, but he did not trust himself with her on a private walk after that last kiss. Now, he only had to get permission to ask her. He would wait and think of a unique way to propose if he were given permission. He would have liked to give her a ring, but his signet ring would have to do. They could choose one together at a later date.

After luncheon concluded, Rick spoke to Ed and suggested they go for a walk in the gardens. Edward was the same age as Chip. There was only a difference of some six weeks between them. The two men had always been close; as soon after he was born, Edward's family had moved to *Pittford Manor* and had lived there off and on for quite some years. They saw each other often. Afterwards, his parents moved their family back to

West Sussex. Then, later, it was too far for him to travel home on weekends from school at Christ's Hospital. As the castle carriage collected Chip, Ed always accompanied him. Their friends at school named them "Day and Night" as Chip was as fair as Edward was dark.

Chip then married his cousin, Tina, when they were only eighteen, and Edward felt somewhat bereft. He stayed away from home for a long time, travelling to see his distant cousins in Scotland, only to find them gone, fighting overseas somewhere; he returned home slowly. It was like a grand tour but of Britain instead of Europe. He had attended the Season in London twice and hated both years. He saw through the shallowness of the people, and by the time he was twenty-one, he had decided to stay at home and help his parents with the injured men they were assisting. He learned to teach, enjoying teaching children to read and write. His mother was a fabulous teacher, and he had kept himself from being bored by keeping busy. When his elderly maternal grandmother died, she left him a treasure chest of money, as she did with all her grandchildren. However, he had nothing and no one to spend it on. So, it sat in the bank, making more money. Some he'd reinvested. He need not work again, but that didn't suit him, so he kept teaching.

When Rick asked him if he could support his sister, Ed just answered, "Yes." Rick knew he should ask more searching questions, but he had a not-so-subtle way of cutting through the dross. He asked, "How?"

After Edward explained his financial situation, Rick's next question caught him off guard: where were they going to live?

That was a curly one, for Edward had no idea. Before he had thought out his reply, he found himself uttering these words. "With what I have in my investment portfolio, she can choose where she would like to live. That may well even be in Australia if she wants to go home." Shocked at his own words, he realised he truly meant them. At least there, he could be useful in the colony. Yes, he would leave it to her.

Rick gave his approval and congratulated him. He also hoped his father would approve, as this brought another of the extended hanger-oner branches into the family fold.

Edward's mother, Amelia, had been in Uncle Ned's special care when she had lived in Australia as a convict. She was wrongly accused of something her father had done; she served seven years before being exonerated by her father's near-deathbed confession.

Rick knew the shame of the convict tag; his own grandparents had all been sent to the colony "at His Majesty's pleasure." However, he knew that at home, no one worried anymore. So many were the children or grandchildren of emancipists that it was a non-event. Here, Lady Amelia Styles was still tainted. She may well have married a Baronet, but people here seemed to have long memories. Edward, too, knew that and hated their narrow-mindedness. Sadly, he did not get a moment alone with Bette all that afternoon or evening. However, he had already made plans with her to meet in the music room to practice a duet mid-morning the next day. He tied a note to his signet ring and left it on the closed keyboard for her to find. He secreted himself behind a curtain at the French door near the music stool. As she opened the piano, she would see the ring sitting on the middle C key. The note read, "Will you marry me?"

Everything went as planned, and he snuck out, kneeling behind her on one knee as she lifted the keyboard lid. She gasped when she saw the ring and note. She still had no idea that Edward was now behind her, and when he gently touched her back, she leapt, and the lid fell, and it hit her on the elbow. Tears ensued, and moments later, she was in his arms, being comforted from the pain. Somehow, she ended up on his lap on the large music stool. Eventually, he got around to proposing properly. He laughed. "Not the romantic way I imagined, but the outcome is the same." He checked her elbow for injury, kissed it, then kissed her.

She giggled after she had recovered from the bang. She said, "Indubitably, yes, just in case you were wondering about my reply. Hitting the funny bone is never funny. I can never work out why it was called so." She gave another wet-sounding chuckle and snuggled close to him, wrapping her arms around his neck, and he did likewise to her waist.

Edward distracted her for some time, neither of them willing to try to move as they were utterly content in their current position. His self-control was sorely tested as she returned his kisses with blatant disregard for propriety. He refused to allow his hands to wander much over her form, other than to find that her waist was so tiny that he could encircle it with both hands with ease. He was also shocked to discover that she wore no corset. Her hourglass shape was perfectly natural. Her body was soft to his gentle touch. He so wished to explore it, but he dared not, and it was just as well.

They had been pleasantly occupied for some time, music for once forgotten, when the Dowager Duchess entered the room unannounced and stopped on the threshold. She laughed. "Edward Christian Ralph Daniel Styles, it seems that once again, I am the first. On the day you were born, I was the first to hold you and tell your parents that they had a son. Now I'm hoping I'm the first to wish you both congratulations?" She chuckled as she saw them both blush.

Bette nodded. "Yes, Aunt Christina, you can. All above board, too, as Ricky has given Edward permission. Look, I've even got a ring." She held up the note with the ring still attached.

Christina came over and congratulated them, kissing both their cheeks. Only then did Bette stand up from Edward's lap.

Edward had been pleased for the few minutes of grace, and he had recovered his equilibrium. "When I left home, I had no expectations of finding a wife, so I am vastly unprepared, Your Grace. My signet ring shall have to suffice until we can remedy the situation."

"I love it, Edward." Bette got him to slip on the ring with the note still attached.

Christina got the giggles, as did Bette.

Christina said, "Just one thing, dear Edward, I have known you longer than your parents. Will you now please call me Aunt Christina, as soon as we shall really be related."

He laughed and agreed that he would. Christina suggested that they play something together, a trio rather than a duet. Soon, the three were laughing hard, and as Christina had left the door open, others heard their laughter and followed the joyous sounds.

Rick had been awaiting a summons from his sister, and as one was not forthcoming, he decided to find them. He had Mary Lou on his arm, and of course, their two eldest children were not far from them. Earlier, both Kitten and Jack had admired the vast size of the toy room and nursery upstairs. Each chose one toy—a ball and a skipping rope— and left to find their parents. Rick remembered the many, many hours of delight he and his siblings had spent in that room as children; he was surprised at his children's lack of interest. Then he remembered the many happy hours they had spent outside with Jack in the garden at home. It now made sense to him. To them, happiness was love, not things. They had an excellent teacher in Jack. Hopefully, they would not forget him too quickly.

By the time Rick, Mary Louise, and the children had found the origin of laughter, others had beaten them to the source.

Luke and Ellen had heard the noise and followed the sound to the music room. Then Chip and Tina also entered via an outside French door. Chip had listened to his mother's laughter from the garden where they were walking and followed the joyous sound. When Rick and Mary Lou finally arrived, everyone congratulated the happy couple. They joined the melee, as did the children. At four and nearly three, Kitten and Jack just stood watching.

Kitten stood holding her brother's hand and started crying. "I 'spose you'll stay here now, and we'll have to say goodbye to someone else we love?" Kitten looked at her beloved Aunt with massive tears rolling down her cheeks.

Bette wasn't sure if the little girl would run away or throw herself into her arms. She didn't want to take the risk, so she picked her up. The child wrapped her arms tightly around her neck. Bette had no answer as she knew that she was probably correct. Edward would want to live here. They had not had time to discuss anything, having been otherwise occupied. Her lips were still red from his kisses. Where they would live was not something she had thought about; she didn't really care. She could not reply.

Edward had heard, though, and came to sit by them both. "Kitten, we may compromise and live half our time in each country. God has not yet opened that door to us, but neither has He closed it."

The look of joy that spread over the child's face warmed his heart.

Kitten looked up adoringly into his face but spoke to his fiancée. "Can we have a sing-along, Aunty Bette?" she begged.

"What do you say, sweetheart? Will we sing of the joy in our hearts?" he asked Bette softly.

She replied with a nod. Her heart was undoubtedly joyous and sad all at once, for she did not know if she would see her twin again after she married.

The family group sang for nearly half an hour. Playing an assortment of requests before eventually folding the top back down on the grand piano and returning to the sitting room for luncheon.

The laughter followed the joyous little girl as she danced around them.

Little Jack, too, had enjoyed the sing-along but was now ready for activity, and he, too, was in a festive mood.

Chip's tiger, Felix, had taken to the lad, and the two were soon seen kicking a ball around on the castle lawns. The lad had been found on the streets of London some years ago. He had been only six years old.

When Chip saw a small, crying boy sitting in the gutter, he stopped his carriage and sat beside him. His story was that his mother had just died, and the landlord had sent her body away and taken her possessions in place of back rent. He had nowhere to go. The child's hacking sobs broke Chip's heart.

On further questioning, Chip had realised the lad had no knowledge of any other family than his mother. So, without further ado, Chip gathered the sobbing lad in his arms and strode into the boarding house. With his groom and coachman assisting, Chip paid the back rent and took the confiscated family's possessions, placing them in the luggage rack of his carriage.

The lad sat either on or next to Chip all the way home. His head groom offered to give the boy a home and suggested to Chip that he be trained as a tiger or junior groom for Chip's carriage.

Chip discovered the lad's name, Felix, and he became Chip's tiger, travelling with him on nearly every trip he made. Now, four years later, Felix had taken three-year-old Jack under his wing. It also gave Felix a purpose. Chip and Rick stood at the window of his study, watching the two boys romp on the lawn in the weak afternoon sunshine. Both lads had been eager to get outside after the weeks of being housebound because of the snow. They had made various forays into the garden to build snowmen for the children, but an extended stay had been out of the question. The two men stood watching as the two boys romped and ran.

"Well, I must say, Rick, I didn't know Edward was going to fall so hard for anyone. He has never looked at a lady before, and he's been chased hard enough." Chip smiled at his younger cousin.

Chip saw the uncertainty in Rick's glance.

"Did I do the wrong thing, Chip? Should I have withheld permission?" Rick asked. He stood some inches taller than his older blonde cousin, and now he looked worried.

"Oh no, Rick, they are perfect for each other. If you are familiar with the family history, which I'm sure you've heard snippets of, then you will know that the entire family has virtually turned its back on that side of society. Edward's father, Robbie, saw through it long before he did. He had fallen for Amelia when she was nineteen, then lost her. He searched, and when he found her to be Jimmy's sister and finally found she had been sent to Australia as a convict. He knew what had happened to her; he waited… and waited for her term to expire. Edward has been teaching at the local school on his father's estate and at his Uncle Danny's school nearby. Not a job that a Baronet's son would normally do, but his mother, Amelia, is not a normal Baronet's wife. You know her story, of course?"

Rick nodded. "So, he's really, um, genuine?"

"Absolutely, Rick, and Edward has been my best friend all my life. We were born six weeks apart, and my mother delivered him. I'm sure you've heard that story as well?"

Again, Rick nodded. "Yes, I had heard that story, but I didn't realise that was him. So why has he not married? He's attractive enough, no squint, stammer, and wealth aplenty."

"Exactly, for he has been chased from pillar to post by everything in skirts and their mothers. Bette didn't chase him. Mind you, she did not need to. He was obviously smitten from the moment he took her hand when she descended from the carriage. Her lack of protocol and disregard for the conventions of society may have been a delight to him as it was for us. The fact that they have similar interests in music was both a surprise and a delight for him. He's always been passionate about his piano and music, and few ladies have the skill that he has. He confided in me that same day that he would pursue the possibility of more and asked for an invitation to stay. Remember, he arrived the next day? We made it sound as if it had been arranged, but he was supposed to be with Bobbie for a month." Chip had heard Rick's quick intake of breath. "He's genuine, Rick, and one of the nicest fellows I've ever met. Try to encourage him to return with you if you can; he'll love the informality of Australia. I'll miss him, as he is my best friend. He's not puffed up and has genuine and strong faith. Bette has chosen well." Chip was a little sad he would lose the closeness of his friendship, but if he were honest with himself, since he had inherited the Dukedom, he'd been so busy they had seen little of each other.

With the engagement now behind them, they had chosen to have only the family present instead of an official engagement announcement party. A formal announcement had, however, been sent to the paper and a telegram to her father.

~

The time for the presentations at court for the young people drew closer. They had rehearsed frequently in the ballroom. The girls had to practice gathering their trains and walking backwards out the door. This would be the most challenging part of the entire evening.

Kit took great pleasure in reading the banns for his cousin for the first time, the Sunday after their engagement. Although he was seven years older than Rick, they had spent many happy hours playing by the various rivers in their childhood years. He had always taken charge of the twins and came to know them well. Rick and Edward had been overjoyed that he would also be presiding over the wedding.

"Keeping it in the family," Rick said.

As much as a Baronet's son and the granddaughter of an Earl could, they kept their wedding small. Bette was content to allow the Banns to be read in the church at Maidstone, but she'd asked Chip if they could marry reasonably 'quietly' at the castle chapel.

On a Thursday morning on April 7, Bette and Edward became man and wife. It was a year to the day after Jack died and was chosen for precisely that reason. They had been brought together because of him. The chapel was small compared to the town church, seating only eighty, and they sat squeezed tightly to make room for everyone. Edward's parents, Robbie and Amelia, sat in the front seats, beaming at the joy of Edward finally getting married. For him to marry in the castle chapel was a delight.

As Bette's parents could not attend, Rick and Mary Lou sat in their place, and Rick gave her away. The Dowager Duchess Christina sat with them. She said she claimed the right to be the first to congratulate Edward once again. He had, in essence, become her sixth child. She adored him in this way, as she had also grown close to Amelia and Robbie over the decades.

It was to Amelia that Christina had turned when her beloved Ned had passed. She had sent word, and Amelia had arrived the next day. They had stayed for a month consoling each other. Robbie had been a rock for them both.

To Amelia, Ned was a special foster brother. He had assisted her in Sydney while she was serving her time as a convict. They had worked to improve the lot of the women in the Female Factory, where she had once been held. They had grown very close but never fallen in love with each other. Amelia had married Robbie upon her return to England, and Ned had married Christina some years later. As Robbie was one of Ned's best friends, the two couples remained close.

Rick had a tear in his eye when he gave his twin sister away. He'd kissed her on her cheek as he said the words. He then placed her hand in Edward's. "Look after her for me," he said softly.

Edward had a lump in his throat already; Rick's words didn't help. He nodded. He knew the bond these two had was beautiful and memorable. Sometimes, he felt like an interloper, but he promised that he would take care of her, and he meant it. Every day with her was a new adventure. She had kept him on his toes and opened his heart to new feelings that he'd never experienced before. Her joyous laughter rang out often, as did her voice in song, and just looking at her fair curls and blue eyes made his heart skip a beat. Her beauty was astounding, but the mischievous twinkle in her eye kept him always expecting the unexpected. Life with Bette would not be boring, of that, he was sure.

The vows were repeated, and his new cousin, Kit, the Reverend Christopher Lockley, pronounced them man and wife.

Edward turned to his wife and lifted her veil from her face; she met his eyes with her grinning, dimpled face. He intended to give her a brief kiss.

"Dare you," she whispered with her own eyes twinkling.

He smiled wickedly and cupped her face with one hand, gently brushing her lips with his. The other hand slowly slid around her neck and then down her back. Hers entwined around his neck, and moments later, she was bent over in the most passionate kiss the crowd had seen outside their own boudoirs. Most of the family were either grinning or giggling quietly, Christina included. Edward had already learned of her edgy sense of humour, but knowing that only family was present and that they were now man and wife, he kissed her as he wished.

Most were managing to hold back their laughter until Jack's small voice piped up, "Why is Uncle Edward eating Aunty Bette?"

Laughter rippled through the silence in the chapel.

Edward stood his wife up from her laid-back position in his arms. He whispered, "Happy, wife?" He grinned.

"Yes," was all she said in reply to that question. "For the moment, but wait until later," she added for his ears only as she leaned into her new husband's chest.

He held that promise close. Utterly content with whatever she had planned for their lives together. Together, they would forge a path for a new life wherever that took them.

The castle staff laid on a spectacular wedding breakfast. Another was to be held in the barn for the staff. Robbie, Edward, and Chip had previously discussed a honeymoon destination. Being the auspicious day that it was, Rick produced a billy from somewhere and made a pot of sweet black tea, as he promised Jack he would do on the anniversary of his death. Mary Lou and the immediate Australian family joined him in the unique toast.

When the discussion about honeymoons had arisen sometime earlier, Chip said, "Trust me, Edward, you will not be sightseeing. There are areas of the garden where you can be totally alone, and then there's the folly. There are rooms in the North wing that are rarely used. Tug the bell pull, and food will be brought. Either is available for you for however long you wish."

Edward agreed and chose a suite of luxurious rooms in the North wing and claimed one of the rooms in the folly if required. He had no place to call his own, and in his mind, he had half decided to return with them when Rick went home. Rick had admitted his plan for *Princhester Court* to Edward when he had let slip something to Chip during a discussion about his house. Edward grinned; now he had some direction in his life.

~

The debutantes were sick of rehearsing. They all knew their roles by heart. They could walk backwards in their dreams. Their gowns were all but ready, just awaiting final fittings. Madam Genevieve, their previous gown designer, had long since retired and fifteen years before, one of Chip's younger twin sisters had worn a Frederick Worth gown to her debut. Worth's designs had taken off and had taken London by storm. He had removed the hoops in the gowns and drawn back the sides to make a bustle. His sons had now taken over his boutique and were continuing to create the most beautiful, frilly designs. Each of the girls being presented had chosen one of Gaston Worth's creations. Now, only the final fittings need to be done.

All the boys were likewise rehearsing. They, too, had the specific requirements of court attire, and they needed to practise for their Levée. Once they were all presented, the following requirement was a round of social outings. Thankfully, Almack's was now closed, and society had moved on from that time. However, there were still the required social obligations. Chip knew that as Duke, they were, in essence, all under his authority. Although he'd been the Duke for some ten years, he still felt inadequate compared to the authority his father had held. He realised that he had inherited that air from his father's military training. It was at times like this that he missed his younger brother, Liam, dreadfully. Liam had always supported him in everything they did. Their father had trained them in every role on the estate. Liam had married, left, and gone to Sydney to prepare for the ministry with Kit. They had married each other's siblings, just as Bobbie and Edward's parents had done. Only Kit and Charl had to return, as Charl had not only become extraordinarily homesick but had also discovered that they were, in likelihood, having twins. It was just as well they did return, as, on the day they arrived, she had delivered their quads. All were healthy and survived. The girls would turn sixteen on the day of the Drawing Room presentation to the Queen. The boy's Levée was to be held the week before.

~

Many years ago, during one icy, wet winter, his father and Reg Hawkins sat down to try to write the extended family tree. The longer they spent on it, the more convoluted it became. Lines were crossing everywhere with the intermarriage of cousins and families. Often, siblings married their in-laws' siblings, and so on. Chip chuckled to himself. His own wife was, in reality, a fourth cousin, once removed. The Lockleys looked strong, and most were fair-haired with blue eyes. Those who had married into the Miller or Turner families had a variety of eyes, ranging from hazel to darker shades. Still, on the whole, the family bore a strong resemblance to each other.

Mattie Saunders's husband Jim had been related, and he, too, had been fair-haired. He was the first cousin of Rick's cousin, John Saunders— a distant connection to Chip. Mattie had no one else, as she was a foundling. So she was claimed as a blood cousin of the Charles Lockley branch in Sydney, which, although tenuous, her children were indeed related. Charles' uncle, Mark Saunders, and Mattie's father-in-law had been brothers, not cousins, as first thought.

~

The week after Easter finally arrived, and the presentations were done. There were five girls of the extended family being presented. Cousins Christie and Lottie Lockley and sisters Margaret and Molly Saunders were joined by another distant cousin, Mattie Corsairs, for their presentation.

Queen Victoria graciously kissed the foreheads of all five girls. They were related to the Dukes or Earls and, as such, were honoured by Her Majesty. Each girl had to walk along past a line of ladies-in-waiting. There were men in uniform on the other side. They had chosen small feathers rather than anything ostentatious. Each of their gowns was in perfect taste, and the simplicity, although frilly, made them stand out from the glittering London girls.

Mattie Saunders' children should not have been included, as they were great-granddaughters of a Baron; however, the Queen knew their stories and allowed their names to proceed. Eighteen-year-old Christie, Chip and Tina's daughter, was the first to be presented, and Queen Victoria spoke with her before calling the four other girls to her. She commiserated with Margaret and Molly when she heard that their father had died at the hands of a bushranger when Molly was a tiny babe.

The cousins stood before the small Queen together. The girls nodded in response to her questions.

Lottie wiped her eyes delicately, as did Margaret and then Christie.

The Queen was asking them about their fathers and grandfathers. She took a few minutes to tell them of her friendship with the previous Dowager Duchess, Susanna. With a final nod, she dismissed the girls.

The five graciously backed away from her. None fully realised the implication that she had just made their season. Margaret and Molly stood holding hands, unable to believe the honour they had received.

Lottie was still weeping when she reached her father's side.

Mattie Corsairs was just stunned. She was the only one of the five who did not have blonde hair. She had inherited her mother's dark hair and green eyes. She had been named Mattie after Mattie Saunders, Margaret and Molly's mother. Her mother, Lucy Corsairs, was her best friend.

Lottie turned to her father with a tearful face. "She asked us all about Grandfather and Uncle Ned. I'm sorry, Father, but I was unable to stop crying. I miss them both so much." With that, she dissolved again into tears. Luke saw the Queen glance at them and smiled.

Luke took her to a quiet section of the room and let her weep on his shoulder. "Love, missing someone you love is hard. You two were so special to him, being the youngest grandchildren. You were also fortunate to have lived close to them and seen them often. Margaret and Molly didn't even have a chance to know their father. I know Margaret remembers him, but Molly doesn't. Margaret will feel his loss deeply. You will need to help her, Lottie." Luke knew that challenging her to assist her friends would help her recover. He also realised that the time spent with the Queen had sealed her success. In a way, he hoped she wouldn't meet anyone here, as he was selfish enough to wish for her to come home again and marry someone close to them, hopefully Jonty Evans. He now felt guilty about having refused her request for his hand. But he would have taken her with him to Africa, and if the newspapers were to be believed, the Transvaal wasn't that safe at the moment. He had not told her yet; she didn't need that worry.

Chip, too, was consoling Christie.

It may have been ten years since the two men died, but the impact both had had on the Empire was immense. The Queen knew this, and as a way of thanking them, she ensured that all their progeny were successful in society. By singling them out from their peers at their presentation, she ensured that achievement.

Luke also spoke to his cousins, Margaret and Molly; they, too, realised the honour they had been given. They had not known their cousin, Lord Charles, as well as Lottie.

The group eventually stood quietly, waiting for the rest of the debutantes to be presented.

The boys Levée had been earlier in the week, and they were waiting with the rest of the family group. The Levée had been a men-only event, and this was the first outing they had made. Jem and Carlo realised that their acceptance by society would be eased due to family connections. Chip's sister's boys, Henry and Anthony, were also presented with CJ, Christie's twin. The five made an impressive sight as all had fair hair and blue eyes. All were tall and exceptionally good-looking.

Once the girls' presentations were completed, the extended family group stood discussing the week's happenings.

A hush descended on the room. None could see what caused it, but they saw the thick crowds parting and bowing low. The person who caused it was heading directly for them.

Rick and Mary Louise were standing together, Rick with his back to the disturbance. His wife should not have been there as she had not been officially presented. As she was married to Rick and attended with Chip and Tina, they said it would be no problem. She stood clinging to Rick's arm; he still had not turned to the crowd.

The parting of the crowd was leading directly towards them. Luke and Chip, being tall, could see who it was, and Rick heard them both gasp, and finally, he spun around. Standing before him was a petite, smiling lady in black. She wore a small crown and a lace-edged veil on her head. Her hair was parted in the middle and pulled back over her ears. She had a smiling face and sparkling eyes.

Finally, Rick and Mary Lou realised who stood before them. The entire family group fell into deep curtsies and bows.

"Richard Lockley?" Her soft, clear voice was heard.

Rick nodded and, stammering, replied, "Y-yes, Your Majesty." He was still bowing, as was Mary Louise beside him.

She looked at them and said, "We do not believe we have had the good fortune to meet this young lady." She put out her hand and motioned for them all to stand.

"M-my wife, M-mary Louise Lockley, Your M-majesty," Rick said, stammering.

Mary Lou had stood on her command. She once again fell into the deepest curtseys she had ever made. Her knee was on the ground in submission to the awe-inspiring lady before her. The Queen leaned forward and kissed her forehead. "Consider yourself presented, my dear."

The Queen turned to Chip. "Now, Duke, bring them all to the Garden Party on Friday." She looked at the rest of the family group and added, "Along with the rest of your delightful clan. We are always interested to hear what's happening in the Antipodes. We always get a true picture of the colony from your family."

Chip bowed in acquiescence. He smiled; she had done the same thing to him and his sister when they were presented some twenty years before. It was because of her that he had been able to marry Tina so soon. He was only just eighteen at the time. She had personally placed Tina's hand on his in front of everyone. That was as good as a Royal Command.

With that, the minute but gracious lady moved on to another person and then departed.

~

The success of the presentations and the social whirl of the family took them in many different directions.

While in London, Rick, Ted, and Chip met with Mr Couchman, who informed them that the final repairs of the restoration were ready for their inspection.

Rick thanked the man profusely and shook his hand. He was in a quandary about mentioning his idea to him and wondered how to go about it.

Rick decided to make another private appointment and explained the entire idea about the house and the earldom to him, asking him to draw up the appropriate paperwork.

Chapter 18 The Earl's Seat

*J*n the end, it was some months before the situation arose that allowed Teddy to learn of his plans. It took a near disaster for the issue to be mentioned. Rick knew his Uncle Charlie had been informed of what Jack had wanted, as it was written in his letter. Thankfully, Uncle Charlie had told Uncle Luke before they left Parramatta. Rick knew that he and Mary Lou would never live in England, and this way, everyone in the family would benefit, and Jack's wishes would be honoured.

The London Season was due to finish in mid-August as usual, but by May, everyone in the family had had enough of the endless round of pointless social engagements. The only one who had shown a preference for anyone was Chip and Tina's daughter, Christie. They left London *en masse*.

It was no surprise to Christina that her granddaughter had fallen head over heels for her second cousin, Steve Hunt. He was the youngest son of Edmund, her little brother's son, so he was her own great-nephew.

Stephen was eleven years Christie's senior and, at just thirty, had matured into a wonderful young man. He had spent the last five years in America working for the English Ambassador. He had returned in time for the season and had, of course, been invited to join the family for all its outings. Chip had not even noticed the partiality Steve had shown for his daughter, but he was delighted when approached for permission to court her only weeks after the presentations.

Edward and Bette had taken temporary residence at *Princhester Court* after returning from his parents' place, so that Edward could oversee the final stages. They had spent the Season with Robbie and Amelia in West Sussex. Rick was delighted when they accepted the offer to reside there while the work was being completed. He had suggested that they turn some of the unused back rooms into small self-contained apartments like Uncle Ned had done for Dr Gerry and some of the other regular visitors to the castle. The estate manager at the castle also had one, although he often ate with either the staff or the family.

Eventually, one entire floor of the Great North Wing of *Princhester Court* had been redesigned internally, and small kitchens, individual internal privies and bathing rooms were added.

Edward suggested that they return there and finish the last of the refurbishments. What he didn't let on was that Bette was expecting and was feeling very ill. She was three months gone with child and due before the Christmas season, around November. She ached for some peace and quiet, which was unlike her, and private time alone with Edward. Bette was peopled out; he was too. Edward referred to this stay as their third honeymoon.

The rest of the family returned to the castle. Teddy and Bella came and stayed from their cottage in Coxheath; Kit and Charl, with their growing brood, came over from the Dower House daily. It certainly was the most magnificent rectory in the country. Kit still kept his hand in at the forge. Years before, even before he had started training, he had needed an occupation and found a disused forge on the edges of the estate. Uncle Ned had approved him refurbishing it, and it became known jokingly as *Lockley's Folly* instead of *Lockley's Forge* as he'd intended. It, however, transformed many of the local lads. Instead of being sent to prison for their minor crimes, they spent time as a striker for Kit at the smithy forge. Within weeks, they were changed boys. Soon, they came back voluntarily and wished to learn the trade. Many went on to succeed in their own smithy shops; others turned their lives around as Kit ministered to them as they worked. All renewed their faith in God.

Kit worked as a curate and continued to grow in strength. When the incumbent had retired, Kit was given the Parish and now had the old minister assisting him. Reverend Hugh and Isabel James lived locally and were always available to assist if needed. He was relieved that Kit had not returned to Australia as he'd initially wanted to. They made a great team, and the area benefited greatly.

~

By June, the word was out about Bette's interesting condition, and Mary Louise was one of the first to congratulate her.

Bette's reaction at breakfast time one morning had finally given her away. When Edward helped himself to scrambled eggs, toast and kippers, her quick exit was followed not by concern but giggles.

"Edward, do you have something to tell me about my sister?" Rick asked with a glint of mischief on his face.

Edward's air of absolute innocence brought on more chuckles around the table. "Now, what would give you that idea, little brother-in-law of mine?" Edward bit into a mouthful of his kippers.

Bette returned some minutes later and apologised. Unable to hide the information any longer, the recently married couple admitted her interesting condition.

Edward was absolutely ecstatic and could not believe he was to be a father, let alone by the time he turned forty. He had been attentive before; now, he barely let her out of his sight.

Rick was stunned that she bore Edward's pandering. Instead, she delighted in it. She did not play on the care he gave but willingly accepted his assistance in many things. He, too, would assist her rather than do things for her. She was capable, and he knew it; he relished just being with her. Rick's twins were now eight months old, and Debbie was crawling everywhere. Danny, too, had started to move, but he would instead point and grunt. Debbie or someone else would get whatever he required, usually a drink. Both were an absolute delight. Each was the opposite of their siblings. Kitten was dark, and Debbie was fair. Jack, too, was darker-haired, but he had Mary Lou's violet eyes. Danny seemed to have mousey hair, but he had his father's bright blue eyes. Both had adorable giggles, and these were heard often.

~

To celebrate what would have been Jack Princhester's eighty-first birthday, the entire family had gathered at the castle for an Australian Christmas in June, as it was hot and more like the Christmases that many remembered at home in Australia. They were enjoying their meal when word reached them that there had been a small fire at *Bramblemere House*.

Ted and Bella wished to go directly home and see if all the staff were well. In the end, all the children stayed, but Chip, Luke and Rick accompanied them.

The meal was abandoned. Knowing what was to come, Chip gave instructions for a team of staff and all available wagons to be sent over, and the house contents to be packed up forthwith.

On the way over, Rick finally had the opportunity to put the next stage of his plan into action. He lay back on the squab seats with his arms folded. "Teddy, I have something to say, and I want you to listen before you comment, please." Rick looked in earnest at his older cousin.

Bella had been too worried to cry. She sat stony-faced and listened. Her eyes were now fixed on Rick's.

Rick continued. "When Jack died, he left a swathe of instructions written in numerous letters to various people. Once the funeral was over, he had instructed Grandmother, Uncle Charlie, Mary Lou and me to be together, you know all that." Rick knew that Uncle Charlie had told Uncle Luke, which was why he needed him in on the conversation now.

Teddy sat listening intently but didn't interrupt.

Bella clutched his hand.

Rick bit his lip anxiously. "Uncle Charlie's letter said that if I felt like making *Princhester Court* the Earldom's principal seat, Jack would be thrilled. Uncle Charlie knows my plan and what was in Jack's will and letter." Both Teddy and Bella gasped. "Well, I was wondering how to get you two to move as you're so settled at *Bramblemere House,* bursting at the seams, but settled." He grinned wickedly at his cousin. "It seems God wants you out. So rather than move back to the castle, we'll move you lock, stock, and barrel into *Princhester Court* tomorrow. Gather what you need for tonight at the castle. Teddy, I have already spoken to the lawyer, Mr Couchman, about this; in fact, I did so the third time I met him. There will be strings attached in that we get to stay when we wish, and so do Edward and Bette. I have converted one wing into various self-contained apartments for this purpose. *Princhester House* in London will also be transferred to the Earldom, and I will sell the hunting box and keep that money myself. I also have some ideas for something I will need some money for, so I'll keep some of the estate funds Jack has left me, too. There is still ample room for running the properties, and a good profit is generated every year under Jonas O'Neill's management. So, in reality, Uncle Charlie will own it, but as his heir and the Viscount, you get to occupy it and oversee it until you inherit it. Chad, in turn, will have to run it. Teddy, I won't add an entail, though, but a caveat to say that my oldest male descendant must be consulted in the event of your line no longer requiring it." Phew, Rick thought, now to have him hit the roof.

"But you can't, Rick; he left it to you. It's your inheritance. It's..." Teddy stopped as Rick put up his hand.

"Actually, Ted, Jack left me other things; I won't go into what that is. The properties he left for me to administer, ask Uncle Luke. Uncle Charlie's letter outlined what he wanted, and as Earl, he gave instructions to Uncle Luke. Teddy, did you not wonder why I have involved you in the redecoration? This has been my plan since Jack died. I get to, um, 'have my cake and eat it too', as my children and grandchildren will always have somewhere to stay and live if they wish to come here. You know, university and the like. That will be specified in the transfer contract. I have not told you about the rest of what Jack left me, but I'm not going to be left penniless, believe me." Rick turned his attention to Bella. "Bell, will you make him see sense, please? This is not for him or for you; it's for the entire family. '*Princhester Court*' will be a beautiful place to live, and it's nearly as close to Chip and Tina as you are now, only in the opposite direction."

Chip could see that Teddy was not convinced. "Oh, for goodness' sake, Ted, you're looking a gift horse in the mouth here. You have to choose between a tiny, overcrowded cottage or a palatial mansion. This is for the family. Rick's not giving it to you; he's making it so the Earldom will be a thing of respect and honour. The silly toffs in this country can't see past money, which means you will have access to many things. It's no different from Uncle Charles buying the walnut farm for you. Father and your grandfather made sure that was put in the Earldom's name. The only issue I see is that the harvest time will now mean longer travel to Yalding. Having said that, it's about time you handed that over to a manager. Jonas may even have someone who can live there. Build a nice manager's house on the place. You'll have access to money now, too, estate money, but you can't be frivolous with it, as it will belong to the family. Rick hasn't told you the whole of the story either."

Teddy swallowed; he didn't know who to look at. His eyes finally fell on Rick again. "Okay, go on."

"Well, the *Court* has over five hundred acres of prime farmland, and well, the productivity of it will make your thirty-acre walnut farm child's play to what it's producing. I'm not saying sell it, I certainly wouldn't, but there will be, let's just say, bigger fish to fry in Aylesford." Rick sat with his eyebrows raised, waiting for a reply.

Teddy finally looked at Bella. "Love, how about it?"

She nodded. "Yes, Ted, as this will be for not just us but our children, but their children as well." She turned and looked at Rick. "I simply love the house already. Rick. I will be gracious enough to accept on behalf of the Earldom." She reached and took his hand. "Thank you, Rick, and I mean it. We were bursting at the seams there, and this will be wonderful."

Luke had stayed silent until now. "Phew, I was beginning to think I would have to throw in my tuppence. Charlie gave me instructions that he wanted you to move in. I would have stood my ground if you had refused. He showed me Jack's letter, and Ted was Jack's wish. And the fire today, or all days, is more than a coincidence, more like a God-incident. The decision was left to Rick's discretion, but it was a 'thank you' to the entire family for accepting him as he was. No questions asked. What is that term he used? Nothing more, nothing less?"

Rick nodded. "Ted, as I said, he left me other stuff that is mine alone, well, shared with Mary Lou, of course." He saw Ted was still listening, "Ted, Jack quoted a Bible verse from Matthew 25 verse 40 in his letter. Luke looked at his nephew. He could still see uncertainty in his face. *For as much as you have done it unto them, you have done it unto me.* Okay, I'm paraphrasing a little, but I'm sure you know it well. It was his way of repaying our acceptance of him just as he was." Rick chuckled, "And today being his birthday, I feel he is almost saying, 'Get on with it'."

Teddy nodded. "Are you really sure?"

Rick nodded. "Absolutely! What's more, your father has already agreed, so the Earldom is getting it, regardless of whether you move in or not."

"Okay. Then, Rick, I, too, will say thank you." He took and released a huge breath. "Fine, then let's pack and move in. No use doing it twice. How about it, love?"

"Yes, please," Bella replied joyfully, clapping her hands with glee.

They had just arrived at the cottage, and all could see smoke still billowing from the kitchen at the back of the house. It was obviously where the fire had started. They alighted and walked around the outside of the building. The kitchens were ruined; most of the damage was done by smoke and the many buckets of water used to douse the flames.

As they gazed at the smoke still coming from the building, a thought occurred to Teddy. "Oh no! Grandfather's pineapples!" Ted exclaimed and took off around the back without waiting for the others.

The rest of the family group followed more slowly, inspecting the devastation as they passed. Finally, they arrived at an extensive glasshouse in the backyard.

"Are they undamaged?" Chip asked, concerned that the crop of priceless fruit might be harmed.

"Yes, thank goodness, they are fine. I have fifteen nearly ready to pick and orders for ten more. I have over one hundred now with fruit and many more with pups. Rick, do you know if there happens to be a south-facing glasshouse on the Estate?" Ted stood in the doorway, looking at the precious fruit his grandfather had sent him so many years ago. They had since multiplied one hundred-fold.

It had been a labour of love, but the crop was almost priceless. In years past, a single fruit would bring thousands of pounds. Even though the price had dropped from the top £10,000 per fruit, it was still a lucrative crop. He could provide perfect and ripe fruit, whereas imported fruit was often green, bruised, or mouldy.

"Actually, there is a huge empty one, Ted. South-facing and with shelves already. It used to have tropical orchids, I believe. I was wondering if it would be suitable for your pines; it's about three times the size of this one." He grinned as he had asked Jonas to make sure it was in good repair, as he knew the pines would need a new home.

"Are you kidding?" Ted grinned and was finally convinced that the move was for everyone's benefit. "Okay, that does it; I'm in. Once we're moved, these will be next. I can't leave them unattended for too long. The temperature has to be regulated, or they go mouldy."

The house itself was overall undamaged, but the smoke had rendered it uninhabitable for a few weeks.

~

The complete move took over a week, but with the assistance of various carts, wagons, and staff from all three properties, it was accomplished with minimal fuss. Everyone pitched in. Bella had prioritised the order of things, starting with personal goods; they each packed enough for a few days at the castle, as it was halfway to their new house, and then the contents were moved. Room by room, the family house was emptied. *Bramblemere House* would once again become *Bramblemere Cottage* as it was no longer the Earldom's principal seat.

Ted laughed. "Rick, compared to *Princhester Court*, it's a stool, not a seat." Once repaired, the cottage would be leased.

Rick and Mary Louise moved into *Princhester Court* at the same time as Ted and Bella. Rick gave Jonas the instruction that Ted and Bella were to have the master suite. He saw his look of surprise. Ted was going to object until Jonas showed them all into the Queen's rooms. Rick and Mary Lou would be in there. Rick had arranged to have these completely refurbished as well. The old tapestries were to stay, but the original bed had wood borers and, sadly, had to be thrown out. The new bed was a replica, a huge four-post one, and Jonas had saved the drapes from the old bed. The room took their breath away; it had been decorated in pale blue, embroidered velvets with dark blue cushions and highlights. It was what Rick called subtle good taste.

"Oh, Jonas, it's perfect, thank you," Rick exclaimed.

Jonas had refused to allow Rick to see it until it was completed, and it was the last room to be done.

Edward and Bette had overseen this work and the completion of the apartments as well. They were also now done. The day the move was completed, and the children had each chosen their rooms, Jonas asked to see Rick in private. Rick sought him out in the new estate manager's office at the back of the house. Jonas was at his desk and looked up when Rick entered. He stood and waited for Rick to come closer.

"Thank you for coming to see me, sir. I'm sorry to ask you to come here, but I found something I think you should have."

Rick had told Jonas about the unusual bequest and that the house would essentially be transferred to the Earldom, but no details were provided.

"As you know, sir, I had not been able to thoroughly investigate the inside of the house until the previous occupant had left. In one room, I found Sir John's private things and a tiny alcove with a desk. The back of the room was lined with shelves, and on them was a row of journals. Sir, these were all written by Sir John before his marriage. These are personal, and I feel he would wish you to have them and for them not to be left here when you leave." Jonas walked over to a large chest. "This one is a chest of his personal belongings from his bedroom, and that one is from the attic room. I removed them and have them here. Some are very personal. I had to check each volume was part of the series, but I didn't read them. I could, however, see that they were not estate journals. These are personal reflections and even some poetry."

Rick bent down and picked up a book from this chest at random. He opened the front cover. He recognised Jack's writing, although it was obviously a much younger hand that penned the words.

Jack Princhester,

24 June 1808

Today, I turned ten, and my mother gave me a journal. She suggested that I write my thoughts in it.

My first one is, I am so lonely. I wish I had a brother; even a sister would be good. Mama has no other children other than me, and she's sad all the time. With Papa now dead, I'll not get any brothers or sisters now. I have asked Mama if I can at least go to school. At least I will be with other children there. Dickon is great, but he's not allowed inside. I pray to God that she will let me go.

Rick couldn't read anymore. His heart bled for the lonely child. He knew that Jack had indeed attended Christ's Hospital School; it was where he had met Paul, Ned, and the rest of the family. Paul had been in his class. Jimmy, too, from next door, had been there with Edward's father, Robbie. Bella's father, Gerry Winslow-Smythe, had made up the group of friends. Although initially set up as a charity school, Christ's Hospital School provided an excellent education, and over the years, many of the local nobility allowed their children to attend. They all adored it. The boys' musical abilities were greatly encouraged. Each student was part of the school's various choirs. Rick himself had spent some weeks there when they visited years before.

Rick smiled; now, all those families were, in one way or another, related. Jack was again the only one left out. Rick thought of the sad, lonely little boy, and a lump formed in his throat. Jack had told him his father had died when he was a child; he didn't realise Jack had been so young and alone, though. He had mentioned that there had been a carriage accident on the return from a trip. He'd obviously grown up at the Court with his mother until she died. Then he got trapped with Elouise Wickham. He stood looking at the diary in his hand. He flicked over the pages. Jack had written something most days, sometimes just a few lines; some days, pages were filled. As he flicked through, a thought occurred to him. In a roundabout way, Jack, too, was related. He'd married Uncle David's widow; a slow smile spread across his face. He raised his eyes to Jonas. "Thank you, Jonas, you did the right thing. I will value these forever. No, these will not be left here. I'll take them home." He tucked the first journal in his jacket pocket. "I'll take this one with me now; it's actually the first one."

Jonas smiled. "I thought as much, sir; I placed them in order that they were in on the shelves. Sir, there is more in that room. I have kept it locked. Here is the key." He handed an old chunky key to Rick. "I'd like to show you where it is, though. When you have time, sir."

"Now? I have nothing on for a bit." Rick was keen to see Jack's special room.

Jonas nodded. He opened his office door for Rick, then closed and locked it behind him. "I keep this room locked, sir, as it has the wages and a safe inside. I'm much happier than I'm now back inside the house, as it's more secure."

Rick didn't reply other than a nod. He followed Jonas, taking his bearings as they wandered through the immense house. It took some ten minutes, but they arrived at a small door at the end of a long corridor and up a few flights of stairs. 'We must be up near the attic,' Rick thought.

Jonas pointed to the door, and Rick opened it with his key.

The door creaked open, and Rick felt like he had stepped back in time. There was a small desk and chair. The room had not been aired for decades and was musty. The sun was streaming through the dirty windowpanes, and the motes of dust were caught in its rays as they flowed through the glass of one window. The room was neither small nor low, but something made Rick duck as he entered, almost as if in a reverent bow; he shivered and wondered why. A book lay open on the desk; it was obviously well-used. Rick did not need to look at the cover or title page to know it was a Bible. The pages were yellowed and faded after sitting in one place for so long. The desk, too, was covered in a layer of fine dust. "Oh, Jack, I can feel your loneliness here," Rick said to himself. He did not realise he had uttered the words aloud.

"He had friends, sir." Jonas volunteered as he stood near the door. "Mr Jimmy from next door was one; Dr Gerry, Miss Bella's papa, was another; His Grace's father, Mr Ned and his brothers, especially Mr Paul; and Mr Edward's papa, Mr Robbie. They all came, but more often than not, they were all over at Mr Jimmy's place with a group of other boys. They were all at school together. Well, Mr Ned was a year older and Mr David a year older again. Mr Paul was Sir John's special friend, and his younger brother, Mr Douglas, was as thick as thieves, so my father tells me. The three younger ones had a wonderful time. Sir's mama, Lady Jane, was a pure delight, sir, so loving she was. My Papa said she was so sad when Sir's father, Sir Phillip Princhester, died, she sort of shut down for some time. I remember her, even though her Ladyship died when I was a lad. She passed when I was about ten. Sir John stayed in the house alone, and I thought he would never get over it. There were only the two of them for so long." Jonas looked at Rick and wondered if he should continue.

Rick looked up at him a little glassy-eyed. "Go on, Jonas, I need to know to understand him."

"Well, sir, he finally went to London some ten years after her

Ladyship died. He was still an innocent. Mr Rick was gone for only a few weeks, and he wrote to my father to say he was bringing his wife back. The father said they were married by Special License. We had no idea, sir, not a single one. If we'd known he was even seeing her, we would have set him straight. Mr Paul did try to tell him to stay clear of her. Mr Ned was only just back, and she had fled from the castle back to her home, but she wasn't welcomed there either. Mr Ned had... No, I won't go into that, sir. I'm sure you know some of the stories."

Rick nodded. "I know about Uncle Ned and Elouise. My father told me before I came that he thought it might be important. As she jilted him to marry Uncle Ned's brother, surely Jack would have known about it? Then they lived apart for so long."

"Yes, he knew it all but was still duped, sir. She had him hooked, with the line and sinker firmly embedded, sir. He swallowed her lies," Jonas paused. He hated speaking like this, but Mr Rick had a right to know. "Well, they came back on their honeymoon. She was all smoochy and lovey-dovey to him, but I saw her making faces behind his back once. He had three weeks of bliss. Then he had to attend a meeting in town, and he said it would probably take all afternoon. Just after luncheon, he arrived back and keen as mustard he was to get back to her; he took the steps two at a time, halting when he heard voices from his bedroom. I was hard on his heels as I saw Michael following her upstairs sometime earlier. I knew what they were intending, but I had no way of stopping them." He took a deep breath before continuing. "Sir John opened the door, and they were at it, if you know what I mean. I could see them from where I stood just behind him. I had tried to stop him, sir; I really did." Jonas looked sad at the memory.

Rick waved his hand for him to continue. He could not trust himself to speak. Jonas nodded and continued. "Oh, sir, Sir John was crushed. He was so in love with her. He thought all women were like his beloved mother, good and pure, not this one, sir. Anyway, she just laughed from the bed when she saw him standing there. It was a horrible cackling laugh like a witch would laugh. Sir John sent the poor lad packing that day, and he followed soon after. She met her match in Sir John, though, sir. She was tied to the house at his instructions. She had a minimal household allowance, and he refused her access to any carriages or riding horses. He sold every horse on the estate except the working ones. If she wanted to leave, it was only by walking, and she didn't do that. The allowance he gave her covered the bare minimum for living. Food was provided, but her menu didn't change for thirty years. A choice was not given to her. Meatloaf, stew, sausages, tripe. Friday was fish, so she was given haddock or cod; Saturday was pie, and Sunday was a roast. She ate that, or she didn't eat. She was forbidden to have visitors unless it was the doctor or minister. The front gates were kept locked, sir; she was tied here all that time. She may as well have been in a straitjacket. Never being allowed to leave. Sir, the week Sir John left, all the men in the house were sent to work in London. So only female staff were allowed to work inside. He even retired the butler." Jonas smiled at that. "The only men were the outside staff, and they had been threatened with instant dismissal and no reference if they even dared to talk to her. Father and I oversaw that."

Rick managed to say, "Hence, all the staff is new," murmuring as if explaining something to himself.

Jonas nodded, "Father was the estate manager at the time, but I remember, sir. Sir John asked Father to move the Estate office to the stables. Not a man of any age was left in the house, sir." Jonas swallowed. "Then Sir John was gone. My father had a letter from Sir John, informing him that all further communications were to be conducted through Jones and Couchman. He said farewell and explained that he would not return until she had died. Well, as you know, she outlived him, sir. I was so sad when I heard that. Sir, I would hear her screaming at the remaining staff. I have no idea why they stayed with her unless it was because they could get no other work. They had all been employed by Sir John before he left. Sir, I don't want to talk about her anymore." Jonas shivered and walked to the dirty window. "Sir, Father took over the running of the estate full-time. He had already been doing most of the work, but when Sir John left, Father took over everything. I had been sent to learn some new farming skills from Mr Jimmy next door, and Father wanted to improve the place here, so it was in good nick when Sir John returned. He accounted for every penny spent." Again, Jonas sighed. "We all so hoped he would come back one day. We worked hard at improving the place. He deserved the best, and we were the only ones who could look after his land for him. We have installed every new improvement we could. Our people were trained and well-housed. Our funds were virtually unlimited, but none of it was wasted, sir. You can see that for yourself. Mr Jones and later Mr Couchman oversaw all the expenditure. Everything was kept in order. Then, about ten years ago, Madam got a bee in her bonnet over something. She refused to spend any money indoors. So, if something broke, it was not fixed. Windows, furniture, and everything else were not allowed to be repaired. We managed to keep the kitchens in order, as well as some areas she wasn't aware of. Sir, it's why there was such a massive job to get it ready for you."

Rick turned to the man. "Jonas, you have done Sir John proud. Mr Couchman kept him regularly informed about your work, and he told me about it himself." Well, in a way, he did; it was in a letter, but Rick wouldn't say that. "He was content with what you were doing. We travelled together for some years, and we became close. He came to live with Mary Lou and me at Christmas 1877. He was with us when he died on 7 April last year after lingering for three days. Jonas, it was one of the saddest days of my life. We buried him next to my grandfather in the family section." Rick stopped talking and choked up again, overwhelmed by the memory of the devastating loss of his beloved Jack. He deep breathed back his tears.

After a few moments, he said, "He adored our children. Jack gave Kitten her nickname; she's really Mary Kathleen. She cuddled up to him like a kitten. And our Jack is Jack William after him, not John, the family name. Jack called him the grandson he never had." Rick drew a deep breath again and released before continuing. "Jonas, when Jack died, he left letters for some of my family. One was for my Uncle Charlie. He's Teddy's father and is the Earl of Coxheath. He won't be coming to live, but he may visit again sometime. Jack wanted this house to become the Seat of the Earldom, which is what will happen. I was going to let you know today anyway. The fire hastened their arrival, but Ted and Bella, or should I say Viscount and Viscountess Lockley, will be your new landowners and employers. I will retain access for my family; actually, it's in perpetuity, hence the apartments, but with Jack's blessing, it will rise to the status it should have. *Princhester Court* will become Ted's home. Jonas, I leave him in your care."

"Oh, sir, really? So, you're not staying?" Jonas was stunned. "But sir…"

Rick interrupted, "No, Jonas, our life is in Australia. I have something to do over there that will make Jack's name remembered forever. This will be Teddy's home. We may well come back again when the children are older. Kitten will wish to be presented sometime. That should be in about 1893 or soon after. You should still be around, so I'll see you again."

They stood in silence for some time, both looking through the dirty windows. Jonas didn't know exactly what more to say. "These are the last two windows to clean, sir. I locked this room as soon as I found the books and left them untouched. I'll get it done as soon as you say, sir."

Jonas walked to the door. He stood looking at the young man. He was sad that he would not be able to work with him. If Sir John thought enough of him to leave him the estate, he must be some amazing man.

Jonas was about to leave when Rick said, "Jonas, I'm selling the hunting box. I'll keep that money so I can do this thing for Jack. I'll write to you so you will know all about it when it happens. He would like that. At the moment, it's just an idea, so I won't elaborate yet. Will the sale of the box affect the estate profits much?"

"No, sir, none at all; it's the one drain on the estate. It eats lots of money, and no profit is produced." Jonas smiled.

"That's good. Will the staff there wish to retire, stay or leave? Are there enough pensioner cottages if they wish to retire?"

"Err, yes, sir, there is. Nice of you to think of it, sir." Jonas smiled again. He liked this man more each time they met.

"Good! One more thing, what do you know about walnuts?" Rick asked his manager.

"Walnuts, sir? Um, not much at all; they pickle them, and the timber is nice." Jonas admitted. He still had his hand on the doorknob. "They have a funny taste raw, I believe. I've never tried one, though, sir."

Rick chuckled. "You're going to have to learn about pineapples, too. Ted has hundreds of them and will be moving them into that empty glasshouse. Some even have fruit on them."

"Pineapples, sir! Really? I've never even seen one." Jonas admitted. "Did you know that some years ago, they cost £10,000 each?"

"Yes, it's why he's growing them. They are a funny plant; the fruit grows from the top. Needs a warm room, though, so Ted uses all the fresh horse manure he can source to warm his glasshouse. This glasshouse here is somewhat larger, so we may have to sort out some heating system." Rick explained. He watched the astounded look on Jonas's face.

"Sir, it was built there as it's got a Roman bathhouse floor under it. I was told it's called a *hypocaust* or some such. Some Lord, some generations ago, had tropical orchids. It's just the way it was built many years ago, I think. None of the plants I've had put in there can stand the heat. If he wants heat, then that's the place for those spiky plants." Jonas's face looked puzzled. "He really grows pineapples?"

"Yes, Jonas, and as I said, you had better start reading up about them and walnuts, as he also has the orchard down near Yalding. He will fill you in, but they will be coming under your banner of authority, too. I suggested to Ted that you build a manager's house on that farm and put someone in." Rick laughed when he saw the look on Jonas's face. He laughed. "Don't stress, though; Teddy is an expert on them now, so he'll tell you all about them. Let's go and see the glasshouse."

Jonas left the room and waited for Rick to lock the door. "I have another key, sir, so you keep that one while you're here." Jonas led the way back to the others.

On returning to the others in the sitting room, Jonas stood at the door waiting. Rick explained the situation, and all were soon on their feet and following Jonas out to the empty glasshouse. Rick had seen it, as had Edward, on one of his walks around the garden with Bette. Neither had been inside.

Jonas called an old, bent man over to him. "Dickon, this is Mr Lockley. Sir John left him the estate, but he's handing it over to the Earldom. Lord Edward and Lady Annabella will be the new occupants. The Earl, Lord Charles, lives in Australia, but he may come for a visit sometime."

"Okay, Mr Jonas." He looked at both Rick and Teddy. "Is that Lord

Charles who spoke in the Lords and won us the vote?"

"No, Mr Dickon, that was our grandfather," Ted said.

"No 'Mr' for me, sir, I'm just Dickon, nothing more, nothing less." He saw Rick's amazed look.

After a gasp, Rick asked, "You knew Jack, didn't you, Dickon? He used to say that all the time," Rick asked as they walked down through the kitchen gardens. He had forgotten that Dickon had been left a bequest.

"Yes, sir, we was the same age. I was all he had as a friend until he went to school. But I were only a gardeners boy and weren't allowed inside. Lady Jane was all that was good and proper, but poor Jack was that lonely. He'd sneak me in, and we'd go up to his tiny attic room that he had set up for himself. Nobody could hear us up there." Dickon smiled. "We had some bang-up feasts up there, we did." His brown eyes shone with happy memories. "Mr Jack, he didn't forget me when the other friends came either, we're all go places and play together. Good times, sir. He didn't forget me in his Will either, Mr Rick. He gifted me a cottage in town and a life annuity way beyond the pension and a gift of £1000." He fell silent and hobbled along the gravel path. "Here we be, sir, 'tis mighty hot inside, I can't even grow veg'ables in there." Dickon opened the door, and the wave of hot air met them.

Ted walked in first, followed by Rick. The ladies decided to stay outside. Edward held the door for them so some air could circulate. "Blooming brilliant, Rick! It's about the perfect temperature for the pines, and it has shelves, and that looks like an overhead sprinkler system. Pines need top watering as they are broms."

"A broom, sir?" Jonas enquired.

"No, Jonas, broms as in Bromeliad plants. They are like spiky crowns, and they are fed and watered from the top." Ted stood looking at the gigantic hothouse. All the shelves had been pushed to one side except for one row. "Rick, I'd say it is nearly ten times the size of mine. They will all fit and then some. I have run out of room, so now I will be able to expand. Dickon, do you know anything about pineapples?" Ted looked at the old gardener.

"No, sir, except them's is ugly spiky fruit." He shrugged. "You're going to use this to grow them?"

Teddy nodded. "I already do, Dickon, have been for years. This will be perfect. I'll get them sent over as soon as I can. Does the sprinkler system work? If so, how?"

"It should," Jonas said. "I think there's a small water wheel that somehow makes enough pressure for the water to spray from the jets. Let me check it before you bring the plants over. It hasn't been used for decades so that it may need repair." Jonas made a note to have the outdoor staff test and repair the overhead watering system, as well as clean all the glass panes inside and out.

~

Some of the opening windows were rusted shut, and the hinges needed replacement. By the time Jonas had finished, it looked almost brand new. Teddy and his team started moving the valuable plants. He decided to start with the youngest plants, as the method of packing and transportation would guide him on how to move the more advanced plants with top-heavy fruit. It took three weeks for the plants to be installed in their new home. Only one pineapple plant had been slightly damaged, but it was repotted and seemed none the worse for its trip. Best of all, no fruit was lost.

~

It was now mid-August. Rick lay in bed at night with Mary Lou snuggled up to him. "Love, we have to start thinking about heading home soon. We've been here longer than I expected, but at least we have Ted installed in the house." Rick was stroking her cheek. It was soft and downy.

"Ricky, I don't mind the summer. It's not as hot as home, but I don't want to be here for another winter. They are bad enough at home with the frosts, but here they are just darned freezing." She pretended to shiver against him.

Every night, he thanked God for letting her live after the twins' birth. They now usually slept wrapped in each other's arms. It had been ten months since they were born, and she had bounced back amazingly well. She had been up on her feet less than two weeks after their birth. She had slept a lot, but that was expected as she had lost a lot of blood. She was also feeding two babies, and it drained her of energy.

Thankfully, Chip's staff were old hands at coping with twins. Everything in both houses seemed to appear in twos. Cots, highchairs, even nannies. Chip had it all organised.

Rick tilted her chin to his, and he gently kissed her.

Her violet eyes reflected the lamplight beside their bed. He could see the twinkle in them and the delicious smile she gave him. "One thing I'll miss is the staff, Ricky. I only have to think of something, and someone is at my feet with whatever I am thinking about. They are amazing." She reached up and kissed his bristly cheek. "Brodie and Shauna are great, don't get me wrong, but they will never replace the castle staff." She kissed him a little longer this time. "...but then, my darling love, you're not a duke, and I'm no duchess, thank goodness." She chuckled. This time, she leaned over him, and the kiss she gave him made him groan with desire. "But Ricky, love, you are my own prince charming."

He reached for her night attire and undid the ribbon of her nightgown.

They stayed somewhat diverted from their conversation for some time.

Some half an hour later, Mary Lou said, "Yes, Ricky, I want to go home. It's been fun here, but I think it's time. Bette's baby isn't due until late November or just afterwards, and as she's not as huge as I was, I am pretty sure she's only having one. Edward is thrilled to bits, as he never thought he would marry, let alone have a family. Have you noticed he still can't keep his hand off her?"

"It works both ways, love. Expecting or not, I've learned to knock when I enter a room, especially the music room. I had to walk back out and in again after knocking yesterday morning." He smiled, thinking of his talkative sister and the previously quiet Edward.

Edward had come out of his shell. They had been married some six months now. Their favourite room, other than their bedroom, was the music room. "I must tell them to lock the door when they go into a room. Were we that bad?"

Mary Lou chuckled. "Yes, don't you remember giving everyone one day off each week so we could have the house to ourselves?"

Rick slowly ran his hand over her smooth body. Her curves delighted him. After three confinements and four children, her curves added to his attraction for her. She called it her 'cuddle'. She was his and his alone. He could not understand the betrayal of an unfaithful wife like Elouise.

Mary Lou snuggled up to him, her nakedness warming him. Soon, he was listening to her rhythmic breathing. He lay thinking about his sister and smiled. One item Rick had purchased at Bette's request was a second grand piano for them. They sat side by side in the vast music room, but often, only one was in use at any given time. However, the double seat of that one piano was usually full. Music filled the room and often seeped from the doorway. More often than not, the door was closed. More than one family member had interrupted a romantic moment after they had finished some complicated piece of music. Even in Bette's condition, their music filled the house. Her physical condition did not stop her from playing, although she found that the swaps in duets were more difficult. The acoustics of the room were superb, and their skill grew the more time they spent there.

Rick also thought about their walk that day, crossing over the beautiful arched bridge onto the island. He had often taken Mary Lou over to the island and gone for a row in one of the boats. The bridge connecting the island was spectacular, and its construction was unique. He had found other interesting design ideas around the estate and was intrigued. Still thinking about their origins, Rick finally fell asleep.

~

Edward had been thinking hard about their future. He still had no home. They had made a trip to his parents soon after their marriage and had stayed a month. Edward's uncle, Daniel, Earl of Meldon, had called them for a visit as he wished to speak to them both together and without others around. Thoughts of the conversation lingered with him.

"Edward, I know you know my story, but you shall listen anyway; Bette here doesn't. I was born to Annie and Sam Corbett, both ex-convicts in Sydney. Father used his mother's maiden name; that's where the Corbett comes in. I shall cut a long story very short and tell you that neither was who they thought themselves to be. Father thought himself to be the youngest son of Earl of Meldon, Phillip Garney, and Mother thought herself to be a foundling; the truth was vastly different. In time, their convictions were overturned. Don't worry how, but they were. Mother turned out to be the illegitimate daughter of the Earl, and father the illegitimate son of the Duke of Malvern; however, the Earl acknowledged him as his own son because of me. I am his real grandson. Hence, I'm now the Earl; yet in a way, that's beside the point, but it's why we started taking in other illegitimate peers' children. Bette, Edward's grandfather, Sir Tim, had been keeping an eye on Mother all the years she was in the colony. He had no idea about their real identities." Earl Daniel was holding an old walking stick with a whale tooth on the top of it. He occasionally bounced it. "Oh well, back to the story beginning. In front of Mother's cottage that Uncle Tim had built for her was a huge rock. I won't go into why, but he built it; it's not necessary to know that. I'm talking about an immense rock. I mean huge, bigger than the house itself. By the time I was a young man, we had outgrown the cottage. It had one bedroom and my lean-to room at the back. Cutting out a lot of the story, Father had the rock split and cut into building blocks, and we built a stone house. We lived in it as a family until I married Vanessa, that's Edmund's mother, and then my parents moved back to the cottage in the front." He paused, thinking back. "Ahh, I'm waffling. But I'll get to the point. Edward, the property is vacant; I have no idea if you want to go there, but if you do, there is a five-bedroom house sitting waiting for an occupant in Sydney. Even if you used it as a base, you could have an extended holiday there." Danny Garney, at seventy-eight, bore a striking resemblance to both his father and his biological grandfather, the Duke of Malvern.

Bette looked at her husband of only a few weeks. They had not discussed where they would live. She had just presumed it would be in England. Her look puzzled him as it was one of absolute amazement.

The old man continued, "I don't want an answer now or even soon, but know that it's there if you think of going back." Danny reclined in his chair and smiled; his stick was bouncing quite rapidly, and his brown eyes twinkled with joy. "I'd love to know that someone loved it as much as I did. Compared to this place, it's tiny, of course, but it's filled with love." As they were sitting in a two-hundred-plus room, an immense, stately mansion that would give the royal palaces a run for their money. A five-bedroom cottage was a gardener's cottage in comparison. It held wonderful memories for Danny, and he would love to see it lived in again.

This put a thought in Edward's mind. Why shouldn't they return to Australia? He hated society here and had no place to call his own. Now that he was married, he had to find somewhere for them to live. A home base. He knew they had rooms at *Princhester Court*, but they weren't his. He wanted to put down roots, but he also didn't want Bette to be unhappy. He realised that she'd do anything he asked of her. "Uncle Danny, can I think about it? I'm... no, cut that, we've not had time to discuss where we're going to live. We'll be helping Rick out for a while; then we have to find somewhere to put down roots for ourselves, but we have no idea where yet. We really have not thought about it." He looked at Bette, and she nodded.

"No hurry, lad, I just wanted you both to know it's there," Danny said. He loved his nephew. Edward seemed to be untainted by the trappings of the social world in London. Few were like him. Danny continued, "Ed, Mother wanted me to keep the place, and I wondered why, but James went and stayed there for a while. Before him, our cousin Fergus and his family lived there for about five years, and he loved it, too. I do feel for you boys; second sons and such often have a difficult time of it. James has not yet found his niche. Timothy, my third son, went into the military. It is much easier for the girls; they marry and have their own families. I have seven girls, too. Mind you, I started early. I married Vanessa when I was not yet twenty-one. Jo-anne was born that year." He gave a wicked grin. "Don't count the months; they won't add up, shh." He smirked again. "Father inherited the Earldom after his elder brother died without a son. I was about twenty-seven and knew nothing of my father's background. I had no idea there were even titles in the family, let alone that my own father had been a viscount for over ten years. Trust me, I was livid when I found out. Your grandfather, whom I called Uncle Tim, had told Father that his brother, Nigel, had died some ten years before. I wasn't even told that Father had a brother. On our return here, there were other revelations; suffice to say, many adjustments had to be made to our thinking." He looked at the walking stick in his hand. "This came from my grandfather, the Duke." He paused and swallowed, a micro-frown crossing his brow. He waved his hand in the air as if to wave them away. "But that's another story as well! That's all I'm telling you, by the way, the house awaits if you want it. It's no palace, but it's yours if you want to live or stay there."

They spent more time with him before re-joining the family. The seed had been sown. The idea stayed with Edward, but he was still unable to decide what to do.

Months passed, and they now had a baby on the way; he was still undecided. He knew he needed to make a decision soon.

Chapter 19 Time to Go Home

*A*ugust faded into September, and no firm decision had been made about when to go home. Rick and Mary Lou were never in doubt about them returning home, but he knew it would be a very long time before he saw his twin again. Rick was undecided about staying until after their baby was born. Rick had finalised the paperwork with Mr Couchman, and the hunting box sold for an exorbitant price. Apparently, because it had not been hunted for decades, it was ripe for the picking. Rick had some nineteen offers and eventually asked Mr Couchman to sort them out. In the end, Mr Couchman put it up for what was, in essence, an auction. The outcome was astounding; it sold for thousands of pounds more than anyone anticipated. Rick, in particular, was astonished. He would have been happy with £2000. *Mulberry House* was now sold. He hadn't even known the name of it. Now it was gone. He knew that if he saw it, he might be tempted to keep it. So, it sold, sight unseen. However, Rick did ask that it be stripped of all personal possessions. They were to be sent to him at the *Court*. Four large cases of items arrived. One was old clothing; much of it was obviously not Jack's, as it included some female items. From the style, they were probably his mother's, as there were some fabulous gowns included, and though outdated, Mary Lou was delighted with them. Another contained some old books, and the rest were assorted items that Rick decided he would leave in the cases and take home to peruse there.

~

One morning, early in September, Edward found Rick sitting in the sun, drinking a large mug of strong tea. Edward joined him, and for some time, they sat quietly, simply enjoying the peace. Edward was swinging his legs, obviously wishing to say something but unsure of how to begin.

Rick could see that he just couldn't find the words; eventually, he said, "Edward?" It was enough.

Edward spurted out, "We're coming with you, but if we're going, we'd better be quick, or she'll have the baby on board. Phew! I wasn't sure I was actually going to say the words." Edward looked at his young brother-in-law. He saw both surprise and delight on his face.

"You mean it? You'll come? Really?" Rick was incredulous.

Very quietly, Edward said, "Yes, we're coming, and we even have a house of sorts lined up. Uncle Danny told me we could have *Rock Cottage* and the house behind it for as long as we wanted. His middle son James has not long returned, and another cousin, Fergus Macdonald, lived there for some years."

"I know him well, Edward. His brother is a dear friend," Rick said, smiling. It was through Hamish that he and Mary Lou had corresponded.

Edward nodded in acknowledgement, knowing the connection. "Apparently, James built a second story on it and has made some other improvements. I know it will be a comedown from *Broome-Hall Manor* or any of the other houses, but it can be 'ours' as such. And Rick, I'm a free agent over there, free as from the confines of society I loathe. I was thinking of teaching. Do you know of any good schools where I could be useful? I don't need to work; I'm flush with funds, but I think I would like to share some of the knowledge Mother stuffed in my brain-box. I might even teach music. Bette and I could both teach from home. She told me she was teaching children before she came." Edward sounded somewhat unsure of himself.

Rick took another mouthful of the black liquid. "Really, Edward? But you're um, well, gentry." Rick sounded awkward.

Edward threw back his head and laughed. "I'm the son of a Baron; you're the grandson of an Earl. Who's the gentry lad?" He turned to Rick and said, "Rick, I hate society here. I hate the shallowness of people, the expectations, the lack of faith. Yes, I hate all that, and yes, I know that people there will probably be much the same, but I'm stifled here. I've floated along, barely being able to breathe. I threw myself into helping Uncle Danny with the adopted waifs he has. I've been teaching them for over twenty years. I love that, Rick. Bette said you do similar stuff over there."

"Yes, Edward, Bette and I were named after our great-grandparents Richard and Elizabeth Childs. Richard was the headmaster of the girls' orphanage in Parramatta for decades. Great Grandmother came to visit with Uncle Ned and his mother, et al. Richard and Grandmother Elizabeth met and married. They had nine wonderful years together. They only retired shortly before Richard died, as the orphanage transitioned from Government control to church management. Great Grandmother was so heartbroken, quite literally, at his loss that she died the same week. We were born later that year. So sadly, I never knew them." Rick frowned and thought of the work they had done. "You know it's not really that different to what your Uncle Danny and his father have done. Only many of those children were illegitimate children of convicts. When the Female Factory closed, the need for housing the girls lessened. The official Government Orphanage school closed in 1850, but when the church took over, it had to find more teachers for all the orphans. There was still a need. We've all worked there at some time, Edward; the teaching is certainly rewarding." Rick explained their involvement in many of the various philanthropic enterprises the family was involved in.

The two men fell silent for some time.

"I suppose I have to learn to drink a strong brew like that. The teaspoon will almost stay upright in it." Edward screwed up his face.

"Puts hair on your chest, Edward." Rick laughed. "The insipid stuff you drink here is not tea. You should have seen how Jack liked his tea. Strong, black and with either three sugars or a teaspoonful of golden syrup or treacle in it," Rick smiled at the memory. "Whenever he could, Jack would buy a tin of the sweet, sticky stuff." Rick finished his tea.

Edward obviously had more questions. "Is there work for me there?" Edward asked with uncertainty. He'd never done paid work before; his teaching had been because he loved it.

"There's work for teachers anywhere, Edward. Probably not much pay in it, but that won't worry you if you're financially secure. We would have you nearby. No, check that... I would love you close." Rick's heart was beating rapidly in excitement. He would not have to farewell his beloved twin.

~

Once the decision was made, the group set about planning their trip home. Edward and Bette travelled to his home and bid his parents and siblings farewell. He also visited his Uncle Danny and Aunt Georgie and collected the address for *Rock Cottage*. The agent in Sydney had the keys, and Danny also gave Edward a letter to take to the accountant. Amelia and Robbie bade a fond farewell to their son and were sad they would not see their grandchild. Edward knew that travelling *enceinte* would be easier than with a tiny babe. Before he left, they grouped together and prayed as a family for the last time, with Chip, Teddy and Edward's family. Danny and Georgie had come to bid them farewell from next door. Tim was there with his wife, children, and grandchildren, and his sisters had come from far and wide. It would probably be the last time they would be together.

Bette was thrilled they were returning home. She would have been just as happy to stay with Edward and move houses whenever they wore out their welcome in one or another. Her only concern was seasickness. She made an appointment to see Doctor Fynn Wilson for a medical check-up before they contemplated embarkation. She insisted that Edward sit in with her. When Dr Fynn heard they were returning to Sydney, he suggested that they book onto the *Norfolk* as his younger brother, James, was the surgeon on board and skilled at delivering babies. The *Norfolk* wasn't due to leave until early October, but it was a steam sailing ship, and the time on board would be only weeks rather than months. Luke and Chip made all the arrangements. They booked passage on the *Norfolk*, with a departure scheduled for the first week of October.

The family celebrated Rick and Mary Louise's twins' first birthday early, as the ship was due to leave only five days before the actual birthday. At least they were leaving from London and not a northern port. The ship was to travel via the Suez Canal, and with the steam assist, the sailing ship would cover the distance in a remarkably short time. The estimated time of arrival in Sydney was just over six weeks.

On embarkation, Lottie clutched a large bag under her arm as she boarded. She had her own reasons to be excited. She missed Jonty so much and hoped he would be waiting for her on their return. Luke looked at her and asked, "Poppet, what is so precious that it couldn't go into your cabin?" Luke was wondering if she had a special souvenir for Jonty. She had barely mentioned Jonty the entire trip. There had been no letters either way, but knowing he was in Africa, he would have been surprised to hear from him. Jonty didn't even know they were not in Parramatta.

Her eyes twinkled in reply; she then raised her eyes and met his with a naughty grin. "You'll see, Papa."

Initially, having wondered which one of their children had brought the streamers on board, he figured Lottie would be behind the antics. She may be missing Jonty, but she was nearly always the life of any group. Carlo would have been involved somehow, but she usually instigated the youthful pranks. It was often something that made people happy, so he wasn't that worried. Sure enough, shortly afterwards, Luke saw her surrounded by the other young people in the group, along with some others they had already met on board. Soon, each had hands and pockets full of rainbow-coloured paper streamers. He laughed and pointed this out to the rest of the older group who stood near him.

Edward wondered what they were for. "Why bring streamers, love?" he asked Bette.

"Watch, Edward. You'll love it." Bette stood snuggled under his arm. She was well wrapped in a fur coat with a hood. Her fair curls were rippling in the breeze.

They stood watching until word came for their imminent departure. Three toots from the funnel, and Luke heard Lottie yell, "Now." While still holding one end, all the young ones threw the rolls of streamers to the family waiting on the quay. The ship soon had a paper rainbow pathway to the dock. As the tugs drew the *Norfolk* away from the pier, the streamers broke loose or were released. Again, the rainbow tails of streamers formed brought smiles to the faces of those left onshore. The fun eased the hurt of the farewell. Everyone waited until the dockland faded into the distance before moving away. Bette looked up at Edward. "Are you okay, Ed? You're not having second thoughts?"

He looked down at her adorable face. The look of concern made his heart skip a beat. "Sweetheart, I have no doubts at all. I said farewell to Mother and Father. If I don't get to see them this side of Heaven, I know I will meet them there. My life is with you now, my darling wife. Only it's a bit in reverse from the book of Ruth, as 'Whither thou goest I go too.' You will get sick of me, my darling one." He looked around and bent to kiss her quickly. He grinned, knowing that they were fully visible to all the rest of the passengers. She should only be holding his arm. For her to even be cuddling him was against protocol. For him to kiss her in public was a total breach of convention.

Rick saw and leaned over to his sister. "Go get a room, you two." Yet he was chuckling.

Bette turned and gave him a dirty look. "We did, and look what happened." Bette was obviously with child, and she poked out her tongue at her brother. At six months, her waddle was not very pronounced. Before her marriage, her figure had been so slender that her condition was more pronounced than that of a less petite lady.

Rick noticed that when Mary Lou was a totally different shape from his sister. Bette looked like she literally had a pumpkin under her dress. He teased her about it. The more time he spent around Edward, the more he liked him. In the days leading up to departure, Edward had pestered him for more and more information.

With a steam tug still assisting them, it took less than a day to reach the sea. The ship hoisted its sails, and they felt it jump when the wind filled them. Knowing how Bette had been ill on the trip out, Luke suggested to Edward that they stay on deck for as long as they could. He showed him where they could stand so they were both safe and out of the wind and steam. Luke and Ellen had done the trip four times now, and although this was the first time on a steam sail ship, the deck layout was similar. He knew his father's favourite place was holding on to the vessel's railing with his mother safely in his arms, but he preferred to be seated and have Ellen next to him. Rick and Mary Lou retired to their cabin. Their four small children were demanding their attention. It was well past their nap time, and they would not settle without them there.

The seas were calm, and the breeze was strong enough to carry the ship along at a good speed. Edward stayed with his arms wrapped around Bette until the cliffs of Dover faded into the distance. He thought that if he distracted her, she might not succumb to the *mal de mer* she had suffered before. As the light was also fading, he bent and kissed her neck, and one of his hands started caressing her bodice. Their fur overcoats kept them warm and private, with hers now undone; Bette turned in his arms and slid her hands under his coat. They cocooned under his fur waterproof coat and kept each other warm. Too warm for Edward. He bent and whispered something to her. She smiled and nodded. Only then did he suggest that they retire to their cabin.

The ship's movement under their feet caused her to be a little unsteady, so he held her close as they walked through the door to the first-class cabins. Once in the corridor, she could walk with her hands on each wall. He still held her steady as her centre of balance was off-kilter.

Dinner was in an hour, and they were expected to join the family group in the dining room. Edward knew that they could have their meal delivered to their cabin if so desired. He desired… and food had little to do with it. As they entered their luxurious double cabin, they quickly peeled off their fur overcoats. The rest of their raiment followed.

Edward locked the cabin door, and dinner time was forgotten.

~

The passage across the Mediterranean Sea was reasonably calm. They had two nights of rough seas, but they abated as fast as they had risen.

Often, Ellen was found assisting Mary Lou in entertaining the four small children; the five young adults were often not far away. Three-year-old Jack had conquered the attention of his much older cousins, Jem and Carlo. When it was calm enough, Jack was often seen tied firmly to one or the other and out on the deck with them, watching the goings-on of the enormous ship. He was generally seen with his thumb in his mouth. Its removal was followed by a volley of questions that kept the two young men occupied. Many of the child's enquiries were taxing their own understanding. One threw them, and they had to seek the wisdom of a sailor to answer him.

"If the sails are square and flat when on the ground, how come they could bellow out like they do when the wind catches them?" Jack had watched the sailors repair a sail that lay flat on the deck while they reattached a rope to it. He had watched as they then hoisted it and saw it fill with air and billow out.

All discovered that they were somewhat stretchy. Both young men looked at each other and said, "Well, who knew that?"

Birds occasionally joined the ship on the rigging, and little Jack loved them. The sailors learned that he was a sponge for information. Often, they would volunteer more than they should. Rick and Luke were often found sitting in the reading room. Each was reading one of Jack's old journals. Every so often, a gasp would emanate from one or the other. They shared many of the things that Jack had designed and viewed the drawings he had done. Rick was discovering so much about the man he thought he knew so well. Old Jack's dreams were of engineering and bridges in particular. Every unique design he saw, he would investigate its construction and design and later add it to his journal. As they slowly read through the chest, one book sat to the side, and this was a larger book of drawings of many bridges and assorted other constructions. It had markings indicating where his ideas differed from those of other existing ones. Each was cross-referenced to a diary entry with a code; some had a tick and some a cross on the top of the pages. Each drawing was signed and was a tweak on another design.

Rick later realised that the ones with ticks that Jack had built.

~

After two weeks of reading, Rick's idea of a perpetual memorial for Jack was taking shape. "Uncle Luke, I had an idea about something, and indirectly it also involves you."

Luke looked up at him from the journal he was reading, his expression one of intrigue.

Rick continued. "You know I've been talking about doing something in Jack's name. After reading all this, I think I have a good idea of what it will be. I had the idea of establishing a general scholarship at the University of Sydney in his name. After spending time reading these, I want to make it an Engineering Scholarship. As you were, in reality, the instigator for the university opening, I would like that somehow remembered too." Rick met his uncle's surprised look with a smile.

"But, Rick, I was just the one they chose. The test subject, if you wish." Luke was flabbergasted.

"It will also cover everything else the family have done too. So, not really just you, but I want that added to the scholarship history." Without waiting for a reply, Rick kept reading.

Luke was stunned. He sat looking at his nephew in shock.

~

When the *Norfolk* reached the entry area into the Suez Canal, their ship had to join a queue to pass through. They had to anchor for a day and wait their turn before their time came to journey down this new passage.

Captain Jasper O'Callaghan steered his way into the canal, and as many as possible stood on deck and watched the slow progression down the canal. Surprisingly, Bette had suffered little to no malaise at all during this trip. It seemed that the interesting state and an attentive husband had solved her problem, at least for the time being. Edward was rarely a few feet from her side. They had even found a piano onboard and had a sing-along most evenings.

~

Once a week, Dr James Wilson had an appointment with them both to check her condition. All was going well. She was well, and he, therefore, was happy. James was very similar in appearance to his older brother, Fynn. Edward found out he was thirty-nine and unmarried. Fynn was fifteen years his senior. He had the same calm demeanour that his brother had and the same confidence in his skills. Edward and the doctor were often found in deep discussions about a wide range of topics. They were the same age, and James found time hung heavily on his hands as no one was ill. Edward was also at a loose end when Bette was resting.

By the time the Suez Canal was slipping behind the ship, many first-class passengers had become friends. The doctor was now included in the family group.

Edward had also picked up on one crewman's accent and noted he came from Kent. Able Seaman William Davy greeted him with a salute every time he came on duty. He told Edward that there were two more crew members from Kent on board: Fireman Cavey and Engineer Spears. William was able to inform Edward about the nature of his work and that Captain O'Callaghan was an excellent skipper.

Late October, they crossed the equator, and a big party was held on board. The passage down the Gulf and across the Indian Ocean progressed without incident. Edward knew Bette's time was getting closer, and he knew absolutely nothing about babies except that they screamed a lot. He still struggled to come to terms with the fact that he would be a father.

Ellen, Mary Lou, and Bette sat talking about her impending birth. Rick and Luke both spoke to Edward. They knew now that they probably would not reach Sydney before the child arrived.

Dr James Wilson had even set up a birthing room on board, and Ellen took Bette into the cabin and showed her around. She explained to Dr Wilson that she, too, had some birthing experience, having delivered triplets and twins herself.

"Ma'am, Fynn sent me a letter saying two things. I must allow the father to be present at the birth and assist if he wishes, and secondly, you knew what you were talking about. He said to ask you about squatting and that you would explain?" Dr Wilson looked at her, very puzzled.

Ellen smiled and gave a small thanks to God for Fynn. "Yes, doctor, we learned years ago that few of the local Aboriginal women died in actual childbirth. Many afterwards from infections, but the births were often quick. They deliver squatting, as I have found women of many other indigenous groups do, too. It's easier on the mother."

"I've not heard of this, but I'll allow you to do what you want, but I will be on hand if required," he said, somewhat interested.

"Oh, I want you there with me, doctor. You'll be doing the delivery, but it will be done with the mother squatting. I'm the one who'll be assisting you." Ellen looked at his surprised face. "Well, you are the ship's surgeon. No one has been sick, so you may yet have to earn your keep." She gave him a mischievous grin.

He roared with laughter. "Oh, you win. I'm intrigued, that's all. If you can set things up when the time comes, I'll do what's needed."

The ship slipped down the western coast of Australia and into Fremantle harbour. It restocked with coal and other stores, then set off to Melbourne.

Captain O'Callaghan warned the passengers that they might have a storm as they crossed the Great Australian Bight. It could get a "wee bit bouncy." His version of bouncy did not coincide with the passengers' definition. He ably steered the ship through the huge crashing waves, taking his vessel further south of the usual route to avoid reefs, islands, and the like. It was, of course, in the middle of this storm that Bette went into labour.

She stood up to use the privy in her cabin, and as she sat, the ship crashed down a giant wave. She screamed in fear and called out to Edward for help. He came and got her back to their bed. She thought she had injured the baby as she was hit by one blindly aching pain. Once it passed, she was lying on the bed in Edward's arms. Some half an hour later, another pain hit. It was precisely the same, only stronger. It, too, passed, and again, they stayed safely on the bed until a third pain shot across her belly. This time was so painful that she screamed. She realised she was now in labour, and she made Edward call for the doctor.

Ellen had heard her scream as they were in the next cabin. She stood at the door and waited. When she saw Dr Wilson arrive, she followed him into their room.

Bette was in the middle of a fourth contraction. Ellen went directly to her side. "Deep breath, Bette; open your mouth and breathe through the pains as I showed you. In... Out... again, until the pain has gone." Ellen did the breathing with Bette. She turned to the frantic husband. "Edward, go and tell Luke, please, and then change into loose-fitting clothing. If you don't have any, borrow some from Rick. His will hang off you."

The hours of her labour passed. Because of the storm, they kept Bette lying down for most of it. Over those hours, the storm had abated, and finally, Bette was encouraged to get up and walk around the cabin. Edward was by her side every step of the way, holding her tightly and keeping her steady.

More hours passed until finally, the pains were about five minutes apart. Edward had learned to stand holding her as she writhed in agony and breathed through the pains. He could do nothing to lessen her torment except hold her. He felt utterly helpless. He prayed silently, knowing what nearly happened to Mary Lou. However, he continually whispered encouragement to her. After some eight hours, Dr Wilson returned. He had to leave and attend to a broken arm and a nasty cut that needed stitching. On returning to the room, Ellen noted that he smelled of antiseptic carbolic and saw him douse his hands in gin before touching Bette. He said that it was nearly time for the delivery.

Ellen smiled, knowing that at least he knew about being clean.

Bette had reached the final stage, and Ellen settled Edward on the edge of an armchair that was bolted to the deck, with Bette squatting between his legs, her night attire lifted to around her waist. The floor was lined with numerous towels, and the doctor was sitting on an upturned coopered bucket.

"I believe we're ready," Ellen said matter-of-factly. "Edward, you have to wrap your arms under her arms and take her full weight. Bette, place your arms on his legs so you can brace yourself against him."

The birth process occurred quite quickly in comparison to the length of time for the labour. John Christian Styles, to be known as Jack as well, entered the world in the middle of the Great Australian Bight on the 13th of November. He was a healthy babe, and as Edward discovered, he had a very healthy set of lungs. He cringed when he heard his son's first scream, yet it was music to his ears.

Bette reached up and noted his cheeks were wet. "We did it, Ed; we're parents." She relaxed back against his chest. She knew the painful bit wasn't yet over. She also knew Mary Lou had nearly died after she delivered the afterbirth.

Ellen saw the flash of fear cross her face. "Bette, you'll be fine. Trust me."

Bette nodded, but was still fearful. Squatting once again, she groaned in pain, her fingernails bit into Edward's thighs. Finally, she let out a scream as the afterbirth came away. "Oh, doctor, that was worse than the birth."

"Ahh, yes, well, the baby is not actually attached to you, so that pain is, shall I say, less intense. The final stage is, I believe, more like a knife cutting you. Now, if you could feed the child, I'll get things cleaned up here, and we'll get you to bed." Dr Wilson started cleaning up the bloody mess.

Edward dry-retched when he glimpsed the sloppy mass that she had just produced. He swallowed his bile. With Ellen's assistance, he carried his wife back to bed and then went to view his son while Ellen arranged for Bette to feed him. His son! Their son! He was a father. He would have his thirty-ninth birthday tomorrow, and now he was a father for the first time. The small wriggling bundle before him was his responsibility now. The weight of parenthood descended upon him as the little boy wrapped his tiny fingers around Edward's thumb and his heart.

Chapter 20 Setting Plans in Action

$\mathcal{T}$he ship continued on its voyage, none the wiser to an extra passenger now on board.

On meeting his young cousin, Rick's son, Jack, had given his cousin a new nickname, and it stuck. "He's John, and I'm Jack, but we are both Jack's boys. So I'm calling him Jax."

The captain informed Edward that the tradition of a child born at sea meant that, often, the ship's name was included as a middle name.

Edward laughed, but when it came time to register him in the ship's log, *Norfolk* was duly added to his name, John Christian Norfolk Styles, born November 13, 1881, in the middle of the Great Australian Bight.

Edward thought back on that year. He started the year before happily single. With no regrets, but something in his life had been missing. He only discovered that on the day he met Bette. Some six weeks into the new year, they were married, and now they were parents.

Rick teased Edward about adding a different name. "Imagine if we had travelled on the *Pericles* or the *Bannockburn*, even funnier if it had been the *Victoria*." All had been possible modes of transport.

After some discussion, Luke suggested that they delay the Baptism to have some form of registration in Parramatta. Luke had discovered years before that it often took decades to complete a ship's log and have the data registered in the appropriate records in London. Some never made it back to port if the vessel was lost at sea.

When Edward had filled in the paperwork, something struck him as funny. He told Bette of it that night as he held her in his arms. "Bette, my sweet, do you realise that Jax was born twelve months to the day from when we first met? It occurred to me when I was adding his information to the ship's log. It's not hard to forget the day you meet your destiny. You, my darling, are the very best birthday gift ever."

"Are you kidding? Oh, dear heart, why didn't you tell me?" She had never realised that it was something she had never asked him. Last year, it had been the day he arrived at the castle, and they had never discussed the date before.

She was still bedridden as the ship was still rocking quite a bit. Their cabin was relatively small, and she was keen to get out and walk. She had missed his birthday and hadn't even realised.

"Can you believe so much has occurred in the last twelve months?" He drew her into his arms. He couldn't believe how protective he had become of his family. He found it hard to believe he even had his own family. "Love, I never expected to marry, you know. I thought I was happily single. It turned out not to be so. If anything had happened to you, I would have gone into a decline. I never understood that before."

Bette looked up at him, "Understood what, love?"

He gently kissed her cheek. "How your great-grandmother died of a broken heart after her Richard died, my beloved. I had never had an attachment that involved the heart to such a degree. Therefore, I never understood the utter grief that could occur. The pain I saw you in during the birth makes me understand not only her feelings but also my parents and their partiality to each other. Rick told me of his feelings when Mary Lou nearly died. He was telling me about how he felt. Love, I could not grasp the emotion he went through back then. Bette, my darling one, when you were in such pain with Jax, and I could do nothing to ease it, I would have done anything to bear that myself and do not wish to inflict upon you such agony again." He thought if that meant their pleasurable activities were curtailed, then so be it.

Bette turned to him, her full breasts pressing provocatively into his chest; she said, "Oh, dearest Edward, that is such a pity because I thought I would like at least six. But maybe a few months to recover before the next one, eh? We can't do anything for a month or so anyway, in case you didn't know, but you're not copping out of doing your duty to me, are you?" she asked saucily.

"But Bette, you suffered greatly and the pain, not to mention the screaming and the blood and…" He got no further.

"So, you are going to leave me unfulfilled?" She feigned sadness and insult, with the back of her hand pressed to her brow, but made him laugh.

"Seriously, you want more? After what you went through?" He was astounded.

"At least five, mind you, being a twin, that may not mean five more confinements. I could have a set, too, or even two. Most couples in the family have at least one set. Uncle Ed had two sets, as does Uncle Luke; well, although one set is part of their triplets, trust me, that's confusing.

Uncle Luke's eldest children are Willy, Mary May and Sally. They are triplets, but Mary May and Sally are also identical twins. They are, of course, Lottie and Carlo's older siblings."

"But the pain, the entire *enceinte* thing, the birth, you want to do it all again?" Edward couldn't believe it.

"Oh, willingly, Edward, because look what we end up with. Jax is perfect, love, and he is the image of you." She snuggled close, knowing their dark-haired baby was asleep. "If I don't get some sleep now, I'll be asleep all tomorrow. I'm just so tired. Ellen and Mary Lou say that it's because I'm feeding him. That is draining, but oh so comforting. When he puts his hand on my breast and looks at me, my heart just melts." She yawned. She kissed her husband a loving goodnight and then settled down to sleep.

Edward was also tired. The emotional turmoil she had created in him was both exhausting and exhilarating.

They settled to get what sleep they could until their son woke for a feed at some unearthly time of the night, or was it morning?

Edward had quickly learnt to change him, avoiding the golden shower his son was willing to produce as soon as his napkin was loosened. Ellen had shown him the secret of changing his son by standing by his side.

~

The baby was a week old before his parents were able to take him onto dry land. As, week after Jax was born, the *Norfolk* docked in Melbourne with an extra passenger now on its manifest.

Bette already felt well enough to be up and walking around. She wanted to feel solid ground under her feet.

They were to spend the day in Melbourne and would be leaving at dawn the following day.

The extended family group took a one-hour sightseeing trip, and then Edward took Bette back to the ship for a rest.

By dawn the next morning, they were once more underway and anxious for the trip to be over. They are expected to arrive in Sydney in a few days. *En route* to Sydney from Melbourne, Edward finally gave some thought to where they would live. He was concerned about taking Bette to *Rock Cottage* without seeing it first. Luke had invited them to stay with him until he sorted out some accommodation, as had Rick and Mary Lou.

They accepted Rick's offer, and Bette chose to stay in her old room at *Roseneath* with Rick and Mary Lou. He was pleased that Bette had chosen her brother's offer.

Edward knew he would have to leave this family to sort out the Sydney house, and it could take some time if he decided to move them there. Even if they decided not to live in it, it might be useful for weekend stays for some privacy.

With that arranged, they settled down to pack their belongings. They would be glad to stand on ground that didn't rock.

~

On arrival at Circular Quay in Sydney, they were welcomed by a bevy of family and friends. Many of the Macdonalds, Evans and Lockleys were there, waving a welcome. Edward knew many from their visits to England.

Lottie scanned the waterfront for Jonty's face, but he wasn't there. A lump of sadness formed in her heart. Had he not waited for her after all?

Wills waited for them at the quay and arranged for their luggage to be transported to Parramatta. He welcomed his new son-in-law and grandson and teased Bette about Rick's 'authority' over her now being terminated. Within an hour of the *Norfolk* docking, they were on the ferry heading westward.

Edward was surprised that they were not to stay in town at all.

Lottie was shattered that she had not even had time to see Mary Lou's cousin, Jonty. His parents, John and Colleen, had greeted them, but they gave no word of his whereabouts. Colleen had aged dramatically.

Wills took her aside on the ferry homeward bound and explained that he had not returned from Africa but was hopefully *en route*. He didn't say that no one had heard from him for over a year. Wills didn't want to tell her of the war in that area. He just prayed the lad would be safe.

She stood looking at her uncle's face. "He's truly okay, Uncle Wills?" At least he had not ignored her. He just wasn't home yet.

"We hope so, love, but he'll have a story to tell when he returns." Luke looked at his brother, and a shrug greeted an unspoken eyebrow raise.

Luke knew that Wills knew nothing more.

They would all have to wait and see what happened.

Lottie turned to her father for a hug. She knew her uncle well enough to know he was not telling her everything, but she would not push him… yet.

Wills left them and went to meet Edward properly. They had barely had time to do more than shake hands in Sydney. He had discovered that The King's School could use more teachers, and Edward would be welcome if he wished to take up a post there.

Luke was nearing retirement. He only had a few years left, and Wills knew that Luke would love the chance to work with Edward.

Music, in particular, was in demand, and they were short of teachers. The school was currently on holiday until February, so they had time to think and make decisions.

Due to their hasty departure from the dockland in Sydney, Edward had not had a chance to view the Sydney residence; they had been collected from the ship and transferred directly onto the ferry to Parramatta.

Two weeks after their arrival, Rick and Edward went to Sydney by ferry, and Rick showed him around the town a little.

Rick had initially hoped to catch his friend Jonty, only to find he was still in Africa. His Uncle Wills had filled him in on the ferry trip on the day of their arrival. He wondered at the length of time he'd been absent, but thought no more about him as he became distracted.

Rick introduced Edward to the rest of the Evans family, as well as Hamish and Effy.

Edward laughed to think that Hamish and Fergus were his cousins, but he had never met them since he was a small boy. Yet, the family here not only knew them well, but Luke was also in business with them.

They were first meeting up with Charlie for luncheon at the hotel, then Uncle Charlie had a meeting at Government House, so that gave them all afternoon to inspect the house and for Edward to make a decision.

The trip to *Rock Cottage* took only about ten minutes by tram, followed by a short walk up the hill. By the time they arrived, it was beginning to get really hot.

Edward's initial vision of *Rock Cottage* did not inspire him to wax lyrical about it. Far from that, he gulped, aghast. It was a shack.

The house behind it looked more substantial. Edward knew James had added a second floor to the rear house sometime before. Edward swallowed his pride, and they went inside. If they lived there, there was no way a grand piano would fit. It would occupy half the front room, leaving no room for other chairs. That was presuming they could get one inside.

In the now extreme heat of an early December day, the coolness of the thick stone walls was impressive, especially in the huge underfloor cellar. He sat on an empty keg for a while, cooling down, before they continued their inspection.

On walking up from the cellar, Edward said, "How do you stand the heat, Rick? I'm melting."

"It gets worse, Ed," Rick chuckled.

"I do hope you are kidding," Edward said as they entered the master bedroom.

Rick wasn't kidding, but left the comment unanswered.

The rooms upstairs were whitewashed and airy.

The staircase was solid but uninspiring, functional, to say the least, but the rooms it led to were welcoming. Each was fully furnished, with feather beds, drawers, wardrobes, and an armchair. Downstairs, not far from the kitchen, there was a bathroom with an indoor flushing privy and a shower, featuring a large claw-foot bathtub. The kitchen, too, had obviously been recently updated, and some items still had tags on them, showing they were unused. It was clean and tidy.

Edward wasn't sure what to expect. Neither upset nor excited; it was all just new to him. He'd never had to think about setting up a house before. His meals were delivered to him, and his father's agent paid all the bills. He realised he'd need to learn quickly if he was going to make a go of things.

Rick saw his concern. "Edward, I'm going to put my fingers in your pie here. I think you should live with us for a while and get used to being a father, for starters. Trust me, that takes some getting used to. We at least have some staff. Here, you have absolutely nothing. Bette would have to cook and trust me; you don't want that to happen." Rick smirked.

Edward found himself unable to trust his voice. He nodded. Then he screwed up his nose and asked, "Is she that bad at cooking? I wouldn't know how even to boil water. I'm floundering, Rick. I thought it would at least have a cook or a gardener." He wiped his brow, perspiring from both the heat and stress.

"Nope! Here is a 'start from scratch' situation. Of course, you could employ them, and they could live in the front cottage, but it's not very private. Come and stay with us. I'm actually looking out for some land and buildings; you could do the same. I'm thinking of a house like Ed's or Charlie's *Willow Grove*. You could even build bigger if you wished to, but here, well, it's not like England. We build what we require and use the community buildings for the larger functions."

"Land, build…" Edward murmured, seeing the light at the end of his troubles. "Yes, I could do that, I suppose; yes, I think I would like to stay close to the family. I already feel part of your family. Bette is happy, and we would have you on hand to assist. Here, I would only have Fergus and Hamish."

Rick was ecstatic. "Really? You'll stay?"

"Yes, Rick, I can't bring her here. At least not to live. She might cope fine, but I'm not sure I would. Uncle Danny hasn't been here since he was young, and in his memory, he made it sound, um, well, bigger." Edward swallowed anxiously again. "My cousin James came and did all this, but even he didn't stay for long. One year was all he gave it."

Edward was still looking around, trying to see the good points of the place, but he was having trouble persuading himself. "I don't know how Fergus stayed for five years before the extensions had been done."

Rick explained that Fergus was just happy with some space of his own. "You know Fergus lived in Hamish's house for years before he came here. It suited them both, but then they built a place a few doors down from Hamish, so he moved back. They now travel quite a bit."

Edward absorbed his words but didn't answer.

They walked out the back door and around the garden; it was neat, tidy, and sterile. The bare minimum had been done.

Edward stood with his hands on his hips, looking around him. "I can't do it, Rick. I'm not bringing her here to live. We may turn it into a weekender for all the family, but not to live in, at least not yet. I might see if I can get a married couple to come and put some life into place. But it's... well, it's just sterile. Even the garden, no flowers or shrubs, it's just sterile."

"Ask the agent, Ed; he may know of a couple who will live in the front cottage. Even if it's to write to Uncle Danny and let him know you've put in caretakers and will use it as a weekender." Rick walked to the back door and held it open for him.

Edward knew that Annie and Sam had loved the house. Danny had been born in the front cottage and lived in the back one for more than a decade. But that was getting on for eighty years ago. His own grandfather, Tim, had built it for Annie. Life had moved on dramatically since then. No, Edward would not bring his family to live in Sydney—a holiday, maybe, but not live there.

They met with Charlie for the return trip to Parramatta on the ferry. The cool breeze on the water was a delight to the overheated Edward.

Their return to Parramatta made Edward's decision to accept the offered teaching position at The King's School almost a foregone conclusion. He had also decided to build a home in town near his family. He started looking the day they arrived back.

Charlie's son, John, met them at the jetty. He had to see Ed at the Emporium, but came to collect a delivery first.

Charlie waited on the wagon. He said, "Hop on the back, you two; I can head your way. I have news for Luke about Jonty. I'll tell you *en route*, Rick."

They climbed on board. Rick was on the back, and Edward was up front with Charlie and John.

"I'm going up to the Emporium and will drop you off. Made any decisions, Edward?" Charlie was one for not saying more than was required.

"Yes, actually, Lord Charles..." Edward started.

"Stop right there, Edward; I'm Charlie or Uncle Charlie if you must. I'm now your uncle, so get used to it. Now, continue, please." Charlie gave him a grin but looked a little embarrassed.

"Okay, Uncle Charlie, I will, thank you. As to decisions, I can't take Bette there. It's a neat little cottage, but, well, it's sterile. James has done some extensions, but I can't say it's much better." He shivered.

Charlie noticed the action and smiled.

Edward continued, "Rick said I should look around for some land. I want to stay close to the family, Uncle Charlie."

Edward looked pensively at the area and houses they were passing.

His mouth twisted in uncertainty. Some were lovely; Luke's house, *Glenmere*, on the corner of Church Street, was what he would like. Finances weren't a problem, and if he could find the land, he would build Bette a beautiful home.

"I think you're in luck, Edward. I read in the paper that fifty-one lots were for sale on George, Macquarie, and Charles Streets some time ago, and some didn't sell. We've just driven along Charles Street, some of them back onto Phillip Street. That nice big paddock next to Eddie's is one of them. It is going for a song because the back corner gets a tad damp in a big flood. Ed's not that happy either, let me tell you. He doesn't want eight new houses next to him. I've been here for over sixty years and have only once seen water near it. The rest of that land is sitting high and dry." Charlie grinned, "What's more, you already know the neighbours, family on hand and all."

Edward's interest was piqued, and he asked for more information.

Rick, too, had been listening. "Any more out this way, Uncle Charlie? We may build, too. Jack left me a tidy portion, and as much as I love *Roseneath*, it's so far from you all. Father also said I had to get our own place sometime. So, I suppose as we have four children, that 'sometime' has come."

John sat listening with a silly grin on his face. His father had taken the reins from him.

As Charlie was passing the Gazette office, he said, "Eh, Rick, hop out and grab a paper from the pile; it's in today's edition." He flicked him a halfpenny as Rick hopped off.

Charlie explained to Edward, "A friend of ours, George, usually has a stand at the front of the office. Honesty system, you know." He waited in front of the Parramatta Gazette office while Rick grabbed a paper and dropped the coin in an honesty box.

Edward noted that they even knew the name of the man in the newspaper office. In England, they would not have even known where it was. He later discovered that George was a long-time school friend of his father-in-law's brother, Wills.

Rick was again on the back of the vehicle as Charlie moved away. "Hey, Uncle Charlie, it said most in George and Macquarie Streets sold after the first auction in September, but some eight are left in Charles Street. How about four blocks each, Edward? Then we can build what we like."

Edward's brows flicked with interest.

Rick settled back to reread the advertisement. "You don't read the advertising, Uncle Charlie; how did you know about it?" Rick read on and saw what would have caused his uncle to read the paper. "Oh, the new hospital in Sydney is open. I suppose you had to go being Viceroy and all?

Hey, they left off your name; that's a bit rude."

"You're the Viceroy, Charlie?" Edward asked, astonished. He had not noticed he had dropped the Uncle.

"Unfortunately, yes, but only for the Western Sydney region, but somehow I get shanghaied into all these official functions because I'm also an Earl." Charlie released a huge sigh. "Not by choice, trust me."

Edward wondered what more he would discover about his new family. In England, as an Earl, Charlie would be courted and kowtowed, too. As Viceroy, even for the western region, he'd be on every official list for any function and on every party invite list. Here, he drives an old cart and runs an inn. Edward grinned; he loved it.

"What?" Charlie asked.

Edward shook his head. No, he could not explain his thoughts to Charlie. The more he saw them, the more he felt totally at home. He just grinned, biting his lips.

Rick had read a bit more. "Royal Prince Alfred Hospital, eh? I presume it was named after the Prince they tried to shoot? So, you were there, eh? Not on the list of dignitaries!"

"Leave off, Rick; yes, I was there; yes, they left me off, but it was because I asked them to," Charlie said somewhat gruffly. Charlie still hated being in the limelight. He would do everything in his power to avoid it. Then, on return home, he'd peel off his official togs and don his oldest outfit. "You know I still hate it."

"Sorry! Trust you, though, Uncle." Rick chuckled. "What about the land, though, Edward? We'll have a look tomorrow, eh?"

"Sounds mighty good, Rick, and, yes, let's build next to each other and to your Uncle Ed. I couldn't imagine anything better. I know a certain wife who would adore living next to her twin. Mind you, I do hope you don't mind listening to the piano. Our house will have a big music room with perfect acoustics." Edward grinned, then totally relaxed. Finally, he could now put down roots. Now, he had to write to Uncle Danny and say, "Thanks, but no thanks." They would, however, use it for holidays and possibly undertake some additional building to make it habitable, including a cool underground basement.

Lottie had found that no one had heard from Jonty since her own letter, which had been sent over a year before. To say she was stressed was an understatement. The spring was gone from her step, and the laugh from her voice. Luke realised his daughter was pining for her lost beloved.

~

By early the following year, both new houses were finished, and the two new resident families of Phillip Street had moved in.

Edward was still getting used to the reversed seasons, but he had settled into life in the colony. He found the hot Christmases were a trial, but the outstanding Christian service they attended was uplifting.

Edward found he had not just settled in; he was relaxed and welcomed. He adored living there. When building, he had insisted on a substantial stone-lined cellar in his house, and on the sweltering days, they would sit in the cool of the basement. He even had an upright piano down there for Bette. As the land was sloping, there was a small window that let in some natural light.

Edward noticed that Bette was heading down there more and more often as the heat of the first hot summer week they were experiencing intensified. He thought she might be expecting again. She had not said anything, so he asked for fish kippers for breakfast from their new cook. The following morning, he helped himself to a serve of soft-set poached eggs and kippers that their new cook presented so beautifully. He smiled; this would do the trick if she were expecting.

Bette knew he would worry, so she had decided she would try to hold it from him as long as she could. Smiling, he offered her a bite of the delicious dish, and she vacated her seat at the table in the back garden.

Upon her re-entry, she admitted to her husband that she was approximately four months along and due in May.

Jax was about eighteen months old, and Edward thought the world of the boisterous little boy. He was often seen riding on his father's neck as they walked along the river's edge.

Edward taught music two days a week at The King's School and learned to assist Rick in the Lockley warehouse. This was a job he loved. Edward had earlier tried a few hours as a striker at the blacksmith anvil, and he had declined further invitations to repeat that torture. It took four days of twice-daily soaks, followed in the big bath with oil of wintergreen, for him to recover, and Bette's massages cured him of the thought of offering to assist. Other than that, he had absolutely no regrets leaving England's shores, none whatsoever except the last farewell to his parents. The letters were exchanged frequently in both directions.

~

Rick and Mary Lou were busy preparing Jack's memorial. Throughout 1882, the Governor, Sir Augustus Loftus, Sir William Manning from the University of Sydney, and Rick had various meetings to discuss his proposal for a memorial to Jack.

Rick needed the idea to be totally approved before it became public knowledge. His father and uncles already knew about it, as did Edward and Bette.

Jonty finally returned from Africa via Europe in December at the end of that year, and Lottie was ecstatic. They married quietly by special license the week he returned, just days before Christmas. She refused to wait a moment longer for him, not even for Banns to be called.

Rick was just glad he was safe. Sadly, he didn't get to see much of him with all the meetings he had in Sydney.

~

By Easter, the final paperwork for Jack's memorial was nearing completion.

Rick was determined to announce the scholarship with an official press release on what would have been Jack's birthday, St John's Day 1883.

Edward, Luke, and he had already drafted a press release. It had taken eighteen months since their return to arrange, but the details were finally complete and now just needed to be announced.

Two days before the unveiling of the memorial plaque on a cairn at the University of Sydney, Rick finally took the article to George Allan at the Parramatta Gazette for publication. Mary Louise's father was to deliver a letter to the Sydney papers so they, too, would carry the story.

A new perpetual scholarship was being formed for the Faculty of Engineering. It was to be named the Princhester-Lockley Scholarship and would be offered annually to the student who demonstrated the greatest need and promise in the field. In other words, the student had to be clever, if not brilliant, but financially challenged and willing to undertake a study of some form of engineering.

Luke and Rick had read every one of Jack's journals on the six-week trip to Australia. After finishing the last book, Rick settled on an engineering scholarship.

However, the idea of the scholarship had been born much earlier, in conversation with Dickon, but Rick had not been able to pin down the field in which to award this new prestigious award. Jack's diaries showed that he had a passion for building things.

While they were staying at *Princhester Court*, one of Jack's designs had caught Rick's eye, and he wanted to know more about it. The unique, arched bridge to the island at *Princhester Court* appeared to be floating. Rick loved it. Similarly, Jack and Dickon joined the kitchen flues to the Roman hypocaust under the glasshouse. Dickon had confessed to Rick some months before they left the story behind, along with some other things.

When young, the two boys, Jack and Dickon, had discovered the voids under the floor of the glasshouse. Jack had realised what they were and worked out a way to use them. He knew that his name, *Princhester*, was of Roman origin. His father had told him about lots of Roman ruins on the Estate. More to warn him about going near them than anything else. They had found the old firebox used to heat the floor, and they worked out how it worked. It had obviously been used far more recently than in Roman days, as the brick flue was still in good condition.

Dickon had said that when about fifteen, Jack had a trench dug and had a clay pipe installed in the flooring from the kitchen fireplaces. He had a vent added to the kitchen stoves to control the heat. They used the glasshouse as a winter playground. Occasionally, they broke some glass, but not very often.

Jack's beloved mother often told the boys to play outdoors, and this place became their winter playground of choice when they were young.

Many other things Rick found in the house Jack had built. Hinges that folded back flat, doors that slid into cavities, secret doors in panelling or hidden drawers. These things had not only intrigued Rick but also the younger men.

Jem and Carlo started hunting for the quirky things that were different. A desk with many hidden nooks, a nest of tables that stacked and turned into a seat. Hidden doorways and even an entrance into a twisting staircase that went to the master bedroom from the office. Each one they found, they added to a list. Soon, the list covered two pages. Many were subtle, but always incredible in their design.

Rick had asked Jonas about them, and either he didn't know or wouldn't tell. He had then sought out Dickon and asked him about them. Dickon both knew and willingly told Rick everything.

About a month before they left, Rick and Dickon sat on the island in the middle of the lake. Dickon had taken him there and shown Rick the intricacies of the floating bridge, then the folly itself, as Jack called it, in the middle of the lake. This building was more like an exotic picnic area that Jack had built for his mother on hot summer days. The breeze cooled as it blew over the water, and the pavilion was a lovely place to sit and relax. Jonas had kept the white marble pristine, and the new white muslin curtains that now adorned it blew gently in the breeze around them. Dickon was more than willing to talk about his long-lost friend. Rick told him of their many adventures. Dickon's smile was his reward.

Rick took notes as Dickon talked and soon added two more pages to the list. Many experiments had since broken; others replaced them. They spent a few afternoons investigating the inventions.

Dickon laughed when Rick asked about the failures. "Mr Rick, Jack never called them failures," he said, "He just learned a way not to build something, so he'd start again, usually from scratch. We did that many times." Initially, one of Jack and Dickon's favourite hobbies was to tinker with building things themselves. "One failed dismally when the project collapsed, nearly injuring us both severely."

Dickon had laughed at the memory, explaining to Rick, "We demolished it, and after that, Jack got appropriately qualified staff to build his things." His eyes twinkled with the memory. "Well, sir, Mr Brian, Jonas's papa, put his foot down and would not let us endanger ourselves anymore. He would endeavour to get them built, whatever Jack designed, as Jack wanted things to look weightless, or seamless or have hidden things." He explained that the old blacksmith, whom Dickon referred to as just "Sooty," was forever making small items to Jack's specifications. "Sooty loved the fold-back hinges so much so that he made many of them for the house. Most doors in the house now use them."

Rick knew Jack was skilled with his hands; he had often seen him fix broken things at *Roseneath*. Even the Morse code tapper was brilliant.

All these inventions had been why Rick settled on an engineering scholarship under the joint name of Princhester-Lockley. As it was also Rick's name, no one questioned the reason; however, the scholarship's paperwork included a complete account of the reasoning behind the endowment's title. Each awardee would receive an explanation of the scholarship. Rick chuckled, sure that few, if any, would ever read it.

Rick had it all figured out, honouring his Uncle Ed's first Emporium; his father, Wills', gold finds, and then preparation for the gold boom of the colony; Uncle Luke's involvement in discovering diamonds, as well as being one of the first students at the university; the two mineral finds at the instigation of Reverend William Clarke. Then, of course, Uncle Charlie, now the Earl, Viceroy, and innkeeper. He'd taken the reins from Rick's Grandfather, Charles Lockley, once a convict, then an Earl. The Lockley name addition was to honour all that the extended family had done for the colony. There was no public announcement of what that was; many already knew. His grandfather had changed the entire Empire by revitalising and pushing the Reform Bill in the House of Lords. This allowed men throughout the Empire to vote. Charles Lockley, 3rd Earl of Coxheath, was a name Rick wanted to be remembered for all time; this way, it would be.

His Uncle Charlie, the 4th Earl, now held the family together. His friend, Jim Leslie, had always been there for him when needed, serving as a confidante. Jim was required for that purpose less frequently now. He was busy training horses for Rick's Uncle Harry at Emu Plains.

Rick missed seeing Jim and Conny regularly, but they still came for family celebrations. Rick remembered many happy hours standing on the slip rails in Jim's training yard, watching him with the beautiful, great horses he trained. Only a few years earlier, he had watched Jim break in a stallion while being watched by some of Jim's poet friends. A man who called himself 'Banjo' Patterson was one, and his friend, Harry 'Breaker' Morant, was another. They watch Jim's skills in utter silence.

The wider family continued to walk the path towards the future. It was one of progress, but one in which all could participate. If a person's job were going to be made obsolete due to a proposed development, they would be retrained and placed in another job of their choice, typically with a pay rise and a better position. If they refused, the family would put the project on hold or change the venue.

Rick's mind flicked back to what Parramatta had been like when he was little. Emu Plains, too, was now vastly different.

"Change, he hated it." Yet, Rick smiled; he thought back to Jack. Rick remembered a conversation with Jack about things he would try to change in the world.

Jack's reply was, "Other than going right back to the beginning and refusing to let the fall in the Garden of Eden happen in the first place, I would change a few things here and there. I may even marry Elouise again because it set me on this road. And lad, I met you; that was worth it all. But Rick, I'd love to make people stand in the sunshine, make them all notice the green things all around them and get everyone to share the load and work together."

Rick thought back to Jack's words, and they brought a tear to his eye. Jack had continued, "The power of people is strong, lad, we could change the world and work together for the future; if only we would all work together, our dreams could take us all down that future road, all working towards the same goal." Jack had then laughed. "Oh, but, Rick, life is about having fun, and this could be such a fun ship that we're on. We've been down this road together, and we have sailed down the river of friendship. You have your life in front of you. Take a look at your own little girl and boy; let their dreams carry them along life's path. Support them as they dream, as your family have done with you."

Rick remembered that Jack had looked him in the eye and said, "But Rick, never stop speaking to the sky." Rick never had. He prayed every day, and he taught his family to do likewise.

Chapter 21 Epilogue
Spring 1884

 hree-year-old Jax ran across the lawn at *Roseneath*, closely followed by his older cousins Jack and Danny.

Jack stopped as he turned the corner and stood looking at an oversized cane chair on the verandah, memories flooding over him.

Rick watched his son as the lad's face melted into tears. He watched the seven-year-old bite his top lip, trying hard not to cry. He failed.

Jack turned to go, but his eyes were so full of tears that he tripped and lay on the grass weeping, his shoulders shaking with sobs.

Rick walked to the prostrated lad and laid a gentle hand on his heaving shoulder. He picked him up.

"Why did Just Jack have to die, Papa?" Jack asked when he snuggled into his father's arms.

Rick brushed the boy's wayward hair back from his forehead, then thumbed away the tears as they continued to fall. "Let's go and sit in Just Jack's chair, and I'll tell you about him." He kept his eye on the two other small boys playing in the yard.

Rick and Bette were visiting their parents, Wills and Cathy, with their families. The children delighted in a different garden to play in. Kitten and Jack both remembered the happy times spent with Just Jack on the verandah at *Roseneath*.

Rick took little Jack and went to sit on the beloved cane chair, explaining death and Heaven to the small boy.

"Can we say Just Jack's prayer, please, Papa?" He put his hands together and bowed his head.

Rick wasn't sure exactly which prayer he meant, so he asked the lad to start them off.

The small head nodded, and in a serious voice, he started the prayer with his hands together. "Our Father which art in Heaven, hallowed be thy name. Thy kingdom come, Thy will be done in earth, as it is in Heaven. Give us this day our daily bread. And forgive us our debts as we forgive our debtors. And lead us not into temptation, but deliver us from evil: For thine is the kingdom, and the power, and the glory, forever. Amen."

As they said the prayer together, Rick's mind went back to that first night together around the fire on the billabong bank near Goulburn.

Jack told him to speak to the sky often. Rick had looked puzzled. Jack had explained, "It's prayer, Rick. God is everywhere and in everything; speak to Him as though you are speaking to a friend, and Rick, sing. Make a joyful noise to God." Jack then proceeded to lie down on his swag and sing hymns of glory to God.

Rick sat talking about Just Jack to his son, named in his honour.

The little boy sat, flicking the cane ties on the chair. He was full of questions about Heaven, which Rick endeavoured to answer.

Edward sat quietly, listening to them on a bench seat just down the verandah. The two other little boys were playing with Brodie, who was now watching them. Edward had intended to spend half his time here and half in England, but after he and Bette had built their new home, they had no desire to return. It had been a topic of conversation regularly, as she felt it was time for them to head back. He kept hesitating. For the first time in his life, Edward was totally content. He turned as he heard the door close and noticed his beloved wife coming towards him. He put out his hand and drew her to him. She was expecting again. Their daughter, Catherine Amelia, fondly known as Kat, had celebrated her first birthday in May. Kat would soon be out playing after her nap. His heart still jumped whenever he saw Bette. She was his heart's desire. She completed him. He reached out his hand to her.

Mary Lou had realised that it was very quiet outside. She went to investigate. What she saw made her stop and smile. Her husband was sitting in Jack's old cane chair, cuddling their eldest son. She had seen Danny and Jax head to the stables with Brodie and knew they would be feeding the horses; both were obsessed with them. Kitten and Debby were with their grandparents. She strolled to Rick and Jack. Both heard her arrival and smiled as she drew close. She reached out and brushed Jack's hair from his eyes.

The child reached up and took her hand, holding it to his cheek. The eyes of her son looked up at her trustingly. He was no longer crying. "Mummy, Papa is telling me about Heaven. Did you know that when our bodies die, like Just Jack's, we will go to Heaven? It's the promise that Jesus made to us. Papa was telling me about the pathway Jesus made for us so we can reach Him. And what forgiveness is."

Mary Lou bent down and kissed him before replying. "Tell me all about it, son." She pulled up a second chair and sat next to them. She sat listening to the child and his simple understanding of the pathway Jesus made for us.

Edward and Bette had their heads together, whispering.

Rick could hear them murmuring, but not the words they were saying. He looked at them, puzzled. After nearly three years in Parramatta, Rick was expecting to hear they would be returning to England any time, and his heart was heavy. He didn't want her to leave. He saw Edward stand and assist her up.

Mary Lou saw a wave of fear pass across Rick's face. She gave his shoulder a gentle squeeze to comfort him. As Edward and Bette arrived beside them, Rick inhaled and held his breath.

"Rick, Mary Lou, we want to have a little chat," Edward said.

Bette saw the heart-crushing look Rick gave Mary Lou. She placed her hand lovingly on her brother's shoulder.

"No, Ricky, it's not what you think! Don't string it out, Ed." Bette almost sounded excited.

Edward was grinning. "We thought you'd like to know we're staying." He slid his arm around Bette's shoulders. "I can't imagine anywhere better to bring up our family. I have everything here I could ever want, and I have no home back there. Here we have our *Rhapsody Retreat.*" He bent and lovingly kissed Bette's forehead. "I thought you might be happy."

Exhaling quickly, Rick lifted Jack off his knee and suggested that he join the other boys. As the four adults watched him run off, Rick turned to Edward and pulled him into his arms after looking him in the eye for a moment. "I'm so thrilled! Absolutely blooming well, heart-throbbingly thrilled!" The look of absolute joy on his face showed his delight.

Edward was shaking with laughter, as was Bette.

Rick pulled back and looked at them both. "What's so funny?"

"Neither of you has asked why we're staying," Edward said, still smiling.

"Well? Are you going to keep us in suspense?" Mary Lou asked.

Bette's reply was to rub her stomach. "We think it could be twins."

Edward once again drew her to him. "We saw the doctor yesterday, and he thinks that there are kicks in two places. We want our children brought up here, Rick. Edward and I don't want them tainted with the shallowness of society in England. So, we're staying."

Edward turned to his wife, lifted her chin, and kissed her briefly.

She went to wrap an arm around his neck.

Rick said, "Oh, get a room, Bette! We're on the verandah. Have some restraint." Rick chuckled.

As he spoke, Edward released her. He replied cheekily, "We did that already, hence twins."

Rick leaned over and kissed his beloved sister himself.

Edward chuckled, "We have a room, Rick, and it's well used."

Mary Lou gathered her sister-in-law into a big hug. "It looks like we're due together, after all, Bette." Mary Lou pulled her gown tight over her stomach and showed her growing bump.

The two ladies giggled.

"I'm twice the size, Mary Lou," Bette stated the obvious. She was already complaining that she waddled.

Wills and Cathy joined their youngest children on the verandah. Each had a child in hand.

Edward related all their news to them, and another round of hugs ensued from his in-laws.

~

Later that evening, after the family dinner, Rick stood on the verandah at *Roseneath* watching the sunset, Jack's words fresh in his mind. More of his words came to mind. "Speak to the sky, lad, as often as you can." Tonight, Rick had much to give thanks for. He had just heard of the delivery of Jonty and Lottie's third child. His father had passed on the information over tea.

They had all stayed for the evening meal at *Roseneath*, and from there, they could see the sunset. Rick missed sunsets at his new house, *Princhester Close*, in Charles Street, as it faced east.

Mary Lou came and stood next to him, putting her arm on his. He didn't take his eyes from the beautiful sunset, but he slid his arm along her shoulder. Eventually, he said, "You know, Mary Lou, when I left here twelve years ago, I meant what I said; I left my heart with you. I only found it when I came back and saw you standing waiting for me on the Gunning platform. In all that time, it was like I was holding my breath. You were never far from my mind, hence all the letters. Your mother was correct; we were made for each other. I had hoped you would wait for me, but I admit there was some doubt. You, my darling, are just too beautiful." He turned and took her entirely in his arms, but didn't kiss her. He stood looking down at her violet eyes in the fading light. "Then, when you nearly died having the twins, my heart stopped for a time. I didn't want to live without you, my sweet love."

She felt the tears on his cheeks. One fell onto her as she looked up at the wonderful man who had stolen her heart when they were just children. "You carried my heart with you every step of your journey, my Ricky dearest. When I had the twins, I heard you when you kept telling me to fight and be strong. I did; I fought as hard as I could. You called me back and I came home to you." She reached up and thumbed a tear away as it rolled down his clean-shaven face. "I, too, would be lost without you." She kissed him. "Ricky, my darling, I knew that if I didn't make it, we would be together in Heaven. As one day we will be, but I don't want that to be for many, many years."

He drew her to him, and they stood locked in each other's arms. Both were lost in thought, and they were facing the setting sun. Each, however, thinking of Jack and with their cheeks together, they watched the sunset.

The golden orb finally sank behind the line of the Blue Mountains, setting the sky alight with a splash of vibrant colour on the evening clouds.

Only then did Rick release Mary Lou. He cupped her face and gently kissed her.

Jack, the wonderful and jolly swagman, turned out to be a titled gentleman. Owner of a magnificent estate and adored adopted grandfather for their children. He had discovered the riches of the world were not material possessions but love, joy, and friendship. He had his shared faith and found his freedom. He gave up the earthly trappings and lived the free life of a swagman.

Rick looked forward to the day he would see him in Heaven. What a joyous reunion that would be.

The last story in the Lockleys of Parramatta series
is Lottie and Jonty's story (Luke's daughter)
Jonty's Journey.
His adventures in Africa were life-changing for both of them.

Jonty's Journey completes the 100-year saga of the Lockley family,
but many of them appear in my other books.

In memory of the wonderful Judith Durham

*The writing of this story
was inspired by the lyrics of twenty of The Seekers' songs.*

Behind the story

As my husband and I travel the roads in retirement, we listen to some amazing music. One of our favourites is The Seekers' Albums. As we travelled in 2021 in the Rockhampton area in Queensland, we passed Princhester Creek. As I'm always on the lookout for names, I decided that this was a good one. Then, I needed a story to go with it. We had The Seekers playing, and I thought of the Mama Mia movie and the ABBA songs; the story fell together quickly, and the rest is history.

As I edit this story, the sad news has been released that Judith Durham's carnival is over, and she has passed away. She was a voice in a million and will never be forgotten.

This story is a THANK YOU to The Seekers for their wonderful and inspirational music.

The Twenty "Seekers" songs that inspired the story.

Goodbye, Mary Lou	After church on Sunday
It's hard to leave	Packing to go
Morning town ride	On the train going south
Speak to the sky (prayer)	Jack finds Rick at Billabong.
It doesn't matter anyway,	Jack re Elouise
With a swag upon my shoulder	Travelling as a swagman
I wish you could be here	Rick missing Mary Lou
The Bush Girl	Mary Lou, missing Rick
Colours of My life	On the way home
Gotta Love Somebody	
Amazing	Meeting Mary Lou at Gunning
Rattler	Returning home on train
Tomorrow isn't long enough	The wedding and honeymoon
A world of our own	
Circle of Love	
Guardian Angel	Jack dying
Love is Kind, Love is wise	In England
Carnival is over	Leaving England - streamers
I'll never find another you	Back in Parramatta
Future Road	The end

Characters

Charles John Lockley b 1800 d Easter '70 son of John Lockley m1 Elizabeth (**Elle**) Staverly d 1855 m2 **Richard** Childs d 1855
m Feb 1820 Sarah (**Sal**/ **Sally**) Shannon McCarthy
    #1**Charlie** John b **Nov 1820** m Nov 1841 **Gracie Miller** b 1823 4th Earl Coxheath
        #1 Edward (**Teddie**) William b 26/9/44 twin – Viscount Lockley
        m 15/8/64 **Bella** Winslow-Smythe 7 children – move to 'Princhester Court'
        7 children (incl 2 sets twins)
        #2 **John** Charles 26/9/44;
        m **Sara Joy Harlow** b 7/1/47 m 1867. 4 children
        #3 Emily (**Emma**) b 25 Aug 46m Dec 1869 **George** Ellison b1844
        #4 **Molly Grace** b 1850 m Oct 69 **Henry** William Harlow b Oct 16, 48
    #2 **Eddie** (Edward John) b 16/10/1821
m Dec 4 1841 Jennifer (**Jenna**) Martha Turner
        #1 **Edward** (**Neddie**) Charles Gerald and b **15 Aug 1842**
        m Jan 1864 **Miriam** Evans 6 children
        #2 Christina (**Tina**) Sarah Martha. b 15 Aug 1842
        m Mar 1859 Charles (**Chip) Lockley 11th Duke of Gracemere**
            #1 Charles John Edward (**CJ**) Dec 5, 1862 twin
            #2 Christina Susanna (**Christie**) Dec 5, 1862 twin
            m 1882 Stephen (**Steve**) William Hunt b 51(Edmund's 2nd son)
            #3 **Gerald** Albert James b Nov 1863
            #4 Elizabeth (**Liza**) Sarah b Oct 1866
            #5 **James** Charles March 1868 twin
            #6 Constance (**Coco**) Marie March 1868 twin
        #3 Jennifer Annabella Elizabeth (**Lily**) 13/4/45
        m 15/8/64 William (**Liam**) Lockley (Ned's)
        #4 26 Christopher William (**Kit**) Jan 1847 reverend in Kent UK
        m 15/8/64 Lady Charlotte (**Charl**) Lockley 26/1/47   7 children
        #5 Nicholas (**Nick**)Calum 2/3/49;
        #6 **Shannon** Mary 1/10/50
        #7 Victoria (**Toria**) b1852;
        #8 **Henry** Charles b 1853
        #9 **Phillip** John b 6th Dec 1856;
        #10 Ruth Alexandra (**Ruthie**) b 6th Dec 1856
    #3 (**Liza**) Elizabeth Shannon **b 1823** m 1841 **Bertie Ellis** – Saddler
    4 children
    #4 (**Anna**) Susanna Grace b **1824** m 1842 **Tim Miller** politician and lawyer
    4 children
    #5 William (**Wills) Wentworth Lockley** b 20/4 /**1826**
m 14/2/1845 **Cathy Turner**
        #1 **Luke** Henry William, b14 Jan 47
        #2 Phillip (**Pip**)Charles; Sept 48,
        #3 Catherine Victoria Matilda (**Tilda**) 3/3/50
        m 1874 **William** George Miller b 50
        #4 Aurelia Lucy (**Goldie**) b 6 July 51
        m 1872 **Alfred** Evans (Phil's son - Mary Lou's brother)
        #5 Richard (**Rick**) Edward b 26 Oct 1855 twin
        m 25/12 1875 **Mary Louise** Evans (Phil's)
            #1 Mary Kathleen (**Kitten**) Sept 76
            #2 **Jack** William Apr 1878
            #3 Iain Daniel (**Danny**) b 7 Oct 1880
            #4 Clara Deborah (**Debby**) 7 Oct 1880
            #5 Eliz**abeth** Catherine Nov 1884
        #6 Elizabeth (**Bette**) Martha b 26 Oct 1855 twin
        m Feb 1881 **Edward** Christian Ralph Daniel Styles b 14/10/42 m aged 39
            #1 John (**Jax) Christian** Norfolk Styles b 13 Nov 1881 at sea
            #2 Catherine Amelia (**Kat**) b June 1883 in Parramatta
            #3 Edward Richard   Nov 1884 twin

#4 William Robert   Nov 1884 twin
#6 **Luke** John b **1828** (March)
m 2/8/1856 – **Ellen** Miller, b 4/10/1830;
   #1 William (**Willy**) Edward 26/4/57 triplet
   m77 Elizabeth Susanna (**Sanna) Harlow** 5/52
      #1 b Jan 78 Henry Lucas (**Hal**)
   #2 **Mary May** 26/4/57 triplets
   m 76 **Marcus** Edward **Harlow** b 2/2/50
      #1 b late 1878
   #3 Sarah (**Sally**) Elizabeth triplets 26/4/57
   m 77 **Jimmy Ant** Harlow b 56
      #1 b late 78
   #4 Charles Luke (**Carlo**) and 20 Nov 60 twins
   #5 Charlotte (**Lottie**) Elizabeth 20 Nov 60 twins
   m Dec 1882 Johnathan (**Jonty**) Evans
Thomas Tindale - b 1800   d 1870's
Margaret Tindale b 1800   d 1870's
Caroline (**Caro**) Evans - Mr Tindale's sister b1805 d 23/Oct1888
Captain **Douglas** Evans-supply ship captain   Pitt Street b 1804 d 1887
Phillip b 1819   Phil, Law   m 1845 **Alice** 4 children
   #1 **Alfred** Phillip b 1846   m 1872   Aurelia (**Goldie**) Lockley b 1851
   #2 **Phillipa** Anne b 1848   m 1874 **Mark** Butler
   #3 Douglas **George** b 1853   m 1875 **Annmarie** Seaton
   #4 Mary Louise(**MaryLou**) b 1856   m 25 Dec 1875 **Rick** Lockley b 26 Oct 1855
Stephen b 1821   Stevie   Law m 1843 **May** 5 children
   #1 **Miriam**   b 1844 - m Jan 64 **Neddie** Lockley (Eddie's) - 6 kids #6 due Jan 1876
+ 4 more
John b 1822 - loved bugs etc m 5/10/55   **Colleen** Murphy; b 25
   #1 Jonathon Finn Douglas Evans (**Jonty**) b 2/8/56 Boer war buying diamonds.
   M 1882 **Lottie** Lockley
      1 Samuel Nicholas (**Sammo**) b 17 August 1883
      2 Patricia Marie (**Patty**) b 17 August 1883
      3 Paul William b May 1887
      4 Charlotte Caroline (**Carol**) Oct 22 1888
   #2 Maureen Caroline Evans (**Reenie**) b 8 Aug 1858   m 1887 **Andrew** Rivers
   #3 William Luke John (**Blue**) b June 1860
   #4 Harriet (**Hettie**) Oct 63
   #5 Findlay (**Finn**) John b 68
   #6 **Cara** Nell b 1873
Effy - convict maid - a convict b 1816
M **Hamish Macdonald** b 1815   m 1857 **Effy** *(see above)*
   #1 Fergus (**Ferdie**) Macdonald in b Jan 1858
   #2 **Elspeth** Caroline Macdonald b Jan 59
   M 1892 **Liam** Henry Wallace
      #1 Callum b Jan 1894
Fergus Macdonald b 1813 m   mid Oct 1858 Catriona (**Katy**) McKay
   #1 **Colin** Hamish   Macdonald b July 59
   #2 **Lachlan** McKay Macdonald 61
   m 1901 **Sarah**   Grace Lockley b 73 (Charlie/John)
   #3 **Ishbelle** Catriona   July 65
   m 1886 **Liam** Poole
      1 Calum b 1887
Major Edward 'Ned' Grace b 16/10/1798 – Parramatta *(His Grace the 10th Duke of*
Gracemere. Edward John Charles Lockley of Gracemere) at Maidstone 48th Battalion
Mother Susanna Bland b – Dowager Duchess – d Nov 1856 – Gracemere House, London
m Dec 25 1841 **Christina Meadows**, née Hunt b 25'12.1808
(daug of Edmund William, Catherine Anne Earl of Riverdell. at Tunbridge Wells (Eames House
London)
      #1 Charles (**Chip**) *Edward John, Marquess Allingmere b 1 Sept 1842 then 11th Duke*
      *m Dec 5, 1861 Christina (**Tina**) Lockley b 15 Aug 1842 (Ed's daughter)*
         6 children – see Eddie Lockley

#2 **Sarah** Christina, The Lady Sarah Lockley (Sarah Joy)b 1 Sept 1842
m Dec 5, 1861 **Ant**hony Winchester
      5 children
#3 The Lord William Edmund (**Liam**) April 1845
m 15/8/64 **Lily Lockley** (Eddie)
      5 children
#4 Lady Charlotte (**Charl**) Jennifer Victoria 26/1/47-in Parramatta – twin
m 15/8/64 Christopher (**Kit**) Lockley (Eddie) (Reverend)
      7 children (quads + 3)
#5 Lady Isabella (**Izzy**) Catherine Grace. 26/1/47 twin
m 15/8/64 Edward (**Neddie**) Winslow Smythe. Future Earl 2 children

Annie White b 26 July 1773 *affair 1790 convicted 1792 served 7 years free 1797 bakery.*
Annabella Phillipa Joy White 'Pitt' arrived as a convict in 1792 died '66
m 10/1802 **Samuel** James Corbett Garney *(Lord Garney/Viscount Clarestow then 6th Earl Meldon) Meldon Hall-mother Anne Corbett – West's farm arr Royal Admiral*
1792 convict b 12/7/1773 d 15th 4/'64, Earl '30
    #1 **Daniel** (Danny) James Corbett Garney b 11/1803 Sydney Viscount
Clarestow; Earl   from
1864 d 1883 aged 80
      m1 1824 **Vanessa** Comfrey d 1831
          #1 **Jo**-anne b 1824
          #2 **Lucy**-anne – b 1826
          #3 **Mary-anne** – b 1828
          #4 **Edmund** Daniel James Garney b 29/5/1831 inherited title 1883
          m 1852 Esther (**Essie)** Black
              #1 Samuel (**Sammy**) James Garney b 1853
              # 2 **Annemarie** Amelia b 1856
      m2 2/7/1833 **Georgina** Styles -   *(Robbie's sister)*
          #1 **James** Samuel Daniel Garney b March 1834 West Sussex
          #2 Georgina Anne
          #3 Adelaide Margaret (**Meg**) m **Bobby** Pittford
          #4 **Timothy Samuel** (Military)
          #5 Sophia
          #6 Christine

Mr Timothy Styles, Sir Timothy Broome-Hall b 1767 d 1862
     m 1800 to **Sophie** 6 children
    #1 **Robert b 1803** d 1884
      m 22 Oct 1835 **Amelia** Black nee Westaweller b 1804 d 1892
          #1 Timothy (**Timmo**) Robert James Styles b 11 August 1836
          m **Elise** Graham
          #2 **Eliza** Anne Caroline Styles b 6 Nov 1839
          #3 **Edward** Christian Ralph Daniel Styles b 14/10/42 m aged 39
          m Feb 1881 **Bette** Lockley b '55 (Wills) m aged 25
              #1 John (**Jax)** Christian Norfolk Styles b 13 Nov 1881 at sea
              #2 Catherine Amelia (**Kat**) b June 1883 in Parramatta
              #3 Edward Richard Nov 1884 twin
              #4 William Robert Nov 1884 - twin
    #2 Timothy #3 **Sophia** #4 **Adam** #5 **Victoria**
    #6 **Georgina** b1814 (m 1834 **Danny Garney**)
      6 children 2 boys 4 girls

Amelia Mary West b 1804 Aylesford Kent d 1892 -see above – Amelia Black
Arrested and Convicted 1827 – aged 23 – Shipped on "Morely" 1828
m1 *Cyrus Black*
    #1 Esther (**Essie**) Martha Ruth West **Black** b 9 May 1830
    m 1852 **Edmund** Garney – Future Earl of Meldon
          #1 Samuel (**Sammy**) James Garney b 1853
          # 2 **Annemarie** Amelia Garney b 1856
m2 22 Oct 1835 **Robert Styles,** b 1803 d 1884 Baronet, Sir Robert
    #1 Timothy (**Timmo**) Robert James Styles b 11 August 1836
        m **Elise** Graham
    #2 **Eliza** Anne Caroline b 6 Nov 1839

#3 **Edward** Christian Ralph Daniel b 14/10/42 m aged 39(Delivered by Duchess Christina)

      m Feb 1881 **Bette** Lockley b '55 (Wills) m aged 25
            #1 **Jack (Jax) Christian** Styles b 13 Nov 1881 at sea
            #2 Catherine Amelia (**Kat**) b 1884 in Sydney
            #3 & #4 twins

Swagman Travels
Bronwyn and Dylan Davies, blacksmith in Goulburn
Daniel Jones the stationmaster

Jack the Swagman. Sir John Princhester b 24/6/1800 d April 1880 (aged 80) –
    arr Christmas 1877 to Rick's - Jack's mother was Jane Buckingham, father Phillip Princhester)
m **Elouise Wickham/Gracemere** – Dowager Duchess of Gracemere in 1843 (Jack aged 43)
Mr Tyzzer the boot maker in Melbourne - Mary Wallace's father
Jock and Mary Wallace, Ballarat blacksmith
1878 trip to London
Rick, Mary Lou, Kitten and young Jack
Luke and Ellen, Carlo and Lottie Lockley
Mattie Saunders – cousin 3 kids **Margaret, Jem and Molly**
Gracemere Castle, Kent
Reg Hawkins – Chip's Estate manager at *Gracemere Castle*
Bartholomew Walters- Chip's Lawyer
Princhester House London
Giles Branwhite – butler
Princhester Court staff Aylesford
Jonas O'Neill
father **Brian** O'Neill -Estate Manager/s
Daniel Quinn – Farm manager at Princhester Court
Tom Hammond – Stable manager
Basil and **Hazel** Hawthorne - Butler & Housekeeper
Lloyd Cartwright – Gatekeeper – *Princhester Court*
Dickon – the gardener – Jack's friend
Lockley/Saunders connection
George and Esther Staverly (3rd Earl, Charles Lockley's grandparents)
2 children – twin girls
#1 **Elizabeth Staverly** m John Lockley – 2nd Earl of Coxheath
    #1 **Charles** m Sarah (**Sally**) McCarthy
        # 6 children
    #2 Elizabeth (**Lilabet**) m **Matthew** Watkins-Harlow
        *(**Bella's** uncle - Matthew's sister was Bella's mother)*
#2 **Emily** m **Mark Saunders** – Baron
    #1 John m **Elspeth** Bland (Else) 22/8/1846 (the duke's cousin)
        3 children
***Mark Saunders** had 1 brother, **John (Jack) Saunders** - storekeeper in Hawkesbury River NSW*
    *#1 James (**Jim**) Saunders (shot by Bushranger Gilbert)*
    *m **Mattie** Paul*
        *3 children **Margaret**, James(**Jem)** and **Molly** Sunders*

Gracemere/Lockley Tree

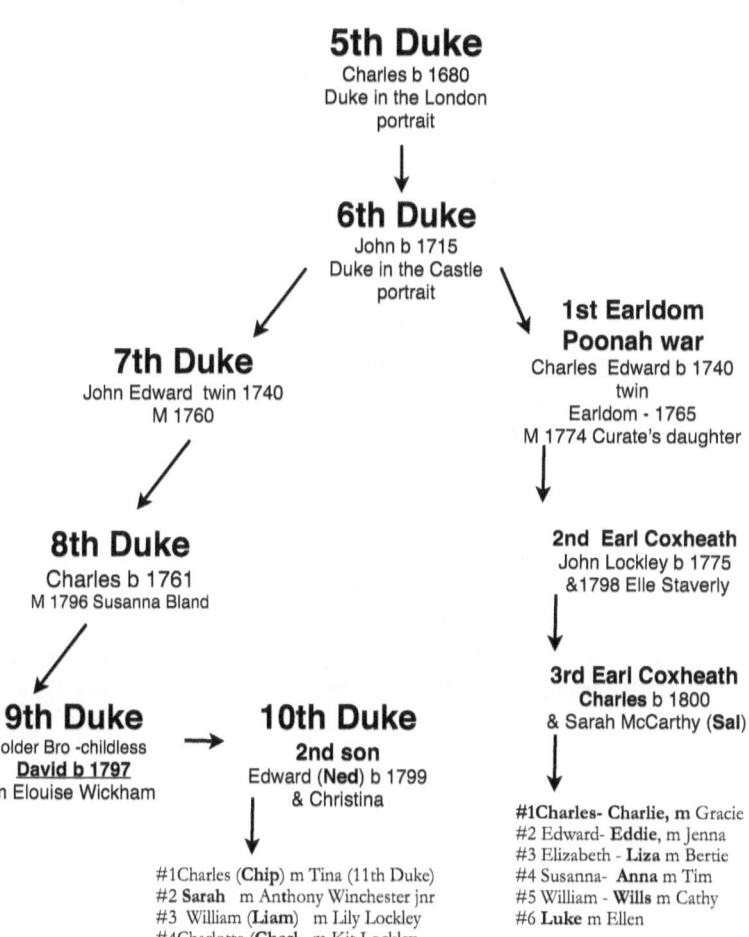

5th Duke
Charles b 1680
Duke in the London
portrait

6th Duke
John b 1715
Duke in the Castle
portrait

7th Duke
John Edward twin 1740
M 1760

**1st Earldom
Poonah war**
Charles Edward b 1740
twin
Earldom - 1765
M 1774 Curate's daughter

8th Duke
Charles b 1761
M 1796 Susanna Bland

2nd Earl Coxheath
John Lockley b 1775
&1798 Elle Staverly

3rd Earl Coxheath
Charles b 1800
& Sarah McCarthy (**Sal**)

9th Duke
older Bro -childless
David b 1797
m Elouise Wickham

10th Duke
2nd son
Edward (**Ned**) b 1799
& Christina

#1Charles- **Charlie, m** Gracie
#2 Edward- **Eddie,** m Jenna
#3 Elizabeth - **Liza** m Bertie
#4 Susanna- **Anna** m Tim
#5 William - **Wills** m Cathy
#6 **Luke** m Ellen

#1Charles (**Chip**) m Tina (11th Duke)
#2 **Sarah** m Anthony Winchester jnr
#3 William (**Liam**) m Lily Lockley
#4Charlotte (**Charl** m Kit Lockley
#5 Isabella (**Izzy**) m Ned Winslow Smythe

Bibliography

'**Australian Daughters**' poem by Robert Wisdom
http://www.australianculture.org/australias-daughters-robert-wisdom-1856/

Trove story of **Horse accident** – 1875 in Gundagai
https://trove.nla.gov.au/newspaper/article/122751703

Welcome Stranger Gold Nugget
https://en.wikipedia.org/wiki/Welcome_Stranger

51 lots for sale George, Macquarie & Charles Sts Parramatta 9/82
Land sale and hospital opening September 1882.
https://trove.nla.gov.au/newspaper/article/107998031?
searchTerm=house%20%20sale%2C%20%22parramatta%22

Old Kings school
https://en.wikipedia.org/wiki/Old_King%27s_School,_Parramatta

Reverend William B Clarke Obit.
https://trove.nla.gov.au/newspaper/article/13419078?
searchTerm=Reverend%20WB%20Clarke

First Fleet Convict Era Trilogy 1788-1800

Gentle Annie Soames

Her dreams lead to unexpected outcomes. An Australian First Fleet story.

A First Fleet story with the descriptions taken directly from the Journal of Doctor Arthur Bowes Smith was the doctor on board the Lady Penrhyn.

Annie Soames is a girl beloved by the community but not afraid to voice her desires. That leads to trouble, illicit love, and a world turned upside down.

Oliver Quilpie, the newly married Marquess, finds his arranged marriage unsatisfactory; he is irresistibly drawn to his wife's companion. Unfortunately, he can't keep his hands off her. In retaliation, Annie copies his every move while riding, dressed as a highwayman. However, she has now fallen in love with him. This ultimately leads to her arrest and banishment to a distant land.

After some years, Oliver's wife dies, and his thoughts turn to Annie. He seeks to find her, but she has vanished. He is horrified to discover she was transported to New South Wales as a convict on the *Lady Penrhyn.* Will Annie want to see him?

ISBN 9780645441574   ISBN ebook 9781923097063   LP ISBN 9781923097346
https://mybook.to/GentleAnnieSoames

Long-listed in the Historical Fiction Company Competition 2024

The Emancipated Potter

Sydney Cove 1788 to Parramatta 1795
Not all felons are convicts, and not all convicts are felons.

Colin Osborne's serene life as a talented potter is crushed by a self-important peer. A single punch sends Colin across to the other side of the globe.

Aggie Gibbs is a young convict girl being hunted by a wayward soldier. The two find themselves in a town of criminals and lecherous men.

Captain John Hunter is Colin's mentor, and he paves the way for a new life for his young friends. Then disaster strikes, and he must leave.

Can Colin keep Aggie safe? Will they fulfil Captain Hunter's wishes to build a decent life for the convicts destined to live out their lives in the penal town? Will John ever return to New South Wales? Paperback ISBN 9781923097476   ISBN ebook 9781923097483

Paternity Unknown

Sydney 1788 - 1800 The Aftermath of the First Fleet landing.
Can forgiveness be that easy?

Connie Waterson is traumatised after she became one of the victims of the attack when the convict women were landed on February 6th, 1788. She finds herself expecting an unwanted child. Along with her friends, she must learn to cope with the challenges of their new environment while protecting the life growing within her.

Nigel Bray is a young convict who almost instantly regrets his carnal actions on the day the prisoners from the *Lady Penrhyn* landed. Knowing that Connie is the unwilling recipient of his base desires, Nigel does what he can to ease her path. He is racked with questions: is the child his? Will she ever forgive him? What must Nigel do to win Connie's trust?

ISBN 9781923097438   ISBN ebook 9781923097445   LP ISBN 9781923097452

The Hunter to Macquarie Collection 1795-1822

When Upon Life's Billows

Sydney 1795-1821 - Governor John Hunter
Keep your friends close, and your enemies closer.

John Hunter loved his life at sea. The wind blows where no man knows, and John is caught in a storm. His ship, the *HMS Sirius,* was wrecked in 1790. Five years later, he became the second governor of the rough and filthy penal settlement of New South Wales. From a place he once loved, he now seems to be in the wrong place at the wrong time, trusting the wrong people.

Helena Rosedale is not your typical female convict. She fiercely battles to prevent the men from abusing her, earning her the nickname *"Helena the Hellcat."*

Crispin Milroy, alone in the world, serves on the new governor's security detail. Can he win the fair lady's heart? Life in 1795 in Sydney Cove was harsh at best. Food is scarce, and disease often ravages the settlement. Life throws everything at these three, yet somehow, they manage to survive. Why does John trust this young couple when others betray him? What trials must Helena and Crispin endure to make their new lives in this unforgiving town bearable? How can John ease their path?

ISBN: 9780645783339   ebook ISBN: 9780645783346

The Saddler's Song
London 1790s to Parramatta 1840s
The Strains of Starting Again.

George Ellis is the son of a tanner, living on the outskirts of London. Alone and hurting after a disease takes his family, he seeks a new life, setting up a business in New South Wales. His beloved violin is his most treasured possession, and his talent for making music is hidden from all but a select few.

Ben Parker, a saddler, is also heading to the colony. Combining their skills to start afresh in a new world, the young men find accommodation with a family. Two of the daughters steal their hearts — but how will the business survive in a stock-starved land where access to leather is limited? What is the saddler's song, and why is it so special?

ISBN: 9780645783353   eISBN: 9780645783360

Tuppence to Pass
London 1800s to Parramatta 1820s
An Unlikely Partnership

Josh Callan is a London lad making the best of the life dealt to him. Stealing from the man who killed his father, Josh gets arrested. The judge belittles him, saying he is not worth tuppence. Transported to the penal colony of Sydney, Josh arrives at the commencement of Governor Lachlan Macquarie's term.

Life in the Colonial town opens opportunities Josh could never have dreamed about and soon proves his worth to the Governor, becoming his confidante.

Can Josh find his niche? Where will this strange friendship take Josh and his family?

ISBN : 9781923097070   eISBN: 9781923097087

His Majesty's Pageboy
London to Emu Plains, Australia, in the 1800s

Jack Turner was born into a life of pomp and privilege that was not rightfully his. He was brought to the royal court for his protection. By the age of ten, he served as King George III's pageboy and was known as Lord John. For years, he struggled against society's immorality and people's shallowness; then, he met an unspoiled young girl whose purity stood out amidst the mire of humanity. He is unable to pursue her before his life hits a wall.

Martha Alexander is the daughter of a wealthy shipping merchant. She has been presented to London's second tier of society, where she meets the young man of her dreams. She is expected to marry well, and Lord John sets her heart fluttering. However, her father's drinking shatters her future. He was made to sign all his possessions away while drunk, unknowingly including his daughter. Refusing a forced marriage changes her life. How did these two young people end up as convicts in Australia?

Paperback ISBN 9781923097308   eISBN 978192309792
Coming 2026

A Fist Full of Holey Dollars
Sydney Cove 1810+

Captain **Rudi Greenwood** is a solitary man trapped in a job without a purpose in a land where alcohol is the currency and rules are frequently ignored in the pursuit of wealth.

Bethany Edwards is a grieving widow expecting her late husband's child. Rudi's attraction to the lovely widow compels him to reassess his views and contemplate someone new. She seeks Rudi's help and support, but is that all she truly feels?

When **Governor Lachlan Macquarie** asks Rudi for help improving the roads, a casual remark alters Rudi's life and affects the entire colony. To tackle the alcohol issue, he proposes creating a new currency. With Bethany by his side, will he rise to the governor's challenges? What actions led to him being despised by the exclusives and free settlers in the colony?   Paperback ISBN 9781923097407   eISBN 9781923097414
Coming 2026

Far From the Whispering Sheoaks
Set in Australia in 1817+

Fanny Little was in the wrong place doing something she thought was legal. Her actions led to her arrest, trial, and banishment. She was assigned from the female prison to ex-soldier Gordon McKenzie and soon found herself in the despicable and humiliating situation of being sold in the public marketplace.

Phil Bentley is a man running from his jealous uncle. He is seeking safety on a secluded farm half a world away. With the community backing them, can Phil save Fanny from Gordon's vile abuse? Why is their relationship destined to spark controversy? And who is Jas? Why does Gordon wish to harm the child? Will they ever escape the shadows pursuing them?

Paperback ISBN 9781923097315   eISBN9781923097322
Coming 2026

Bound Down in Iron Chains

An Australian Historical Tale, set in the Boys' Orphanage in Sydney in 1818+
Smuggling, Rum and Ructions

Howard Marlow is a studious and honest London bookkeeper. When asked to help a friend's brother with his bookkeeping, he unknowingly helps a crime gang. He is arrested, convicted, and transported. On arrival, Howard is assigned to the boy's orphanage, where a possibly crooked soldier is in charge. He is asked to use his skills to decipher bookkeeping entries that make no sense. He discovers his love for the affection-starved boys at the orphanage.

Naomi Buckingham, a convict girl, is thrust into the harsh reality of the orphanage alongside Howard. She is assigned to the orphanage, but it is far from the refuge she had hoped for. The supervisor is a man who does not respect women. With no one to rely on but the new accountant, she grapples with the question of trust.

Naomi is the key to breaking the bookkeeping code and cracking the case wide open. Can Howard use his brains to save them both? How do they become involved with some of the worst criminals in the New South Wales penal colony?

Paperback ISBN 9781923097353   eISBN9781923097360
Coming 2026

Unlikely Convict Ladies Trilogy 1792-1840s

Dancing to Her Own Tune

Co-authored by Sheila Hunter and Sara Powter
Sydney 1790s to England 1830s

Annie White is released after serving seven years as a convict in Sydney. She has a visitor who helps her start a baking business. Annie is then asked to assist another ailing man, **Sam Corbett**. She nurses him back to health, and a relationship blossoms between them. They settle into a life together, barely making ends meet, when she realises she's expecting a child. Sam's past is laid bare, and he must come to terms with the revelations. They both must confront their accusers and discover that the answers to their questions are not what they anticipated. Their life experiences seem to cling to them, and, unable to shake them off, they end up back in England. They must face their ghosts and recognise they are not who they think they are. How can they transform their anger and spite into love and forgiveness? The Dance of Life goes on.

ISBN 9780645110715   ISBN9780645110722

Long-listed for the Historical Fiction Company Competition 2022

Amelia's Tears

Parramatta 1828 – England 1840s
From Tears of Sadness to Tears of Joy.

Amelia Westaweller awaits her assignment in the Parramatta Female Prison. Forced to leave the relative safety of gaol, she is assigned and now faces her worst nightmare. A foul man claims her and makes her life a living hell. Then, her world goes black. A glimmer of hope arises when she hears from her brother, Jim, who has enlisted a friend to help her. She writes to Jim, pouring out her heart and telling him of the horrors of her new life. He encourages her to stay firm in her faith. All she can do is pray. When Major **Ned Grace**, her brother's friend, enters her life in Parramatta, he starts to ease her path. Things have changed, as now she has a child in tow. How can Amelia forge a new life for herself? What man could want her with her background and a child at her side? Who is the gentleman who turns her tears of sadness into tears of great joy?

ISBN: 9780645110739   eISBN: 9780645110746 Hard Cover ISBN 9798420617953

A Lady in Irons

England 1800s Parramatta 1808+

Katy Harrington is mourning the death of her husband after he died in a shooting accident. Barely coping, she awaits the birth of their child. If it's a girl, she must hand the family home to her husband's brother. The day after giving birth to a daughter, she and her daughter are left on the side of a road. She collapses and is found by someone she thought had died in a fire ten years before. **Perry White**, badly scarred himself, nurses her back to health. They marry and move in with her widowed friend, Mary.

After some years, she discovers her husband and friend in each other's arms. Now living in a love triangle, she flees. Grasping the only straw available, she intentionally gets arrested and is sent to a colony far away. By doing this, her marriage can be annulled.

What happens in the Colony is different from what she expects. Governor Macquarie comes to her rescue, but what of Perry and her children?

ISBN: 9780645110784   eISBN:9780645441505

NO MORE, MY *Love*

Hunter Valley, N.S.W, 1820s

Jess Elkin is distraught when tragedy ravages her family. Now widowed, she becomes the victim of a carriage accident and is nursed back to health by the driver.

Marcus Ryan, a hard-headed woollen mill owner, was not expecting to fall in love. Yet, when Jess's fortunes suddenly turn for the worse, Marcus must decide how far he will go to pursue her. Years after following her to Newcastle, Australia, Marcus vanishes. Jess is left wondering if he will keep his promise to return to her… Will she ever see him again?

ISBN: 9780645441536   eISBN 9780645441581

Long-listed in the Historical Fiction Company Competition 2023

The Vine Weaver

Hawkesbury River area 1820s+
New Beginnings and Old Threats

In the 1820s, **Joel and Hetty Walker** lived on a secluded farm on the Hawkesbury River, which became a haven for the protection of young convict women. A series of events brings **Fran Rea** to Hetty's attention, and she is taken to the farm. Fran and Hetty develop a cottage industry under the compassionate eye of farmhand **Hector Macdougal;** Hector's loving words change lives. It is to him that Fran turns when threatened.

The vines now must draw them close to survive the future revelations, and of those, there are many.

ISBN: 9780645441512   eISBN: 9780645441529

Long-listed in the Historical Fiction Company Competition 2023

https://amazon.com/dp/0645441511   https://amazon.com/dp/B0C6Z552Y2

The story continues in "Scotch at The Rocks"…

Scotch at The Rocks

Glasgow, Scotland, early 1800s to The Rocks, Sydney 1830s

Orphaned children Brodie Stewart and Heather Anderson live on Glasgow's streets. Although hungry, they somehow manage to survive and stay out of trouble. Heather finds a job and looks to be settled; things go pear-shaped for them both. Eventually, they marry by declaration, but even that gets complicated, and they are both arrested soon after exchanging their vows. In 1838, they were transported to Sydney as convicts. Heather arrives within weeks of Brodie, and they are assigned close to each other. They are now living in the docklands of Sydney, known as The Rocks. They now have to forge a new life halfway across the world from their homeland.

Adventures abound, and Brodie gets press-ganged. While he's away, Heather's life changes and soon, she's officially selling Scotch Whisky at a shop in The Rocks.

You can take a Scot out of Scotland, but where did the Scotch come from?

ISBN 9780645441550 ebook 9781923097001 Large Print 9781923097254

https://mybook.to/ScotchatTheRocks

Waiting at the Sliprails

The Bathurst Road 1830s

A Convict's Tale

Bea Dawes's term of conviction nears an end, and she has few options other than marriage to a stranger or going on the street.

Jack Barnes, the hired drover, wants a wife. Bea accepts his offer; then, she discovers that he could be gone for months, leaving her alone with **Billy and Netty**, part of the tribe of an Aboriginal tribe who live on his secluded farm. Bea learns to love her husband and also this wonderful Aboriginal couple. Drought ravages the farm, and Jack must hit the long paddock with the flock. In his absence, a visitor arrives, threatening to destroy everything she has worked so hard for. Can Bea touch her heart? Can she cope? Will the drought ever end? And when will Jack return?

ISBN: 9780645441543   eISBN: 9781923097032

https://mybook.to/WaitingattheSliprails

PenCraft Award Winner for Literary Excellence
Christian Historical Fiction 2024

Convict Shadows of the Past

Two Jennifers, two hundred years apart

When she discovers her convict family history, eight-year-old Jenny Kellow learns that she was named after a convict from nearly two hundred years ago. Inspired by her grandfather's stories, she delves into her ancestors' convict past. From him, she hears tales of bushrangers, convicts, and life in the early colony of Parramatta. She embarks on a journey to retrace the footsteps of her convict great-great-great-grandmother to honour her. Jenny's quest begins with microfiche in the 1960s, where she discovers a small tin mining town in Cornwall and the production of a cheese that set London alight. She uncovers that her ancestor, **Jennifer Kellow,** brought her cheese-making skills to Parramatta, where she taught others the craft. Echoes of the past can still be heard if you know where to listen. Who was the first Jennifer, and what does she have to do with cheese? Why is she so elusive? Did Jenny's ancestor, Jennifer, ever see those two small crosses carved into the bricks of the Female Factory? Would Jenny ever uncover her ancestor's story? ISBN: 9780645783315
ISBN ebook 9780645783322

A NaNoWriMo 2022 book winner

In Defence of Her Honour

London 1800s to Parramatta 1819
Will the real man of quality please stand up?

Bill Miller was raised and educated with the sons of the family. The youngest, Bert Edison-Browne, had been his best friend. However, jealousy intervenes when Bill's excellent schoolwork begins to curtail their friendship. He wins a scholarship and enters Oxford University. When Bill's father dies unexpectedly, Bert insists that Bill take over as butler, but it's more to oppress him. Bert's jealousy grows and festers. He is now looking for a way to rid themselves of their new butler. A ruckus ensues, and Bill is arrested for assaulting Bert.

Molly Ross, the housekeeper's daughter, will vouch for him. It's too late; Bill has been arrested and is soon to be sentenced and transported. With Bill gone, Molly now fights to defend herself from Bert. After hitting him with a pan, she, too, is arrested and sent to Sydney. Bill and Molly arrive with letters of introduction and compensation from Bert's father. Soon, they will be running the best inn in Parramatta with an endorsement from the governor.

ISBN 9780645441567   ISBN ebook 9781923097049

Long-listed in the Historical Fiction Company Competition 2024

I Can't Stop Tomorrow

Irish Famine 1840s to Avoca Beach, Australia

Escaping bigotry and prejudice in Ireland, the O'Shane family lives on a secluded farm on the west coast of Ireland. The potato blight soon decimated their farm. It's always darkest before dawn, and the two remaining girls cling to the hope of a new life. With the kindness of strangers, the eldest girls, **Clare** and **Kerry O'Shane**, head to their cousin, Sal Lockley, in Parramatta, Australia. A new, wonderful life awaits them both. **Shéamus Connor** is the annoying teenage boy who reluctantly draws Clare's affection. However, living in a convict town means ruffians abound.

John Moore is a bad-tempered and troubled Irishman who is content to live alone on another secluded farm until he discovers Clare and two other lads need rescuing.
Can John protect her from the pain inflicted by an evil world?
Can Shéamus find his lost love, who has fled?

ISBN: 9780645441598   ISBN ebook 9781923097056

Madeline's Boy

England 1830s to New South Wales 1840
The race to protect an Orphaned Boy
All is not straightforward when money and titles are involved.

Orphaned, afraid and on the run, Chip must flee.
Madeline was his mother's best friend. Maddie now needs to keep her charge safe and alive. She must give up her life to protect the boy she has loved since birth.
Months after Chip's parents' demise, Maddie sets out to deliver Chip to his Uncle Humphrey, who lives in Sydney. Through him, she meets Chip's uncle's friend, Tim, who falls for Maddie—but will they find happiness?
The menacing presence soon finds Chip, and Maddie needs to hide him again. They are relocated from hidden farms to secret valleys, ultimately ending up in an Aboriginal encampment. Can Tim find a way to be with Maddie? And if so… Will Chip ever be safe?

ISBN: 9780645783308   ISBN ebook 9781923097094

Long-listed in the Historical Fiction Company Competition 2024

https://mybook.to/MadelinesBoy

Jam or Marmalade for Tea

England 1820s to New South Wales 1825 (Governor Brisbane Era)

Martha Hamilton is the eldest of four orphans struggling to survive on their own. She is caught stealing, tried, convicted, and transported to New South Wales. With her family gone, she becomes despondent. Life holds no meaning for her, and the ocean waves look inviting.
Captain Guy Manning is a frustrated and injured redcoat soldier returning to Sydney for a new assignment. He notices Martha trying to jump overboard and rescues her. How do two cats bring them together?
A convict ship is no place for romance, and she's far too young anyway, isn't she?
Can Guy save her and forge a life together for them? What connections does he have to try to save her siblings? Why is marmalade important for their future?

Paperback ISBN 9781923097933   eISBN9781923097285

A NaNoWriMo 2023 book winner

https://mybook.to/JamorMarmaladeforTea

A prequel to 'The Lockleys Parramatta' series

(Free novella with newsletter signup)

Unshackled Lives

Set in England & Australia in the 1800s
Australian historical fiction of early colonial days

Ned Lockley is the second of four sons of the Duke and Duchess of Gracemere. As his mother's favourite, his childhood years were blissful, but he needed to grow up, and quickly. A whirlwind romance is followed by a loved one's betrayal. The following emotional turmoil is particularly challenging for Ned to cope with, especially amid a collapsing and immoral society. Ned can't stay as his family is falling apart. His mother's words to remain true to himself and his faith make him leave everything he knows. How did Ned end up in New South Wales in charge of placing female convicts? Will he ever find happiness or discover who Charles is?

ISBN 9781923097377   eISBN 9781923097384   LP ISBN: 9781923097391

A 100-year, six-part Australian Colonial series

The Lockleys of Parramatta 1800-1900

Hands upon the Anvil

A blacksmith's life and love are more than work
Parramatta 1830s

Eddie Lockley's parents were transported for their crimes. Can a steadfast lad rise above his origins and guide others to succeed in a land of opportunity?
Ten-year-old Eddie longs to help his mum and dad. Living in a convict town with his family, the keen youngster has been working with the local blacksmith since his sixth birthday. But when a lieutenant doesn't stop abusing his older brother, the young boy yearns for the day when he can stand up and end the torment. Though he's thrilled when his mentor offers to send him off to learn his letters, Eddie fears he won't be around to watch his siblings' backs. But as he takes on the biggest adventure of his life, the brave believer soon discovers that God is looking out for everyone he loves. Does this young man in the making have what it takes to change everything for the better?

ISBN 9780994578235 Ebook ISBN 978-0-9945782-5-9 Hardcover 9798496177368

https://mybook.to/HandsUponTheAnvil

Out Where The Brolgas Dance

Gold is found, and so is love
Parramatta 1840s

How can a question change so many people?

It's the 1840s, and discoveries across the Blue Mountains continue. Major Mitchell's new road is complete, and towns are planned and being built. Abundant land is available for those who want it. Eighteen-year-old **William "Wills" Lockley** has laid a solid foundation for a respectable career as a blacksmith, but the Lockley lust for adventure flows deeply within his veins. He dreads the monotony of work at the blacksmith's forge and yearns for adventure in a new frontier. Wills meets six Englishmen (*Coping with what is now known as PTSD*) who have the means to make his dreams come true. What they discover changes the Colony and their lives forever. Gold fever ensues. While in the West, Wills must deal with an uncertain romance. Does Cathy even want him?

ISBN 9780994578242 Ebook ISBN 978-0-9945782-6-6
Hardcover ISBN 9798755445504   LP ISBN 9781923097155
https://mybook.to/OutWhereTheBrolgas

Diamonds in the Dirt
Diamonds, love and money… but there is much more to life.
Parramatta 1850s

The youngest Lockley son, **Luke Lockley**, has completed his university education, and his life lacks direction. No job, no money, and no love. Desperately alone, he prays for guidance. How can Luke trust that God has a plan for him if he can't even find a job? He does the only thing he can … he prays. Within a week, life has changed … oh, how it has changed as his brother Wills turns up with a suggestion. Would Luke be interested in joining the expedition with John Evans? **Reverend William Clarke** needs assistance with a government mineral survey. The challenges, adventures and finds are life-changing for many. However, it gives Luke meaning, purpose and direction. The condition of his heart problems also takes a turn. Can he walk away? Will she wait for him?

ISBN: 9780994578273 Ebook ISBN: 978-0-9945782-8-0
Hardcover ISBN 979-8788011141
https://mybook.to/DiamondsintheDirt

The Earl's Shadow
Who or what is the 'shadow'? How does it affect so many?
Parramatta 1860s

Charles Lockley, the Earl of Coxheath, spent his youth as a convict in Parramatta, unaware of his noble birth, with limited education and few social skills. Now, after a near-death experience, Charles must decide how to live the rest of his life. He is thrust out of his comfort zone in London. There, Charles discovers his purpose. He delivers a speech in parliament—an action that will reshape the empire.

His eldest son, **Charlie**, shares many of his father's shortcomings. However, the past continues to haunt Charlie.

But how does **Jim Leslie,** the Cobb and Co. coach driver, fit into their story? And what exactly is 'The Earl's Shadow' that he mentions?

ISBN: 9780645110708 Ebook ISBN 978-0-9945782-9-7
Released June 2022
https://mybook.to/TheEarlsShadow

Once a Jolly Swagman
An old black Billy Can contains the secrets of an incredible life
An Australian Historical Novel Inspired by the songs of The Seekers
Set in 1870s Parramatta and Kent, UK

Rick Lockley, struggling to escape his family's expectations, runs away to find himself. **Jack**, a jolly swagman, takes him under his care. Even after years together, Rick knows little about the old man.

On his death, Jack leaves Rick his precious billy can; the contents reveal Jack's identity. Stunned, Rick must travel to England to finalise Jack's wishes. There, he uncovers Jack's life of love, betrayal and a link to his own family. Rick also discovers there is much more to learn about this enigmatic man.

ISBN 9780645110753   Ebook ISBN 978-0-6451107-6-0
Released Sept 2022
https://mybook.to/OnceaJollySwagman

Jonty's Journey
Gems, Love, Artists and a Golden Lion
Australia and South Africa 1880-1902

Sydney Jeweller Jonty Evans's passion for gems takes him to Africa at a volatile time. There, he finds the diamonds he wants and is given a lion cub. However, Jonty is all but kidnapped. His experiences in the Transvaal plunge him into questioning everything he knows about life. Soon, nightmares haunt him. (This is now known as PTSD.)

Upon returning home, he nearly ruins his chance with **Lottie** before it even begins, and he finds adjusting hard. Lottie's father, **Luke** Lockley from Parramatta, takes him under his wing and directs him to someone who can assist.

Jonty is then called back to Africa as a liaison and reunites with his lion, Chimbu, after saving the life of his security detail. His life journey introduces him to remarkable artists, politicians, poets, rebels, and the scapegoat soldier, Harry Breaker Morant. Can Jonty lay the past to rest and find his lost peace?

ISBN 9780645110777 HC ISBN 9781923097124   Ebook ISBN: 978-0-6451107-9-1
Released Feb 2023
https://mybook.to/JontysJourney

Sheila Hunter's Australian Colonial Trilogy 1840s

Co-Winner of 1999 NSW Senior Citizen of the Year, In the Year of the Senior Citizen

Mattie
The Story of an Australian Convict Child
An Australian Historical Story inspired by real Life.

An orphaned child, Mattie, is convicted of petty theft, sentenced to seven years, and sent to Australia. She meets another convict woman who, at her death, gives Mattie a chance for a new life. She makes the most of everything that comes her way, earning her freedom, falling in love, marrying, and becoming a mother. But life is not kind to her.

She meets bushrangers, moves to the gold fields in Bathurst, and starts a store. Yet, she is the kind of woman who made Australia what it is today. Can she survive alone in a man's world? She is a remarkable woman who breaks down all her barriers.

(Mattie's story continues in The Lockleys of Parramatta - bk 4 & 6)
ISBN 9781503252370 & ebook AISN BOOTTEDBTO
(The story continues in The Earl's Shadow & Once a Jolly Swagman)
Released 2015
https://mybook.to/Mattie_sh

Ricky
A boy in Colonial Australia

Ricky English and his mother immigrated from England to join his father in the new Colony of Sydney. Upon arrival, there was no sign of his father. Ricky's mum uses the tiny amount of money they brought to get lodgings in a run-down building. Things go from bad to worse when his mother dies; he is thrown out of the hired rooms, and the caretakers confiscate all their possessions.

Ricky lives on the streets of Sydney Town as a street waif. Ricky finds safe places to sleep and befriends freed convicts who can help him survive. One day, he encounters a lost child and helps reunite her with her family. These people try to help him, but he insists on doing things his way because of his stubbornness. However, he has found a mentor and confidante. The story follows him through his life. He survives and turns his life around, helping others along the way. *(Will's story continues in Jonty's Journey)*

Paperback ISBN 9781500770570 Kindle ASIN: B00MLYN6IG
Released 2014
https://mybook.to/Ricky_sh

The Heather to The Hawkesbury
Four Scottish families brave a new life in a strange land.

Torn from their homeland by starvation, four Scottish families are forced to leave the Isle of Skye and seek a new life in Australia. **Mary Macdonald**, her husband **Murd**, and their family, her brother **Fergus** MacKenzie, sister-in-law **Caro** MacLeod, cousin **Alex** Fraser, and all their loved ones are compelled to emigrate from Scotland because of the Potato famine and Clearances.

The story follows these families as they journey from Scotland to the New South Wales colony in the 1850s. Mary struggles to cope with the changes and losses in the first months of settlement. Although the other women rely on her, she is nearly overwhelmed. Mary can't settle in this fierce land and pines for home.

Together, the families endure hardships such as accidents, loss, floods, and relentless work, ultimately forging a strong bond with their new homeland. Trials, tribulations, and triumphs mark their saga as they establish themselves in Australia. Will Mary ever find peace and contentment where danger and sickness have taken loved ones? Can her love for Murd sustain her through the turmoil of life? And what becomes of the brooch given to Mary as she leaves her mother?

ISBN 9781503251434 ebook 9781923097025 Large Print ISBN1533473641
Available on Amazon/Kindle & Large Print
https://mybook.to/TheHeathertTHawkesbury

244

Sara's Author Bio

Sara Powter
PACIFIC WANDERLAND PUBLICATIONS

Sheila Hunter and Sara Powter were a passionate mother-and-daughter team of amateur genealogists. While working together on their family tree, they made many captivating discoveries. Our most significant discovery was finding four convicts who held very different perspectives on life in the colony from the military. These four felons were transported to Australia between 1792 and 1814, during the height of the convict transportation era. Before her passing in 2002, Sheila adapted some of these histories into enchanting stories, known as her Australian Colonial Trilogy. Sara later had these published. Sheila left a fourth unfinished story, inspiring Sara to complete it. However, before she did, **the Lockleys of Parramatta** were created to see if she could do justice to her mother's work. The first two in the series were completed before attempting to finish **Dancing to Her Own Tune** for her mother. (*Sheila wrote the first 30k words*)

Vividly living through the Colonial Era, these books delve further into the theme of overcoming adversity in Colonial Australia, and how it developed, the demise of the Convict system and the discovery of mineral wealth.

Sara skilfully intertwines precise archival data with a captivating narrative to craft a collection of stories about faith, love, loss, and redemption.

Two hundred years after her family arrived in Australia, Sara continues the Australian Colonial stories that start with **Gentle Annie Soames**, a saga about the First Fleet. Her **First Fleet Trilogy** is now complete. Following this chronologically are **The Hunter to Macquarie Collection,** the **Unlikely Convict Ladies Trilog**y, and The **Lockleys of Parramatta**. **The Convict Birthstain Collection**, set in the mid-1800s, follows. All the stories are Amazon Aus QR stand-alone novels. There is a chronological list of her books on her web page.

See Sara's web page to keep up to date with more stories.
An online store is available for a signed copy of Sara's books.
https://www.sarapowter.com.au/   (*Australian Postage only*)
Feel free to email her at
saragpowter@gmail.com
BOOK BUB
https://partners.bookbub.com/authors/6273615/edit
FACEBOOK https://www.facebook.com/profile.php?id=100063887262514
Do you want the book *"Unshackled Lives"* *for free?*
Download from Book Funnel after you sign up.

FREE Newsletter signup
From my web page.

www.ingramcontent.com/pod-product-compliance
Lightning Source LLC
Chambersburg PA
CBHW031945240626
47153CB00003B/869